Lieutenant Jacob Starke in Cuba

Michael T. Ribble

Copyright © 2022 Michael T. Ribble

All rights reserved. No part of this book may be reproduced or transmitted in any form or by any means, electronic or mechanical, including photocopying, recording or by any information storage and retrieval system without permission in writing from the publisher.

Apalachicola Publishing—Dumfries, VA
ISBN: 978-1-7330842-3-9
Library of Congress Control Number: 2022906865
Title: *Lieutenant Jacob Starke in Cuba*
Author: Michael T. Ribble
Digital distribution | 2022
Paperback | 2022

This is the fourth book of a series following one fictional American navy officer during the period just before and during early days of the Spanish-American War. The United States Navy and Revenue Cutter Service worked to prevent military supplies and fighters from entering Cuba, until just before war was declared. Fictional activities described are interwoven with actual events and while they did not occur, could have. The timeline is accurate to the extent feasible, as are ancillary events inserted to capture this environment. Certain long-standing institutions, firms, agencies, and public offices included are mentioned and their activities taken from historical sources, or given fictional tasks that might have occurred within normal operations. Similarly, people who occupied political, military, and public positions were included and fictional discussions fit what they might have said and done. All fictional characters are wholly imaginary and any likeness to actual persons living or dead is coincidental.

Cover photo: *Cover photo courtesy of Library of Congress, Prints and Photographs Division, item 2016816177; from an original in the Detroit Publishing Company photograph collection.*

Dedication

To:
Commander Philip A. Smith, USN,
Chief Engineman Carl Allen Cayson, USN,
Chief Personnelman Kenneth G. Zahn, USNR,
and most especially, Baerbel, my love and muse.

Other books by Michael T. Ribble:

Lieutenant Jacob Starke and Calypso
Lieutenant Jacob Starke and the Anarchists
Lieutenant Jacob Starke and the Spanish Gunboats

Table of Contents

Chapter One
Return to Cuba

Off Havana and ten days into 1898, the first officer of the New York & Texas Steamship Line's *Concho* brought his large ship to port, aimed her foremast slightly right of Morro Castle lighthouse, and began bleeding way. The pilot schooner loitering in deep water below Morro Castle's gray-brown ramparts sheeted home and moved to intercept this latest arrival. A few flickering city lights were visible under darkening skies but *Concho* would transit the entrance channel, snatch a buoy, and moor in the bay before tropical evening turned night. The schooner heeled as it set up to approach the liner's large boarding port. Minutes later, she eased gingerly alongside the square opening, port side aft, compressing three rope fenders. Four uniformed men scrambled aboard *Concho*, the pilot boat twisted away, paralleled the larger ship briefly, slid into its wake, fell-off to catch the wind, and returned to station. Three boarders went to conduct health and customs interviews in the dining room while the pilot was escorted forward.

This was *Concho*'s first port since leaving New York City's Pier 20; and some days later would be her final stop on a Caribbean circuit. The cargo-passenger liner was 320 feet long, displaced nearly 4,000 tons, and carried a marginal schooner rig for emergencies and passenger confidence. Her pilothouse on the main deck aft of the raked foremast was integrated into a single-level, white deckhouse containing master and navigator cabins. A midship deckhouse over the engineering spaces encircled a raked, black funnel anchored by wire rope stays and displaying the star logo. Bell-mouthed ventilator cowls forward of a pitched-roof skylight on the centerline were spread across its top. An aft deckhouse contained cabins, skylights, the raked mainmast, and white boats slung from davits on either side of her weather deck. The fantail was encircled by stanchions supporting an off-white canvas awning rigged for port. A black hull beneath the low superstructure included her plumb bow, a counter stern, large boarding ports aft, and two rows of portholes for the cabins, a dining room, and other spaces.

Concho entered the short channel alongside small fishing boats inbound with their day's catch. She ghosted beneath two fortresses' stone and concrete ramparts on the high ground to port that overlooked Havana, on a low peninsula to starboard. Small forts and batteries lined that side then a city dominated by red-tile roofs amidst an eclectic mix of buildings, steeples and domes. Once this short passage ended, the liner came smartly starboard into a broad bay, slowing further as she made for a battered buoy off Machina Wharf with its three-legged derrick towering over the customs pier. This mooring was roughly a quarter ways across the bay. Santa Catalina peninsula was on the far side; containing Regla's coaling piers, rail terminals, bull ring, active smuggling population, and various communities. Foreign ships would moor or anchor out, to be served by water taxies and lighters, although Compañía Trasatlántica Española passenger ships did go pierside. This was partly due to the company being Spain's premier shipping line, but also because each transatlantic crossing brought nearly 1,000 troops besides regular passengers; and every return carried sick and wounded soldiers.

Once the forecastle crew and small rowboat's buoy jumper finished, *Concho* payed out enough anchor chain for her stern circle to clear surrounding ships then locked heavy chain stoppers. The liner settled easily to a mooring buoy streaked with guano stains. Her stern was pointed up-bay; Havana to port, Regla to starboard. The large Spanish cruiser *Alfonso XII* and handful of steamships clustered nearby with schooners, barks, brigs, and other rigs scattered around the bay. Lighters moved slowly over dark water while jostling multicolored bumboats surrounded the liner, took care of business, and returned to piers, wharfs, and slips.

The evening grew still once this traffic cleared and night fell over the bay; severing *Concho* from encircling countryside, fortresses, villages, towns, and city. Ships, buildings, and wharfs vanished into the dark or were silhouetted by lights ashore. Lighted ferries of two competing lines traveled between Havana's Muelle de Luz Wharf and Regla's piers. This tropical stillness was complete except for intermittent steam whistles and muted sounds floating across from Havana. Flickering and steady lights surrounding the liner increased as night blanketed city, bay, and waterfront; many reflecting off placid, ink-black water gently lapping against a hull less than two miles from the sea. This port seemed more tranquil than the one she left four days earlier but war was just beyond thousands of soldiers guarding the city; with many times that deployed to the island.

Cubans seeking independence and Spanish loyalists devoted the months since 1895's summer to clawing each other with guns and machetes. This included the largest army Europe sent to the Americas; one now struggling to overcome a maelstrom of allegiances, factions, and loyalties. Upwards of 200,000 regulars and conscripts fought to retain Spanish control alongside voluntarios and guerrilleros who gave no quarter. Facing them was an improvised army whose commanders exerted semi-discipline on its insurrectos; some fighting near-conventional war, some a guerrilla one, and others marauding. Led by the Cuban Revolutionary Party, these nationalists also instituted a mobile island government supported by their sophisticated Junta based in New York City and spread across the United States.

José Julián Martí Pérez, known as Martí, created a shared vision of independence, organized the Junta, and then died soon after reaching Cuba. Without him, independence factions were united only in driving out Spain. The primary split was between Cubans with African ancestors, mainly slaves freed eleven years before, and those claiming Spanish descent or coming from Spain. Martí's plan to gain independence through a short, popular uprising was another early casualty and the replacement strategy was to destroy the island's value to Spain while escalating the cost of remaining.

Cuba was a bewildering political mosaic. The most dedicated to a status quo, besides foreign investors, Barcelona business interests, and Spanish aristocracy were people from Spain, or peninsulares. These formed a social elite, whether they planned to stay long enough to make their fortune or permanently. Autonomists occupied the middle ground. These were primarily well-off creoles that saw a Spanish self-governing region best serving their interests. Independence factions varied in loyalty to the Junta since they included some autonomists, those committed to independence, anarchists, adventurers, and more. A small number viewed annexation to the United States as the solution or second-best alternative. Pacificos supported no faction but were preyed on by insurrectos, often forced to support them, and distrusted by the government.

When the governor-general informed Madrid he was unwilling to do what was needed to hold Cuba, the focused, energetic, and professional Valeriano Weyler y Nicolau came as captain-general and governor-general to crush the revolt. He completed three fortified trochas to segment the island then began pacification by province, beginning with Pinar del Río. A reconcentration policy was announced that forced rural populations into cities for protection and to reduce insurrecto support. Reconcentrados leaving farms and villages by necessity or decree required care a bankrupt Spain was unable to provide so rural pacificos, insurrecto sympathizers, and refugees gathered in makeshift, unhygienic camps and buildings. Clustering in and near fortified cities and towns, they expired by the hundreds then thousands from disease and malnutrition. In some areas drafted Spanish soldiers let famished children lick what remained of their own reduced rations. The American press accentuated this suffering and pressure increased until Congress appropriated funds, the administration asked for contributions, and Clara Barton was approached about the American Red Cross overseeing relief. None of this was in place so the cargo in *Concho*'s hold would soon be Consul-General Fitzhugh Lee's responsibility.

Weyler outraged a hostile American press but loyalists believed the end near when an anarchist assassinated Spain's conservative prime minister. Elections brought a liberal government that moved to establish autonomy and replace Weyler. Ramón Blanco Erenas Riera y Polo was their choice. Respected, skilled, and popular, he established an autonomous government, initiated efforts to negotiate with insurrectos, and continued aggressive military activity. Loyalists felt their government was abandoning victory and yielding to a foreign nation that offered insurgents a base, sustenance, and safe haven. The Junta was convinced independence lay within sight and declared anyone treating with Blanco a traitor.

The Spanish government worried Cuban autonomy and placating an American public could fail individually or in unison. War preparations began but their treasury was bare and European support needed, especially nations with navies or influence. Continental governments neither favored nor trusted Americans but hesitated to openly support Spain except en masse. Austria and France faced internal conflict. Great Britain, Germany, France, and Russia were committed to Mideast, African, Indian, or Chinese campaigns; confronting each other in the Mediterranean; and adapting to Korea, China, and Japan's changing realities. Spain's reluctant and belated autonomy initiative was welcomed as the least disruptive resolution.

Lieutenant Jacob Starke, United States Navy, sat on *Concho's* fantail under the taut awning obscuring a nearly full moon; reclining in a canvas deck chair and mulling his immediate future. The January evening was warm and ship seemed almost stationary at her mooring off Havana's waterfront. Remnants of afternoon heat passed through his light, cotton sack suit. Wisps of smoke rose slowly from a browned meerschaum pipe following each long, slow draw. He finished two glasses of wine earlier then came on deck to relax before retiring, but found it hard to ignore what must begin in the morning.

He was ordered to Havana at Consul-General Lee's request on temporary duty while still commanding *Calypso*. His barkentine-rigged, steam gunboat was rammed by a liner while moored in Hampton Roads and now under repair in Newport News. *Calypso* was constructed years before by his uncle's firm, Starke Shipping & Shipbuilding, as the merchant ship *Illusive*. She was designed to be one of four that could be converted for commerce raiding or sale should war come. This was viable with the existing Navy little more than a collection of relics masquerading as men-of-war but then came the *Virginus* seizure and mass executions. When a naval war with Spain seemed inevitable the public saw how inadequate their fleet was, the Navy began rebuilding, and *Illusive* class rationale collapsed. Only that ship completed, without her sail rig, and began carrying cargo throughout the Caribbean.

She was destined for the breakers with few aware of this secondary role buried in a cache of old drawings. However, Captain Sidney Albert, at the Navy's Bureau of Navigation, was searching for a suitable candidate to serve as ferret to disrupt Junta filibusters using a long-legged ship with roving commission. He discovered *Illusive* by chance; about to be overhauled or sold. The firm was willing to negotiate so the Navy bought her for a reasonable price considering the warship skeleton. Overhaul and conversion began using faded builder's drawings. The intended barkentine rig was installed along with modern water-tube boilers, a triple-expansion engine, and 4-inch breech-loading rifles. She was commissioned *Calypso* then assigned to the Special Service Squadron for disrupting filibuster expeditions smuggling arms into Cuba.

This precarious scheme needed a composed, aggressive commander with the expertise and diplomacy to operate independently. While negotiating with Immanuel Starke, Captain Albert became convinced the nephew, Jacob Starke, fit. Albert observed him as a naval cadet on *Apalachicola;* he was familiar with the ship, and increasingly ambivalent about the Navy. The last quality swayed Albert since *Calypso*'s commander would be more proactive if expendable, so he offered her to Starke less than two years earlier.

Exhausting a faint smoke cloud, Starke recalled Albert as captain of *Apalachicola*, an obsolete sloop off Alexandria, Egypt, during the British bombardment. His own father, Jefferson Starke, served with Albert before the war and subsequent expatriation to Rio de Janeiro. He saw Albert occasionally since *Apalachicola*, but more often after they were ordered to Washington's ornate State, War, and Navy Building. The *Calypso* offer came without warning just as he was preparing to resign or request leave of absence to join his uncle's Baltimore shipping firm or the father's in Rio de Janeiro. Commands were scarce, usually required influence, and nonexistent for junior lieutenants. His uncle enjoyed a first-rate reputation within the shipping community and Republican Party but the father stuck in a number of senior officers and politicians' craws despite the passage of time. Jefferson Starke submitted a formal resignation because he refused to fight fellow Americans and believed reconciliation or peaceful succession possible. The Lincoln administration summarily dismissed him and many others, so he offered the new nation his services and hunted Northern merchant ships during the war. This would have incurred sufficient enmity but he also took *Woods Rogers;* a paddlewheel steamer carrying gold bullion to replenish New Orleans banks. His cartel ship with passengers and paroled sailors sent to Havana was lost without trace so many still wanted him charged with piracy.

Calypso had played havoc with Junta expeditions for more than a year; including a string of engagements sending three filibusters to the bottom and a Spanish gunboat sufficiently damaged to leave for repair in Spain. That cruise ended when she was accidentally rammed off Norfolk while preparing to sail for Haiti. She limped to the nearby navy yard, was patched up, and then towed to Newport News. She was still there; with repairs completing under her executive officer, Lieutenant (junior grade) Benjamin Watson, engaged to Albert's oldest daughter Olivia, and newly designated chief engineer, Passed Assistant Engineer William O'Leary. Albert was able to keep Starke in command but the cost was a month or more in Havana, after Consul-General Lee used *Calypso*'s temporary state to request him. The ex-Virginia governor and Confederate cavalry general appointed by Cleveland's administration was retained under McKinley. He met Starke at the family mansion while exploring the possibility of obtaining assistance from the father's company. Jacob Starke's connections and performance afterwards convinced Lee he might prove useful as an ersatz naval attaché while negotiating visits by American warships; perhaps even *Calypso*. The detail was also supported by the Chief Intelligence Officer, Commander Richardson Clover; respected in the Navy, influential outside it through his wife, regular host of society affairs in a stone mansion off Dupont Circle, and desiring information on Havana port fortifications, the arsenal's shipyard, and massive dry-dock towed from Britain.

Starke was considering this, the dark harbor, and enjoying his last tranquility for some weeks when Edward Curtis rounded the deckhouse. The Englishman was coming to determine if autonomy and increasing stability supported rebuilding the unused mill and plantation his investors bought from the Starke firm. Both lay outside Artemisa, a city in Pinar del Río on the Mariel-Majana Trocha. It was a bargain when sold but a year had passed without return on investment and he wanted Starke to repeat their first trip to the properties. Darwin Tyson, running *The Sun*'s Laffin News Bureau in Havana, already agreed to a second excursion by cable.

Curtis not only shared a stateroom with him from New York, but was Starke's potential brother-in-law after revealing two weeks earlier his widowed sister, Katherine Ledford, gave birth to a son some four months earlier; the product of an unintended tryst at Hotel Inglaterra over a year ago in Havana. Katherine was drawn to Starke's door by one of his intermittent nightmares ashore. Perhaps exotic surroundings played a hand, but passion overwhelmed propriety for a night then both resumed their previous arms-length relationship. They parted awkwardly the next morning and she returned to Britain soon after. Their correspondence continued with her letters growing inconsistent as months passed. He attributed this to her affections shifting and knew nothing until approached during the Starke Christmas ball. Katherine endured her confinement and birth without telling the father despite her brother's urging. Starke knew the child was his and proposed marriage but Curtis cautioned she might not accept. Especially since her father nursed an inveterate distaste for colonists he must weigh against his widowed daughter and illegitimate grandson. Starke's aunt and uncle supported marriage since their ersatz grandchild existed and his aunt thought highly of Katherine.

Her brother was younger than Starke; thin, athletic, invariably dressed well, and, except for a light brown mustache, clean-shaven. Curtis' lips resembled his sister's; precisely midway between pronounced cheekbones, moved little when speaking, and about as full as desirable in men. A straight nose fit his face and the thin brown hair was neither excessively long nor short. His demeanor was open and he might be thought a dandy but was fully capable of standing or acting, endowed with an inquisitive nature, and vigorously pursued topics until reaching a conclusion or wringing out all possible information. Starke was an only child and Cynthia

Jefferson the closest he came to a sister, but believed the future baronet was a first-rate brother and protector. Katherine clearly benefited from this after her husband, Philip Ledford, went down with HMS *Victoria* off North Africa and the dowry fell under her brother's control.

Curtis paused as he walked aft. Surrounded by war, the American was relaxing in a deck chair enjoying his evening pipe between sunset and moonrise. The enigmatic navy officer touched his sister far more than she admitted, even to herself. Starke spoke little of himself but the night before their last excursion to Artemisa mentioned being with a captain surrounded by hostiles on a bluff. It seemed he observed then adopted what was admirable of that officer's ability to accept, evaluate, and act. The results showed in *Calypso's* accomplishments. Curtis had worried about revealing Katherine's secret but received a reaction far different from many who suddenly discovered they were fathers; and better than his own conflicted response. It took his favorite in an upper class sporting house, one of Katherine's school friends, to see the sister as a woman. Her counsel and what he remembered from childhood made the tryst with Starke less surprising than how she avoided anything similar for so long; and convinced him of her strong feelings.

Katherine's husband had a cultured demeanor Starke lacked, although Curtis thought some women might find him appealing. He was average in height, wiry, and exuded earned confidence. Unlike many younger naval officers and others, Starke wore a short, neatly trimmed beard; which failed to add sophistication because it lacked the thickness to fully conceal a roughhewn and gently scarred face. Faded blue eyes emplaced under arcing eyebrows constantly surveilled all unless locked unswervingly on something of interest. His mouth showed little movement, the lips invariably slightly compressed, and he exuded self-control except for a single strand of rebellious hair. He was as reserved as Katherine after Philip passed, causing Curtis to doubt Starke's intimacies with her sex approached his own dalliances; and there was an openness that suggested he engaged no woman for sport. Katherine's brother liked and trusted this man who broached the armor she built plate by plate from before coming out, through marriage, and during widowhood. His unexpected nephew equally affected him and he enjoyed holding the boy despite spittle and other natural distractions. He was weighing Starke's chances with sister and family when the American looked up then pointed his pipestem at an adjacent chair, "You're pensive this evening?"

"I'm hoping we don't find what your Washington friend predicted."

Starke introduced Curtis to Maximilian Falk y Machado at their Christmas ball. Falk worked for one of Albert's Justice contacts on filibuster prosecutions and Cuban issues in Congress. The young New Yorker was well-connected, educated, read law, and solitary offspring of an Austrian engineer and woman from Cadiz who met and married in Cuba then immigrated to the States.

"Falk's a good judge but Tyson's been down here with *The Sun*'s news bureau."

"Look forward to seeing him again; always generous with that hip flask. Good chap but strange. Hard to believe he was with you in military school."

"Jefferson Classical & Military Academy; and he did well there."

A steam launch chugged past close aboard under their fantail, plowing a long dark furrow and releasing noxious vapors to drift on the barely discernible breeze. Caught unaware as he sat down, Curtis muttered, "My God, that fellow brought up a stink."

"Always. Streams and sewers empty to the bay but with only a narrow passage out much of what comes in settles and rots so disturbing the surface releases gas. Water's not fit for anything. Ships take fresh water from lighters. No one even washes decks with it; more than once anyway."

". . . and swimming's unpleasant." Curtis chuckled.

"I'd relish one now. Use to swim in the York River at a steamboat landing below my mother's plantation, Oxen Grove."

"Katherine swims."

"She mentioned it on the Hygeia pier after we left the dance for air; complained about wool bathing costumes."

Curtis laughed, "Not that she wore many. Brydian Grange's pond is surrounded by woods so she wore little or nothing; then a light chemise as nature took hold. Father finally decreed she must wear a bathing costume; even though he preferred swimming in the altogether before it was banned. After that she never swam with us but slipped away and returned wet. Father knew she regressed, but never took issue."

Starke nodded, inserted the pipestem then drew, raising a glow below the bowl's flat rim. When Katherine brought up swimming he assumed she meant rolling into the sea in a bathing machine. The young woman Curtis described was nothing like the devout Katherine thoroughly wedded to propriety he experienced; except for their one Havana aberration. She denounced him as a free thinker for preferring a horseback ride over Sunday mornings on a hard bench. Her brother and Aunt Constance's counsel forced him to suspect the woman he hoped to marry was more a mystery than once thought; and he remembered the oft-revised proposal letter on the stateroom bureau required additional polish.

He pointed the pipestem to a relatively close shape, hoping to change subjects, "Look there, Edward. The large structure shaped like a long building."

"I see it."

"Floating dry-dock built in Britain by Swan & Hunter then towed here last fall. It's 450 feet long, 109 wide, with a lifting capacity of 12,000 tons and completed in record time. Spain's dredging to position it and complete lifting tests this month. Why install such an expensive dry-dock at a barely functional shipyard while their army goes unpaid?"

"Didn't they build ships here once?"

"Yes, but local forests are gone and wood's not used for as many warships; so what's their motive and why the priority? Some think they plan on returning the yard to operation and make Havana the Caribbean Gibraltar. A functioning yard would mean their West Indies ships would no longer be forced to choose a North American shipyard or return to Spain."

Starke later finished the awkward letter to his son's mother before retiring. It was stilted and imperfect but Katherine needed his formal proposal in her hands to explain it did not come from duty or social pressure. He saw complications innumerable but the desire she accept was genuine. If not, he hoped she would agree to establish their son's legitimacy.

Chapter Two
Havana

Starke and Curtis went to breakfast early then boarded a lighter. Swarming bumboats descended as it pulled away. Several hawked goods but most were water taxies run by or chartered to firms, chandlers, and hotels. Their lighter plowed steadily through a placid bay heated by the morning sun, rupturing its thin membrane, and releasing putrefaction's noxious vapors to a light morning breeze; prompting another comment by Curtis.

They came ashore by the Machina Wharf derrick, walked under an arch, and entered the customs house to register. Uniformed officers inside seemed to lack urgency and ignored the *Concho* inspection, if inclined. The thorough examination was especially meticulous for American correspondents. Starke understood their barely disguised anger. Reporters were viewed as indistinguishable from newspapers that regularly printed maddening fiction. It was even rumored correspondents had placed a small bomb at the American consulate offices; and their cavalier view of Spanish law and regulations was undisputed. Starke explained he was with the consul-general's office in Spanish, which eased their passage; as did Curtis' upper-class accent and British passport.

In reasonable but not record time they were on the street. Starke recalled the main post office was nearby and mailed Katherine's letter while the shipping company's agent sent their luggage to the hotel. Starke hailed one of several cabs hovering near the customs house entrance and they settled in for a thirteen-block ride. He chose what foreigners called a volanta rather than the more fashionable victoria. Highly decorated and uniquely Cuban, these open carriages had two large wheels, long shafts, and operator astride one of two-horses.

Their driver took them west from the customs house under clear sky. After paralleling the harbor's wood and steel piers they entered city proper where buildings blocked any breeze. The population, around 250,000, had expanded beyond the old city wall to fill the peninsula. Houses were yellow, pink, green, blue, or white; with red-tile roofs and internal courtyards for the more affluent. Commercial and government buildings of brick or stone stood out and above this carpet with domes, steeples, and clock towers rising further. The volanta rolled easily over relatively wide, paved streets shared with carts, carriages, pedestrians, and horse-drawn streetcars. Most side-streets, however, were unpaved and only wide enough to keep vehicles from brushing walls. Fighting delayed or halted improvements but there was a telephone system, Red Telefónica de la Habana, S.A., and the three-year-old aqueduct bringing clean drinking water from springs in the hills.

The Starke shipping firm's Havana representative and Aron Sharett, a Jewish chandler in Norfolk, arranged for Inglaterra lodging. Sharett recommended Hotel Mascotte on Oficios Street since the former mansion offered harbor and sea views, but Starke preferred the Hotel Inglaterra facing Havana's central park. It provided fashionable accommodations for diplomats like Consul-General Lee and the more well-heeled correspondents. The Navy would reimburse most expenses but Starke seldom limited himself to what was allowed since he maintained no house besides that at Oxen Grove plantation, his personal income was more than sufficient, and the Inglaterra offered other advantages.

The hotel's name could be seen on a small circular roof facade centered over the main entrance and it occupied the corner across from Parque Central and immense Teatro Tacón. Two floors were built in 1873 and third in 1886. The first opened onto the boulevard below arches and narrow patios with gasoliers. The second and third were lined with small cast iron porches, louvered double-doors for individual rooms, and ventilation grids between their doorframes and next story.

After working through people and carriages, they pulled in front of the hotel. Starke climbed from the volanta's black leather seat, cleared its large red wheel, and paid their driver. He looked across the broad Paseo del Prado once the vehicle rolled away. On the far side lay Parque Central's paved walkways, ornate cast-iron street lamps, and numerous monuments. One memorial honored Isabella II while another resembled a large stone urn and contained flowers. There were trees but the park was dominated by low shrubs and flowers segmented by pavement covered with park benches, tables, and chairs. Except for a swath where Paseo del Prado ran north to the sea, sizable buildings surrounded its perimeter.

The Inglaterra lobby had a telephone, high arches, and intricately carved ceiling above tiled floors. They crossed to the front desk and registered. Out of its eighty rooms, Starke received the one his son was conceived in. It was high-ceilinged, comparatively large, and opened to a compact balcony overlooking street and park. Its iron bed frame boasted an ornately carved headboard and there were electric lights. A common bathroom was available down the hall but a marble-topped commode and chamber pot were provided for night.

Starke settled in then passed through the lobby to meet Curtis for siesta refreshment at a table under the arches. Darwin Tyson, longtime friend and journalist, left word they had supper reservations once *Concho* moored. His absence was odd since the custom, like most tropical cities, was to begin work early, break for afternoon heat, and finish in late evening. Curtis motioned from a small iron table surrounded by four wicker chairs; encircled by reporters believing them new competitors. Starke ordered his preferred Havana libation, a balloon glass of fresh fruit, Spanish gin, and tonic water with a liberal dose of quinine. Horses clopped by and people threaded through surrounding tables while he passed Tyson's invitation to Curtis. They sat in deep shade with a Caribbean sun warming nearby street and park. Starke slowly sipped his concoction; interrupting their conversation only to ensure malaria was held at bay by ordering another.

Starke was back in the lobby that evening to wait for Tyson and Curtis. Supper was at El Palacio de Cristal on the corner of Consulado and San José Streets. This popular dining establishment was about two blocks away, behind Teatro Tacón. It required dressing well, but no more; and Starke added a hardwood cane with brass head. Tyson arrived in a light tropical suit and broad-brimmed boater of fine white sennit. Starke shook hands while looking into a bony, clean-shaven face as his friend grinned, "Let's have a drink on the terrace before Miss Evans arrives. She believes our office reputation is best served by keeping everything to proper hours; which is unfortunately true."

Tyson in public without his silver flask holstered under the left arm was unnatural; as was ordering a gin and tonic rather than whiskey or bourbon. Starke was curious if the indomitable female correspondent joining them influenced this, or managing *The Sun*'s Havana news bureau. In either case it did not extend to Turkish cigarettes. Tyson sat back in his chair, extracted the familiar gold-trimmed jade cigarette case, made his selection, lit it, and casually tossed a smoking match into the ashtray.

Recalling Curtis' observation regarding military school, Starke agreed it was difficult to picture Tyson in a gray cadet uniform. His oldest friend was a volatile concoction of eccentricity, intelligence, and perception with reliably dismal views. Naturally stoic, he embraced arcane poetry, military tactics, and philosophy with equal enthusiasm while holding to a personal view of honor and discipline that chafed against the school's. He left for University of Michigan's College of Literature, Science, and the Arts; where his degree came with less effort than most students. Tyson's father became reasonably wealthy during the war when his watch factory fed an insatiable weapons demand and thought his son would join him but Tyson was drawn to scandals, debates, crime, and war so he wrote for a succession of papers climaxing with *The Sun*. Cigarettes and alcohol may have fueled this professional climb but success came from ability, drive, and insight. Across the table, Starke saw a thin column of smoke lift from the cigarette and considered Tyson's odd relationship with his aunt. There was a definite black mark by his name in her social ledger because he yet to marry and might be impairing her efforts regarding the nephew; but Tyson spoke as though she was their aunt and Starke often felt his friend reminded her of someone from the past.

Tyson noticed his friend looking at him. It was hard not to with Starke's piercing gaze. He crushed a dying cigarette, "Word's out the Weyler faction will demonstrate against autonomists tomorrow. Some army officers are involved so it's best to keep off the streets. Blanco's bringing in outside troops but their loyalty may not match the senior officers' since most haven't been paid for so long bordellos trade in 8mm rounds. We're becoming less popular here as well since Weyler's removal."

"Perhaps, but I report to the consul-general tomorrow morning."

"You'll likely find him here at the hotel."

"Perhaps."

"Which reminds; it's odd you're here yet still command *Calypso*. Local authorities are unusually close-mouthed about the *Pedro Menéndez de Avilés* affair; saying only that the torpedo gunboat completed voyage repairs and returned to Spain. Rumor has it she was shot up and *Calypso* involved. I checked with Norfolk. They say *Calypso*'s repairs were due to a collision."

"And?"

"The Hampton Roads collision's in court and *Calypso* besting a steel gunboat without damage sounds unlikely."

Starke felt uncharitable even as he welcomed his friend's frustration. Tyson's Gila monster grip on leads was no secret. He never experienced it since their friendship was never exploited and Tyson accepted Starke was always truthful but not equally forthcoming.

Curtis arrived wearing a lightweight suit fresh from the tailor. Like Starke, he still lacked obligatory headgear. Their waiter spotted him sitting down so another drink order went to the bar. Their conversation moved on, to Starke's relief, since Curtis was there to evaluate reopening his syndicate's holdings. Falk's prediction of a violent, unstable situation outside Havana proved accurate. Media Luna plantation was attacked days earlier despite nearly 100 soldiers defending its rudimentary fort. The army reported 200 insurrectos with artillery and their own troops barely held. Others believed the assault was never intended to take the plantation; only intimidate workers, destroy equipment, and drive away oxen. Pausing while Curtis' drink arrived, Tyson went on to observe the governor-general's efforts to restart the economy and establish autonomy encouraged General Gomez and the Junta to step up efforts to destroy both; so Blanco was issuing rifles to any willing plantation. This meant the Pinar del Río properties Curtis hoped to rebuild would require fortification along with reconstruction and machinery. Even so, the young Englishman wanted a second site visit despite Starke arguing against it.

Cassandra Evans ended debate by floating confidently through clusters of reporters and visitors on her way to the terrace cafe. Starke first noticed her the year before while riding a Washington streetcar home on the day Albert offered *Calypso*; but they never met until introduced during his aunt's interview for *The Evening Times'* Women's Page. She later invited Cassandra to a dinner party and dragooned Starke as escort, no doubt for veiled matrimonial purposes. They met several times afterwards but not since her joining Tyson to work for *The Sun*'s news bureau.

The men rose from their chairs as she approached and Starke saw she was adopting upper middle class Havana fashion. A light cotton skirt, lifted above the floor by her left hand, exposed black shoes. The long-sleeved white blouse of identical material had an upright ruffled collar. That and a gold-buckled black belt obscuring her waist created the illusion of one garment. The line of buttons was hidden by a long white necktie wrapped twice around her high collar before falling forward and out between breasts elevated by a light corset. Her right hand clutched a smallish purse and the roundish hat emulated a shallow bowl filled with ribbons and flowers. She was classic beauty with floor-length auburn hair up in a pompadour and hat pinned to cant slightly forward. He observed her face was still gently scored with a few pleasant lines converging on glistening brown eyes beneath flawless eyebrows; exactly as he recalled from their evening at Delmonico's. She had tanned more than fashionable; a fact of life for those out and about in the city, but it failed to lessen the appeal and helped her blend with the population.

Starke was relieved she also appeared disarmed since her battered brown Brussels carpet bag and small notebook were absent. Evans was nearly as tenacious as Tyson but they lacked the concordat developed over the years with his friend. She was intelligent, impervious, and single-minded; so much so she once persuaded *The Evening Times'* editor to dispatch her to Havana. During the trip south she met Starke and Tyson in a Key West restaurant by chance. Although she proved as aggressive gathering stories in Havana as Tyson, it nearly cost her life. She was stricken by some unknown fever spawned in the low-lying city's open soil drains, street sewage, and refuse flowing into the bay. It was no surprise since she visited reconcentrado camps and buildings where endemic diseases flourished. Tyson and the Starke shipping firm's agent cared for her until fit enough to pass through quarantine then put her on a steamship for New York.

Evans recovered and was in New York City for the Grant's Tomb dedication when *Calypso* entered Brooklyn Navy Yard. She visited unannounced and Starke found her changed by Havana and affliction. A youthful countenance and figure had yielded or evolved to one conveying an experience that enhanced her natural attractiveness and imparted greater poise. Even the thin lines lightly etching her face suggested brittle tenseness had given way to greater depth and character. Seeing her, Starke sensed this evolution continued and she was all the more alluring for it. Evans wore scent, as in New York. It was not customary but noticeable only with an obliging breeze due to evening streets' competing odors. She greeted Tyson casually before extending her right hand to Starke then Curtis.

Rather than force her to sit then immediately rise, they began walking a block west to Consulado Street, past the massive theatre, then another south to the square corner building that was El Palacio de Cristal restaurant. Once inside, they were seated at a circular table covered with white cotton cloth surrounded by four dark-wood chairs and attended by a waiter in jacket and white gloves. Starke and Curtis offered news from Washington and Britain before the talk turned to Cuba. Tyson addressed local politics while Evans slowly brought after-dinner coffee to her lips, blew gently, and set it down. Her eyes had acquired a gentle firmness, "I try to capture the other Havana; the one beyond uniforms, fighting, and places reporters frequent."

Curtis leaned forward, his interest peaked, "And what have you discovered?"

"Many things; of some you must be aware and others perhaps not."

Starke lit his pipe and Tyson retrieved a Turkish cigarette from his distinctive case. She took a minute to think then, "The city's mostly on low ground, a few feet above sea level, so heavy rains bring the bay and whatever's in it through the streets. There're acres of fill settling constantly with the same effect. Not only are homes and businesses mixed but social classes. The more well-off have better houses built around courtyards but their ground floors are still inches above street level and flood just as readily so most are given over to horses or other animals. Many houses use iron bars rather than windows and local cesspool ordinances aren't enforced.

There's been little money to improve this and what existed went to the new aqueduct and fortifications. This is partly driven by local revenue going overseas to government and big business."

Curtis listened intently and when she paused to think and finger her cup, he leaned forward into the table, "You mentioned people?"

"Survival's everything but most are passionate and industrious. Upper classes follow Spanish custom so status is everything and the city a cauldron. Spanish and creoles dominate but look across the room where the Negro gentleman is dining with a mulatto wife. Work laws enacted after slavery also brought Chinese and Filipinos, so Cuban customs aren't even completely Spanish."

Tyson released a thin stream of cigarette smoke that floated skyward, "And bullfights?"

Starke detected slight squirming beneath her constraining white outfit, "Bullfighting and baseball are popular. Neither's prohibited. Authorities patronize bullfights since they're favored by peninsulares but creoles and women prefer baseball. Many females have been educated in Europe or the States so I don't require translation at the games. There's cockfighting but once was enough; and in some rural areas men gallop past a tethered goose trying to rip off its head from the saddle."

She fingered her cup then continued, "Darwin and I often attend the weekly bullfight at three o'clock in Regla since the Havana ring is closed and filled with reconcentrados. They're put on every Sunday after Mass, since people go to baseball games on Saturdays. He felt it would be overmuch, and it was disquieting, but there's a forbidden fruit sort of fascination with the tragedy that repulses and attracts. Besides, important military and civilians attend regularly so there's a wealth of information."

Tyson leaned forward in a low voice, "That's where we heard about tomorrow's protests. Stores will close and shutter their windows; especially theaters and cafes. There won't be any military bands in Parque Central for a few days either."

After Curtis and Evans went to their rooms, Starke and Tyson located a table. Whiskey being scarce, they ordered rum. Starke assessed his re-acquaintance with Evans. She seemed to accept Tyson as mentor, or something more, and a scattering of his friend's mannerisms clearly found fertile ground with her. He mused, more to himself than Tyson, "Miss Evans seems different."

"Perhaps; I'm with her every day so don't notice. She's too willing and I worry she'll get hurt or sick. Yellow fever's gone for now but summer will come and I hear a Ward Line steamer's master just died of typhoid."

Starke disguised his discomfort whenever typhoid was mentioned. His mother was sent to Washington for safety during the war and died of it; along with Lincoln's son William and many others.

Tyson remembered, "Sorry Jacob; forgot."

"My problem, not yours, but thanks."

"Anyway, Cassandra files good reconcentrado stories and wants to visit camps outside Havana. I've been putting her off and doubt Blanco allowing reporters to leave the city includes women. She could find herself in trouble or fall ill; and the last time nearly did for her."

"I understand her interest. There's never been so many begging. Reconcentrados I take it?"

"You've visited India. Some claim it outdoes their plagues. Situation's intolerable in Havana but worse outside. Adults little more than skeletons; bloated children with sunken faces and bones for limbs. It's beg or starve. Young men are forced to take sides so that leaves the elderly, women, and children. Some are in camps and others in derelict warehouses but there's little real shelter, pitiful food, and no sanitation. So many are dying the towns lack coffins. Starvation mostly; but there's consumption, pneumonia, typhoid, typhus, and malaria. It'll get worse when yellow and dengue fevers return. I give what I can; so do some Spanish officers. The soldiers are going without pay and on reduced rations but often let children lick their plates. Blanco obtained funds and is trying to import beef from Texas. He's also encouraging a return to the farms but those venturing outside fortified areas risk their life. Guerrilleros treat them as insurrectos and Gomez ordered anyone who returns to work, surrenders, or negotiates to be shot or hung. That means the machete. Some Spanish officers let reconcentrados go home without having the authority; believing their chances better than in the camps and they don't have to watch. There's no way to reverse this for now, even if peace came and money available tomorrow."

"So Edward won't be restarting the plantation and mill anytime soon?"

Tyson sipped some rum, took a long draw from a half-burned cigarette, and thought for a moment. Looking at the shadowy park across the street, city lights, and rising moon, he concluded, "Too risky unless there's no choice. Gomez is intimidating or killing those working, confiscating oxen, and threatening to destroy every operating mill or plantation. Tobacco operations, cane fields, and plantations are burning. Trains are attacked, along with towns, mills, plantations, and even small garrisons."

"What's the army doing?"

"Blanco's campaigning but not with Weyler's energy. Still, he's pressuring insurrectos, and with autonomy some are surrendering, including generals. They're clearly hurting but still make life dangerous outside fortified cities; and those won't remain safe when insurrectos get more light artillery."

Starke and Tyson were about to leave when a portly gentleman with white hair parted down the center, mustache, and powerful, square-shaped head approached. Both rose to greet Consul-General Fitzhugh Lee. Wearing a dark suit with wing-collared shirt and long white tie beneath his vest, the large figure firmly gripped each extended hand in turn. Since commanding Confederate cavalry, the Virginia governor and Democratic Party leader championed reconciliation; arguing the war decided those issues causing it. He ran for Senate, was appointed consul-general by the Cleveland administration, and retained this position after Republicans prevailed in the 1896 election.

"Gentlemen. It's good to see you in Havana again, Captain. Join me for breakfast; I doubt we'll go to the office tomorrow morning."

He smiled at Starke's friend, "I expect Mr. Tyson knows why. Which reminds; if you visit in a day or so Mr. Tyson, there may be a statement. Gentlemen."

Lee left them then cut through schooling reporters like a warship breaking the line. It was clear that mob hoped to learn what was said and irritated he spoke to one table then ignored them.

Tyson observed with a grin, "It seems I'm unpopular tonight, Jacob. Lee knows who's accurate but keeps the pack hungry without alienating them. You'll see he sometimes just shrugs and says, 'quién sabe' to avoid statements."

Starke soon settled in soft cotton bedsheets for a fitful night of semi-sleep disrupted by heat, upcoming events, Katherine, his son, Cassandra Evans, and reconcentrados. He wanted to be back with *Calypso* at sea; or anchored off Key West with open cabin windows, a breeze, and Yamashita's eggs and rice to look forward to.

Chapter Three
The Riots

Starke breakfasted between the Inglaterra's arches Wednesday morning; observing people mass across the broad Paseo del Prado's tree-lined median. Loyalists viewed autonomy as betrayal and autonomist papers insulting soldiers intolerable. The day began with voluntarios, some army officers, and others parading past the governor-general's palace cheering Weyler and Spanish pretender Don Carlos.

This group joined another gathering in Parque Central. They milled, debated, and reacted across the street from Starke; but remained in the park so he felt reasonably safe and it was not his affair. The pulsing murmur reminded him of what refugees on American ships off Alexandria described preceding the British bombardment; before shelling collapsed all semblances of order, encouraging mobs to attack foreigners and property. Egyptian soldiers and police that had been reluctant to act, unable to resist, or sympathetic were swept into a swirling mass demanding independence while satisfying personal whims from theft to murder. Havana might be similarly vulnerable if Tyson's sources were accurate about police and army units, especially voluntarios. Some variation of Alexandria appeared possible with a large foreign population, especially Americans, living in the city. Starke was vying for his waiter's attention when the bulky consul-general saw him, approached, extracted a chair, and, while settling in, smiled, "Good morning, Captain, may I join you?"

Starke added another coffee to his account as Lee ordered. Two reporters appeared at their table, trolling for quotes. Their quarry's imperturbability before, during, and since the war resulted in an unruffled Lee responding politely; often parrying with quién sabe. Starke noticed reporters at nearby tables and in the lobby display airs ranging from anticipation to near panic but all furtively eyeing that growing assemblage in the park. Lee's order arrived and he began eating as though nothing was abnormal. Starke added three spoons of brown sugar to the coffee, retrieved his pipe, charged it, and passed a flame over the bowl's moist tobacco. Lee smiled then touched his mouth with a white cotton napkin, "Captain Albert says you have good sense of position."

"Sir?"

"Looking at the terrain and reading its strong and weak spots. Spotting where events will happen and where to force them. Said it was one reason he wanted you for *Calypso*."

The consul-general nodded across Paseo del Prado, "Like this morning. Come to my room. It's far too public here."

Lee's Inglaterra apartment overlooked Parque Central where the crowd pulsed with demonstrators arriving or leaving. Chants supporting king, regent, army, and Spain grew in volume as Lee opened the porch door. A rising sun instantly flooded his room and reflected from black cast-iron railings and marble floor. Turning to Starke, he picked up the thread, "Well, Captain, it looks as though we won't be in the office this morning. Let's talk."

Lee began as they sat facing the porch door, "I'm to promote our nation's interest while protecting citizens and property. With that in mind I've encouraged the administration to send warships to Havana and other Cuban ports on routine visits. Some argue this would upset Spain but *Maine* was ordered to Key West where she's less than a day away. Captain Sigsbee and I've agreed on two coded messages to bring her here and test our system daily. The first is an alert and the second a request. Albert said you were at Alexandria; any thoughts?"

Starke recalled Albert losing *Maine* to Sigsbee, a far better connected junior, at about the same time his Washington tour was extended and portfolio increased. He did not know Sigsbee but met her first commander, Captain Crowninshield, during *Calypso*'s Key West visits. That captain relieved Rear Admiral Ramsay as Bureau of Navigation chief and promised Albert would have *Maine* after Sigsbee. Why Albert wanted her was a mystery. She was built to offset a similar pair of Brazilian battleships although her sail rig was abandoned before commissioning and replaced by two fighting masts. Such en echelon designs passed from favor in most navies before completion and this first American designed battleship took so long to commission she entered the fleet too slow for an armored cruiser but too weakly armed and armored for a first class battleship. The similar but faster *Texas* was in the same predicament so the pair were designated second class battleships and became known for accidents, incidents, mechanical problems, and design flaws.

Both were still useful. *Maine* may not equal the new *Indiana* class but four muscular 10-inch 35 caliber rifles in twin turrets rose from a broad deck with three superstructure islands. She was always white and straw-yellow but one color or the other dominated each repainting. There were also a number of white boats in davits or cradles on and between islands. The midship one contained two substantial boat cranes, pilothouse, two stacks, and ventilators. The forward one began at her ram bow and incorporated the foremast and anchor machinery. Her mainmast and tall searchlight platform rose from the aft island that housed a commanding officer's cabin and matching flag officer accommodation. Each island mounted two 6-inch 40 caliber rifles.

Starke gazed through the open door at clear skies over the city then refilled his pipe bowl; a useful ploy to gain time. He slowly lowered the lit distraction, "Alexandria was open to the sea but Havana's narrow channel is a gauntlet no ship could survive except through subterfuge or surprise. It would also take more than a fleet to do other than board refugees; and only if the Spanish allowed it. I agree with Goodrich's report. The British fleet pressured Ahmad Ourabi but not the mob and then attacked fortifications rather than appear impotent. When that only silenced coastal guns and made matters worse, an army was sent. Of course, France surrendered any hope of influence when their fleet left. Our squadron took refugees of all nations and persuasions. The small German one established a hospital; and the same *Gneisenau* due here sailed with that squadron. They also made use of merchant steamers so that might be an option here. Spain will want to control this mob, which is not unfriendly to the government, and one or two passenger ships would not be threat or insult."

"That's worth considering but we cannot risk repeating *Virginus* or Haiti. As it stands, *Maine*'s arrival would risk Spanish support and could cause war unless everything was agreed beforehand; and the press would portray it as a step towards intervention in any case."

"*Maine*'s not the ship I would suggest but she's in place. Do you plan to alert Sigsbee?"

"Not just yet. What do you know of him?"

Lee was probing. Warships were independent and could work with or against State's representatives, even one of his stature. The course taken during *Maine*'s stay would be her captain's choice and the consul-general's best leverage through Washington since commanders were only required to consult local consuls. He obviously desired an impartial evaluation. Starke grazed his beard with one hand, "Not a lot. His Academy tour occurred while I was away. I understand he was promoted and received *Maine* almost concurrently. He fought in the war, commanded other ships, and served with the European Squadron, but his specialty's oceanography and he's known for precisely following orders and protocol."

The consul-general stood, hands clasped behind his back, looking over Parque Central, "Calm, stable, and predictable."

The crowd began limited stone-throwing with the inevitable broken windows. Around midmorning a sortie left for the autonomist papers *La Discussion* and *El Reconcentrado* where they damaged presses, shattered a satisfying number of panes, and intimidated employees. Tyson later mentioned two Spanish generals faced down this group, which paused before returning to the park where constant chants supporting Spain and its army continued. A second sortie for *El Diario de la Marina* was met and dispersed by infantry and cavalry, despite their officers' reluctance. Businesses remained closed or shuttered as Cuba's midday sun reached full intensity; just before protesters wandered off to the palace chanting, "Viva Don Carlos" then "Viva Weyler" and a small band leaving for the civil governor's home was broken up. Shortly after that, most troops were ordered into barracks while reliable units cleared Parque Central and Plaza de Armas.

The British consul soon joined Lee and Starke. Sir Alexander Gollan was almost six years into this posting and well-versed in Cuba. He believed the unusual restraint, along with absence of shooting, meant the entire affair was orchestrated. Starke rejoined Lee that evening for a stroll through the park after the consul-general sent a message placing *Maine* on alert. Despite representing a nation demonstrators blamed for forcing autonomy, the bulky man in his light suit was well-received. Whether because he refused bodyguards or they believed rumors he would take the field with Blanco, Starke had no idea.

Starke ate supper alone since Tyson and Evans were out then began a letter to his aunt and uncle before retiring. He slept uneasily and finally found himself among Alexandria's dead, dying, and debris. That woke him so he opened the balcony door, pulled a chair to it, and watched the sun rise over park, city, and distant Morro Castle.

The city was calm enough after breakfast for walking six blocks to the consulate at 92 Aguiar Street armed only with his cane. However, Starke and Lee agreed it would tempt fate to roam; especially near the arsenal with its floating dry-dock. Contacts would also be thin on the ground since senior Spanish military and civilian leaders were in the Captains General, or Governors, Palace overlooking Plaza de Armas, four blocks away. The rumor was they would continue into the night deciding how to control rioting, so Starke reviewed documents and read local newspapers.

Lee wanted a navy officer to evaluate Havana's defenses from that perspective and considered hiring one no longer in service or Academy graduate denied a commission. Just before approaching Walter Scott Meriwether, an ex-officer reporting for *The New York Herald*, he learned of *Calypso*'s collision and cabled Day to request Starke's temporary assignment as ersatz naval attaché. His proposition aligned with Office of Naval Intelligence interests so *Calypso*'s commander was detailed to monitor foreign traffic and develop a written appraisal of port defenses. The consul-general was among those convinced the island lost after centuries of misrule but feared Spain's precipitous departure would leave political, social, and racial factions at odds. Like many, he was concerned the island could become a new Haiti just off the mainland or subjected to European intervention. American investments and citizens were at risk but war with Spain could mean disaster. Havana and other major cities were heavily fortified so taking them would difficult, costly, and not accomplished quickly with the entire American army numbering less than a third of what Spain had in Cuba; and a blockade could initiate chaos. Autonomy might resolve the issue with less risk, but only if all parties bought in.

When Starke visited the navy commander's waterfront office he learned a small torpedo detonated near their dry-dock on New Year's Eve. He also spoke with one of Captain Manuel de Eliza y Vergara's officers chasing down paint requisitions for *Alfonso XII*. The man was polite but aloof, despite Starke's language ability, until realizing the American in civilian clothes commanded a ship that drove off then sank the filibuster attacking *Francisco de Montejo*. He loosened further after asking about *Calypso* and learning of the collision. It seemed he was requesting transfer to one of many small gunboats working coast and rivers. *Alfonso XII* was inescapably tethered to Buoy 2 by flagship duties and worn boilers; which Starke interpreted to mean funds, parts, and port repair capabilities were limited. The officer found this duty monotonous since very little changed except during more comfortable winter months, but midmorning breezes were still followed by unpleasant afternoons. Heat and disease turned summer months into purgatory but he conceded duty afloat was more desirable than a small army garrison or thrashing about the interior for insurrectos. If unable to get a gunboat, he hoped to join sailors from his ship's 400-man complement defending shore batteries.

Their conversation ended just before the flagship's steam launch left the quay. Starke watched it chug through the pungent bay. Admiral Manterola's flagship since November was the unprotected cruiser *Alfonso XII*, named for Queen Regent Maria Christina's late consort. Commissioned in 1887, she was bark-rigged with square sails on main and foremast; fore and aft on the mizzen. Below a vestigial bowsprit her gold-leaf figurehead was integrated into the white hull. Two large, ochre funnels thrust up aft of the mainmast. An elaborate captain's walk surrounded the stern and tan awnings were rigged over the main deck. Two obvious gun sponsons protruded from either side that theoretically gave four of her six Hontoria mounts a clear field of fire. Every boat was riding to booms alongside, emphasizing her extended stay and flag duties.

Starke took supper with Lee at the Inglaterra that evening, with constant interruption by reporters crafting stories on anti-autonomy riots and rumors of a battleship coming. The consul-general explained no request had been sent and no warship would come without one. He also emphasized the absence of disturbances, besides shouting around Parque Central's periphery, no Americans were threatened, and none had requested protection from the consulate. One asked if Starke was a bodyguard since Lee regularly walked alone, talking with residents. He replied Starke was a naval officer assigned for a few weeks to assist the consulate in a city where his family had commercial interests.

Sporadic gunfire was heard around ten then nothing overnight. When Starke joined Curtis and Tyson for breakfast he learned Blanco and the civilian government remained in the palace past midnight. Several officers were arrested for participation or refusing to act against any mob that supported Spain and the army. Two generals, Garriche and

Solano, confronted protestors and their officers; then guards were posted at newspapers attacked during the day.

The days' disturbances did delay offloading *Concho*'s condensed milk, glassware, and foodstuffs. Blanco had also begun establishing committees under provincial governors, working with local consuls, to coordinate relief from Spain, Europe, and the States. Puerto Rico's captain-general, however, flatly refused to implement autonomy and resigned; which followed one predecessor's recall and a second dying within hours of taking office. Curtis was more concerned the tobacco crop of Artemisa's mayor was burned since his investors' properties were nearby. Starke pointed out this meant rebuilding and starting operations must be postponed but Curtis remained firm about visiting the property and Evans was apparently pressuring Tyson to let her come.

In Washington's State, War, and Navy, Building, Captain Albert began his week's last workday at the huge dull-white edifice most officers referred to as the Building. His small east-wing room was in the Department of the Navy section of an enormous structure containing around fifteen acres of offices in five above ground floors. Southwest of the Executive Mansion on rising ground, its French architecture stood apart from most government buildings' Federal or Grecian themes. He found mornings especially enjoyable when an orange sun illuminated the view from his large four-paned window. Buildings appeared to glow; including the Executive Mansion, Presidential Grounds, Treasury Building, and multitude of smaller red-brick or wood structures. This New Yorker found the capital's winter days enjoyable and, despite a steady northwest wind bringing colder weather, today was clear with the potential of sixty degrees. His office lacked a fireplace so it could be chilly on cold days; but only at first and that pleasantly ameliorated by warm coffee from a worn, white china cup with embossed gilt eagle. That agreeable aroma permeated the room as he sipped, and would linger until the first pipe.

He studied the Treasury Building, then President's Grounds' walkways, trees, and statuary before focusing on an avenue populated by moving people and horse-drawn vehicles. It was beyond the Executive Mansion and leafless hardwood trees that once obscured much of the view each summer; until culled by a fast and deadly hurricane that leveled Cedar Key on Florida's west coast then swung north to Washington. A Metropolitan Company streetcar rolled west on steel rails in the asphalt above Lafayette Square, dispersing carriages, bicycles, and people. Horse-drawn cars and overhead wires were prohibited in the city so its power cable lay underground below a slot between rails. Capital Traction Company's line ran along the square's south side but carried only the occasional horse-drawn trolley since its powerhouse burned and that line still rebuilding. As true every morning, he observed those headed for offices, hotels, and stores were primarily men but with steadily increasing numbers of women. His redhead wife Abigail and recently engaged eldest daughter Olivia chose marriage but the youngest, Isabella, spoke of university then perhaps joining that morning throng.

Short, stocky, and slightly heavier from a long Building tenure, Albert's rolling walk, even ashore, combined with thick, powerful arms and legs to assure observers he could still climb ratlines, cast the lead, or row a pinnace. A short neck, close-cropped receding gray-white hair, and absence of mustache or beard accentuated this. He wore service dress blue, although civilian attire was allowed in the Building, and his uniform updated to the new regulations. Its blue blouse with standing collar was trimmed by braided black mohair, as were four sleeve stripes. His white cotton shirt rising slightly above the blue collar with anchor and eagle devices was sufficiently tight to wrinkle and redden skin. The formfitting blouse emphasized a respectable paunch and smartly creased trousers, stressed by thick calves and ankles, partly concealed polished, black calfskin shoes.

The junior captain steadily gained influence working the Building due to his abilities; and less than 50 of that rank were on active duty. As Secretary Long's special assistant he coordinated the Department's efforts with Treasury and Justice to limit filibusters supplying insurrectos for almost three years. To this end, he created, commissioned, and controlled *Calypso*; a converted merchant ship now under repair in Newport News after being rammed at a Hampton Roads mooring. He occasionally served as a sounding board when Secretary Long's assistant strayed and staffed Theodore Roosevelt's memorandums; this week's batch advocated restructuring the Navy for war with Spain despite both nations working to avoid confrontation until autonomy was allowed a chance.

Theodore possessed two speeds, full stop and full ahead. Albert had yet to see the first and it proved a conundrum for him, amongst others. This failed to vary even with his wife Edith faring poorly; serious enough their children were removed from the family home near Britain's embassy. He was intellectually and physically active with a passion for debate and hyperbole that thrived on confrontation and attracted reporters trolling for copy. Those with differing views found themselves in a vigorous, intellectual sparring match. His less obvious qualities included insight and passion for all things naval. Roosevelt's public image was that of the fearless crusader but he had never seen the elephant; unlike *Calypso*'s commander. The young men also differed regarding libations, although both rode and preferred hunting to shooting. The assistant secretary had exerted this energy to ensure Starke kept *Calypso* although they never met; which satisfied Albert since he could not guess how the two would mesh if brought together.

Albert wanted a last ship before retiring but his reputation for insight, honesty, and effectiveness trapped him in the Building and temporarily cost *Maine*. Without her or some other he would continue in similar assignments, or perhaps a large shore command, since promotion was unlikely with a minuscule cadre of rear admirals, the courtesy rank of commodore bestowed sparingly, and Congress having abolished the admiral and vice admiral ranks. He ended the morning musing, walked to the carved oak desk, set the coffee cup on one corner, pulled out a rolling chair, settled in, and inched forward over the faded Persian rug. Shifting his chair required well-considered movements during winter or changing weather to ameliorate knee pain; a consequence of too many years balancing on rolling and pitching decks. A wood correspondence box occupied his desk's far right corner alongside a mahogany pipe stand. Directly across was the small wooden box with rollers displaying "THU JAN 13 98". Overhead was a gas lamp of white glass and brass suspended from an ornate medallion on the high ceiling.

The Evening Times from yesterday was there with its reaction to ongoing Havana riots less animated than Roosevelt's diatribe and equaling its Dreyfus coverage. The paper confirmed Albert's inquires at State and Consul-General Lee's cable that Blanco's government retained control with attacks aimed at autonomist papers. Spain's minister to Washington, Dupuy de Lôme, was also correct in pointing out their consulates and officials around the States often experienced worse treatment. Albert's sources claimed de Lôme believed autonomy would never prevail over an intransigent Junta and war inevitable. Even so, the minister carried out instructions to support the first and prevent or delay the second.

Albert remained indoors the next Sunday, except for church, due to near constant rain but Monday was cloudless and more spring than winter. The Building's climate was less agreeable after Friday's *The Evening Times* parroted New York papers dedicating the previous week to false war reports, a Havana consulate besieged by Americans seeking protection, and *Maine* steaming for Cuba. These malicious accounts were retracted . . . after offending editions sold out. Although less jingo, *The Evening Times* blamed Weyler for the riots then implied the North Atlantic Squadron and torpedo boat flotilla steaming south for winter drills were to threaten Spain and back *Maine*. Albert found the last particularly galling since exercises off the Dry Tortugas were announced and reported long before any Havana disturbance.

Chapter Four
Thrust and Parry

Albert had a meeting with Secretary Long scheduled before noon that added to a week consumed by details concerning filibuster patrols during the North Atlantic Squadron's winter exercises and *Calypso*'s absence for repair. The squadron commander, Rear Admiral Sicard, agreed to allot several ships for patrolling but with *Calypso* in the yard and her alter ego, the Revenue Cutter Service's *Vanguard*, pulled for other assignments, no specific ship was dedicated to disrupting filibusters.

Maine was increasingly taking center stage. The Navy was set on drilling the squadron as one unit but State believed a port visit would reduce press claims she was on standby for Havana and would show improving relations. They also saw an opportunity to curb their Spanish counterparts' bombast that her entering Havana would be a national insult, if not act of war, since other nations' warships recently visited Cuba and it was equally appropriate for her.

The squadron would also sweep up *Montgomery* and *Detroit* on its way to Dry Tortugas for coal and drills. Less capable ships unable to steam with it would continue patrolling but two unprotected cruisers' absence would weaken filibuster patrols off the lower Keys during a period when *Maine*'s steam cutters would be unavailable and it was an open secret the Junta planned three expeditions. Spanish gunboats had apprehended several filibusters off the Cuban coast after

Treasury Secretary Gage pointed out past lethargy but it was still more effective to patrol known departure ports than every potential landing spot along the Cuban coast.

Albert wanted his ferret operational to fill this gap but was competing with calls for more ships to support other missions. Not even *Calypso* could escape. She was put forward to replace *Maine* or make Cuban port visits; the argument consisting of her being less provocative, had assisted a Spanish gunboat, and ended several filibuster expeditions. Albert derailed the momentum by reminding Long her repairs would take another month or more and she also pummeled a Spanish gunboat. That temporarily removed *Calypso* from contention while leaving her in Secretary Long and Assistant Secretary Day's minds once repairs were complete; which might gain her some priority in the Navy bureaus.

The very capable Lieutenant Watson was overseeing her repairs at Newport News while Starke was detailed in Havana but the shipyard's Government Department was busy with two battleships on the ways and the bureaus notoriously arbitrary. Albert was supporting the executive officer's constant struggle since Watson could work framing, rebuilding, copper sheathing replacement, and less critical tasks but lacked a commanding officer's leverage in Washington. Replacing her forward 4-inch mount was the most recent imbroglio. Rebuilding or condemning it at the Washington gun factory became the critical path to getting *Calypso* underway once her keel was confirmed to be undamaged so Albert cajoled a mount out of new construction stock at the shipyard.

The Bureau of Construction and Repair's Chief Constructor Philip Hichborn also asked him to speak with Immanuel Starke about his brother Jefferson helping persuade Brazil to sell several ships under construction in European yards. Long,

Day, and Roosevelt hoped to accelerate expansion while denying these assets to Spain. The elder brother lived in Rio de Janeiro where he operated a shipping company and possessed influence with his adopted country's government but Albert insisted the expatriate lacked motivation or reason to assist. He was not only still accused of piracy by Radical Republicans but never shed anger and resentment over his dismissal after resigning. The war also left him a widower who continued to mourn his wife after forty years. Albert could not decline because Hichborn and his chief clerk, Darius Green, helped obtain, convert, and repair *Calypso*; but anticipated only a pleasant Wednesday afternoon at the northwest Washington mansion.

The erudite Falk also passed through his office after visiting the Department of State's south wing on his travels to Department of Justice offices scattered around the city. Shrewd, connected, personable, and enigmatic; he guided Albert through a congressional hearing and continued advising in other matters. He also provided insight on dealing with the Junta and was Justice's link with Congress on Cuban issues. Today he told Albert the Democrats, more jingoist Republicans, and those members habitually opposing the administration were trying to add Cuban recognition to several bills leaving committee or on the floor for amendment. Speaker Reed, however, treated these as flocks of pigeons to be dispatched and sent fluttering to earth. The Senate, meanwhile, was in turmoil over Hawaiian annexation; which the administration did not support.

Several newspapers attributed sinister purpose to port visits by German training ships on winter cruise, demanding the administration act. They also accused the government of being unwilling to protect Americans and ignoring European schemes to colonize the island or establish a coaling station.

Equally spurious articles exaggerated the riots or reported Lee's kidnaping before returning to reconcentrado stories that conveniently left out the insurrectos' role. Even the delay off-loading *Concho*'s relief supplies was used to justify claims Spain refused to allow shipments through customs. Lee exposed this falsehood by announcing cargoes were marked American government property; the Red Cross was supported by Spain's regent, government, and governor-general; and the Havana consulate ensured it went to reconcentrados with the help of Spanish soldiers who were often sick, poorly fed, and unpaid.

Albert wore a brown sack suit, overcoat, and bowler for his Wednesday afternoon visit with Immanuel Starke. He left through the Building's elaborate east-wing portal after subtle jests about being out of uniform. Walking north over gravel then asphalt, he soon crossed Executive Avenue, where the new Capital Traction Company rails were freshly embedded, to Lafayette Square. Waiting for the Metropolitan Company car provided a pleasant break on a mild, overcast day so he contemplated the street corner shared by St. John's Episcopal Church, Arlington Hotel, and duplex mansion occupied by the Hays and Adams clans. Theodore might be there visiting since the assistant secretary often stopped by for a midday repast and repartee. Albert boarded the next streetcar then rode it northwest past the new Spanish Legation and Dupont Circle before reaching the St. Margaret's Episcopal Church terminus. His last few blocks offered an enjoyable walk down a familiar street to the mansion. The Albert family was invited there for a formal dinner and last year's Christmas ball. He also made several calls since the *Illusive* negotiations and Constance Starke hosted his two daughters for a Newport season at the family cottage.

Albert's family home in New York was a local showplace but this mansion was built to meet family and business needs. Located a few blocks northwest of Florida Avenue, it had broad lawns on three sides and narrow front one along a sidewalk set back from the curb by a second grass strip. To the rear was its stable, conservatory, and carriage house. The redstone, four-story Romanesque structure's large whitish-gray stone porch rose above a ground floor service entrance to kitchen, heating, and storage areas. The same stone was used for its foundation and single course separating each story. Three corners were rounded but a turreted tower with cone-like top and massive lightning rod served as the fourth. Facing the street was a smaller half-turret between the porch and far corner. The roof was a conglomeration of peaks, gables, small glass-globed lightning rods, and concrete-capped chimneys with translucent fumes rising from two or three.

He climbed the marble porch stairs sweeping up to massive double doors. After twisting a mechanical brass doorbell and hearing it ring loudly inside; the Starke Shipping and Shipbuilding's former purser Joshua Altman greeted him warmly, closed the door, and deposited Albert's bowler, overcoat, and gloves in the cloakroom. Immanuel Starke emerged from his library off the two-story paneled hall's rear to walk through a space that split the house then ended with curved staircases below Tiffany stained-glass windows. Jacob Starke's uncle was closing sixty but still dominating. His full beard was trimmed; he invariably dressed well and habitually moved in smooth, rapid thrusts. Developing hoods over piercing eyes below short, thinning hair contributed a ponderous authority.

Business or social, Albert found him clear, precise, seldom jovial, and nearly devoid of trivialities. He was a shrewd negotiator with a disciplined inclination for action; which accounted for Starke Shipping & Shipbuilding's profitable operation. That firm's blood-red swallowtail house flag with three interlocked black "S's" flew from a dozen or more freighters and liners working Caribbean and East Coast ports. The fleet's ships were largely small, heavily worked, sail and steam ships; although Starke recently acquired controlling interest in *Eveleth*, a large steamship designed to carry passengers and cargo. The firm also had railroad interests and, until recently, a Cuban sugar operation and small shipyard in West Point, Virginia.

Albert thanked Altman just before Immanuel extended his hand, "Welcome, Captain. It's good you've come. Let's adjourn to the library."

The elder Starke thought Albert, or "the good captain" to his wife, must have singular business to come in mufti. Since first meeting during negotiations for their elderly bark *Illusive*, Starke respected the stout officer who ascertained every risk or benefit then extracted essential points. Albert's only misstep was suggesting *Illusive* might go to his nephew once commissioned as *Calypso*. Jacob was edging towards joining the business and command was the one enticement that might dissuade him. He still hoped the nephew would leave the Navy to join the family business but reluctantly avoided interference in his life or upsetting an arrangement benefiting the firm and its people. His nephew again seemed on the cusp of resigning at Christmas, after the collision and learning a tryst with one of Constance's distant cousins produced a son, but that fell through when *Calypso* was back in the picture.

Jacob was more son than nephew. Immanuel's marriage to Constance was a blessing that brought no children. His brother's wife, Florence, died from typhoid during the war while staying with them. Jefferson went with the Confederacy after his dismissal for submitting a resignation letter and unwilling to return with Radical Republicans boasting they would arrest him and confiscate his property. His son remained with the family and Jefferson settled in Rio de Janeiro to start the Southern Caribbean & Atlantic Shipping Company. Immanuel hoped this visit was not a proposition that would keep Jacob in uniform longer but knew there was no chance it would encourage his leaving.

The masculine library had large bookcases along its walls and windows overlooking a broad lawn with streaks of spring green in the winter brown. Its furnishings included oriental rugs, floor globe, the large wood desk with brass lamp, and two wingback leather chairs. The black-marble fireplace trimmed with square brass rails occupied a large portion of one wall beyond two chairs on either side of a small varnished wood table. Immanuel motioned Albert to one then poured brandy from a crystal decanter. A cigar was also offered, but the captain preferred a pipe. He began charging it while the host prepared a cigar using his silver cutter before moistening the tobacco skin.

Starke lit his cigar with a safety match, drew several times through his beard, and began, "How's the family, Captain? Your girls were the life of the Christmas ball."

"They're fine, sir. We are looking forward to Olivia's wedding and appreciate your offering the ballroom."

"I'm happy to see it used and Constance thrives on social occasions."

"I didn't see Mrs. Starke. She's well I trust?"

"With Miss Barton at State; meeting with Addee about reconcentrado relief. Apparently, they've an appointment, or at least as much as Clarissa ever has."

"So, meeting with State's second assistant secretary, the President's Committee for Cuban Relief must be picking up speed. No surprise with Miss Barton; but she must be nearly eighty."

"And suffers fools less gladly with each passing year. Constance's working our acquaintances, friends, and business associates. Ward Line and some railroads have offered to ship without charge, and Plant's considering. We don't run liners to Cuba so I've agreed to ship supplies at cost but Constance thinks its good business to follow their lead."

Albert was aware Starke was best approached directly so he shifted topics, "Sounds like Abigail when the bit's in her teeth but that's not my purpose."

Starke smiled, releasing a puff of smoke, "Of course."

"Our minister in Brazil, Edwin Conger, leaves next month. Charles Bryan should be his relief but it may be some time before he arrives. Meanwhile, the Navy's working with State to buy some of their ships under construction. The most useful are *Amazonas* and *Almirante Abreu* in Britain since they're protected cruisers, but the coast defense ships, *Marshal Deodoro* and *Marshal Floriano*, in France will also be considered."

Albert took a draw from his pipe as Starke extracted the cigar, "Spain's after them as well I take it?"

"If we can't buy them, it's best they don't. Chief Constructor Hichborn feels the cruisers would be useful but their coast defense ships are less capable than *Maine* and *Texas* so keeping them from Spain would be sufficient."

"Where do I come in?"

Albert paused to delay the unpalatable, raised his pipe, took a draw, exhaled slowly, and looked directly at Starke, "Hichborn and Day, with the secretary's support, would appreciate your asking Jefferson's involvement until Bryan arrives. Our relations remain fragile after the Naval Revolt and he seems to have their ear."

Starke's beard moved as if concealing a smile, "Did you draw the short straw or were you seen as the least offensive envoy?"

"I suspect both; and I owe Hichborn and Addee favors."

"You offered your opinion?"

Albert twisted his brandy glass, "It would have been remiss not to."

"You served with my brother on *Saratoga* before the war so I doubt it was optimistic."

Albert took a slow sip of excellent brandy as his host knocked ash off the cigar tip into an ashtray then replied, "Perhaps Conger knows something we don't. Jacob did speak with his father while *Detroit* was there but I don't know what was said."

"Jefferson's views have not changed to my knowledge and his loyalty is to Brazil so he will act accordingly."

"I've had no contact with Jefferson since Secretary Stanton dismissed him but he railed at the dishonor, like others."

"Stanton's betrayal forced his loyalty south. As you know, Florence's death during the war then accusations of murder and piracy put paid to any inclination for reconciliation and destroyed all loyalty. He's had nothing to do with the States beyond commercial necessity, and little of that. Consul-General Lee asked that I make inquiries just before his appointment. He returned a polite declination, which I thought encouraging, but Lee's a Democrat and was a Confederate cavalry general. I'm certain any Republican would have been ignored outright."

Starke crushed the cigar's remains then allowed himself a swallow of brandy. Albert exhaled a bluish gray cloud of smoke, "What do you suggest?"

"My brother's now Brazilian so any appeal to patriotism would fail from the start. He will not compromise his adopted nation or appear to. I suggest Navy and State build a proposal favoring Brazil to such an extent his not supporting it would be disloyal. I could forward such an offer and mention you. He's followed *Calypso* and is aware of your support for his son."

"Jacob's success is entirely his own, I assure you."

"Perhaps, but I doubt he'd be on active duty without *Calypso*."

Albert was sensitive to Immanuel's desire for his nephew to permanently enter the firm. He had twice thwarted this and yet the amiable man finishing a brandy beside him was not only gracious but treated his family exceptionally well. Sensing this must be addressed, he began, "Immanuel, I understand you want Jacob in the firm. He was the best match for *Calypso*, I've not pressed him to remain, and will not do so in future."

Turning to look beyond the desk through the window, Immanuel considered a second brandy but sensed Albert must soon leave. The man was sincere so he replied, "Never thought you had, Sidney. I do want him with the firm, but in his own time."

Starke then looked at Albert, "Which reminds. What are your thoughts in that regard, if I may ask?"

Albert was seldom taken by surprise, but Starke was probing to see if he might join their shipping firm. The captain achieved success through hard work then advanced to his current position without planning what came after. Albert recharged the pipe to gain time, considered the best response, and defaulted to honesty, "I've spent most of my life in the Navy and not certain where to go from there beyond time with Abigail and perhaps grandchildren."

"I understand but please give it some thought."

Albert was thankful Starke began to rise, signaling the visit's close, and tapped his pipe on the rim of a partly filled glass ashtray. Starke shook his hand at the door, "Take care, Sidney and let me know when you fancy a change."

Albert did not return to the Building but considered the offer while on the streetcar and later walking. Starke provided no details. Abigail would prefer having him at home but one more sea tour was alluring and Crowninshield promised he would relieve Sigsbee on *Maine*. While climbing the row house's brick steps, Albert felt he understood Jacob Starke's dilemma that much better.

Albert reported to Hichborn the next morning and then helped Secretary Long prepare to meet President McKinley on Monday. The secretary supported American warships visiting Cuban ports and Spanish port visits along the East Coast, but was uneasy with State's request to continue holding *Maine* on station waiting to support, protect, or evacuate. Spain's minister, Dupuy de Lôme, initially opposed any visit; stating his nation would consider one unfriendly and any landing an act of war, but weakened late week when British, French, and German port calls were pointed out. He still emphasized any visit required several days' notice for Madrid and Havana to confer. Albert proposed the unprotected cruiser *Montgomery* since her accommodations better suited the climate, she matched the other nations' warships, and her class could achieve any reasonable purpose. She was also, like *Calypso*, known for pursuing filibusters.

Chinatown's New Year celebration could be heard in Albert's office that Friday but he was oblivious. The day was spent shuttling between the Navy's east wing and State's south with information on foreign ships present in the Caribbean and their port visits. Britain's North America and West Indies Station operating out of Bermuda, Halifax, and

Jamaica had the new battleship HMS *Renown*, cruisers, and gunboats. French Atlantic Division ships regularly came from Europe, and smaller nations like Austria less so, but State's focus was Germany after the unprotected cruiser *Geier* joined their training ships on winter cruise. That nation possessed significant Haitian investments and the recent Port au Prince incident tarnished State's Venezuela success; so they argued sending *Maine* to Havana would send a strong statement to Germany and Spain.

The Havana consulate was approaching German, British, and French legations about ship visits as Starke walked the waterfront to observe and confirm there were no foreign warships before the consul-general replied to a cable requesting numbers. The Compañía Trasatlántica Española passenger steamship *Alfonso XIII* was moored near Machina Wharf's tall tripod derrick. Over 400 feet long, the single-stack liner had four masts; two squared-rigged ahead of two fore and aft. Her black hull displaced nearly 10,000 tons with four white boats below davits on either side of a white central superstructure. Each crossing from Spain brought hundreds of fresh troops, but today she went home. Most of the nation's dead remained in Cuba so it was primarily sick and wounded loading through her boarding port. Something like 300 wearing loose-fitting light blue uniforms, shuffled past a sharp officer checking names, then over a brow that hardly shifted under the weight of listless soldiers walking out of habit; a common sign of malnutrition, disease, or combination. Several moved carefully to avoid jarring wounds; especially those returning home with missing limbs from medical amputations or insurrecto machetes. Several in litters might not survive the passage. He remained transfixed until all had disappeared into her black hull, the boarding port closed, and mooring lines cast off. Two tugs eased *Alfonso XIII* from the quay, leaving small black whirlpools of pungent water speckled with floating debris. She was slowly coaxed around until her truncated bowsprit sighted on Cabana Castle. There were several short steam whistle blasts then head and stern lines were passed over carefully to avoid the putrid bay. Gray-white-black foam erupted from beneath her counter as she slowly gained speed then turned north into the short ship channel. He wondered how many sick or wounded draftees aboard would never see their homes, fields, and towns.

Lee cabled two German warships were expected then turned to reconcentrado relief since he had the city governor's agreement to distribute aid in and around Havana. Washington and Madrid's actions allowed Secretary of State Sherman to announce Spain's readiness to support the Red Cross effort managed by Stephen Barton. A few Havana papers called for peace and acknowledged the calamity's magnitude but this did not extend to wealthy residents supplied through its harbor. It was a constant surreality Starke was forced to accept and did; perhaps because the Montana expedition eliminated much of his youthful naivety and what survived was shielded by an internal bulwark segregating action from emotion. While it made him an effective commander, and occasionally helped to survive, the hardness required abraded sympathetic inclinations. While in Havana it built a routine divorced from *Calypso*, left to the care of her able executive officer; and Katherine, in England with her family and illegitimate son. Even so, he looked for status from Watson and Katherine's reply to the letter posted when he arrived.

Starke stopped at the Inglaterra desk during siesta to check his mail and leave Curtis, Tyson, and Evans invites to join him for late Saturday supper at El Louvre. His favorite restaurant brought a Parisian atmosphere to Havana with French cuisine, refreshing libations, eclectic mix of colorful Spanish uniforms, and cliental that included loyalists, pacificos, autonomists, foreigners, Weylerites, insurrecto supporters, and reporters with generous expense accounts. They hired two victoria carriages pulled by small horses through a pleasantly warm evening. The men wore light sack suits and new straw hats from Obispo Street shops. Starke carried his heavy cane and Evans wore her white dress. She and Tyson took the lead carriage since they had grown inseparable operating the Laffin News Bureau's Havana office and Starke wanted to speak with Curtis. As their driver, perched on its raised box seat, eased them into evening traffic, Starke began, "What's the plantation and mill story?"

"Darwin's correct. The amended reconcentrado order requires all businesses outside fortified areas underwrite their protection and there's enough insurrectos opposing autonomy to keep tobacco and sugar crops at risk."

"Blanco's probably acting in good faith but few insurrectos trust Spain."

"I still need the Artemisa trip to see the property and approach people required to rebuild then operate. If we can't reopen shortly, perhaps offering a stipend will hold them."

"A trip's feasible but trains travel in pairs and never at night since the first is still armored to provide protection and repair track."

Starke visited the Artemisa mill and plantation for his uncle's firm before the fighting so he was acquainted with some people Curtis wanted to meet and help. His uncle did what he could until it became impossible and finally sold his properties to the English combine Curtis represented. Starke had no idea how many of these people were alive, fighting on one side or the other, and suffering in reconcentrado camps. He was last there a year before to complete the sale, also at

Curtis' insistence. Tyson went with them on the train from Havana to Artemisa then horseback to the mill with a dozen voluntarios. Weyler killed, captured, and scattered many Pinar del Río insurrectos but enough escaped to harass plantations, mills, and lightly defended towns.

Curtis raised his head and sniffed as their victoria passed a side street, "I thought we're far enough from the harbor to avoid that." Starke smiled, "Covered cesspools. There are regulations, but not closely observed, and reconcentrados use the side streets."

They rejoined Tyson and Evans at El Louvre and were escorted to a table where waiters in gloves and white jackets brought food and drinks in the French style. Evans seemed captivated by Curtis' Bridport estate, London society, and observations on New York. Tyson, absent his flask, took advantage of the wine list then after-dinner drinks once the table cleared. He was tempted to extract his gold-rimmed, jade cigarette case and finish with a Turkish cigarette except local custom was to avoid smoking in restaurants or near ladies. Starke recalled Evans mentioning she enjoyed the smell of her father's pipe but passed for the same reasons. Curtis seldom smoked except at accepted times and in proper attire.

Unfortunately, in Starke and Tyson's opinion, Curtis raised Artemisa so Evans brought up going along. She and Curtis held their ground and the other pair eventually began to yield. Starke did not support it but knew most active correspondents were chaffing at the bit to see what lay outside Havana and Blanco was not only more lenient than Weyler but took every opportunity to demonstrate an improved climate. In truth, his army controlled little more than major cities and fortified areas in the eastern half. The western provinces, including the countryside Artemisa, were allegedly pacified but the small insurrecto bands remaining ensured normalcy remained a dream; so Starke half-expected authorities would view the trip too hazardous for any female reporter. Evans remained undeterred and the question unresolved when they returned to the Inglaterra. Tyson and Evans retained their carriage for an evening circuit of Paseo del Prado; a north-south avenue consisting of two broad streets along a median lined with Indian laurel and evergreens; as much long park as thoroughfare. Tyson used the warm Havana evening under a clear sky with caressing breeze to dissuade Evans.

The next day, Starke's three supper companions crossed the bay on a late morning ferry for Regla's Sunday bullfight. He remained behind composing a letter to his uncle that reiterated Oliver Barrington Curtis was his son and sole heir.

Chapter Five
The *Maine*

Before Starke left the Inglaterra lobby for the consulate at 92 Aguiar Street on Monday morning he listened to Lee assure schooling reporters *Maine* would not come unless summoned and no justification existed at present. After studying a cable waiting at their office, the consul-general's jaw clinched as he passed it to Starke. Day informed them arrangements were being worked for the battleship to visit Havana. Lee wrote an immediate response advising several days or a week to negotiate with local authorities since the timing would link her to the riots.

Starke took that reply to the naval commander's offices near Machina Wharf since the cable office was nearby. He stepped outside after sending it, to find a Spanish officer observing the white German schulschiff *Gneisenau*, one of those at Alexandria in 1882, clear the narrow channel near Plaza de Armas. Turning smoothly starboard for mooring Buoy 3, she crossed the bay; her stack trailing an expanding flat column of translucent, light-gray smoke.

The *Bismarck* class corvette's hull was almost 270 feet long with midship gun ports for five 6-inch guns on either side. Displacing over 3,000 tons, her wood-sheathed hull incorporated false stern galleries and gold-painted figurehead. The ship-rigged corvette slowly approached a large mooring buoy under steam with sails harbor-furled; led by a small boat carrying jumpers to bend her anchor chain to a stiff steel ring.

The forecastle party wore white uniforms with blue collars and flat hats. White boats were stacked midship and two swung from radial davits near the stern where a whaleboat hung athwartship. Groups of uniforms were forming around boats and davits as they were readied for lowering. Milling waterfront crowds paused to observe this mooring process and bumboats began circling.

The naval commander's office would be busy arranging support, preparing salutes, and setting up courtesy calls so Starke returned to the consulate. *Gneisenau*'s arrival also required adding to the day's final cable. Lee was balancing reconcentrado relief and arranging an audience with General González Parrado, acting governor-general, but looked up when Starke entered, "Hopefully, our cable delays *Maine* until Blanco returns from the field. I've heard a French warship may come from New Orleans and another schulschiff, *Charlotte*, arrives this week. If you could confirm that with the port captain I would be grateful."

"Yes, sir."

"Blanco gave *Stein* a banquet last month and the French ship carries a rear admiral so brace for official functions," then Lee smiled, "I've no doubt *Maine* will receive precisely what custom and courtesy demand."

As Starke turned the consul-general added, "I'll bring up your Artemisa venture with General Parrado since a look outside Havana before the rainy season might be instructive. Tyson's no problem since his reputation with Parrado is better than most. The general may not risk a woman but I should have an answer before week's end."

Starke revised a letter to his uncle after returning to the Inglaterra and went downstairs to eat amongst reporters trading information or cajoling tidbits. Afterwards, he crossed the broad Paseo del Prado to Parque Central and found an open bench near the white-marble fountain dominating the park. Fuente de la India was a female figure seated over four dolphins; with bare breasts, cornucopia, and shield. Starke lit a pipe and waited for the military band to start its evening concert.

He left for the consulate following an early breakfast, arrived after sunup, and sifted through the mail looking for status on *Calypso* repairs. Finding nothing, he carried outgoing letters to the post office, passing through Plaza de Armas in front of the governor's palace. On the way, he trailed three horses towing a boxy, round-roofed streetcar over rails embedded in cobblestone. Once at the post office, he went to the "Nacional" and "Extranjero" boxes, slid his uncle's letter through a slot, asked for anymore consulate mail, and left for the public telegraph and cable office.

Starke recognized the young alferez de navio standing near the naval commander's offices as one who was just down the pier when *Gneisenau* moored. It seemed only the uniform differed from naval cadets ordered off *Calypso* after her collision. They would be missed when she returned to service but competing for commissions after two years at sea could be impossible if they had remained. The young man noticed Starke, introduced himself, and suggested a better vantage point between buildings.

Several seconds were needed to adjust to the brilliant sun reflecting off a dark, placid bay. The wharf's planking and gray concrete would soon be unpleasantly hot and metal parts untouchable. *Alfonso XII* floated serenely at a buoy south of *Gneisenau*, but his attention was instantly diverted to the channel beyond Plaza de Armas that the schulschiff transited a day earlier.

Maine was entering Havana unannounced. *Calypso* had anchored near her in Key West and along the East Coast but three superstructure islands, distinctive bow, and sponsoned turrets erased all doubt. The only Navy ship resembling her was *Texas*; but she had one stack and a single rifle in each turret. The battleship swung slowly starboard then made for a vacant mooring buoy, trailing a translucent gray cloud streaked with darker veins. Spain's royal ensign flew from her foremast and an American at the main. An outsized rudder turned the 6,700-ton hull, over 300 feet long and sixty wide, between two moored ships, leaving a wake spreading over the surface. Backing began once lined up on the large buoy, momentum bled off, and she stopped almost over it. Some tense moments followed while bending anchor chain to buoy before sailors in blue uniforms and officers in frocked coats began stowing items about her wide decks, lowering boats, and setting an in-port watch.

Maine dominated, even at 400 yards, and her unexpected entrance startled the city; but she was soon securely tethered to Buoy 4 across from Machina Wharf. The white and straw-yellow battleship's bulk and 10-inch guns would cause debates on intent and stir political factions. Starke calculated she must have left the Keys yesterday afternoon or early evening then steamed overnight. Spanish authorities obviously received no more warning than Consul-General Lee since a lieutenant rushed past to a waiting steam launch. He would be conveying required salutes, arrangements for formal calls, and other protocols. Starke abandoned his errands, hailed a victoria cab, and left to alert the consulate. He arrived ahead of *Maine*'s Naval Cadet Holden who formally reported her arrival. Captain Charles Sigsbee had believed his ship was expected but sufficiently concerned about what he would find to prepare her for fighting behind the peaceful facade.

Protagonists spent the next week regaining equilibrium and composure. The protocols started with port captain Vice

Admiral Jose Pastor sending the tense Lieutenant Alberto Medrano to welcome *Maine* and arrange salutes. Lieutenants also arrived from *Alfonso XII* and *Gneisenau* to pay their commanders' respects. These were returned by *Maine* officers then Captain Sigsbee in full dress uniform called on Rear Admiral Vincente Manterola that evening at the Admiralty Office. Lee and Sigsbee quickly developed a rapport, which was providential since *Maine*'s captain had authority to act as he saw fit so long as the consul-general was consulted; and they agreed on the volatile situation created by her early arrival. Sigsbee reassured Lee he would observe all customs and courtesies, expected the same, and enlisted men would remain on board to avoid an incident like *Baltimore*'s in Valparaiso. Officers would be allowed ashore only in civilian dress.

Starke proved the distraction. *Maine*'s commander was unaware a naval officer was in Havana, especially one who still commanded *Calypso*. He asked Starke pointed questions suggesting justification for his assignment would vanish if *Maine* remained over a week; and wanted information gathering shifted to his intelligence officer, Lieutenant Jenkins. Starke was asked to assemble what he had for inclusion in a *Maine* intelligence letter that would be routed through the North Atlantic Squadron's Rear Admiral Sicard to the Office of Naval Intelligence. Starke was obligated to unofficially pass local authorities' dismay *Maine* failed to provide medical clearances and nearly quarantined her. This did not help with Sigsbee, whom he suspected would have been less than cordial except for his commanding *Calypso*.

The opening moves were badly played and irretrievable so both administrations tried to recover, prepare for a war neither sought, and delay long enough for autonomy to take root. Lee was cabling status twice daily while *Maine* was in

Havana and Sigsbee put on an evening show for the city by playing searchlights off the harbor fortifications and arsenal. This may have been well-received by Key West's residents but Starke thought it inappropriate for Havana.

The schulschiff *Charlotte* arrived Wednesday. She resembled *Gneisenau* but was larger and slightly newer. Her ritual of salutes, courtesy calls and visits were repeated for a British cruiser from Key West and another round readied for the French warship coming from New Orleans.

Consul-General Lee made his official return call on *Maine* the day *Charlotte* anchored; accompanied by Starke with his intelligence notes. Lee went with Sigsbee after arrival honors and left Starke with the executive officer, Lieutenant Commander Wainwright. Their paths crossed occasionally at the Building but Wainwright's precise, courteous demeanor always seemed contrived; unlike *Maine*'s last executive officer, Lieutenant Commander Adolph Marix. The rail-thin, heavily mustached Wainwright was humorless and less inclined to conversation than Starke. He was rumored to totally immerse himself with any ship assigned and seldom leave; along with a death-grip on discipline accompanied by total adherence to hierarchy and custom. He wrote, but primarily advocating for a well-known naval reformist clique. Wainwright lacked combat experience but sailed in Bering Sea patrols, served as flag secretary, and was stationed in the Far East. He never officially held command but relieved a sick captain, earned a Columbian University law degree, and served on a Coast Survey ship. Starke's primary exposure came through the Hydrographic Office; where Wainwright worked under Sigsbee until becoming Chief Intelligence Officer about the time Starke received *Calypso*. What he knew of Starke's Havana assignment was only a guess since Wainwright reported to *Maine* in December but there was no doubt he wanted intelligence work transferred to Jenkins; which strengthened Starke's case for returning to *Calypso* at Newport News.

The warships dressed ship for the Kaiser's birthday on Thursday. Sigsbee, Lee, and two lieutenants made their formal call on General Parrado since Governor-general Blanco was still in the field. Starke later heard they went to the wrong building before a reporter directed them to the correct one. General Parrado received them cordially and made a return visit to *Maine* on Friday. He was greeted with full honors and provided her wardroom with a case of sherry and cigars. The Spanish military made almost no unofficial calls over the following days but hundreds of Cubans toured *Maine*. The port surrounding her saw large ships passing in or out and was alive with small fishing boats, bumboats, water taxies, and more. Many of the smallest had thatched roofs over their cockpits. Hearst's press boat *Buccaneer* was not among those welcomed and quickly detained on rumors a fugitive reporter was on board, along with a half-dozen small artillery pieces. *Buccaneer*'s arrival so close to the battleship's caused Starke to suspect the trim steam-schooner yacht was bait for some *New York Journal* scheme to put *Maine* at odds with local authorities. Lee agreed to avoid being drawn in but the paper's headlines still proclaimed Spain had declared war on it.

Starke spent Saturday morning writing letters. Katherine's would leave with *Olivette* on her next crossing then be mailed from Key West. There had not been any from her since Curtis revealed the birth; so he pondered what would come. Evans suddenly begged off from supper with Starke, Tyson, and Curtis after a morning shopping Obispo Street, like most local women, where she bought souvenir bullfight fans from La

Especial. She claimed to be indisposed with an affliction both temporary and familiar.

The men converged on Inglaterra's lobby in dinner dress then hired a victoria for El Louvre. Starke patronized this French-style restaurant most Saturdays and El Palacio de Cristal on Sundays. Each man contributed coins when the destitute converged on them between carriage and restaurant. One nondescript man approached Tyson to ask for a light; a local custom since most smoked and such requests were unrestrained by class, circumstance, or familiarity. The evening was surreal; their leisurely supper in unsustainable contrast to reconcentrados starving outside.

Later at the Inglaterra, Tyson pulled a Turkish cigarette from his gold-trimmed jade case, tapped the thin tube on its edge, and lit up. Starke's pipe languished in his room; but he did not like cigarettes and seldom smoked cigars anymore. The light blue smoke rose over their table. Starke leaned back in his chair, "If *Maine* remains, my time here will end."

Curtis' interest peaked, "What about Artemisa?"

"You still want another look at the property?"

"Of course; arrangements are needed for rebuilding."

Tyson interjected, "Pinar del Río fighting's increased despite Weyler's pacification claim. My sources say large insurgent units are gone but small groups still burn, intimidate, and kill. They favor plantations, small towns, and trains. Blanco's increased voluntarios and guerrilleros since they're from here, know what to expect if Spain leaves, and often eager to avenge loss of family, friends, or property."

"True, but my business must complete before summer, especially if Spain and the States sign a tobacco treaty."

Starke looked at Tyson then Curtis, "The yellow fever season's also approaching. I'll see what can be done."

His illegitimate son's uncle smiled, "And I can return home to plead your case."

Starke said nothing but Curtis' subtlety failed to escape Tyson, who paused lifting his cigarette for another drag. To divert curiosity, Starke asked, "Long week, Darwin?"

The thin correspondent holding his cigarette European fashion looked around, "Spent it covering the Germans. They've returned to training after Haiti but have a great deal of Cuban investment and want their nationals to know they're protected. Perhaps you had the opportunity to use your German, Jacob?"

Starke's friend was fishing, so he responded, "No more than polite social gossip at one of Blanco's weekly receptions."

Tyson pressed on, "Anyway, the top story is Spanish troops killing Nestor Aranguren. He was promoted to brigadier general after executing Joaquin Ruiz, a Spanish officer who went to treat with him. Gomez ordered those talking autonomy executed but the engineering officer apparently felt knowing Aranguren would provide safe passage. They spoke and ate before he was executed by machete; along with two men accompanying him. That was December. The Spanish have been after Aranguren since, learned he often visited some lady near the city, and surprised him during a rendezvous. Women were killed in the shooting and family members returned for trial. Aranguren was quietly buried yesterday by the Spanish, who've apparently located the lieutenant colonel's body. I'm still digging, but several insurrecto leaders met suspiciously similar ends."

Tyson took a puff, "Cassandra's working reconcentrados and their relief. Everyone says its horrible then blames the other side."

While Curtis' attention wandered to a well-dressed and chaperoned lady with dark hair being escorted to a table,

Starke added, "*Seneca* brought relief supplies this week and more are coming so the consulate's pressing for someone to manage it. Red Cross is my guess. Cassandra might find a story there."

"Much appreciated; I'll pass that on. Spain's planning to reciprocate *Maine*'s visit by sending *Vizcaya* down the East Coast then Havana. Our administration learned it from the press but claims all Spanish ships are welcome."

Starke was familiar with the armored cruiser *Vizcaya*. Her three-ship class was thought Spain's best since their only competition was a battleship and several unique cruisers; some still under construction. The type was well-armed and designed to outrun what it could not outfight. They also possessed a high freeboard that gave them an air of grace and power. Starke was considering this when Tyson continued, "Also heard they've added more boat patrols around the dry-dock; sounds as though they're worried about a torpedo."

Curtis interjected, ". . . and anything's possible given the right provocation."

Tyson took a final draw before crushing the cigarette, "You're right. Blanco's sworn in the autonomy government and relaxed press restrictions. He's respected but nothing's settled. Spanish newspapers are reporting riots there so more than Cuba may be at the brink. That's unsettling European monarchs and we don't rate very high over there so Spain would have gained allies if Sigsbee had forced the entrance."

They discussed France's lingering Dreyfus affair, Europeans aligning with or against Japan on Russia's Manchurian initiatives, and annexing the Sandwich Islands; but Curtis ensured Artemisa remained primary. Tyson dined recently with *The New York Herald*'s Sylvester Scovel and learned Blanco permitted him to interview General Gomez on autonomy. Scovel and Tyson attended the same university and were in Greece during that war. That evening's engagement apparently kicked the pins from any argument about Evans accompanying them to Artemisa once she and Scovel's wife, Frances Cabanne, compared notes. The Scovels had been married less than a year but were already together in the Klondike and traveled around Cuba for months. With that revelation, Starke saw little could be done to prevent her coming and agreed to approach Lee at the Havana Yacht Club breakfast for *Maine* officers.

Chapter Six
Excursions

Starke was awake when church bells for early morning mass began ringing at six since Lee was hosting a midday affair in Marianao at the Havana Yacht Club. That city was eight miles west along the coast so they were to meet early at the waterfront then go by boat. After passing through Havana's waking rituals they boarded a wealthy Cuban's meticulously maintained steam launch. Consul-General Lee and Vice-Consul Joseph Springer sat beside him on a cushioned bow compartment seat as they sliced through placid waters towards the white battleship catching a rising sun. When *Maine*'s duty officer hailed, their driver replied, slowed, and came expertly along the accommodation ladder's lower platform. Sigsbee boarded after nine officers and cadets in civilian dress. Starke recognized her chief engineer, surgeon, and chaplain since he spoke with most during the last week, onboard or at the consulate. Wainwright stayed with the ship, as his nature and regulations demanded.

The launch backed, paused to turn, and then started forward, merging quickly with departing fishing boats. Most were sparsely rigged with a mainsail held aloft by two poles, stern canvas shelter, and midship oars. These trailed or remained clear of a pilot schooner nearing the short channel separating the low-lying city, Captain-general's Palace and small batteries from Fortaleza de San Carlos de la Cabaña on high ground to starboard. The launch started to lift and roll before Castillo de los Tres Reyes Magos del Morro then turned west after La Punta Fort. The dark blue sea turned blue-green close off their port beam then exploded clear and white as it smashed into large, grayish-brown rocks along the shore. Havana's coastal tides ran less than two feet and the day calm but Starke had often seen an energetic north wind whip the sea into a frenzy that completely inundated this rugged coast and sometimes areas of Havana.

Starke surveyed the shore as they worked their way along; memorizing what he saw to avoid any charge of spying. Except for the small San Lazaro inlet, exceptional skill and luck would be required to land boats. Besides La Reina battery, a large, obsolete half-circle emplacement above the inlet, there was Santa Clara Battery. It was modernized, partly concealed, and contained three 11-inch, two 12-inch, and smaller guns. Lesser batteries and watch stations were under construction, modification, or repair along the coast. Most had been dug into coral underlying the topsoil, were difficult to spot, and incorporated underground passages. He recalled a British fleet's heavy guns silenced Alexandria's formidable defenses fairly readily, despite doctrine giving the advantage to shore emplacements, but an army was required to do more.

Unlike the nearly opaque bay and bottomless water off Cuba's coast, the Havana Yacht Club's approaches were crystalline with a bottom visible to twenty feet or more. They disembarked well ahead of Lee's eleven o'clock breakfast, walked across coastal sand to the large clubhouse, climbed a dozen steps, passed between a set of pillared arches, and entered. Starke observed the local garrison was patrolling streets, stationed on the clubhouse roof, and sweeping higher buildings. Lee's guest list was just under forty; did not include local Spanish officials; and most attending favored independence or were neutral. Diplomats were scarce since many were not invited to avoid their discomfiture, declined to prevent appearing biased, or, like Britain's consul-general, favored Spain. China's vice-consul and chancellor did attend and both questioned Starke at length about his experiences during the recent war with Japan then explained a large number of their citizens were in Cuba on work contracts or lived there. The half-dozen American and British correspondents included Tyson's recent dinner guest, Sylvester Scovel, and Honoré Lainé, a Frenchman driven from his plantation and no friend of Spain. The remainder consisted of yacht club members, including the steam launch's owner.

The dining room was large with high wooden ceilings, board floor, and porch looking out to sea. Its tall windows were designed to have the bottom half shuttered or left opened for sea breezes. Breakfast was on a long table covered by white linen under place settings, food, and libations; with tall flowers down the center. Waiters and staff worked quietly with practiced ease in black shoes, dark pants, matching jacket, white shirt, and bow tie. Most guests, including Lee, chose dark jackets with tails, starched white shirts, and ties. The more pragmatic dressed in white cotton. Sigsbee appeared unnaturally thin beside Lee and easily mistaken for a banker with his three-piece suit, white bow-tie, and gold fob. He also wore a derby and carried an umbrella. Starke was among those favoring a cane. All such accoutrements lay on a table by the door where they created an array of felt hats, top hats, bowlers, and soft straw boaters.

The consul-general sat at the table's head, facing porch and sea with Sigsbee to his right and, as the meal ended, stood to offer, "Captain Sigsbee and the splendid officers of the *Maine*." The captain responded with, "The United States and Consul-General Fitzhugh Lee, its representative in Cuba."

Group pictures were taken just before guests were encircled by emaciated reconcentrado children. Word apparently circulated about this breakfast or, like train stations, the yacht club was a regular haunt. Everyone dredged pockets and purses. Starke thought it a sobering and disagreeable finish to an otherwise enjoyable outing. He did not join the others on their special train to Regla's la corrida de toros that afternoon where Parrado arranged box seats to see the "Gentleman Bullfighter" Mazzantini. The starving Cubans cast a pall on Starke's mood and during the trip out Lee mentioned the office received approval for his Artemisa excursion. Starke wanted to alert Tyson, Curtis, and Evans since the trip had been less certain the day before when officials seemed unapproachable. Lee's influence proved decisive since a guerrillero escort was also arranged. Starke would mention that to Curtis since their officer would be local and know contacts for protection and workers should the investors opt to reopen.

Curtis already assembled clothing and gear before leaving the States while Starke took the same course as their first trip; buy most items in Havana then discard once they returned. The best material was that used for Spanish uniforms but it was too distinctive, and unsuitable for other reasons, so he chose a nondescript cotton outfit, straw hat, and high-topped riding boots. Tyson and Evans wore traditional traveling attire since their focus was the Mariel-Majana Trocha, local politicians, reconcentrados, and Artemisa businessmen. The party met Thursday morning in Inglaterra lobby and hailed a cab for the railway station west of Castillo de Santo Domingo de Atarés for the only first class car on one of two daily Cardenas & Jucaro Railway runs into Pinar del Río. Extremely well-appointed coaches existed in Cuba but this was not one. Wicker bench-seats and shuttered windows lined either side under an emergency stop-cord running below its long cupola. The small Baldwin locomotive with tall, straight stack, prominent steam dome, and largely open wood cab was just ahead, with second and third class cars behind. Coupled to them were half dozen wooden freight cars with exterior framing then an armored car. Cuba's stifling heat permeated the train, but Starke thought this last car must be an oven in winter and torture chamber during summer since the side entrances were shoulder-high with rifle loopholes; and its two round roof vents would offer little ventilation.

On the same track was an escort train to repulse insurgent raids or repair sabotage. It consisted of an armored boxcar, freight car, and a flatcar with ties stacked in a redoubt; and would remain about 2,000 yards ahead throughout their thirty-five-mile journey. The procession would go south from Regla through La Salud before curving west through Güira de Melena and Alquízar then enter Artemisa. The city lay in Pinar del Río's lowlands, nine miles southwest of Guanajay and south of the rich province's mountain backbone. Once called Nuevas Filipinas, the region was known for fertile, reddish soil, exceptional landscape daubed with palm trees, and unhealthy summers.

Starke and Tyson stepped up to the open platform between cars then entered and took a bench seat behind Curtis and Evans; since all pews faced forward. When their fellow passengers were seated, body odors merged with steam and smoke in stagnant air. The escort locomotive's slow panting finally changed to a strained burst of flat coughs then short sequence of rapid blasts and squeals. Large driving wheels spun against steel rails while gaining traction. The labored chugging slowed as they steadily picked up speed. Starke studied their escort's box-like locomotive until the conductor explained it was French and as common as their lightweight

Baldwin; then returned to punching tickets. Starke felt the car jerk rearward several times, signaling they were preparing to depart, and then lurch slowly forward. He visualized the glowing firebox under the engine cab and white steam shooting from cylinders on either side. They would travel at less than half the speed expected in the States; with light Cuban rails ensuring an unpleasant ride.

The swaying cars finally achieved a steady rhythm and steel wheels clicked loudly over joints. Left behind were the station's starving women and children that once farmed small plots or labored on plantations. The multitudes forced to rely on others' largess continued to swell and even Havana forced to acknowledge the disaster. Lacking consistent government support, reconcentrados emerged from inadequate lodgings, including some encamped in the abandoned moat, to seek work, assistance, or scraps. This caused a surreal contrast with the morning's light-blue sky, high silk-like clouds, and spectacular vistas.

His language skills allowed him to speak with people and once more reaffirmed the desire for independence enjoyed far less support in western provinces. This was equally true during the Ten Year's War and contributed to its failure; which drove Gomez to focus on them from the first. Weyler also understood this, concentrated mobile forces there, caused Maceo's death, and scattered insurrecto forces. The dispersed fighters then formed small independent bands with varying loyalties that threatened fortified cities' suburbs and rural areas in the Havana and Pinar del Río provinces.

Appalling accounts and pathetic Cubans refugees failed to convey what passed the coach's wood-framed window. Voluntario and regular soldiers patrolled the railbed or garrisoned small guard shacks at every bridge; with stations hosting large contingents. Villages and towns were encircled by blockhouses, deadlines, trenches, and barbed wire. The roads, primitive and few before, were neglected, destroyed, or reclaimed by vegetation. Wood structures between cities vanished, marked by chimneys, while only blackened ruins remained of stone houses. Reconcentrado settlements visible from the train had burgeoned since Starke's last visit; and filled with emaciated women and children using sticks or rail spikes to till small vegetable plots.

Starke dredged a worn briar pipe bowl through the tobacco pouch, tamped this mixture down, and then lit up. He heard the countryside was lifeless except for birds but now saw it was not exaggeration. Weyler's reconcentration policy separated insurrectos from rural support while Gomez tried to starve fortified cities into submission so farmers were forced from their land, buildings and crops burned, and fences destroyed to prevent raising animals. Goats, chickens, and other domestic animals were macheted then consumed or left to rot; including feral pigs. The stillness was unnerving, even from the train.

The tracks curved smoothly west towards Güira de Melena after La Salud then through Alquízar before Pinar del Río. Excluding short stops, its open windows and ventilators ensured the full aroma of land, locomotive, and town permeated their car. Wherever vegetation allowed, rust-red or nearly orange soil could be seen once they crossed into Pinar del Río. Green grass carpeting the track bed left only shiny rail crowns exposed. Palms became more plentiful; tall, emerald-tufted trees with near-white trunks or a squat variety's scaly stems. Distant mountain peaks appearing light purple through thin wisps of clouds drifting above lush landscape grew clearer as Artemisa neared and the Mariel-Majana Trocha could be seen off the left side.

This trocha was commanded from Artemisa and the most sophisticated of three fortified lines girding Cuba. Two to three-hundred yards was cleared along the entire length for Mauser rifles and a narrow gauge rail line built to serve its many whitewashed forts separated by small blockhouses linked by fortified guard posts. These defenses included miles of barbed wire in coils or pulled straight, electric lights, and waist-high stone walls. Areas favored for nighttime crossings were covered by artillery and sown with land torpedoes on tripwires. Thousands of soldiers and voluntarios were deployed in light blue uniforms with leather equipment harnesses, straw hats, and rifles. Away from soldiers on guard duty, working, or resting, were large mobile forces that backed up outposts and could meet large incursions. Lee advised Starke not to be overly impressed with numbers since troops committed to trochas, plantations, towns, and railroads reduced those available to locate and destroy insurrectos.

Starke observed Artemisa's nondescript wood station and covered platform beyond the right-side coach window as they slowed. The city lay just north of it so their trip would end without incident. A water-tower, off-white picket fence, and trees across two sets of tracks running past the station dominated scenery to their left. Socializing restarted as the station neared. Starke and Curtis were left undisturbed but Tyson and Evans' scribbling in black notebooks attracted passengers' interest as their train squealed, shuddered, and jerked to a halt. Once alongside the wood-plank platform, passengers rose and then shuffled down the narrow aisle. Starke joined the flow and saw Curtis assist Evans leave the car as a uniformed army officer approached.

Chapter Seven
Artemisa Return

Teniente Gerard Ildefonso Arango y Mendez commanded the voluntario detachment protecting local sugar plantations and its small guerrillero unit. He appeared younger than Starke but more sinewy with bronzed skin and close-cropped hair that would be glossy black if the long, well-tended mustache was accurate. Arango's cavalry-striped trousers and blouse insignia conveyed rank and specialty. His uniform was of the obsolete loose-fitting Guerrera style, not the Guayabera type based on Cuban work shirts; since voluntarios bought their clothing. This faintly striped, light-blue rayadillo outfit included worn, comfortable brown boots reaching the knee, flap-holster on the right waist, and Smith & Wesson revolver with lanyard. A light cotton shirt beneath was visible above the collar and brown leather gloves completed his outfit.

Arango's manners were impeccable but barely cordial. After introductions, he escorted them to his uncle's town house for siesta in its central courtyard. The elder Arango was more gracious, partly from Spanish hospitality but also, Starke surmised, as prelude to negotiations with Curtis. Teniente Arango had been educated in New York and his uncle fluent in English from years of business so conversation flowed with information useful to the correspondents and for commerce. The patriarch explained tobacco required higher skills but less land so coffee supplanted it and sugar as Pinar del Río's largest crop; and left an immense plantation decaying in nearby mountains. The Arango family owned several sites but only operated one due to the fighting.

The family was Spanish loyalists from the Canary Islands who reluctantly supported autonomy and paid men to protect their plantation. They viewed Weyler's removal as instigated by the States so Starke solicited thoughts on the military with great care. They revealed most officers estimated only a quarter of army in Cuba was effective on any day due to disease, with newly arrived conscripts the most vulnerable. Filibusters smuggling men and weapons into Cuba were another sensitive area since it needlessly prolonged the fighting, especially in Pinar del Río. Evans inadvertently improved relations by injecting, not entirely accurately, that *Calypso* sank two filibusters and put a third out of business. Arango became less aloof and described fighting with Maceo's army two years earlier when it assaulted the city then began burning sugar mills. A guerilla war continued ever since with most commercial properties destroyed and half the province's homes. This drove refugees into the city even before the reconcentrado policy but their numbers increased afterwards and the provincial governor's attempts to care for them were soon overwhelmed due to lack of funds and food scarcity. Almost everything came in by rail once insurrectos began executing farmers who sold crops to cities or towns; including Arango's father who was bound to a tree and macheted.

What agriculture remained was on fortified plantations like theirs. The old walled slave quarters on it, used in preference to a barracoon, was deserted when those enslaved were freed and Chinese workers preferred living elsewhere. It was now repurposed as a strongpoint manned by voluntarios with the ex-classics student's guerrilleros sortieing from it to scout for army columns and hunt down insurrectos. Guerrillero, voluntario, or insurrecto, none expected or gave quarter but the province's regulars, voluntarios, and guerrilleros were gaining enough ground for garrisoned mills and plantations to start rebuilding, tobacco to begin a slow recovery, and some sugar plantations to hesitantly reopen.

The uncle offered a place to stay after Teniente Arango announced they would be off for the Starke sugar plantation and mill ruins early since insurrectos made it prudent to leave at first light and return by sunset. While Starke and Curtis were away with the nephew, his uncle offered to introduce Tyson and Evans around the city. Once the older Arango and Curtis went off by themselves late in the evening to negotiate, Starke retired and slept fitfully until morning enduring flashbacks of Montana, Egypt, and China; waking impatient to rejoin *Calypso* and return to sea where he slept strong, well, and without ghosts.

Arango's twenty guerrilleros cantered down the street leading their officer's mount and two more. Starke was grateful Tyson and Evans believed the city would prove more lucrative than a deserted plantation and mill. He also, reluctantly, decided it best as a serving navy officer to not go armed while riding with guerrilleros; but Arango had extra weapons if needed. The escort sat small, hardy horses and were outfitted as mounted infantry with Remington 11mm rolling block rifles; their socket bayonets long since replaced by an assortment of sword-like machetes dangling from leather belts. Starke observed Spain's Model 1891, Collins Company's Paraguay models, and some local, handmade, or obscure varieties. Belts and harnesses were locally made with a belly pouch for spare rounds. Wineskins substituted for canteens. There was no parade ground consistency in the uniforms, except for flat straw hats with small red and yellow cockades, but all were similar and satisfied individual preferences and means. Before this fighting began they had been farmers, merchants, laborers, and miscreants but were now hardened veterans; comfortable with a rifle resting easily across each saddle. Only their officer carried a cavalry carbine; swinging from its saddle ring as they left Artemisa.

Starke sensed this detachment anticipated action once beyond the barb wire and trenches, but especially west of the trocha. As they passed a recovering tobacco plantation outside Artemisa's outskirts, he studied its rebuilt drying shed and sorting house, tobacco plants, and thatched roof huts of Chinese and Filipino laborers. The old French-style residence on raised ground appeared fortified with earth and barb wire to serve as barracks and redoubt. Its defenses were laid out with experience but would not fully prevent raids on crops, buildings, oxen, and workers. If these could be discouraged until the month's end however, last fall's seedlings would have matured, been harvested, and placed in drying sheds; and a useful field of fire created. One of the guards raised his hand to Arango as if to say, "Good hunting!"

He found this excursion tenser than the previous year's. That lieutenant later died of yellow fever and his command was uneasy about insurrectos. This one was eager for a fight and saw escorting ancillary to their hunt. It was the same anticipation he remembered on another expedition long ago and experienced the result. Besides, they might meet a pacifico or reconcentrado returning to his farm. Some Spanish officers, and even Maceo, issued passes or turned a blind eye to people risking return over starvation. These guerrilleros, like insurrectos, would see anyone about without their permission as traitors and Starke hoped to avoid involving himself and his son's uncle in a sanguinary event.

Despite concerns and late morning heat, Starke's attention settled on the present as he eased into the rocking saddle and closely scanned their verdant surroundings. Curtis intermittently disturbed him by riding alongside to raise a question. It was irritating but preferable to his distracting Arango who must focus on his trade. Periodically, Starke pulled a linen cloth from his pocket to wipe sweat from his eyes or lean forward to brush a multicolored insect feeding on his mount. Unnatural stillness settled on the small cavalcade, except for morning birds, as the road, little more than a lane, narrowed until becoming mostly grass. Where stubborn bare earth remained, or the shod horses of riders on point cut through, small red dust puffs rose in still, humid air. Starke glanced back and saw the soldiers riding drag had bandannas over their faces. Lush vegetation on either side was too dense to deploy flankers, but these guerrilleros had the experience and discipline to keep quiet and avoid bunching; leaving only their horses' intermittent snorts and gentle slap of machete scabbards.

Arango did not avoid the abandoned railroad spur to the central but led his men onto the roadbed rising several inches above a vanishing path. As they followed its rusting rails, the horses adjusted their gait to deal with ties barely visible in the overgrowth. A sense of expectation kept everyone from nodding off from heat, horses, and terrain as they approached the mill's abandoned work-area. Once there, two riders carefully scouted its tall grass and scattered gravel then probed partly concealed debris. The red-brick chimney was all that remained of the mill, and slat-sided railcars from Starke's last visit were now on the trocha's narrow gauge rail line. Vegetation completely encased scattered piles of corrugated tin sheets pierced by upright poles marking the structures' collapsed remains. What outbuildings left partly intact were burned long enough ago to have their charred and blackened carcasses cloaked in light vines. The two rusting fire-tube boilers and milling machinery were now fully encased in green foliage and main house reduced to a partial arch marking its low rectangular debris mound on rising ground.

The guerrillero leader signaled with a nonchalant hand motion and his men fanned out to enter the complex as if flushing game from a broad meadow interspersed with detritus and ringed by royal palms. As Starke expected, this visit replicated the previous year with their escort remaining in the saddle while Curtis surveyed, made notes, and took pictures with a camera. Taking photographs was new, but also Arango's behavior; compared to his predecessor. Defense was not the guerrilleros only interest since they eagerly scouted overgrown lanes into unplanted fields for signs of recent insurrecto activity.

Returning to Artemisa was executed with equal precision, the same tension as coming, and no one dropped their guard until checkpoints, trocha, and reconcentrado camps were behind. Starke felt free to urge his mount alongside Arango and learned small insurrecto groups rarely engaged armed parties of their number after Maceo's death and Weyler's campaign; preferring brief attacks against vulnerable people, buildings, crops, and livestock. Plantations, their managers, laborers, and livestock were, not surprisingly, favored targets. Larger bands would raid a small town or village, kill any loyalists, create confusion, and disappear; then emerge as a great victory in the American press. At this point, Starke understood why Arango's picked detachment was small enough to be tempting yet capable of giving a good account. He was primarily hunting.

Tyson and Evans enjoyed an evening drink at the town house while Curtis went off with Arango and his uncle. Starke took evening air in its interior courtyard; standing near a column under the porch overhang. He charged a pipe, lit it, relaxed, and looked up at a clear tropical sky. Within minutes he sensed someone moving nearby and turned to find Evans. They first met almost two years before; at the same time Captain Albert offered *Calypso* and she was with *The Evening Times*. His aunt dragooned him into escorting her for a mansion dinner party, since unmarried women needed one. They next met by chance in Key West while he dined with Tyson and she was traveling south to Cuba, hoping to make a reputation. She instead caught some unknown fever. Tyson helped her recover enough to return home on a liner and pass through quarantine into New York; where she recuperated with friends and family. While covering the Grant's Tomb dedication she discovered *Calypso* was at Brooklyn Navy Yard, paid him an unannounced visit, and boldly intimated an evening out. They ate at Delmonico's and attended one play before she returned to Washington. He was almost certain Evans was Havana's only long-term female reporter; and enjoyed an odd professional relationship with Tyson on *The Sun*'s news bureau there.

"Jacob?"

"Yes, Miss Evans?"

"Cassandra, please."

"Since we're alone."

There was an odd look as she responded, "Very well. Did you get what you came for?"

Her features added a slight smile as Starke looked into distinctive eyes under smooth auburn hair. The light, attractive lines gently etching her face seemed deeper but added dignity to an agreeable carriage and figure. He exhaled, "Avoiding insurrectos was enough for me. Edward must judge the rest."

"Nothing else?"

"The consul-general wanted information."

"Darwin said as much. We're lending our notes."

"And, you?"

She edged closer speaking softly, "Yes, but I'll never forget the reconcentrados, especially their faces and bodies little more than skin and skeleton. The worst cases won't survive if help came tomorrow. What rations they're given only prolong suffering. It was more discouraging than Havana; something I thought impossible."

"The western provinces are worst; for African Cubans especially. Insurrectos control most rural areas in the east and Mambises make up a large part of the Cuban army so farming is probably safer there."

"Darwin arranged an interpreter but most won't speak. Any opinion, from pacificos in particular, risks retaliation. Insurrectos and loyalists are destroying the farms of those suspected of supporting the other so anyone neutral suffers both. Blanco's trying to give reconcentrados work but his troops aren't often paid, and always poorly fed. He's also issuing farming permits and allowing licensed pistols and machetes but people are convinced someone will kill them if they leave; besides it will take seed, tools, and time before any harvest. No one accepts blame. Some loyalists even claim our aid is another scheme to turn the island against Spain."

Evans seemed in the midst of a personal catharsis so Starke listened, pulling another draw from the pleasant-smelling pipe, as she continued, "They say this governor does more than most but conditions and stench are indescribable. Some died while we walked past. I've seen nothing like this."

Starke took a satisfying draw, saying nothing. She reached out, briefly touching his arm, then the slight pressure vanished, and smile returned, "Good night, my captain." With that, Starke was left by the column. He attributed the odd turn of phrase to literary proclivities, emotional agitation, and mock admonishment for his earlier greeting.

Saturday morning broke clear and bright under Pinar del Río's expansive, azure sky kissed by thin cotton cloud tufts stretching to distant mountains. Teniente Arango took their party from town house to station. The horse soldier and Curtis seemed to have a solid relationship; perhaps because he was British and could help rebuilding. The party boarded what seemed the same train from two days ago, although Starke paid little attention to engine numbers. A similar guardian angel stood by just ahead with its odd, sighing locomotive dripping condensation as soldiers in light-blue uniforms boarded armored cars pierced by gun slits; or barricaded flatcars for a better field of fire. Curtis sat beside Starke on a cane-backed bench seat while Tyson and Evans compared notes on the next forward. Sweating bodies, steam, and smoke prompted Starke to break out his pipe and prepare a bowl of moist tobacco from the worn leather pouch. Their escort's cycle of strained, flat coughs began while lighting up and he was well into the bowl when their train lurched back, then forward, and scenery beyond his shuttered window transformed from town to country.

Curtis, uncharacteristically, lit a cigar, "Well that's over, Jacob. I appreciate the help."

"It's the least I can do since we sold you the property. Did you get what you wanted?"

"Senor Arango was most candid. Believes the end will come without local capital to rebuild so it must be foreign money or Cuba stays in ruins. He sees autonomy as the best of several bad resolutions but says there's little support since insurrectos don't trust Spain enough to stand down again. If they succeed, he's certain Cuba will become two states, like Santo Domingo, with the eastern provinces another Haiti. Without that separation, he sees rival factions fighting throughout the island and this is encouraging people to sell. Even those determined to hold on may still do the same since there's no money to rebuild and Spain's bankrupt. However, for those with resources and willing to take the risk this could be an opportunity."

"And your intentions are?"

"Our host is confident this cannot continue and willing to approach local owners. I'll propose our investors consider acquiring more property. Meanwhile, his nephew will contact locals, including those who've taken Blanco's amnesty, about returning to begin the cleanup. It's too early to rebuild but limiting work to clearing leaves little to attack and can be easily defended. There're also tax advantages for allowing reconcentrados to farm it for now. Most owners offer poor acreage for tax breaks but we're not building or operating so reconcentrados can take the risk, receive the benefit, and transition to a loyal workforce later on."

"Then you plan to rebuild?"

"Perhaps not for sugar since Pinar del Río's known for tobacco. I'm negotiating with an English processing firm, Henry Clay and Bock Company, in Havana. They've also said tobacco requires more skilled labor but fewer people and less acreage than sugar cane. Rebuilding for it would also mean a smaller investment and larger profits later. I need to go over the figures again before returning home but would start tomorrow if autonomy looked feasible."

"You seem taken with Cuba, Edward."

"An ancestor, Captain Oliver Barrington Curtis, was in a regiment of foot when Pocock and Keppel took Havana. We gave the island back a year later. He died of yellow fever and is buried somewhere around the city. There were rumors Oliver Curtis had several affairs but no legitimate issue so the baronetcy and property passed to my father's line. His portrait hangs above the main staircase at Brydian Grange and intrigued my sister, at least as a girl."

"He's the man her . . . our, son is named after?"

"Absolutely; and you'll find Katherine's deeper than what she reveals."

Starke prepared another pipe, said nothing, shifted conversation to passing scenery, and replied to Curtis' questions on closed ship versus open locomotive steam plants. They arrived at the Inglaterra late that evening after visiting a bath house where most clothing was discarded or donated. Exhausted and relieved, Starke slept soundly and woke to early morning bells for Sunday mass. He crossed to Saloon Brunet for breakfast, a cafe in the large Teatro Tacón building. Several clusters of loud reporters were similarly occupied, including Walter Meriwether of *The New York Herald* who also lodged in a third floor room, and allegedly served in the Navy before turning correspondent.

Meriwether was leaving as Tyson entered. The two spoke then parted when Tyson spotted his friend at a table. Starke stood as the thin frame ambled towards him. They sat down and a waiter was soon away with Tyson's order, leaving steaming coffee to be nonchalantly fortified from his worn silver flask. That quickly returned to an inside jacket pocket and the companion gold-trimmed, jade cigarette case, was extracted then placed gently on the table. Tyson looked at Starke, grinned, and spun the case a quarter turn, "Its Sunday and Cassandra's on an errand. We worked a story until late and she's off to the censor. They cut less when she goes but it's getting harder with *Maine* in port; reconcentrado or autonomy stories especially. When it becomes too difficult, the *Journal*'s press boat, *Buccaneer*, sometimes carries uncensored copy to Key West and other papers' correspondents."

Starke felt the locals' frustration with foreign press. Many correspondents in Havana, or their papers, never printed any Junta responsibility for the reconcentrado debacle that left starving and emaciated Creole, Colored, Mulatto, Negro, Chinese, Filipinos, and others wearing rags and trapped in the makeshift shelters filled with people lacking nourishment or sanitation. Many were dying in the streets while the living performed natural functions where they stood or walked. Women and children beggars were gathering on streets, near stores, and around stations. Blanco was struggling to provide relief but lacked funds and forced to work through an incipient autonomous government that delayed or ignored many of his initiatives. Tyson had the reputation of a straight-shooter, even if his paper favored independence, so Starke asked, "You can't be singled out for attention?"

"*The Sun*'s news bureau isn't now but the paper did have Eduardo García arrested then expelled last year. Rumors are Madrid's preparing a response to our ambassador's formal suggestions to avoid conflict. They sound like demands so Spanish papers are livid and many in government say no more. Pessimism about autonomy and Blanco's military campaigns is increasing, along with hostility for the States; even during the few days we were away in Artemisa. Today's rumor claims our fleet drills off Dry Tortugas are preparation for a blockade and assault; with *Maine* sent ahead. Sigsbee's ignoring laws about medical clearances and circumventing customs to bring in supplies has not helped; especially since he's not called on the autonomous council; and *Montgomery* left Matanzas yesterday for Santiago so there're two ships in Cuba."

Starke wrinkled his brow as he lowered a cup containing only damp grounds, "I'll raise those points with Lee."

"Relations for the moment are polite, proper, and tense. Bumboats avoid *Maine* and, excluding official business, only Cubans tour. The Navy's small boat practice on the bay is also said to conceal spying."

Starke replenished his coffee as Tyson's breakfast order arrived, and considered what his friend said. It was accurate. Sigsbee scrupulously followed protocol but probably had not considered the local autonomous government; and their boat practice was at least scouting since Jenkins confided as much. He was, hopefully, not venturing too near military facilities or taking photographs openly. Tyson lowered a half-consumed pastry then reached for coffee, "There's a rumor large American and European financiers are buying Spanish bonds and if Cuba becomes independent want those loans covered. Their profits could exceed 200% and Cubans believe it could become an indemnity like the one Haiti still pays to France."

After breakfast they met Curtis and Evans at Belot's bath house and spent a good part of the morning taking saltwater baths and showers. Starke spent a few moments that afternoon contemplating Parque Central then left for the consulate to read correspondence from *Calypso* that arrived while they were away.

Chapter Eight
Clarissa Barton

alypso left the dry-dock with frame, hull, and sheathing complete due in large part to her interim chief engineer, Lieutenant (j.g.) William O'Leary and Watson, aided by Captain Albert, successfully navigating shipyard vicissitudes. Starke was pleasantly surprised to read her hull was re-coppered despite added expense and they were about to mount a 4-inch rifle replacement on her rebuilt deck; but work remained. Albert was struggling to buttress *Calypso's* priority in an expanding navy preparing for war and hungry for officers, sailors, and engineers. He and Watson skirmished constantly with Navy bureaucracy to limit transfers and maintain a core crew; while turning a blind eye to the chiefs' contrivances to preserve their quarters. Ensigns Walter Dunbar, Gideon Blair, and Carl Martyn avoided transfer, as did Paymaster Matthew Wiggs. Cabin Steward Yamashita was protected, as were senior stokers, coxswains, and deck sailors. Thaddeus turned out to be another stalwart according to Watson's postscript. The gray feline scoundrel rescued from a Key West bartender's wrath spurned French leave to continue roaming the disrupted ship searching out morsels, places to nap, and occasional affection.

The second letter came from his aunt. She noted several Washington events then added longtime friend Clara Barton would leave for Havana on the fifth to support the Red Cross effort and asked Starke to call on her. Katherine and his son appeared in its closing lines. She was obviously bonding with a baby she had yet to see and saw marriage as little more than formality. Starke felt guilty for keeping her ignorant of Curtis' warning any union was even odds at best. Setting it aside, he turned to official correspondence and arranging intelligence notes then joined Curtis, Evans, and Tyson at El Palacio de Cristal; the restaurant a block away and behind Teatro Tacón at Consulado and San Jose streets. He fell asleep that night resolving to extract a release date from Consul-General Lee.

Reconcentrado relief and arrival of the Red Cross consumed most of the consulate's morning conference; before discussion turned to lack of relations between Sigsbee and autonomist authorities. Lee suspected this resulted from a situation not described in Navy regulations and, to be fair, State was more vague than normal. He and Springer favored independence but worried a sudden Spanish departure and autonomy fail the Cuban factions would fight each other. Consequently, Lee decided to cultivate the best relations possible with the autonomist government and approach Sigsbee on his own.

Starke approached Lee after Springer left with their clerk, Henry Drain, to suggest his presence was less useful with *Maine* in Havana and *Montgomery* likely to relieve her in mid-February. Jenkins had his revised notes, the cruiser would bring her own intelligence officer, and the consulate could arrange to review reports before they went to the squadron for forwarding. His departure might also provide a rationale for the Army's Military Information Division to participate. Starke felt this last point should be mentioned but not pressed since the infant Army organization was far less proactive than Navy's and Lee possessed significant military expertise. The consul-general's primary challenge was absence of operatives and only reliable source the Pinkertons.

The lieutenant partly made up for this deficiency with contacts through two family shipping firms represented in Havana, a language capability, and his reputation within the local Spanish navy. Giving away this advantage was no easy decision for Lee but both navies were preparing for what promised to be a naval war. America lacked Spain's financial curbs so it was exploding in size with more senior officers politicking fiercely for commands like *Calypso*. Starke could lose her if held in Havana and the old soldier did not want that on his conscience so he agreed to cable Albert for orders.

Starke's final week began with *Buccaneer* anchoring near *Maine*. The schooner-rigged, single-screw steam yacht was a *New York Journal* dispatch boat and Karl Decker, the man who arranged Evangelina Cisneros' escape four months earlier, was reported on board. Spanish police conducted a search then ordered her out but, probably on Hearst's orders, her master refused then ignored a resulting fine. The authorities responded by stationing an officer on board to ensure good behavior and prevent departure until the fine was settled. Lee and Sigsbee were drawn in when the press reported a *Maine* officer boarded *Buccaneer* to offer protection and assure them Spain would be forced to turn Decker over if arrested. Although the palace remained silent, their police chief and captain of the port were openly furious; so a reluctant Starke in civilian attire was dispatched to *Maine* and *Buccaneer*. Starke did not volunteer since Crowninshield and Marix no longer ran the battleship and he enjoyed no rapport with Sigsbee or Wainwright. As anticipated, it was a stiff, awkward interview that failed to elicit clear denial or admission the source was one of their officers. However, Starke was confident they understood Lee's warning if aware; and learn truth if not. The issue would stay within *Maine*'s lifelines and dealt with either way but his involvement did nothing to improve their view of him.

Starke returned to Machina Wharf on the steam cutter cycling between there and *Maine;* where he hailed a water taxi for *Buccaneer* to avoid giving correspondents an opportunity to bolster previous claims. The master was wary with his ship under armed guard and initially unwilling to do more than complain about the fine and libeling. Starke responded by pointing out what a foreign ship behaving similarly might expect in New York City harbor; *Maine* or consulate could do little; and *Buccaneer*'s prolonged confinement in Havana would achieve nothing. The master's subsequent manner allowed Starke to step onto Machina Wharf with some confidence the fine would be paid after another day or two on the front page. Lee was satisfied and Vice-Consul Springer not. That was expected since Springer viewed the fine as a national insult from the onset and made a point of being unhelpful; even when it seemed *Buccaneer* might cause an incident and escalate a minor issue for the *New York Journal*'s benefit.

The unprotected wood cruiser and French flagship *Dubourdieu* entered port on Tuesday; ship-rigged with a black hull like *Calypso*'s. She apparently sailed unexpectedly from New Orleans after a secret cable from France. Following courtesies and salutes, the formal governor-general's reception took place Thursday and her admiral's official call on the autonomous council Friday; where a state dinner was planned later in her visit.

The Red Cross contingent arrived with *Olivette* on Wednesday. Besides Clara Barton, protesting she exercised no management role, it included a John Elwell to manage and distribute relief supplies, one doctor, and five nurses. Starke reintroduced himself to Barton at the Inglaterra on behalf of his aunt and Consul-General Lee, offered to set up a consulate visit, asked what she required, and volunteered assistance over the next few days. The longtime friend of his aunt recently attended their Christmas ball and the women visited each other at the mansion or Red Cross headquarters in Glen Echo. Starke instantly picked her from the crowd but she was easily spotted even if they had never met. Not only was her likeness known across the nation and manner unmistakable; the seventy-seven-year-old entered the lobby with an entourage and bearing comparable to a dowager empress. She stood ramrod-straight with smooth skin, rounding features, and tightly bound jet-black hair. Her heavy, dark dress spread broadly from waist to just over the floor. Starke remembered his aunt remarking Barton took meticulous care with appearance, dyed her graying hair, and seemed energized by adversity.

She surprised Starke by recognizing him before he introduced himself, passed on his aunt's regards, and briefly recounted taking trains to Port Tampa then *Olivette* through Key West to Havana with no overnight stays. Despite this, she dismissed invitations to rest and immediately probed Starke for observations and information. He found her persuasive, organized, and committed although actual management was to be under a Mr. Elwell who once lived in Santiago, Chile, ran shipping interests there, and was fluent in Spanish. As in previous relief operations, they would not only feed and clothe but start rebuilding, establish orphanages, and return people to self-sufficiency. Starke was due to leave Havana and limited in what he could do, but her drive was contagious so he offered his Inglaterra room to her party as they were short one. Before leaving, Starke assured her of the consulate's help arranging an Artemisa trip and promised to put her in contact with useful people, including the Stark firms' agents, Tyson, and Evans.

The lobby's conspicuous arches and painted or colorfully tiled walls enclosed a frantic scene Thursday morning when Starke passed through to breakfast. Correspondents eagerly pumped each other for information or interviews with local notables. Tyson broke from the swarm and wasted no time escaping with Starke. He explained during breakfast that the *New York Journal* published a stolen personal letter written by Enrique Dupuy de Lôme, Spain's minister in Washington. His candid thoughts on autonomy, President McKinley, and Cuban insurrectos aligned with jingoes, Roosevelt, most of the press, and others but newspapers were deeming it a national insult, calling for dismissal, and demanding an apology from Spain. The tumult pushed *Montgomery*'s departure from Santiago to the back pages.

Tyson and Evans joined Starke for a light meal before Friday's siesta. Curtis sent his regrets as he was meeting with Henry Clay & Bock Company about tobacco treaty negotiations between Spain and the States. The trio found a round iron table encircled by wicker chairs under the Inglaterra's arches. Evans sipped wine across from Starke who enjoyed a balloon glass of medicinal Spanish gin, tonic, quinine, and fruit. Tyson satisfied himself with rum after several aborted attempts to extract the silver flask.

Evans wore a cotton walking dress, was lightly corseted, and bound her rich auburn hair in the pompadour style under a flat straw boater. The woman's skin glistened with a delicate sheen of sweat and she smelled faintly of lemon. Starke's forefinger traced his glass's rim as he recalled her unannounced appearance on *Calypso* in New York, their evening out, and recent conversation in Artemisa. Strangely, there were also flashbacks of Katherine in Havana a year before, their irrepressible passion, and resultant son. It seemed the two women began to merge and he imagined Cassandra, not Katherine, at his door. She cleared her throat, "What are you thinking, Jacob?"

Her amused expression suggested she had been studying him. Tyson extracted his flat jade case, removed a Turkish cigarette and prepared to light, which allowed Starke time to recover, "Only a momentary distraction; *Maine* should be leaving for Mardi Gras. I expect she'll have orders when *Cushing* brings dispatches this weekend or early next week."

To reinforce his evasion, Starke extracted the pipe Evans preferred to Havana's pungent atmosphere then began a diversion. The meerschaum's light-brown bowl dredged slowly through a pliable leather pouch and resulting moist tobacco pressed lightly with a finger. When just right, a small central spot was lit, allowing the fire to burn down and towards the outside. Tyson, thin wrist resting on their table's rim and smoldering cigarette in his fingers, was not taken in. It was a familiar ploy, but he ignored it and observed, "Seeing *Maine* leave might ease tensions. The local press is seething over de Lôme's stolen letter receiving attention while Aranguren executing Ruiz was not only ignored but our papers vilified the soldiers who caught and killed the general. It's made reporting difficult. People won't speak and censors avoid passing anything."

Starke released a light bluish puff of smoke, "That was discussed at the consulate. They were popular, and friends as I recall. Lieutenant Colonel Ruiz was an engineer on Blanco's staff who thought he could discuss autonomy with Colonel Aranguren but Gomez ordered anyone speaking with the Spanish executed so Ruiz was macheted with his two guides. Lee tried to save him but there wasn't time. The authorities believe they've located the body. Aranguren was promoted to brigadier general before he was killed and recently buried."

Tyson took a drag, "That agrees with my sources but they also claim Aranguren wasn't the only insurrecto dispatched this way and if assassinations become popular, Havana will be even less safe for correspondents. The loyalists I still speak with are convinced we support insurrectos so I've suggested Cassandra work from Key West."

"And I've declined," Evans interrupted with a tight smile, "the reconcentrado story must be told and Clara Barton's work made known."

Tyson exhaled light gray smoke, "I no longer press the issue. Port au Prince expects two Italian gunboats to enforce their claims. Is that why *Montgomery* left Santiago?"

Starke could respond with candor, "Consulates don't receive information unless they're involved. I thought she would relieve *Maine* but there's talk she will be off Jamaica on filibuster patrol."

Barton's Artemisa visit became the topic then Starke went for a nap before returning to the consulate; leaving the journalists working some new story. He learned Evans' typing speed apparently exceeded Tyson's; who added two machines to the local office besides his personal Underwood. One went to Evans and the other shared by part-time typists. That either correspondent typed was unusual. Most did not. Some were proficient in shorthand but the majority dictated or used longhand. The pair seemed a strong team and those they worked with appeared satisfied so Starke guessed Tyson was doing well in his forced transition to management.

The bottle-green torpedo boat *Cushing* was anchored near *Maine* that afternoon when Starke left Machina Wharf in a steam cutter. She could theoretically sink her larger and vastly more expensive neighbor; a fact driving world naval debates.

Everything concerning these razor-thin boats was contentious except atrocious seakeeping, a fact proven by this trip. *Cushing* crossed from Key West in heavy weather several days early due to a decoding error. An officer was washed overboard and drowned in spite of two sailors' effort to save him; which might gain both Medals of Honor. Ensign Breckinridge was the Army inspector general's eldest son and nephew to a vice-president who later served as a Confederate major general.

Today's visit was partly because Springer asked Starke to confirm Navy plans for the ensign's remains but primarily to arrange Clara Barton's Sunday visit. The first was straightforward since *Cushing*'s commander, Lieutenant Albert Gleaves, and Captain Sigsbee already agreed the torpedo boat would take the officer's body back to Key West. The second required negotiation. Sigsbee invited her group for supper with his officers and prevailed on Starke to shepherd Red Cross guests. The Sabbath was chosen because *Maine*'s commander was hosting the autonomy council that Saturday and she would be delivering food and clothing during the week; trailed by Evans. It was also scheduled around Sunday services and funeral for *Cushing*'s ensign; conducted by the formidable, John Chidwick, one of the Navy's few Catholic chaplains.

Cushing was steaming to Key West before Barton's party boarded *Maine*'s thirty-three-foot steam cutter for the short passage through pungent water. As it backed from the substantial wharf with dark water lapping against pilings, Starke told Barton his Inglaterra room was transferred so her entire party could be lodged there. He also assured her it was no inconvenience since Starke Shipping & Shipbuilding's Havana agent booked him a two-day stay at Hotel Mascotte on Oficios Street; then pointed it out between buildings close to the wharf rapidly falling astern. The renovated mansion was across from where the boat to *Olivette* would depart and its rooms, above a ground floor of shops, overlooked the harbor. Aron Sharett, his uncle's Jewish friend, chandler, and business associate often recommended it but Starke invariably chose the Inglaterra. He noticed Barton addressed him as captain when in public, and when he brought it up she replied he commanded *Calypso* and observing civil or military protocol was in her upbringing and useful in relief work.

Coxswain Aufindsen was a Norwegian sailor Watson failed to poach from *Maine* and today his white cutter sliced easily through the bay to her starboard accommodation ladder; across a broad main deck from the aft turret. Her stern pointed at the city, a position that never seemed to vary, probably due to easterly breezes over the bay and sluggish current. From habit, Starke scrutinized canvas awnings rigged above nearly white deck planking that ran most of the ship's length then traced the starboard anchor chain to where it submerged; before resurfacing at the large mooring buoy caked with droppings. The starboard boat boom was not swung out or rigged so her other white-hulled boats with varnished, dark-wood strakes must be on the port side hanging from davits at deck level or secured to that boom; ready for training, errands, or Jenkins' intelligence excursions.

Aufindsen' crew anticipated difficulty when a woman of Barton's age wearing dark, heavy clothing stepped from cutter gunwale to the ladder's platform. Starke's aunt said Barton maintained herself and, except for dancing, did not shy from physical activity. While he considered this, the petite figure crossed easily, climbed the gleaming wood steps, paused briefly to honor the motionless flag, and stepped onto quarterdeck. Sigsbee and Wainwright greeted her party on the immaculate deck then took them across, below a steel bridge between superstructures with boat cradles on either side, and into her aft island. Beyond its door, they walked by offices lining the short passageway to her flag cabin; port side aft and a deck above half of the trapezoidal wardroom and its adjacent staterooms.

Starke left Barton with the executive officer then went below to locate Jenkins; confident Wainwright and Sigsbee's cabin steward John Bell would care for their famous guest. Starke first met Bell while visiting the battleship in Key West and the two ships' stewards collaborated there. He was also aware *Maine*'s Negro steward was known and respected throughout the fleet for years of good deeds; so his health and situation were of interest to officers and enlisted whenever his name came up. There was also a mystery. Watson once asked *Maine*'s first executive officer about Bell's history and discovered the sailor's service record had him enlisting in 1871 but he was on the Grand Army of the Republic rolls, which required serving during the war. There was also a relationship with a White family, or naval officer, since his leave was often spent at their home. Marix had no idea whether the family was Northern or Southern, but understood him to be fond of their children, brought them presents, and followed their lives. Beyond that, his family was the Navy and when overseas he visited sailors' graves to tend them and leave flowers.

Starke found several officers in service dress blue uniforms lounging about the paneled wardroom near her stern. Although shaped by hull and staterooms along either side, it was furnished to mimic a gentleman's club. The dark rug with its intricate pattern hid a steel deck and deadened noise while paneled walls and wood doors contributed to this effect; which instantly vanished when visitors looked up to white piping, ducts, steel girders, and riveted plates surrounding a skylight. This refuge was attended by a bow-tied steward from some Asian country moving inconspicuously from one cluster to the next. Two of Starke's classmates, Lieutenants Blow and Blandin, were assigned to the ship but only Blow was present. When he rose from a chair, Starke immediately saw the change since they were cadets. Blow seemed more distinguished and almost professorial with eyeglasses, retreating hair, and small mustache that only slightly lagged the scalp in turning white. Starke heard he was awarded a medal from Queen Liliuokalani while an aid to retired Admiral Brown; Norfolk's commandant during *Calypso's* conversion. Blow confirmed this and added Congress finally allowed him to accept the honor a year earlier so it was safely stored in a stateroom drawer. Like Starke, he was caught between the Navy and a family firm, except his situation resulted from marriage.

Starke crossed the room to speak with *Maine's* intelligence officer. Jenkins was relaxing in a large, cane armchair with soft cushions beside a small table near the mainmast that passed through room center. Chief Engineer Charles Howell and Assistant Engineer Darwin Merritt were also sitting at it with pencil and paper tracing a rough drawing of condenser piping. In front of an empty chair lay *Facts and Fakes About Cuba.* Chaplain Chidwick had been reading it before called to the flag cabin. Starke already turned over his notes to the large lieutenant with prematurely white hair and dark mustache so there would be little difficulty creating an intelligence report. They spoke until a steward announced Barton's party was leaving for the officer's mess.

That mess was near the wardroom, along the starboard side and across from the aft torpedo tube. A pantry separated it from the junior officers' mess just forward. The inboard wall was fitted with varnished wood cabinets and along the outboard was a long, plain bench to wait for a place at the long table running down its center. Precisely sited on a starched and bleached cotton tablecloth were white china plates ornamented by a thin gold line with eagle and anchor insignia. Polished silver flatware with similar engraving lay by silver rings clutching rolled cloth napkins. Several varieties of crystal stemware, shaped for water, wine, and other drinks, rose near each setting. Aligned down center table were crystal decanters and square silver serving pieces crowned by an elaborate tureen. The paymaster, mess treasurer, and Bell had ensured all was perfect since Barton was arguably the nation's most well-known woman after launching the American Red Cross, two wars, Ottoman Empire relief, Michigan's thumb fire, and reconstruction of the South Carolina Sea Islands after a devastating hurricane.

The main entree was fresh fish followed by turtle soup, salad, pudding, fruit, and nuts. Navy regulations allowed only wine so, while the table was cleared, Starke leaned back in his chair near the far end desiring an after dinner brandy. Barton received complete attention so he spoke sparingly, followed the conversation, and observed. Bell was often at the door but always where a glance from Sigsbee would bring him to the table. The cabin steward was thin, short, perpetually anxious, perhaps in his late fifties, and had a soft, light-brown complexion. His head was more oval than round with a narrow, short face below tightly curled, receding hair. The mustache and goatee he probably wore most of his life were no longer black but like his hair transitioning to white.

Barton complemented the clean, well-lit, and disciplined battleship before contrasting it with Havana's diseases, poor sanitation, and instability. While explaining what the Red Cross offered she emphasized the necessity to survey places like Artemisa then extend relief efforts across Cuba; glancing down table at Starke when speaking of their planned excursion.

She was uncharacteristically pensive after leaving for the Inglaterra then put off bidding Starke goodnight until her retinue left the lobby. She then led him to a quiet corner and spoke in a soft voice, "I offered Lieutenant Commander Wainwright our services should he require them. He doubts they will, as I do, but disaster plays no favorites and comes without warning. These things stay with us. I've known Constance since the war and she mentioned your nightmares."

Starke was irritated his aunt revealed that but admitted anyone around him long enough was aware; one episode brought Katherine to his room and bed. He fumbled for a pipe, observing, "Only ashore Miss Barton. At sea, I sleep quite well."

She touched his arm, smiling, "And you enjoy riding I understand. Constance said Immanuel thinks you sit a horse as if born to it. We have like interests and afflictions. My black periods vanish when the call comes."

She then looked directly into Starke's eyes with an intensity he was often accused of visiting on others, adding with a sigh, "Jacob, if I was sixty years younger; Godspeed on your journey back to *Calypso*."

Chapter Nine
Havana Farewell

Starke spent Monday and Tuesday preparing to depart Wednesday afternoon on *Olivette* for Port Tampa, with a Key West port call along the way, then Washington by rail. Meanwhile, Dupuy de Lôme and family were similarly occupied in New York City. Their furnishings had been auctioned off and family lodged in a hotel until White Star Line's *Britannic* boarded; while diplomats in Madrid and Washington negotiated a response to his personal letter that would placate their publics. Spain disavowed it without apology on Tuesday. This was accepted and State informed Luis Polo de Bernabé Pilón would take his role as minister. The jingoes, *New York Journal*, and war parties were infuriated.

Spain's armored cruiser *Vizcaya* was steaming for New York when Starke made his last courtesy call on Captain Sigsbee, senior naval officer in Havana. Doing otherwise would have been discourteous and it was customary to provide an opportunity to send material to the Building; he already had several letters for Day. Starke ignored harbor vapors and enjoyed the calm, bright Havana morning with its fitful land breeze while *Maine*'s steam cutter prepared to leave Machina Wharf. The battleship's ram bow was pointed at the waterfront instead of her stern or quarter. She had never settled in that position before, but it controlled the harbor perfectly. Her port turret's 10-inch rifles covered the inner harbor; and starboard the fortresses and entrance channel. It was a fluke that meant nothing now and even less in days, if not hours. More boilers would be brought on line, steam raised, the buoy slipped, and she would pass through the short channel below La Cabaña fortress and Morro for New Orleans and her second Mardi Gras.

Today's six-man crew was the same that carried Barton's party so Starke spoke briefly with Coxswain Aufindsen. Precisely at the scheduled departure time, he backed clear of the wharf, came ahead, and started cutting through a thick, murky bay trailing faint, light-gray smoke that settled some distance off. Liners, freighters, and ferries were surrounded by a profusion of coastal shipping, craft, and boats enlivening Havana's wharfs, piers, quays, and anchorages. Along Regla's waterfront across the bay large ships were going pierside to work cargo, coal, or complete voyage repairs.

Starke decided the battleship's new position would offer her crew a fresh view of harbor and city. Their excitement of entering Havana had long since dulled by routine, work, training, quarter watches overnight, and pungent harbor's unrelenting heat. For more than three weeks they were confined to a sweltering steel island surrounded by life but without shore leave, except for a few officers in civilian dress. Contrived events offered brief distractions but even watching ships arrive and depart held little interest.

The French unprotected cruiser *Dubourdieu* leaving after something like a week must have brought mixed emotions. She was underway for New Orleans' annual festival. *Dubourdieu*, *Texas*, and other ships were there with *Maine* during last year's celebration so many sailors were no doubt resurrecting and embellishing stories of exuberance and desertions. During other visits, Starke heard talk of the baseball team's victory in Key West, but their ship's reputation for calamities was never far away: a newly discharged sailor falling dead by the brow, three drowned during a storm, ramming a New York City pier, and an officer with them in New Orleans just died on *Cushing*. No doubt their endless confinement at the buoy had joined this list.

Starke contemplated the unique white and straw-yellow command Albert desired and offered him a billet on. Her stem was almost at the buoy. A blackened anchor chain left its mooring shackle, plunged into filthy water, and then emerged on its journey to a starboard hawsehole. Both anchor davits were swung outboard for symmetry; with the port anchor and chain rigged for emergency or heavy weather. The two boilers kept on line to power her main battery and auxiliary services exhausted through one stack, creating a faint haze above its funnel cap. Below the mahogany pilothouse to port were two whaleboats with varnished strakes intermittently catching the sun. They hung from small davits below towering midship cranes secured fore and aft. Straw-yellow superstructure islands, bridged by walkways and boat cradles, were surrounded by taut, bleached-white canvas awnings and the large, black searchlights topping tall platforms near bow and stern were center-lined. The union jack's white stars spread over a blue field on the bow jack staff, and ensign at the mainmast gaff, hung listlessly; except when a puff of air entered limp folds. The same effect could be seen on a tubular canvas windsail suspended from her foremast gaff to ventilate a berthing deck home to nearly 300. Sailors moving about topside wore old uniforms relegated to work clothes while marines with 6mm Winchester-Lee rifles stood to their posts or walked prescribed routes. One warned off a bumboat, but those normally persistent vendors had been ignoring *Maine*. Rigged as she was now, Starke thought the battleship resembled a Great Lakes passenger steamer. Her roughly 320-foot length, near sixty-foot beam, and 6,500 tons vastly exceeded one; but two black barrels protruding from each sponsoned turret dispelled any misperceptions regarding purpose.

Two Spanish gunboats were allegedly in port but Starke was unable to locate either and assumed they were at the arsenal or Regla's coal pier. However, *Legazpi* and *Alfonso XII* were moored to buoys near *Maine*. The transport *Legazpi* lay just north of their cutter's course and became first to drift down their port side. This recent arrival took *Gneisenau*'s buoy since both schulschiffs had sailed. Her merchant origins were obvious in brigantine rig, central superstructure, single stack, launch on both sides, and white deckhouse aft contrasting with the black hull. Starke met her master once. Teniente de Navio Francisco Javier Tiscar y Croquer said she began as *Formosa* then became *Zamboanga* before the navy bought, armed, and renamed her. Since then she moved troops and supplies between Philippine, North African, and now Caribbean ports.

Admiral Manterola's flagship *Alfonso XII* was moored to her buoy long before Starke's arrival, with many of her sailors drafted from Spain's coasts. They endured a situation similar to *Maine* but with little prospect of change since the boilers were so badly worn their unprotected cruiser moved only under tow or using her bark rig. She was named for the monarch's father and one of a three-ship class built in the late 1880s for colonial service. A sister ship, *Reina Mercedes*, was at Santiago de Cuba and the other, *Reina Christina*, in Manila. Despite these infirmities, *Alfonso XII* presented an impressive appearance. The vestigial bowsprit thrust flatly out over an ornate figurehead fixed to her straight stem. The hull was black like *Calypso*, but her masts appeared more ochre than straw-yellow and matched the yards. An ornate iron-railed captain's walk encircled her stern and three sponsons along each side gave six 5.5-inch Hontoria guns a broad field of fire. Her fore and aft-rigged mizzen sails were perfectly furled; like the main and foremast square-sails. Rising between her first two masts was a pair of large, cream-colored funnels flanked by empty davits. A slight distortion above the aft stack meant at least one donkey boiler was on line. The class was reputed to fall short of expectations despite their striking appearance; which probably contributed to the lethargy repairing her.

Coxswain Aufindsen guided his steam cutter down *Maine*'s port side towards her stern. The boat boom was swung out and rigged. As her midship ash chute and scuppers passed, Starke saw most were idle but some emitted a steady discharge or pulsed sporadically; and all used in port showed light lip rust. He also caught brief glimpses of the unusual green antifouling paint below her waterline. After hooking around the stern, Aufindsen replied to a hail from the starboard gangway on the main deck forward of her aft turret near the accommodation ladder. He maneuvered his cutter easily alongside the platform; reversing the same instant his Danish bowhook, Seaman Nielsen, snagged a pad eye rather than pass lines. Starke thanked the coxswain, climbed to the gangway, paused momentarily for the flag, and then escorted over an immaculate deck into the aft island.

Once inside, Starke passed through an open space pierced by the main mast surrounded by baths, a pantry, and ship's office. As he entered the vacant flag officer cabin Sigsbee expropriated for an office, he saw Peggy, the captain's pug, and one of their three cats. Sigsbee and Wainwright greeted him while his eyes adjusted. Neither was especially warm but both cordial and Sigsbee grateful for his offering to carry documents since the captain was finishing a report for Roosevelt on cruiser and battleship torpedo tube use. He promised to deliver it the next morning, then requested Starke convey his verbal proposal that *Maine* be relieved by a battleship or armored cruiser. Starke felt rotating ships through Havana unhelpful, but cruisers like *Montgomery* or *Detroit* were better suited, would cause less offense, and be far more habitable. Sigsbee did not ask his opinion so he agreed, knowing it would prove awkward if his own thoughts were solicited upon delivery. Before taking leave, a satisfied cabin attendant entered with a note from the quarterdeck. Sigsbee replied then added after the Colored sailor left, "Pinckney's a good man. Plays an excellent banjo; I suspect Mardi Gras rumors have him in high spirits."

Starke stopped a deck below in the wardroom to invite Lieutenants Blandin and Blow to join Tyson, Curtis, and himself for a final Havana outing. They were classmates and he especially hoped the recently promoted Blandin was free. That large, squat gentleman sporting a well-manicured beard far fuller than his own seemed withdrawn after denial of the latest request to transfer from *Maine*. Starke planned to offer his services by approaching Commodore Farquhar in Norfolk. Blandin had been one of the commandant's officers during the Samoan Hurricane when Farquhar captained *Trenton* and Blandin swept overboard. However, he was with his division now and would relieve Blow as Officer of the Deck until midnight so Starke was forced to leave a brief message when gongs signaled the cutter's impending departure for Machina Wharf.

Starke walked by the huge tripod derrick looming over the wharf, crossed Alemeda de Paula, and entered Hotel Mascotte. The triangular three-story hotel's lobby was behind the ground floor arches over its entrance and small shops. He checked for messages then picked up *El Diario de la Marina*. Some reporters were also at the hotel but he slipped past unnoticed. After entering his room, Starke opened a window then briefly watched ships and boats moored, anchored, or moving about the bay. He would start a letter to Katherine before leaving since none came during his stay and Curtis never mentioned any. It was possible they were somewhere in the pipeline and his brief stopover in Washington before rejoining *Calypso* might provide an opportunity to find out but resolution was needed since Katherine and their son preyed on his mind.

Evans was in the Inglaterra some twenty blocks away finishing a draft story on the Rea book's denial of female insurrecto companies striking fear into the Spanish army with machete attacks or fighting to the death. Rejection of similar claims already exposed him to personal attacks so she made inquiries. Women were active as spies, couriers, or in schemes similar to Evangelina Cisneros' alleged plot. A few fought alongside their man, but Amazon stories were concocted in Havana, Key West, Jacksonville, and New York without basis. At one point, she set her pencil aside to stare through the window over Paseo del Prado to Parque Central. *The Sun* and its late publisher supported Cuban independence but Tyson, like Dana, demanded accuracy. Her boss was interested in this article because it exposed one of many false stories assailing readers daily that often included executed prisoners, innocent women defiled then murdered for sport, soldiers butchering nurses and patients, feeding prisoners to sharks, insurrecto armies winning great victories, and myriad of others. When she first approached him to advance her career he seemed more interested in top-grade alcohol and Turkish cigarettes. After a Key West dinner with him and Starke they met in Havana where she fell ill. He helped her survive and filed her stories. That was when she started to see there was more to the thin reporter; and he valued her work enough to offer this position.

Tyson's rum-fueled analysis the previous evening confirmed her mentor saw Cuba as a Greek tragedy. He concluded Spain's departure after ruling abysmally for decades was inevitable but leave or stay it could bring down the monarchy. While slowly twirling rum around the glass' bottom he looked at Evans; conjecturing how American readers would respond after learning Gomez' army was not gallant heroes fighting hand-to-hand or winning the day with machete charges, but a relatively small, hard-pressed, poorly equipped army that included many Mambises and focused on ambushes, destroying Cuba's economy, and killing. Tyson's words were unsurprising but this openness was not a side he often showed, except with Starke. It emphasized she was involved with three very different men. Tyson was successful and of their profession. Curtis was attractive, amiable, wealthy, and someday be titled. Starke was unsettling but having an odd attraction that seemed a volatile blend of apprehension and desire. She considered visiting Hotel Mascotte before he left then quickly dismissed the idea.

Evans' three men dined at El Palacio de Cristal while she worked but Starke left early to finish packing. His final carriage ride through Havana was pleasant and enjoyable with consulate duties finished and *Calypso* still in the future. The streets were alive with people in bars, cafes, and restaurants since a subdued festival was being celebrated. A shipping company would take his large trunk in the morning. The smaller one would go as baggage on *Olivette* to Port Tampa then north by train and his cabin trunk would remain with him. The evening muggy and room warm so he opened a window overlooking street, wharf, and bay. A slight breeze blowing east over La Cabaña carried the harbor bouquet while a peculiar twilight settled on the city soon after sunset. Moonrise was hours away, the overcast sky obscured most stars, and humidity was unusually high as night approached and scent of rain permeated the air.

Maine's anchor lights confirmed she remained almost bow-on to his room, with *Alfonso XII* at the next buoy towards the channel. That cruiser's bulk and rigging were shades of black and gray. The hardworking *Legazpi* was less distinct at her mooring nearest the channel entrance. A tall bark at some Regla coaling pier was less than half mile from *Maine* and only just visible; probably relying on oil lamps and pier lights. More shapes were anchored across the glistening black water but very little movement since harbor traffic ceased. He interrupted packing when a passenger liner cleared the channel and made for a buoy beyond *Maine* towards Regla. Timing, shape, and lighting told Starke it was *City of Washington*; a regular sailing under the New York and Cuba Mail Steamship Company, or Ward Line, house flag.

City of Washington's master would likely have preferred entering before dark but it was a familiar harbor and there was the schedule. After boarding a pilot she steamed under the Morro then through the narrow channel with dark cliffs to port and brightly lit city on lowland to starboard. Starke saw her often enough while *Calypso* patrolled the East Coast and Caribbean seeking filibusters. She had an auxiliary sail rig but was designed as a steam ship. A tall funnel rose between fore and main masts over a sleek black hull with straight stem and pronounced counter. Her wheelhouse was forward and boats hung in davits along the white superstructure. She left the channel, turned smartly right to avoid entering shoal water off Regla, and passed between the three moored ships. Havana was a regular stop between New York and Panama City so her crew was already at work rigging awnings as they prepared to snatch a buoy just over 400 feet beyond *Maine*.

Once she moored, a line of four ships off Machina Wharf was visible from Starke's open window. He returned to the small table; curiosity slaked and tropical night adding to this quiet interlude. *Calypso* was beginning to eclipse friends he would leave, and there was still an onerous trip north in the morning. Several stray thoughts of Evans, Tyson, and Curtis interrupted attempts to finish Katherine's letter. He paused at the sound of La Cabaña's evening gun. It once announced the city gates closing, but now let Havana know it was nine in the evening. Later, he paused to enjoy a faint but fine rendition of *Taps* drifting across the bay; its plaintive notes adding to an intensely peaceful mood, perhaps enhanced by the violence encircling Havana.

He could easily visualize *Maine*. Blandin was well into his watch, probably lounging near the port turret, and Blow in his cabin. Her crew included a mandolin player, like *Calypso*'s coxswain, and earlier he thought accordion music was coming from the ship. Sweating marine sentries would be at their posts or patrolling topside with rifles growing heavier as time passed. Their thoughts would be on hammocks in their barracks, even if the warm berthing deck made sleeping difficult. *Calypso*'s executive officer often allowed her crew to sleep on deck in hot weather, but *Maine* was too large and Wainwright did not seem one to relax rules. With their in-port routine established, those on duty could anticipate the hours left to be relaxed, night quiet, and very few boats or ships to worry about. Time would pass on mundane tasks and talking as surrounding ships, waterfront, city, and countryside become little more than silhouettes with lights reflecting from the tepid surface's dark gloss. Night sounds would carry quickly and easily; even water gently caressing boats secured at the port boom would be heard topside.

Starke set Katherine's letter aside to begin a shorter one to his father in Rio de Janeiro. They seldom wrote but it was past time to reveal the grandson. Ink began running out as the first paragraph finished so he dipped the pen then began lifting it when his room exploded in a blinding flash followed by a massive detonation and air blast that shattered unopened hotel windows. Electric lights flickered out soon after glass shards finished striking floors and people outdoors. Hallway doors flung open as terrified lodgers emptied into Alemeda de Paula below and others gathered at Machina Wharf.

Seconds before, a rumbling came from *Maine*, moored between *Alfonso XII and City of Washington*, as her forward magazines below enlisted berthing detonated in a single small explosion followed by an enormous blast. This energy thrust irresistibly upward, crumpling steel bulkheads until checked briefly and channeled by the armored deck before it too was thrust aside. Everything in blast's path was destroyed, disintegrated, or turned to powder as the explosion burst up and out through steel, armor, and wood-sheathed decks. Exploding into a dark sky, it illuminated the bay and turned night into sharp, fragmentary flashes of black and white images. Bodies, steel, cordage, wood, cement, and burning cellulose rained down on water and ships as far away as Regla. Forward crew berthing ceased to exist and her starboard turret was catapulted through the air to land and sink unnoticed. Sailors awake or in canvas hammocks suspended from beams under steel decks were incinerated, crushed into the overhead, or atomized. As the reddish-yellow plume shot up and out from *Maine*, a bright, blue flash raced through intact passages aft of the explosion. A few sailors on deck were thrown into the sky before landing in the bay. Her hull forward, including the 12-inch armor belt, was blown out, boats destroyed, and other ships damaged as the eruption peeled back a main deck section; twisting it to starboard. The shocked, stunned, and dying battleship shuddered. Her forward sections were ripped open leaving only the keel and twisted shards of plating to support her bow so it curtsied unnoticed then dropped thirty feet to the rank, black bottom.

Her aft third was suddenly open to a bay that inundated remaining spaces with a rushing wall of filthy, nauseating water; causing a port list as she settled. Gushing through this pitch-black, disrupted, and unfamiliar world, it pushed debris and men to safety or cul-de-sacs; forcing air out every avenue to generate a moaning sound. Her port turret remained in place but steel bulkheads and frames were ripped open or resisted until only the aft superstructure's deck remained above water. Secondary fires lit the scene and small explosions went on intermittently. Those escaping the flooding wardroom and staterooms found little more than mainmast, aft searchlight, and shredded awning. Some ventured forward searching for survivors to discover two-thirds of *Maine* was tangled wreckage. Her steel foremast and battered searchlight lay twisted amongst mangled girders, plates, and deck. The mooring buoy vanished with most of her boats. A capsized steam cutter drifted away; brass screw, black rudder, and rust-red condenser protruding from a white hull reflecting flashes from exploding ordnance.

Ships like *Deva* alongside Regla's wharf were pelted with debris, windows in Havana and Regla shattered, the city convulsed, and electrical supply disrupted. When power was restored searchlights were turned on the smoking wreck, illuminating it and the surrounding water. *Maine*'s carcass continued to settle, burn, and launch rounds into the night. Tugs soon emerged from the waterfront to move *Alphonso XII* and *City of Washington* away from the burning and exploding wreck.

Chapter Ten
The Return

Starke left immediately for the consulate then spent the night with Lee and Spanish authorities while sailors and civilians worked desperately to reach survivors. Almost none of *Maine*'s boats remained. Some of *Alfonso XII and City of Washington*'s were holed but their sailors manned what was serviceable and rowed for *Maine*. Others joined in, picking through floating debris around a wreck eerily lit by searchlights and rocked by explosions throwing fragments into the night. Calling out in English and Spanish, they continued until Sigsbee ended it, believing the danger too great and no chance that survivors floated near the wreck or remained in flooded compartments. Starke heard these calls, closed his eyes, and returned to translating or separating fact from rumor.

Recovery began at first light. Searching boats returned with mangled bodies and those parts overlooked during the night or worked free since. Remains not entangled in the smoldering wreck were found adrift, against hulls, along the waterfront, and floating near the channel as if making a last effort to reach deep, clear water beyond. Flags were half-masted across the city, concerts and theater performances cancelled, and normal port activity subdued or halted; especially around the mutilated steel cadaver settling into its bottom. Little more than her aft third remained, and not much of that, above water. The stern superstructure island Sigsbee stepped from into a boat was barely visible in the pungent harbor. Her mainmast remained defiantly vertical but the deformed foremast lay near a battered funnel that collapsed into the wreckage. The aft searchlight platform rose above the water; as did two massive boat derricks despite their missing foundations. Positioned like a tin can lid over ventilator tubes and cowls poking through lapping water was the main deck section blown up and to one side. Still attached were I-beams that had been crew berthing's overhead. Starke heard two human imprints marked what little white paint remained. Grotesque, black vultures came early to circle above Admiral Manterola's boats detailed to keep them and reporters away; securing the smoldering wreck until divers removed the dead still aboard.

The sun neared its zenith with *City of Washington* sending bodies ashore and wounded to San Ambrosio Hospital before continuing to Veracruz. Three new ships had entered Havana's broad bay. *Olivette* anchored off Machina Wharf where boats converged on her forward cargo port. Trailing astern were the coast survey steamer *Mangrove* and lighthouse tender *Fern* Sigsbee cabled for. Starke saw *Fern* snatch *Alphonso XII's* old mooring buoy but Havana was no longer his concern. *Maine* was not his ship and her captain ordered all officers to leave. Consul-General Lee sent him a note confirming the orders returning him to the Building and Albert cabled his presence was essential with Jenkins missing, along with his work and notes. The intelligence office wanted Starke to recreate his contribution before rejoining *Calypso*.

Tyson and Evans surprised him in Hotel Mascotte's lobby before leaving for *Olivette*. Both were staying in Havana, so Tyson's efforts at persuading Evans to retrench in Key West failed. He also mentioned Sigsbee and two sailors were to be lodged in the Inglaterra by late afternoon and remain until an

American warship arrived, most likely *Montgomery*. Wainwright went to *Fern* since her commander was a friend. Sigsbee had demanded *Alfonso XII* not be returned to her old buoy so it could be held for the cruiser. Starke guessed Spanish authorities acquiesced despite viewing it as insulting. He was not surprised since Sigsbee and Lee suspected a torpedo or improvised mine and *Maine's* commander was convinced all mooring buoys except that one were mined.

Starke firmly grasped his friend's bony hand then gently repeated the gesture with Evans before entering the customs building. After threading through its inspection room he waited on the wharf with others to be ferried to *Olivette*. This trip would be crowded with *Maine* survivors going to Key West to wait out the inquiry. Among them were the less critically wounded because Sigsbee declined Clara Barton's offer to care for them. Nineteen would remain for a funeral then burial in Colon Cemetery; with more to follow once divers and decomposition lifted them to the surface.

Starke shared stateroom and clothing with Blandin, Blow, and the Marine detachment commander, First Lieutenant Albertus Catlin. The three spoke little and periodically left to check on their men. A subdued Blandin stared at the passing sea through a window. He had been officer of the deck, doubted Spanish involvement, and was distraught over his second sinking. Key West was entered that evening and once *Olivette* moored the station commander directed survivors to temporary quarters or the Marine Hospital. Commander James Forsyth's large head, once massive body, and oversize goatee that failed to mask the lack of a chin were familiar from previous visits, but Starke decided against approaching him. Forsyth was occupied sorting survivors and keeping them from schooling Key West correspondents. Starke had no reason to go ashore so he returned to his stateroom, endured a fitful night's sleep, skipped breakfast, and went on deck the next morning at ten o'clock. From *Olivette*, he looked to the Northwest Channel breakwater construction then *Calypso's* old anchorage. While leaving for Port Tampa, he watched the three-story, white Marine Hospital building with its long pier, then Fort Taylor, pass down their port side.

Olivette glided past St. Petersburg the next morning then up a flat, mirror-like Tampa Bay, bordered by green foliage and sugar-white beaches. She went alongside the Plant System's massive Port Tampa pier complex. Starke could look across the pier and mark exactly where *Calypso* had moored; just after a large bend and south of the small customs house he must visit. The fish houses and towering phosphate dock north of the pier were busy. Only a short walk was needed after customs to board a waiting train with the last coach's coupler just feet from a pair of buffer stops. White letters on the restive locomotive's tender let him know the South Florida Railroad would carry him past the Tampa Inn Annex and Tampa Inn, off the pier, and down a single track across nine miles of swamp and sand to Tampa. From that city, a Florida Central & Peninsular train would take him to Jacksonville before continuing to Charleston where the Southern Railway would bring him through Richmond to Washington.

Later, from the station platform, he saw a large bonfire marking Plant's Tampa Bay Hotel and passengers boarding a train on the spur to its west entrance. The complex was excessive for a hotel but designed as a tourist destination during winter months. Constructed in a Moorish motif with minarets and domes, the red-brick building had five stories with 500 rooms, private baths, electricity from a separate generator building, and casino with an indoor swimming pool under its retractable floor. The hotel's other enticements included dancing, hunting, fishing, bicycling, and sailing.

Four days after leaving Havana, Starke watched the Virginia countryside slide past his Pullman car window. As the train slowed to enter Washington, its conductor cautioned passengers local temperatures were below freezing; colder than Starke expected but no surprise since the thermometer dropped steadily as passenger diversity increased. It seemed some Southern states, but not yet Virginia, began segregating Colored from White passengers despite any clear racial demarcation. After coming over the rise that provided a broad panorama of Washington, his train rolled across a small island then over the Potomac River's Long Bridge. Once on the other side, it crawled slowly up Maryland Avenue under billowing clouds of smoke and steam.

Left-side passengers were treated to brick, wood, and marble structures dominated by the State, War, and Navy Building on a low rise above Washington Monument and mall. Those on the right took in the waterfront where Starke boarded *Newport News* for Norfolk and command of *Calypso*. The people, cargo, and gear crowding its wharfs, piers, and wood buildings showed Washington's port had recovered from the hurricane that razed Cedar Key then slashed up the East Coast. *Newport News* was somewhere downriver but waterfront and channel were alive with river freighters, ferries, schooners, and workboats. White and gray-white sea gulls spiraled above scanning for food; reminding Starke of the coal smoke, steam, mud, raw sewage, and decaying garbage bouquet that attracted them. Metal wheels squealed against steel rails as the train continued slowing. He turned to observe the Mall, and beyond it the Building, Executive Mansion, and Treasury Building pass the far windows; and standing out from brick, wood, and marble structures surrounding them.

The train continued up Maryland Avenue shunting aside vehicles and pedestrians then Virginia Avenue until it halted beyond the wye junction. Switches were thrown and it backed up 6th Street alongside a wrought-iron fence, to the Baltimore & Potomac Station's train shed. Center Market was to their northwest; the large red-brick building beyond a broad street laden with people, carriages, and streetcars. As Starke's train slowed to a walk, he saw the Treasury Building, Executive Mansion, and the Building just off a long undulating parkland west of the station bordered with a conglomeration of wood, brick, and marble structures; although populated by far fewer trees than before the hurricane. To their east he saw the white Capitol on high ground; dominating everything about it.

Washington had two unconnected railroad stations due to competition between the Baltimore & Ohio and rival Pennsylvania Railroad. The first ran a branch line from the northeast with its terminus the smaller New Jersey Avenue station. The Royal Blue Line to New York used that. Pennsylvania Railroad's Baltimore & Potomac Station was less than a dozen blocks west and midway between the Capitol and Executive Mansion. It was larger, more impressive, and served several lines entering from the southwest over Long Bridge. A large clock tower rose above lesser fellows and gables on three stories of red-brick, black mortar, and stone trim. The attached train shed went 130 feet south along 6th street with walls pierced by tall windows and its roof capped by a rectangular housing filled with small vent windows.

Starke's train eased to halt inside after passing the east wall's loading platform arches where small groups and individuals milled, stood, or loitered. When certain the train was stopped, he rose from his seat, joined passengers leaving, and stepped off the car's steps to a stool. The platform was crowded with individuals and parties. Some approached his train, or another preparing to depart on the second track. A number were better dressed than Starke, who traveled in his comfortable, nondescript sack suit with hat, gloves, and heavy cane. Many smoked, conversed, or studied newspapers with front pages consumed by *Maine*. One agitated cluster included a booming voice damning Spain for the loss then McKinley for not demanding Congress declare war; sentiments heard often enough during the trip. Starke passed the cigar-smoking, overfed group on his way to heavy wooden doors separating station from shed then walked a short hallway between baggage and private rooms into the main waiting area. At the baggage office on its far side, he gave the uniformed man his claim ticket then waited for handcarts piled with trunks to come from the train's baggage car. A Negro porter rolled his luggage past the ladies' waiting area, newsstand, restaurant, and out the B Street entrance.

Beneath the station's clock tower a doorman stepped off the curb and motioned at some queuing taxies while Starke waited under the canopy considering Cuba's effect on his weather tolerance. A shiver confirmed his decision not to be met by the Starke groom, Darius Sutton. The weather would be difficult enough for the 10th Cavalry soldier struck by a nearly-spent .45-70 round almost eighteen years earlier, ran their stable, and built a local reputation for equine expertise. That, however, meant foregoing his uncle's well-sprung black landau pulled by Gemini and Castores; their eight-year-old bays with black tails, manes, and socks.

Today's substitute was a single-horse, yellow Herdic cab that rapidly crossed the street to roll alongside its cement curb. His baggage was loaded, the porter given a generous gratuity, and he climbed through the rear door to take a bench seat along one side. His cab reversed direction then headed west past Center Market for a short distance before turning north on 7th Street. The mare was oblivious to activities beyond her blinders as she pulled them around Mount Vernon Square then up Massachusetts Avenue through bicycles, pedestrians, wagons, and carriages to Dupont Circle. Once there, they turned north on Connecticut Avenue; seeing several Metropolitan Company streetcars before reaching St. Margaret's Episcopal Church. During this journey to Florida Avenue, they passed legations, mansions, businesses, houses, and shacks; a heterogeneous mix of wood, brick, and marble common throughout the city.

The Romanesque mansion became visible once they turned left off Florida Avenue and was unchanged since he was last there. Surrounded by leafless trees and brown grass, the red stone building with three round corners and a fourth replaced by the tall turret counted four stories if its ground floor and staff accommodations under the gabled roof were included. The tallest turret was capped by a cone-shaped roof and lightning rod while the second, a smaller half-turret, was grafted to the front wall on the other side of its center entrance. The main entrance perched atop the whitish-gray stone porch flanked by marble staircases sweeping around arches obscuring a less obvious set of concrete stairs leading to the domestic area. Construction material for the lower wall and single courses separating each story was the same stone used for the porch. Several gables sported glass-globed lightning rods and brick chimneys capped by gray concrete that emitted flickering, translucent fumes into the cold air. A grass median barely separated building from sidewalk but the rear yard was expansive. From the same-shaped conservatory and carriage house at each end of a concrete apron and central rear door, it stretched beyond a large red-brick carriage house and stable for horses, inhabited by Gemini and Castores.

The main entrance consisted of two heavy oak doors then a short passage between the butler's office and cloak room opening on a large, wood-paneled, entrance hall splitting the mansion. Its two stories ended at the building's rear with curved staircases to the second floor below Tiffany stained-glass windows. The parlor was on the first floor off the left side with its front corner formed by the larger turret and pocket doors for converting it to a pair of small rooms. The library behind it contained walls of books and a marble fireplace. Several oriental rugs, a floor globe, leather wingback chairs, wooden desk with brass table lamp, and captain's chair were included in its furnishings. Off the hall's right side was a Louis XVII ballroom running most of the building's depth with a small band dais in the rear and front alcove incorporating the partial turret. Three cut-crystal chandeliers over a parquet dance floor provided light. Large mirrors between windows on the exterior wall and two wide entrances on its interior gave the illusion of a grand ballroom. The formal dining area was directly above; although slightly shorter to accommodate a breakfast or morning room with dumbwaiters to the ground floor.

The lowest floor housed kitchen, pantry, scullery, bathrooms, laundry room, boiler, china closet, storage rooms, small office, and old smoking room converted to a servant's hall. Its front door was under the porch but the rear was more often used. A boiler generated steam for safety-valve radiators with wood and red velvet covers; supplemented by stoves and fireplaces that burned wood, coal, or gas piped in for lighting and the massive range. There was indoor plumbing with tubs and showers in second floor en suite bathrooms. A washroom was beside the breakfast room and third floor guests shared male and female bathrooms; with a similar arrangement on the servant side. A first floor powder room abutted the cloakroom and its male equivalent beside the butler's office. Two bathrooms, with cage showers, were on the ground floor.

Four primary bedrooms, with dressing rooms, were above parlor and library. Rear stairs led to more spartan guest rooms on the fourth level's left side; shaped to accommodate its turrets and gables. Servants' quarters on the right were arranged similarly except one additional small staircase wound up from the ground floor.

Starke announced his arrival with the mechanical brass doorbell. Their butler, Altman, opened the door and they shook hands. After releasing the Herdic cab, servants began carrying trunks down through the ground floor door. Starke had just surrendered hat, gloves, coat, and cane to Altman when his uncle emerged from the library and aunt from her parlor. Senior maid and ersatz housekeeper Cynthia Jefferson walked slightly behind his aunt; but the cook, Martella Young, and groom, Darius Sutton, would expect separate visits.

Immanuel Starke neared his nephew with a powerful and purposeful stride. The family patriarch was closer to sixty and slightly less energetic than Jacob remembered but still dominated any room. Never overtly jovial or trivial, the more noticeable hoods over his eyes increased that air of imperturbability. A full beard was starting to show the same gray streaks already streaking his short, thinning hair. The physique was less hard but still conveyed natural authority and inclination to act. Starke had thought his uncle unapproachable as a boy but experience brought greater understanding of the man who loved him as a son and constantly tried to instill self-reliance with rough kindness. The right hand shot out, "Welcome home, Jacob. Havana sounds interesting. Your aunt worried you might have left the

Inglaterra for *Maine* and people are still trying to find out who survived."

Aunt Constance came to her husband's side, listened, then moved forward and hugged him. It took years to understand their relationship. Although the firm might appear his uncle's solitary passion, it was clearly a distant second to his slightly younger wife. She changed little since they were last together. The well-formed face, frame, and confident manner created the reputation of a classic beauty before coming out in New York; then years of increasing poise, security, and experience enhanced it. Her figure was never thin, and filled slightly over time, but remained one women many years her junior envied; and hair changing to silver-gray added elegance. Capable, intelligent, and devout; she oversaw their domestic realm, complemented his uncle, and dedicated years of benevolent scheming get her nephew married. Instead, the baby she could not wait to grandmother came first and his aunt assumed their union would follow shortly.

Unlike the unrestrained hug waiting with Martella, Cynthia's welcome was genuine but formal and reserved. She was an enigma since her mother's passing and father sent her from Oxen Grove plantation to live with the family. They spoke sporadically when he was at home and she felt like a cousin. Cynthia developed into a woman of average height with well-proportioned figure that defied efforts to conceal or obscure it through dress. Her face was a near perfect oval with dark eyebrows, translucent cinnamon-brown lips, and pleasant nose between two slightly hooded almond eyes. Rich, black hair framing these attributes was piled on her head leaving only earlobes visible; but probably swept the floor when let down. She was intelligent, well-read, efficient, and proper. Throughout their acquaintance he seldom saw a smile, much less a laugh, but the few times this occurred it began demurely then ended with a crescendo of flashing white teeth. Her relationship with Katherine was particularly odd because both seemed punctilious to a fault when addressing each other. He suspected Cynthia suppressed as much passion as Katherine and thought it odd she never married since Washington's Colored women customarily continued to work outside the home after marriage, unlike their White counterparts.

The trio sat for hot cocoa at his aunt's favorite parlor table in an alcove formed by the large turret. She passed a cup to his uncle, who nearly lit a cigar, then one to Starke before beginning, "How long can you stay, Jacob?"

"It depends on what happens at the Building, but probably a few days. I've been away from *Calypso* far too long."

"Can't Benjamin continue longer?"

His uncle placed cup and saucer on the small white-lace doily, "With war talk and his having had *Calypso* for some time, Jacob's concerned she will go to someone else."

Starke looked to his aunt, "Watson's also due some relief."

Her eyes twinkled as she lifted the cup even with her lips, "Olivia Albert will thank you."

Immanuel added, "You mean the Albert family," then paused for what passed as a smile, ". . . well maybe not the younger sister."

Starke's aunt finished a sip, "They compete, as all sisters do, but the eldest should wed first and Abigail claims Isabella is thrilled."

Lieutenant Watson and Passed Assistant Engineer Adrian Osbourne had been introduced to Albert's daughter Olivia and younger sister Isabella at a dinner party two years before; igniting a steady correspondence exchange between that household and *Calypso*. Watson proposed to Olivia in December and, if her father survived that long, a June wedding was scheduled. Neither Albert nor his thin, redhead wife Abigail could be described as tranquil and their offspring energetic and competitive, so preparations probably kept the house in perpetual chaos. Starke's aunt offered the mansion for their ceremony and reception. She was fond of the sisters, even hosted them to a Newport summer, but also saw the event as an opportunity for the firm to increase its exposure with influential Navy people.

His aunt began probing, "Katherine's agreed on a date?"

She clearly did not think less of Katherine or intend to treat his illegitimate son, Oliver Barrington Curtis, as anything but the ersatz grandchild she craved. The question confirmed no correspondence had come from Katherine or her mother. Curtis warned Starke their father, Sir Curtis, appeared more irritated his grandson's father was American than the boy's illegitimacy so absent correspondence was not surprising.

"I wrote from Havana, but no response yet."

"Then a letter's probably in the post. A cable would be too public. Will you marry at Bridport?"

"Nothing's set, aunt."

"Yes, yes, of course."

Constance clearly believed her subtle but persistent matrimonial and baby campaign was nearly concluded despite the sequence juxtaposition. Starke was less certain. Although a son kindled unaccustomed feelings and deepened his attraction for Katherine it would not alter the fact she disliked the States, her father's views on Americans, and *Calypso's* more pressing claim. He already proposed, acted to ensure his son received the Starke name, and enlisted Curtis to plead his case; leaving Katherine the unknown factor. Starke loved his aunt and was contemplating whether to explain this when his uncle offered escape, "So you won't get a Sunday ride?"

"I'm afraid not but would like to since the last time I sat a horse was in Cuba; and that not very relaxing."

"There's another issue requiring your attention before returning to *Calypso*."

"Yes, uncle?"

"Newman Pearce. I last visited Oxen Grove while closing our West Point yard and since we no longer have business there have not been back."

"You're right, uncle. I'll stop on the way to Newport News."

Oxen Grove plantation came through his mother; an arrangement orchestrated by the families to prevent Radical Republicans from confiscating its remnants. The Starkes assumed quasi-ownership, paid taxes throughout the war, financed its recovery, and arranged for Jacob to inherit directly. Even so, only part of his York River plantation between West Point and Chesapeake Bay was saved. Most of its 3,000 acres were confiscated or sold. The enslaved community fled to Fortress Monroe with the first union troops; although some tried returning later to the place they saw as home. What carpetbaggers did not get, confiscated for taxes, or taken by the Freedmen's Bureau was managed by Pearce and provided Starke a steady income. Pearce needed little oversight but owners must periodically visit, review accounts, inspect property, and agree on future plans. Starke was aware of his neglect but often away or procrastinated because it required travel by train to West Point; about forty miles east of Richmond, then downriver by boat since local roads ensured a long, slow trip in the best weather.

"I'll arrange for one of the shipyard's tugs, Jacob. Her master's buying it from us."

Constance Starke saw where this was going so she rose. Her husband and nephew did the same as she announced, "This seems business so I'll take my leave. I'll see you in the morning, Jacob; and don't be long dear."

She glanced back while climbing the stairs. Her husband and nephew were entering the library and Cynthia was clearing away.

The library had not changed. Its black-marble fireplace's brass accoutrements framed logs spanning andirons and glowing embers were scattered over white ash. A matched pair of high-backed leather chairs faced it, separated by a small table holding bourbon, whiskey, and cognac decanters. Starke glanced through a window to the barren trees beyond as his uncle filled two bourbon glasses. Curtis contemplated the same view before revealing Katherine had borne Starke's son.

Immanuel retrieved a cigar from the humidor, clipped its end, and then ran it past his lips, "Too bad you've gone over to pipes; this is an excellent Havana."

Starke began his ritual with the worn pipe used in Cuba, "I'll stay with this."

His uncle's cigar tip glowed red, "What about *Maine*? We can't trust the papers."

Bourbon pleasantly clawed Starke's throat, its bite presenting an unnatural contrast to such a smooth, flowing name, "Nothing but opinions. Most officers suspect a coal bunker fire, like *Calypso* off Jacksonville last year, but torpedo, sabotage, fire, or boiler explosion have supporters."

"Newspapers favor a torpedo or some sort of mine."

"*Maine* swung to a new position that day and some speculate military torpedoes were planted near mooring buoys so ships would settle over them. Something impromptu is also rumored since she was resented by several factions. I read Weylerites have been accused but they don't want us involved. Insurrectos attempted to mine the new dry-dock but want recognition or a blockade; not our involvement. Perhaps the inquiry will determine a cause."

"If there's war, we've no Cuban property except our leased Havana office. Your father can look after our interests and Edward's investors are British, so they're protected."

Starke took another sip, "You think there'll be a war?"

"Same mood as 1860, except North and South are unifying. Jingoes shout everyone down, even president and Speaker. Spain's apparently no different and the queen regent's barely restraining her war faction. The Europeans don't support us but should one ally with Spain the rest will choose sides for their own reasons. War's mass insanity and shipping either profits or gets destroyed; depending. Our masters have been directed to avoid Spanish ports and not sail unless they can make safe harbor before hostilities. Sharett and his contacts are helping but insurance rates are already rising."

When his uncle's cigar and whiskey were expended, the patriarch excused himself, "I'm off, Jacob. Constance doesn't appreciate my waking her."

Starke left for his second floor bedroom over the library where he slid, exhausted, under a down comforter. It was excellent sleeping weather but his thoughts shifted between *Calypso*, meeting Albert tomorrow, his son, Katherine, and friends in Havana. He finally drifted off but found himself groping through canted, dark passageways filling with putrid water; fighting to get past people frozen in terror as distance between water and overhead vanished. Jenkins, John Bell, Coxswain Aufindsen, the cutter crew, and wardroom steward eyed his struggle with indifference until he dropped off; knowing they would return.

Chapter Eleven
Benign Interrogation

Starke rose early, folded comforter and sheet back, embraced the morning chill, and went to his dressing room where he trimmed a too-long beard, mixed shaving soap, and lathered. A safety razor was preferable at sea but the straight type left a cleaner feel so he opened his favorite with mother-of-pearl handle and stropped it against the heavy leather razor strap. He began with short, gentle strokes and entered the morning room just before seven-thirty, where an eggs, ham, toast, and coffee buffet waited. Returning briefly to his dressing room, he used a boar's hair toothbrush, finished dressing, and left for the front door.

Altman intended to hand him coat, bowler, and cane until seeing he was in uniform; an unusual selection. Starke spoke briefly then left carrying a satchel; walking briskly towards Florida Avenue. Turning right took him to St. Margaret's Church and northern terminus of the Metropolitan Company line. He could have turned left for the Capital Traction Company line but it was still rebuilding from the powerhouse fire and using horse-drawn cars until April. The day was warming and only a few minutes passed before boarding a car headed south towards its Lafayette Square stop across from the Executive Mansion.

Captain Albert could see Lafayette Square from his office in the nearly deserted Building. It was George Washington's birthday but he wanted to meet with Starke before spending the afternoon watching parades with his family then attending an evening function. Young men still wore red, white, and blue ties but now walked past flags half-staffed for *Maine*.

The last days had been unnerving. They began when he woke to find his twice-promised command a twisted wreck, most of her crew dead, and well-connected officer given preference over him facing inquiry and possible court-martial. That morning's coffee was not enjoyable and interrupted by a clerk before finished. He entered the Executive Mansion with Long just before nine o'clock.

Crowninshield was away from Washington when Sigsbee's late evening cable arrived, so the duty commander sent a messenger to the president and Long's apartment in the Portland off Thomas Circle. A second from Consul-General Lee confirmed the disaster. Orders were sent for the lighthouse tender and a coast survey ship in Key West to sail for Havana. McKinley claimed technical ignorance, suspected an accident, and refused to act on opinion. Everyone agreed since Havana's chaotic politics and *Maine*'s checkered history supported several possibilities. Long confirmed with Albert that Navy regulations forbid public discussion before any inquiry finished and the president extended this prohibition across government; and emphasized war must be avoided for a number of reasons but especially risk of igniting Europe.

Albert spent that afternoon arranging divers, supporting the inquiry, and mitigating a growing conflict between the Bureaus of Equipment and Ordnance over responsibility if not from an external cause. Public rumors and conjectures also required tamping down; especially after a second Sigsbee cable suggested mine or torpedo. Albert's review of it for the secretary concluded it added nothing new. Governor-general Blanco visited Sigsbee at the Inglaterra where the captain and two sailors were staying. He offered assistance, condolences, and an official funeral for the seventeen dead recovered. Sigsbee visited *Alphonso XII* to express his gratitude to Captain Manuel de Eliza y Vergara for her crew's response.

Roosevelt's wife growing ill before Starke's return might have weakened the assistant secretary's self-control. Despite heading a board to investigate coal incidents he was busy muzzling all opinions except a mine while telling people to wait for the inquiry. Albert's frustration peaked after Admiral Manterola proposed a joint inquiry to Sigsbee during an awkward Inglaterra visit. Roosevelt argued strenuously against it then observed there was almost no chance the truth would ever be determined or accepted.

North Atlantic Squadron commander Admiral Sicard convened a board of inquiry while divers were still recovering bodies. Captain William T. Sampson was designated president and Lieutenant Commander Marix judge advocate. It convened on *Mangrove* the same day Starke arrived in Washington. There were also rumors Sicard would request relief due to his health, and favored successor was the popular and energetic Captain Winfield Scott Schley.

Albert heard through Falk and other contacts that Spain was unable to assign a new minister until Dupuy de Lôme returned home so First Secretary Don Juan du Bosc must bridge the gap. There was no other choice but his ongoing conflict with de Lôme was so intense the bachelor du Bosc moved from the legation. He apparently claimed some French ancestry, spoke several languages, and regularly attended local athletic clubs. He was a stalwart Weyler supporter viewed as obdurate in diplomatic circles so Day delayed recognizing him until de Lôme was recalled officially; an action Madrid was resisting since the letter was personal correspondence stolen by the Junta.

Albert's thoughts of preceding days ended with a knock and Lieutenant Starke entering in uniform. Command and a tropical tan enhanced the officer's presence and reminded him of the uncle and father. Both possessed an ability to inspire loyalty and the son clearly inherited it. His naval cadets petitioned to remain on *Calypso* after the collision despite knowing it would hurt their chances for a commission. Osbourne sent a similar request to Steam Engineering Bureau chief Melville after his lieutenant's examination; and the ship's surgeon, Sydney Conrad, declined transfer to Brooklyn's naval hospital then arranged a Norfolk detail until the bark was repaired. Even more surprising was a personal letter from the Norfolk receiving ship's commander. Captain Terry wrote *Calypso*'s chief petty officers politicked to stay on board and were working his command to achieve the same for their sailors. Albert viewed such élan as fragile and valuable so he pressed to keep sailors for repair work and Bureau of Navigation permission to request Norfolk's commandant limit poaching. This was only feasible because Rear Admiral Ramsay was no longer bureau chief. He had been known for honesty and directness, but also for strongly believing officers and enlisted were interchangeable.

Albert rose and rounded the desk to greet Starke, "Welcome back, Captain. Please take a seat."

Starke settled into the small settee's leather upholstery as the captain retreated with his familiar rolling gait to the leather swivel chair behind a cluttered desk. Albert observed, learned, and ultimately thrived on Department, Building, and capital politics. Slightly heavier than two years before, when he offered *Calypso*, his frame remained short, stocky, and powerful with the round head perched on a short neck. Starke knew from their old steam sloop *Apalachicola* he seldom acted without reason and in this latest position weighed everything from uniform to social life for how it would affect his position. Every personal, social, and professional event was considered for value to the Navy, his portfolio, and then himself. While working for him, Starke discovered influence within the Building invariably rested on a man's reputation for honestly, consistency, and follow-through that could be easily lost

Albert reached across his desk, extracted the meerschaum pipe from several in a stand, and dredged it through the supple leather pouch, "Sorry about bringing you in on the holiday."

"I had to report my arrival to the Department anyway."

"Yes, of course. I've arranged your interview with the intelligence office for tomorrow and you'll want to leave for Norfolk soon after."

"Yes, sir; but I must make a side trip."

"For what purpose, may I ask?"

"A long-overdue talk with my plantation manager."

"Watson'll survive another day or so in command. How do you think he's panned out?"

"Couldn't ask for a better executive officer."

Albert carefully pressed tobacco into the bowl then passed a match over center while creating a draught. His first puff was followed by the expended match arcing into an ashtray, "I hope he does equally well as Olivia's husband," then continued, "I've got the conference room we used before. Commander Richardson Clover will bring Lieutenant Commander William Driggs, his assistant. Maximilian Falk will sit in for Justice. Our assistant secretary cannot. He's off tilting windmills when not looking after a sick wife and son."

"I'm sorry to hear that."

Albert's forehead wrinkled as he grinned, with two nearly black eyes meeting Starke's, and mused, "Probably just as well; never could decide how you two would fare," before shifting topics, "Roosevelt, Senator Lodge, and others see *Maine* as their opportunity since Madrid and Washington want to avoid war but must now prepare for it. Speaker Reed supports the administration, but jingoes have the advantage with our press; and Spain's papers are also pushing for war. Where's your correspondent friend by the way?"

"Darwin Tyson? With the Laffin News Bureau in Havana; and Miss Evans is there as well."

"A strange pairing but they seem competent. Anyway, *Calypso* must get to sea. Spain and the Junta cannot think filibuster patrols have stopped."

"My uncle would agree. He's worried about shipping."

"And rightly so. It appears Admiral Pascual Cervera y Topete has been given their best ships; *Vizcaya*, now in New York, and her two sisters. That's a powerful squadron; faster than the *Indiana* class and capable of defeating one of our large sailing independently. He could easily attack shipping from a port in Spain or the Canary Islands."

"With respect, sir; that assumes they're maintained. The Havana ships seemed in poor shape although whether that holds beyond the West Indies I couldn't say. Spain's nearly bankrupt and trying to buy ships, so maintenance and fuel must be a problem. In his position I'd preserve the squadron, make gestures, harass our blockade, and attack commerce with converted merchant ships that could work trade routes under sail; but that's not possible without abandoning their army in Cuba."

Albert chuckled, ". . . and responding to a vocal public expecting we'll crumble. Don't build a reputation for strategy too early. You'll lose out on sea commands and end up on a staff like me. Even so, I would not want to be in Sigsbee's shoes. Never warmed to him or Wainwright but they've managed *Maine*'s loss about as well as could be expected."

"Yes, sir."

"We'll meet here in the morning then go to the conference room. Intelligence's bringing a stenographer so you won't need a written report. That should get you out of here on Thursday and back on *Calypso* by Monday. For now, check in and enjoy what's left of the holiday."

Starke reported his arrival and sooner than anticipated was walking past the Executive Mansion to Lafayette Square for a street car then the mansion. The next morning they walked to the same small conference room where *Calypso*'s mission to disrupt Junta expeditions was described and Spanish gunboat inquiry conducted. The entryway was still indistinguishable from others along the corridor; having the same color, transom window, and framing. Inside, its large rectangular oak table encircled by plain parlor chairs with cane inserts continued forcing occupants to edge along either wall. Beyond it, and opposite the entrance, was a single, large, four-pane window that helped light off-white walls with row of ship photographs that contrasted with the dark pine floor and oft-repainted chair rail.

A woman with writing pads and array of pencils was sitting beside Falk and remained seated when he rose. Female stenographers were increasing, with many becoming expert in shorthand or typing. Most were young, well-educated, and usually quit work when married; but some chose career over family. Starke suspected the second course here since she seemed nearer his age, with coal-black hair pulled back tight like Katherine's when he first saw her, a tailored traveling suit with white blouse, and no jewelry. She was very thin with corset and bustle struggling to mold a figure from very little material. Fashionable pince-nez glasses rested on her nose and slightly magnified dark eyes were surrounded by a light-brown shadowing. Starke guessed Mediterranean or southern

European descent; which was confirmed during Miss Renata Turchi's introduction.

They arrived minutes before Albert and Starke, which perturbed the captain because it disrupted his routine. The attendant bringing a water pitcher and glasses late did not help but everything was in position when Clover and Driggs entered precisely on time. Driggs was an armaments expert operating his own weapons firm and initially seemed more interested in *Calypso*'s duel with the gunboat *Pedro Menéndez de Avilés*. Albert allowed a few questions then put the meeting on track by asking Starke to summarize the notes surrendered to Jenkins. Starke was milked for information into early afternoon while the captain dispatched several pipes.

Miss Turchi began writing as Starke responded and expanded. The massive floating dry-dock built by Swan & Hunter in Britain then towed to Havana absorbed the most attention. He spoke to dredging and problems met installing the largest of its type and insurgents' attempt to plant some manner of torpedo under it. Clover voiced some doubt but noted they did mine the river gunboat *Relampago* and a few sources claimed the Junta consulted one South American country about torpedoes. Accusations the harbor moorings were mined came up but Starke could only state Jenkins said he was looking into it. He could add little about warship visits except *Almirante Oquendo*, an *Infanta María Teresa* class armored cruiser like *Vizcaya*, was rumored to be coming. Starke was able to accurately summarize fortifications, describe emplacements west of the harbor entrance, and predict six Hontoria guns from the immobile *Alphonso XII* would be mounted as shore batteries. Clover and Driggs also probed the city's mood. Starke relied on Tyson and Evans' notes suggesting Cuban society centered in Havana had been devastated by members taking sides; which was corroborated by what he overheard exercising with foils at one local gym and numerous duels occurring. Starke also emphasized the difference between urban and rural areas, as well as eastern and western provinces. Towards the end he took the liberty to observe, based on the Alexandria bombardment, that shelling Havana would risk Americans along with some Europeans; however evacuating citizens from Cuba on short notice would prove impossible and delaying it extremely perilous.

Starke settled on the settee when they returned to the office while Albert pawed through papers spread over his desk. The result was a handwritten letter on Department stationary from the Bureau of Navigation chief. It ended Starke's temporary duty and directed his return to *Calypso*. Albert smiled, "Get her to sea, Captain. Jingoes want war and will have it if Junta expeditions continue. Today's transcript can be sent for your review but in the meantime you're set to leave and these orders allow the delay needed."

Albert stood and, while firmly shaking Starke's hand added, "Remember this time at sea is different. Every Spanish warship could be a threat and every filibuster an ally."

"I understand, sir. My uncle already cautioned his masters; and *Calypso* should show her heels to most Spanish warships except the *Infanta María Teresa* class."

"Perhaps, but *Calypso*'s hull was damaged so it's best to find out during a full speed run and not by racing some Spaniard."

Starke left through the Building's eastern entrance then walked past the Executive Mansion's greenhouse complex to Lafayette Square. He was soon on a street car rolling northwest to pack for the trip. Early next morning, Darius harnessed Gemini and Castores for a Baltimore & Potomac station run. The matched pair was driven from an open seat above the unmarked black landau's front wheels, just forward of two carriage lanterns. The light, fashionable carriage with glossy wood body was trimmed in silver and ebony with retracting windows in center half-doors. Two oiled leather upper body clam sections raised and lowered with the entire assembly riding on elliptical springs and narrow rubber-tires under equally thin mudguards. The riding quality was further enhanced by two red-leather bench seats facing each other with coil spring cushions. A folding luggage rack behind the body and between its rear wheels was loaded and strapped down. Starke boarded after his aunt and uncle.

Locomotive, tender, and part of one coach protruded from the Baltimore & Potomac train shed when they arrived. The group went inside after Starke said good-bye to Darius then stopped at the baggage room before entering the train shed. A light haze floated over the engine's stubby funnel. Steam periodically vented to the gravel, and black steel covering boiler insulation shimmered in cold morning air. Starke ensured the hand cart with luggage reached the baggage car, hugged his aunt, shook his uncle's hand, and took an unoccupied seat on the Southern Railroad local. He was well settled when the train jerked several feet backwards, shuddered, and rolled ahead; gathering speed as it made for Long Bridge. Beyond Potomac River lay a sequence of stops and starts on its trip south to Richmond before slowing at that city's northern limit then rolling along the James River. After pausing briefly, it backed up a spur to the Virginia Street station. He took another local that afternoon. The express linking Richmond with West Point's ferry to Baltimore only ran three days each week; and today was not one.

Chapter Twelve
Return to Oxen Grove

West Point's Terminal Hotel overlooked York River with three floors and 200 rooms. Tall windows and broad porches connected corner turrets while the nearby amenities included a seafood restaurant and casino on the long pier. His uncle had been a patron since it opened nine years earlier for wealthy guests; although the Grove Hotel, Beach Park Hotel, and others also served Richmond's port city.

Starke registered, enjoyed a catfish dinner, and returned as dancing began under the first stars freckling a clear sky. He stopped by the desk, arranged for morning, and sent a note to the tug master; who was not on the local telephone system. Darkness came soon after but electric lighting allowed him to start another letter to Katherine. It was awkward since nothing had come for some time. Meanwhile, Oxen Grove increasingly consumed his attention. He knew it was time to become more involved or sell since his uncle no longer visited West Point on shipyard business.

A single-horse Studebaker brougham arrived after breakfast. Starke climbed in then sat back, leaving its windows open. The driver maneuvered around an ice delivery van, then passed rapidly through city streets lined with stores, churches, oyster shucking sheds, vacant buildings, piers, moored schooners, and barges. The deserted shipyard wharf was abandoned to dead weeds and matted grass invaded its thinning gravel, now serving only as a bed for debris piles. Lifeless industrial areas were depressing but Starke found shipyards especially wretched. This one felt even more forlorn because it once belonged to his family and would never be resurrected.

Starke Shipyard No. 1 had been renamed for the new owner's young daughter and was now *Sally Anne;* with the change painted across her stern. After he boarded the veteran yard tug it backed from the wharf into a still York River reflecting the rising morning sun, then churned downstream for Oxen Grove landing. Standing in her eyes and feeling somewhat pensive, he watched a blunt bow plow the broad, flat river lined with pine forests and fields. Hiring *Sally Anne* was more convenient than a scheduled steamboat; and either beat the sandy, unimproved roads populated by flights of biting insects with clear speed advantages. The tug soon turned smoothly from the channel to begin its approach on Oxen Grove landing. They moored at a rough wood pier projecting into the river. It had belonged to his plantation but was now run by another further inland to ship crops and restock a general store. It was not a regular steamer stop so landing and nearby shore were deserted. As Starke walked the half-mile to Oxen Grove, *Sally Anne*'s fires were banked and her master joined fireman and deckhand on the fantail. After cool pails of beer were retrieved from the bilges, three faded-yellow cane poles were rigged and cast; then wine-bottle cork bobbers studied for movement.

Two packed-sand roads led up from the river. The first curved quickly right through a pine forest to emerge a mile inland where shotgun houses and the general store occupied a clearing. The second led to the plantation; set back from the river on high ground to counter pirate attacks. It was now little more than a passage through new-growth pines whose sharp scent overpowered competitors and density stilled any breeze. That, and sun reflecting from light brown sand, ensured most days were either warm or hot.

Oxen Grove generated income and existed as a personal memorial but was no longer a self-sufficient plantation. Its cotton gin building housed machinery unused for decades and its abandoned slave quarters was only identifiable by crumbling stone chimneys in matted grass. While many buildings had been dismantled then scavenged or moved to other locations by White and Freedmen farmers; the outlines or foundations of several could be seen, surrounded by fields in various planting stages. Buildings still in use were meticulously maintained; including the unoccupied plantation house looked after by his manager's wife.

That brick house was built in the Federal style by indentured servants, skilled slaves, and local artisans. Its central hallway had doors along either side with both ends left open in summer to catch passing breezes. One set of double doors led to the dining room and the second a parlor. A crystal chandelier hung from centered medallions in each room. Its library, adjacent to the parlor, included a white-brick fireplace with dark wood mantle under a brass chandelier. Unlike the British approach, with external kitchens, this house was built in the German style with one behind the dining room. The second floor hallway serving six bedrooms was accessed by stairs on the ground floor hall near the back entrance. That oversized door opened onto the covered porch overlooking a neglected flower garden's outlines and pier where *Sally Anne* moored. The front porch looked down a sand and gravel path lined by large oak trees that ended at a dirt road beyond several pastures. It could eventually get a traveler to West Point but primarily connected sharecroppers, tenant farmers, and homesteads. Most small farms that once raised their own produce and made what was needed were now dedicated to tobacco or cotton. Everything else came through the general store; bought with profits or, more often, on credit.

Starke went first to his overseer's home situated between the main house and vanished quarters. The manager, Newman Pearce, opened its door. Raised along the river after the war, his extended nose, narrow head, ungainly walk, and slow manner suggested lethargy but he was competent, energetic, and locally respected by White and Colored. Circumstance limited his formal schooling, as it had many, but he read steadily, mostly the Bible or agricultural periodicals, wrote in a strong hand, and summed better than most. He not only became a successful manager but was known as an astute trader; wise to every trick used for concealing scours and quick to spot spoiled seed corn. Several men ran Oxen Grove after Tribbs Jefferson passed on but only Pearce had the knowledge, initiative, and honesty to reliably farm its remaining 1,000 acres. Except for living in the main house, he treated the plantation as his own and kept it profitable, even when those nearby failed; which allowed Starke to keep it and enjoy a second income.

His thin spouse Mandy joined Pearce and Starke on their walk to the main house then eased ahead to unlock its entrance. In a small side room serving as office, the men began reviewing records and accounts before discussing future plans. The open doors and windows allowed a fitful breeze to flow through, gently ruffling the rooms. Starke drifted through the house while Pearce pulled additional files. He paused at his father and mother's charcoal portraits, beside oil paintings of her parents, then considered a few small items remembered from previous visits, especially in the small upstairs bedroom where he stayed.

Sally Anne's crew lifted fishing poles when her master spotted men coming downhill, twirled lines around their lengths, and anchored them with still-baited hooks. Starke remained on the pier while boiler fires were spread and steam pressure climbed; reviewing a supply list Pearce asked to have shipped from West Point. When the boiler reached operating pressure, they shook hands, Starke boarded, and Pearce cast off. The small tug backed away, stopped, pivoted with a hard rudder, and chugged upstream trailing light smoke. Starke wondered when he would next see Oxen Grove as pier and shoreline merged. It felt like home but not somewhere he could live; partly due to its seclusion but also because farming required a dedication and interest he did not possess.

River then port smells, taken with the warm late afternoon, hinted at what summer would bring as *Sally Anne* approached West Point. A railroad shipping change ended its time as a major cargo port but there was a growing tourist trade and the harbor was still in use, albeit less active. They met or passed three riverboats, including the white side-wheeler *Accomack* with general cargo and passengers; distinguishable without reading the name by its thin black stack, two decks, and small pilothouse. *Sally Anne* moored alongside the long, covered wharf behind a white Baltimore, Chesapeake & Richmond Steamboat Company side-wheeler. Starke spoke briefly with the tug's master then hailed a cab for the Terminal Hotel.

He found a comfortable chair on the second floor porch after revisiting the seafood restaurant and walking along the river. A *Richmond Dispatch* kept his attention since insects had yet to reach his altitude. The *Maine* inquiry was well-covered; including an article about some bodies the divers could not dislodge. Mine conjecture was plentiful and the paper saw fit to include a story about coal torpedoes and Roosevelt's effort to expand naval militias. *Vizcaya* had departed New York for

Havana and Norfolk's navy yard was no longer working nights readying the monitor *Terror* and torpedo boats. Britain and France were facing off in West Africa, Zola's trial refused to fade despite a verdict, and Germany's Kaiser was touring the Holy Land. Booker T. Washington held a conference at Tuskegee, a Negro postmaster was murdered by some South Carolina mob, and the trial of sheriff's deputies charged in the Lattimer strike shootings a year before revealed deep-seated animosity between northern and southern Europeans. He paid particular attention to *The Sun*'s reprinted article about Cuba since that paper never used bylines. Tyson or Evans could have filed the story since they were in Havana and it matched their notes.

Starke slept unexpectedly well throughout the cool, clear night. Roused early, he dressed, breakfasted, boarded the Richmond train, and arrived late morning. Newport News passengers were shuttled to another station for a late afternoon Chesapeake & Ohio train running down the peninsula. He read and dozed in the waiting room until the call for boarding then took a vacant window seat. There was a series of noisy jerks, steam whistle blasts, and the train shed alongside its two-story, red-brick station passed from sight as they rolled through the James River waterfront and shipyard on land and over trestles. He watched the river flow around, through, and over rocks, shoals, and small islands as the local gained speed, turned inland and headed southeast. There were short, intermittent stops along the way. His traveling companions changed but the coach never filled so he was left undisturbed. As they worked down the Peninsula Extension trailing black smoke and exhausting steam, Starke made himself comfortable and was soon lulled into a half-asleep by the monotonous click of steel wheels crossing rail joints; waking briefly for a sortie to the dining car. Impatience to reach *Calypso* caused him to pass on spending the night at Warwick Hotel and go straight to the shipyard pier where his ship was moored with a reduced crew. That freed Sunday to discuss the indignities she suffered while in the yard and reconstituting her crew.

Starke worried his pipe as double tracking began and Newport News appeared off the right side. What began as little more than village was expanding over surveyed streets, cross streets, and long rectangular lots. His train turned east on the Old Point Comfort Branch when halfway past the city, went several blocks, and paused. Minutes later, it was backing across a switch that sent it, still in reverse, down the main line to the station. Two tracks became a dozen curving towards coal trestles and piers, towering grain elevator, and the Pier 1 railroad station; downriver from the casino and downhill from Warwick Hotel. Starke caught brief flashes of the massive eleven-story grain elevator and coal trestles south of the station as the train backed slowly through a series of switches then into a red, wooden train shed built on a pier to facilitate rail and ship passenger transfers. He stepped onto a platform serving double tracks under its gable roof with open sides then walked to the light-yellow, brick station steeped in the smells of coal dust, riverbank, grain, and fish. The weather was warmer than Washington but still pleasantly brisk.

Starke arranged for delivering his luggage to *Calypso* then left through the multi-gabled station's main entrance below its tall clock tower. Once outside, he paused to look up the gentle slope to Warwick Hotel, dominating its surrounding buildings two blocks west and a long one north. His cab was drawn by an old horse more familiar with plows but still pulled the cab smoothly up West Avenue along the James River. A jumble of open areas, row houses, and other buildings followed after the pleasure palace and Newport News Academy. At the shipyard boundary they turned right then left onto the broad street fronting it. The main entrance, a white-framed gate and gatehouse, was near the corner. His cab paused while its driver conversed with a watchman then they were waved through, rumbled over a single set of tracks, and passed between a long red-brick shop and the southeast fence. Starke was unable to see *Calypso* until clear of the building and on the pier since his carriage offered no forward vision and he refused to stick his head out and appear to gawk.

The motionless steam bark was moored bow out, starboard-side-to at the shipyard's south pier. Downstream along the James River were large tracts with houses obscured by trees, the pleasure pier, and casino. The ferry landing, rail station, coal piers, and massive grain elevator were also visible; as was the Warwick Hotel on slightly higher ground away from the river. The industrial waterfront upstream was dominated by *Kearsarge* and *Kentucky*'s massive hulls, about a month from launching.

Calypso's square-rigged masts rose from a 245-foot black hull, separated by her single large funnel, then fore-and-aft rigged mizzen. The lower sections were straw-yellow with bowsprit, upper masts, yards, and gaffs black. Bowsprit and jibboom, clipper bow, and fantail stern emphasized the elegant lines disrupted only by two large rifles just visible above her bulwarks. White canvas flying bridge windscreens and deck awnings accented the varnished wood deckhouse and collapsible bridge wings. Boats under canvas covers hung from radial davits or rested on skids inboard. Her design included provisions for a cruiser conversion and sailing rig, but one was forgotten and the other not installed while she sailed as *Illusive* under Starke Shipping & Shipbuilding's blood-red swallowtail banner with three interlocked black "S"s.

Except for Captain Albert's requirement for an inexpensive ship free of the fleet to harry filibusters, *Illusive* would have entered the breakers an obsolete merchantman. She was instead sold to the Navy, converted, discarded her past, commissioned as *Calypso*, and operated along the East Coast and into the Caribbean. This temporarily ended when she was rammed while moored in Hampton Roads. Starke coaxed her to the Navy's Norfolk shipyard where enough repairs were completed for towing to Newport News. The yard that accomplished her original conversion had spent the last three months replacing and repairing. This resurrection was incomplete but Watson and O'Leary, with Albert's help, achieved miracles while Starke was in Havana.

The cab was rolling away when Starke started across a heavy yard brow spanning dark, dirty water that lapped and cupped between hull sheathing and pier. The duty watch, using their spyglass, had tracked his cab from main gate and was standing by. Their captain paused midway across the brow, briefly faced the national ensign, and then stepped through the gangway to *Calypso*'s deck. After a nodded response to Watson and Blair's salutes, he added, "Thank-you, gentlemen. Mr. Blair, please log my return."

They followed Starke to the day cabin where Yamashita already laid out his service dress uniform. Starke shifted into the high-collared blue blouse and trousers then selected a pipe from its stand on the desk. He brought it, a leather pouch, and lighter to the table then resumed his habitual demeanor with Watson and Blair.

Calypso's executive officer might appear languid but enjoyed a hunter's ability to stay motionless until action was needed then respond instantly. Only his eyes betrayed this by constantly scanning everything in range. Starke noticed Watson gained several pounds since they met at the Building but remained lanky with his thin face perched on a long, narrow neck with distinct Adam's apple. He joined *Calypso* after removal from *Winston A. Capps*; an obsolete barkentine in the Treasury Department's Coast and Geodetic Survey Service. Albert gently pressured Starke to reconsider this accomplished navigator who displayed an aptitude for gunnery and possessed like qualities in shiphandling and seamanship. Over one dinner Watson let slip that mathematics, except for some arcane theories, was a discipline he enjoyed because accurate results were almost certain when all factors had been included and calculations correct; with every error traceable to some cause. Albert already pointed out this propensity to Starke and mentioned Watson relied heavily on logic for decisions. Although it got him through the Academy with remarkably few demerits, Starke served with many of a similar mindset who failed to consider more than one solution; which could demoralize crews and prove fatal in combat. However, Albert was firm and his ability irrefutable so Starke finally acquiesced. It became obvious soon after that *Calypso* gained an executive officer who was professional, consistent, and fair; strict without favoritism; seldom intemperate; and never berated or admonished publicly.

The same could not yet be said for the dark-haired Ensign Blair; struggling to appear nonchalant. Nature permanently affixed a pugnacious expression to a squarish face with compact nose, small mouth, and chalky complexion that only reddened in the sun. Watson claimed and Starke agreed he was a romantic who proved capable, energetic, and could balance initiative with good sense; providing no exceptional amount of patience was demanded. He often hesitated before requesting help and proved susceptible to premature decisions so *Calypso's* leaders worked to mature him and running mate Ensign Bernice Martyn. That officer led deck division and the port section. Martyn worried hard decisions to distraction, avoided challenging others, and preferred having senior officers present. Starke felt reasonably confident both could be the exceptional officer their third ensign, Walter Dunbar, was. This senior ensign was formally designated *Calypso*'s navigator and third in line for command, since steam engineering officers were excluded.

Starke bulged the supple leather pouch while dragging his bowl through moist tobacco, tamped the result carefully, and lit its center, "It's good to be back and seems I needn't have been concerned about the ship."

Watson barely edged out Blair, "Thank you, Captain. The Government Department and yard have been helpful but only because we distract from battleship construction; and there's still the inclining test Tuesday, then a Board of Inspection and Survey before fitting out."

Blair added, "Captain Albert helped get a new 4-inch mount. *Iowa*, some cruisers, and gunboats are getting them but not battleships; and one was still here as a construction spare. It was on its way back to the gun factory in Washington but he was able to twist some arms and substitute our damaged mount."

Starke drew on the pipe as Watson continued, "We have been fortunate, sir. Captain Albert's worked the bureaus so our main challenge's down to crewing. Every command's short with ships commissioning. Even naval militias are being tapped."

"I see, XO. Please prepare a list for Commodore Farquhar."

"The Government Department's weekly status meeting's at the administration building tomorrow afternoon, Captain; but it's now like every other shipyard with inspectors working directly through the commandant to their bureau. The senior officer's now Commander Pigman. He only tolerates us with the two battleships working towards a March launch, so any priority we receive is only to get us out from underfoot."

Albert already advised Starke no naval cadets or cadet engineers were available; a real loss since *Calypso* integrated Academy graduates into steam engineering and deck watches. The previous chief engineer transferred but O'Leary fleeted up and Albert was cajoling the Steam Engineering Bureau to continue him. Similarly, the naval hospital medical director and *Franklin*'s surgeon contrived to keep Assistant Surgeon Conrad in the area and available.

Starke cracked a window that evening, felt the cool breeze, and slept easily under his harshly comfortable, dark gray blanket of tightly woven wool. It seemed more like returning home than resuming command but he nodded off thinking of Katherine and their son. The new day broke cool and was heralded by the familiar sound of Yamashita boiling coffee in the pantry; a prelude to eggs and rice.

Starke's first call was Commander Pigman at Government Department spaces on the second floor of the administration building; a two-story edifice of red-brick with cement trim, central square tower, and chimney at either end. After passing through its main entrance, a glass-filled arch over double doors, he climbed some stairs then went through a wood door with frosted glass window. Inside were rows of desks and people in and out of uniform. Pigman welcomed him, offered to arrange the meeting with Commodore Farquhar in Norfolk later that week, and let Starke spend the morning speaking with each inspector representing their bureau.

The weekly status meeting began after lunch, with *Calypso* following the battleships. Naval constructor Lieutenant Joseph Woodward led for *Calypso* since he ran the department during her conversion. The timeworn ritual began by introducing inspectors, shipyard counterparts, and *Calypso* officers. Steam engineering inspector, Passed Assistant Engineer Claude Price, briefed first. *Calypso*'s boilers were repaired, water tubes replaced, condensers cleaned, and pumps rebuilt. This was a formality for O'Leary since the two steam engineers spoke before the meeting and were in agreement.

Calypso's chief engineer was first generation Irish so the accent was less obvious than his father's dark hair and mother's green eyes. The O'Leary family was staunchly Catholic, loyal Democrats, and Tammany Society stalwarts. His father was once a draughtsman at Harland and Wolff's Belfast shipyard before immigrating to the States where he found work in public and private yards. When and where depended on the party in power until civil service reform ensconced him at Brooklyn Navy Yard. It was no surprise the son gained a passion for shipbuilding and steam engineering while growing up in a Drydock District row-house with three sisters. Before joining *Calypso*, O'Leary was a junior steam engineer at the embryonic Newport News Government Department. Her unplanned conversion needed an officer at the Starke West Point yard to oversee initial work and tow preparation. He was offered the assignment only because no naval constructors were available then; after *Calypso* arrived in Newport News, kept the assignment through commissioning. He found the bark with her modern steam plant alluring and requested to be assigned as assistant to the chief engineer. That officer was transferred to a larger plant after the collision and Captain Albert arranged to keep him as interim chief engineer.

Bureau of Equipment and Recruiting inspector, Lieutenant Rogers Gault, reported all canvas in storage ashore. Running rigging was inspected and renewed where needed. Damaged standing rigging was replaced and the whole tuned then slushed. All major equipment damaged was reported repaired or replaced. Before closing, he added the new patent log for measuring speed had been received then assured everyone this model was more reliable than its predecessors.

Chief Boatswain Mate Braddock Weaver was taking notes for his department officer who was on watch. Powerful, roughhewn, and seemingly ungainly, he could be surprisingly agile and whatever knowledge assimilated became indelible. He was also an expert seaman whose only other passion was the home and family in Newport News. During her conversion he was offered a civilian yard position but remained with the Navy despite family separations and lack of a pension. Weaver was a leader who generated loyalty, built morale, achieved results, and one of few sailors awarded the Medal of Honor for combat since the war. He seldom spoke of it but while on *Detroit* Starke heard Weaver, at the time a landsman, became involved in hand-to-hand combat with cutlass and pistol protecting wounded when sailors and marines took three Korean forts.

The Hull Department claimed they finished rebuilding a medical storeroom and the sickbay so both were ready for stocking. The allowance of equipment and medicine had been requisitioned and Assistant Surgeon Conrad was working to replace baymen and the apothecary. He arranged to remain near the ship, despite medical department damage, through temporary duty at the naval hospital by arguing the bark remained in commission. Conrad also held regular sick calls on board to bolster this position, which also helped morale. The assistant surgeon, with relative rank of ensign, was another officer Albert cherry-picked. He held a medical degree from University of Michigan and was a listerism devotee interested in tropical diseases. His diversions included mystery literature, singlestick, seamanship, and photography. Conrad was also extraordinary taciturn which obscured his intelligence, curiosity, and insight; making his decision to begin practicing in the Navy, much less shipboard, curious.

Assistant Naval Constructor Robert Stocker and Carpenter Alonzo Burroughs attracted Starke's greatest attention. They reported no obvious keel deformity despite replacing a dozen frames and other structures, restoring hull sheathing, and repairing or rebuilding the damaged interior. Both officers also championed the chief carpenter mate's request for copper sheathing to be cleaned, inspected, and the damaged or thin plates replaced. This was now complete, despite constant threats it would be cut back due to expense. Stocker's final topic was a light displacement inclining experiment required by the Board of Inspection and Survey or INSURV. It required halting all other activity for two days and would begin the next morning if calm weather held; since *Calypso* was already stripped for repairs. Three large pendulums would be fixed on her main deck's centerline then, during high slack water, she would be moved to a spot free of current where a crane would lower heavy lead weights in calculated deck locations. Multiple pendulum readings would be taken then sent to the drawing department for recalculating stability.

Naval Constructor Woodward returned to *Calypso* with Starke afterwards for a detailed inspection before the next day's events, and to discuss Friday sea trials. Only at sea would they learn what effect damage and rebuilding had on handling and speed. Preparing for this short underway required bunkering enough picked coal for the run; examining boilers, piping, and valves for leaks; setting relief valves; testing electrical systems with shore power; and checking navigation equipment. A small Newport News tug would accompany them out, and then return to the shipyard; leaving *Calypso* to enter the Navy's yard in Norfolk for fitting out.

An unusually frustrated Captain Albert paced his Washington office after a morning meeting with Long. He just cancelled the day's appointments and his blood pulsed uncontrollably while intermittently glancing at the mechanical desk calendar clinging stubbornly to February 25, 1898. His self-enforced seclusion would continue until the possibility of showing anger over Roosevelt's Friday actions and Long's reluctance to deal with his assistant passed. Albert believed professional navy officers should not ally with any political party and avoid their machinations, except to accomplish Navy tasks, so all appointees, Democrat, Republican, or Whig received his support. He worked several items with Theodore, the man stepped up after *Calypso*'s collision, and none more actively promoted the service; but his energetic self-confidence and unapologetic jingoism proved a constant risk. Theodore was eager for war, especially with Spain since it would be mostly naval, end the last major European foothold in the hemisphere, and free Cuba.

His insubordination and disloyalty finally burst all bounds Friday afternoon. Crowninshield had just returned from the Caribbean, where he was riding *Montgomery* since before *Maine* exploded, and a fatigued Long left at noon. His assistant was directed to take no action without the secretary and president's approval.

Albert was meeting with Treasury, Justice, and State about sending *Calypso* back to sea after filibusters and the secretary had not traveled far beyond Lafayette Square before Roosevelt implemented a war plan developed over several months without consulting Crowninshield, or ignoring him. Guns were removed from storage and shipped without preparation, coal was bought, the Asiatic Squadron ordered to Hong Kong, funding requests sent to Congress, ship recommissions directed, foreign warship buys authorized, and personnel actions initiated. Roosevelt's only justification was having the opportunity since these actions were neither unplanned nor urgent but placed the Navy on a war footing without department, administration, or congressional approval; and dared Spain to declare one. The United States would have done exactly that if the situation was reversed. What made it more perverse was Roosevelt's mid-January memorandum to Long requesting such actions; one the secretary, on Albert's recommendation, decided was premature as a whole but did implement those items that made sense. Disloyalty spread suspicion and distrust so Albert even began wondering if Crowninshield, a man he respected, was involved; but he would never ask.

Long was a steady, controlled secretary so Albert was shocked to find him furious as he described the risk Roosevelt caused department and nation; and possibility he did not act alone. Apparently, the powerful jingo who pressed for Theodore's appointment, Senator Lodge, was reported in the Building that same day. Albert believed this a jingo coup and the assistant secretary should be shown the street immediately but felt it was not his place to propose it. Long was also aware such a dismissal could worsen matters, so he instead fretted over Roosevelt's actions and need for tighter reins. It was doubly hard for Albert to restrain himself while the secretary spoke of Roosevelt's ill wife and a son since the captain's sympathy did not extend to a subversive insubordinate who risked others' lives and families in some personal quest for war. Seething, he left Secretary Long's office with direction to recommend actions for undoing the more egregious or costly directions, avoid any appearance the Department was in disarray, and ensure Roosevelt would not become scapegoat, martyr, or hero. Albert forwarded a memorandum proposal to Long then went home to reconsider Immanuel Starke's offer

about joining their shipping company; and Abigail spent her
evening avoiding the urge to offer an opinion.

Chapter Thirteen
Resurrection

Watson seldom used the main cabin while Starke was away and Yamashita ensured nothing changed so it felt as though returning from short trip. While comforting, it reinforced his belonging to *Calypso* and she to him; some would say a warning he was too long in command.

Watson stood in for Starke before but with the ship anchored, crewed, and only routine tasks to confront. This time, *Calypso*'s repair and crew preservation were down to him. This greater exposure to command responsibilities perhaps salved some lingering bitterness from Commander Fredericks ordering him from *Winston A. Capps* then trying to end his career by letter. Captain Albert had derailed the scheme; his old ship was another disintegrating Caribbean wreck and her captain's career ended following investigation of the grounding. Even so, Starke believed Watson's loyalty to *Calypso* and his benefactors, then amplified by proposing to Albert's eldest, had driven him close to exhaustion.

Ensign Dunbar, their lanky, sandy-haired navigator, was equally relieved by his captain's return. Like Watson, he temporarily experienced the next rung when their executive officer was on leave, but that was underway with Starke on board. This tenure was longer and during a period when executive officer duties multiplied; and his eagerness to focus on navigation demands and electrical equipment could not be clearer.

O'Leary was, like *Calypso*'s last chief engineer, convinced steam engineers should not be limited to boilers and propulsion machinery; and Starke overlooked a certain amount of territorial overlap. Unfortunately, O'Leary was too junior for his current role which made its tenure uncertain. He constantly risked being superseded or supplanted and his excellent reputation within the Bureau of Steam Engineering only increased the possibility he would be pulled. Starke had received no indication of a plan to transfer him, and preferred not advertising the situation, but that bureau controlled all steam engineering assignments and officers were in demand for ships commissioning; so he chose to work through Captain Albert. Hopefully, losing their chief engineer and O'Leary's efforts at managing the baseline conversion and latest repair would be enough to support his formal designation or extend the interim arrangement.

Line officer assignments were controlled by the Bureau of Navigation and they also eyed the wardroom. Commodore Farquhar had summoned Watson to the receiving ship *Franklin*, moored across the Elizabeth River from Norfolk's navy yard, to ask if he desired transfer with his temporary command ending. Watson declined but used the time to make his case for keeping their three ensigns and pass on their desire to remain. While returning on the steam pinnace, he concluded the Navy must be assembling wardrooms for the Newport News battleships launching that month.

Any shipyard period's final weeks, then days, grow exceptionally onerous as deadlines for specific tasks approach and dormant problems surface. This required balancing of time, resources, and priorities; leaving winners and losers. Watson, Dunbar, and O'Leary pushed hard early on when there was leeway so the remaining hurdles were primarily coaling and canvas. Chief Weaver wanted sails raised during sea trials. Martyn backed him with more vigor than the executive officer observed previously, so Watson persuaded Starke to consider it despite fewer sailors. Coaling proved the greater conundrum because *Calypso* did not decommission. New construction ships, or those out of commission, ran sea trials on picked coal with no more than needed; but *Calypso* was in neither category so regulations required a larger amount for stability and margin. This caused several tense meetings between Watson, Dunbar, O'Leary, Wiggs, and a Government Department driven by bureau interests. Paymaster Wiggs quickly discovered the root cause was which account would be charged for additional coal. Starke agreed with his officers the ship should fully bunker but also understood Newport News would load bituminous coal. That type traded stability and smoke for power; and he wanted some anthracite, with opposite characteristics and higher cost. The resulting compromise Farquhar approved was a three-quarters load-out going into trials with anthracite filling empty bunkers during fitting out.

Calypso was coaled and sails harbor furled by Thursday evening, but O'Leary and Chief Machinist Mate Emery Baasch worked into Friday morning lighting boilers, tracing lines for steam leaks, and cycling valves. Chief Baasch emigrated from a German state bordering the North Sea so his language was blunt. This reinforced the chief's authority but left a black gang thinking him unsympathetic despite his siding with them more than not behind closed doors. The two lead stokers probably suspected this and were influential because they guided the trimmers, passers, and stokers who broke coal into usable lumps, carted it to boilers, and then spread it evenly over white hot coals behind each boiler's three heavy doors.

This was strenuous and dusty work in humid heat invariably above three digits so the black gang received higher pay for an existence that ground men down. *Calypso*'s lead stokers and others still found this preferable to their state before the Navy. Dylan Jones hoped to reenlist as a water tender, the boiler operator rating, and saw this work vastly better than descending hundreds of feet into a mine's noxious air, flooding, and explosions. His parents were Welch immigrants so he was born into that world and began working below ground as a child. Mine owners cut wages after the 1893 panic and threatened more so a Navy recruiting poster offering fair pay, lodging, meals, and travel for similar work was inducement enough. Strong, healthy, and unmarried, he enlisted. The United Mine Workers struck in the spring so things grew worse at home while he advanced from coal trimmer to lead stoker. He now plied water tenders for information and dedicated free time to engineering texts. His close friend was the port section's lead stoker, Delmar Kemp. This large, powerful Negro with those African features exaggerated in cartoons was good-natured and respected by most on board; and those testing him found it took days or weeks to recover. The family's western Virginia farm may have seemed attractive but he began working the brutally hot, dusty fields while a child. His parents encouraged education and Bible reading along with hard labor so he spent any free time poring over machinery articles and becoming fascinated by steam tractors. This eventually drew him to Norfolk's shipyards and suppliers but without relatives, or sponsors it was his size and farmer's acceptance of backbreaking work employers were interested in. After several months he spotted a Navy flyer offering stoker jobs and potential of becoming a water tender or machinist mate. Kemp enlisted, discovered he loved the sea, enjoyed its society, and found a home with *Calypso*.

The black gang worked through early morning lighting-off and warming two Normand water-tube boilers generating 180-pound steam for a Navy-designed triple-expansion reciprocating engine. Her modern plant was also planned for some new gunboats so given to *Calypso* during conversion for operational testing. The new engine successively reused steam three times to increase range, power, and economy. Its massive cylinders, solid frame, and heavy base rose from sliding feet to almost the main deck; completely filling the cavernous compartment aft of *Calypso*'s fireroom. The plant was more economical than her double-expansion engine yet produced 1,227 horsepower. This increase was almost a hundred but being designed for warships meant maintaining full speed for any long period risked damage. Maintenance was also greater so engine, boilers, piping, and condensers would have brought *Calypso* back to a shipyard yard by June even without a collision. Along with propulsion boilers, the black gang also lit her auxiliary, or donkey, boilers; a reliable fire-tube type producing low-pressure steam for pumps, winches, dynamos, water distillers, and other equipment.

Chief Boatswain's Mate Weaver inspected rigging with his mast captains at first light, confirmed the port anchor was readied for dropping, checked mooring lines that now wedded *Calypso* to the pier instead of chains or poles, and visited a yard tug to confer with her master. The chief led with a passion for seamanship but those testing him could spend days recovering. Weaver was on *Franklin* with orders to *Maine* when he learned *Calypso* was crewing under Starke. The chief served with him on *Detroit* during the Brazilian Naval Revolt and preferred the bark over a battleship where seamanship enjoyed less status. A chief with orders to *Calypso* was willing so Weaver went to the bark and his benefactor now among those missing in Havana Harbor. It was not the first time fate favored him. While a confused, panicked, and trapped landsman during the 1871 assault on three Korean forts, he fought blindly with pistol and cutlass to survive. An officer believed he was protecting wounded on the ground around him so he received a Medal of Honor with its small pension. Knowing the truth, Weaver seldom mentioned the episode and wore his medal only when required.

Paymaster Matthew Wiggs was taking morning coffee in the wardroom. Any observer might think him a dandy except for a strange flat nose mashed against his face through accident, incident, or natural growth. He was, however, a master at navigating supply regulations and laws. Albert hoped to avoid a paymaster who might constrain his ferret's ability to disrupt filibusters so he visited the Bureau of Supplies and Accounts during the selection process and called in some favors. Wiggs was a passed assistant paymaster with relative rank of lieutenant (j.g.) and could have declined the more junior assistant paymaster billet but did not. Starke found only two faults with Albert's choice. He habitually advocated for a general mess to replace the many small ones maintained on warships and was a temperance man. Neither proved more than mildly irritating and his contribution exceeded professional expertise because he was a Baptist deacon.

Calypso had no chaplain. The Navy employed fewer than two dozen so most went to large ships or shore stations. This would have been satisfactory since most officers disliked having them on board, but without one all religious responsibilities fell to the captain. Starke was raised Protestant like most officers, and baptized Episcopal, but did little more than go along at sea and evade religious instruction while ashore. Katherine labeled him a freethinker. He considered her observation and found it hard to deny but decided he tended towards agnostic and saw religion based on a faith he could not claim to possess. Since he abhorred hypocrisy and refused to buy or write sermons, meeting this responsibility seemed insurmountable before Wiggs. The paymaster was devout, enthusiastic, and capable; with no inclination to proselytize, harangue, or be a missionary. Starke had heard their paymaster deacon's spouse was more pious, wedded to church doctrine, and less tolerant; a domestic situation Watson suggested was one source of Wiggs' diplomatic skills and agility with regulations.

Conrad sat across from Wiggs, holding his saucer under a wardroom china cup with Boothby's novel *Lust of Hate* on the green table cloth in front of him. He was physically fit with an inclination towards girth. Articulate when inclined, energetic, and keen researcher, his current professional interests were seasickness and yellow fever. Reading mysteries was his primary hobby but he recently developed an interest in photography. Conrad relished life at sea despite its boredom and prospect of entering another slaughterhouse like the Spanish gunboat off Cuba. Captain and crew appreciated his return from temporary duty at Norfolk's naval hospital.

Starke completed the last lines of a report while calls for getting underway were passed. Watson already walked the crew through Watch, Quarter and Station Bill assignments but there would be a level of confusion best left unseen by the captain. What remained of their original crew had been on board since commissioning but the ship was too long in port and going to sea with less than her already minimal complement of 135 enlisted and wardroom of twelve. On the ledger's positive side there were unused bunks and hammocks for riders from the shipyard trades, Government Department, and INSURV. *Calypso* regularly sailed with a smaller crew during merchant service when Starke was a mate and supercargo so he expected little more than some watch confusion before completing sea trials and returning to Norfolk's navy yard across Elizabeth River from *Franklin*.

A weekend at sea would also avoid *Maine* questions. The inquiry was releasing nothing to government or press so what was published came from every source imaginable or none. Naval officers were common targets but the shipyard fence somewhat shielded Starke from reporters. For that he was grateful. The explosion could have resulted from sabotage, torpedo, or a bunker fire like the one *Calypso* faced off Jacksonville so any remarks or conjecture were grist for the press. Even Secretary Long was caught out when he opined the inquiry no longer thought Spain a culprit, if one existed. This chilled his relations with McKinley although most experienced officers believed the president leaned towards a coal bunker fire. Officially, speculation was to be avoided until the inquiry finished.

There were several competing press stories. Britain and France were embroiled in colonial wars. Spain and the States competed to obtain two Brazilian cruisers building in Great Britain. Zola's trial kept Dreyfus on front pages. Even the reconcentrado disaster was surpassing *Maine* due to Senator Proctor's fact-finding trip and Clara Barton's Artemisa visit. Most newspapers' lead story was a South Carolina mob murdering the newly appointed Negro postmaster and his daughter while attacking their combined home and office. Colored and White lynchings, failed or successful, were also increasing. Some were carried out, others thwarted, and a few participants fired on. They were seldom condoned but often rationalized by readers as delivering justice the law or courts would not.

Navy ships were somewhat insulated because their closed societies had defined classes under the same regulations. Any alternative was chaos since roughly two-thirds of *Calypso's* crew were citizens and through birth or extraction counted African, English, Irish, Germans, Poles, Scots, Swedes, British Canadians, Newfoundlanders, Norwegians, Frenchmen, a Finn, Japanese, Spaniards, a Sandwich Islander, and others who often did not know or care. This mélange of accents, languages, experience, and religions under one flag was portrayed as a weakness by many but familiar to American naval officers who often recruited merchant sailors off the waterfront when sails were the primary propulsion mode.

Starke finished morning coffee then snapped open his father's gold Patek Philippe & Cie hunter to check the time. When satisfied the delay was long enough, he adjusted his white standing collar, pulled a visored cap from the wall peg and went through the door. It was a short passage to the main deck where *Calypso's* starboard side lay against the yard's southern pier. Her superstructure mostly blocked the view downriver; but upriver was a waiting harbor tug, more piers, a dry-dock, and some building ways. Two large battleships taking shape dominated, but other ships were in various stages of building or repair. The day was cold, overcast, and just below freezing so some water puddling on the pier was lightly frozen. It would quickly thaw with more sun, although temperatures were not expected to climb more than a dozen degrees. The day was gray with a promise of rain and air pregnant with smells of river, shipyard, coal, steam, and fresh paint.

Coxswain Clement Melvin crossed Starke's path near a ladder to the pilothouse. He was not only their best coxswain but played mandolin. The sailor paused to salute on his way aft to the steam pinnace; where its' two seamen, a fireman, and coal-passer waited with the crew detailed for a whaleboat swung outboard for their lifeboat. Starke halted briefly at the ladder's top to scan south past leafless trees along the James River shore to the casino, ferry pier, and rail station; all dwarfed by tall coaling trestles and massive grain elevator.

Blair called out his arrival in the pilothouse; a rectangular structure forward of the main mast and stack. Tall windows pierced three varnished mahogany walls while doors on either side led to collapsible wings and ladder to the flying bridge encircled with canvas windscreens. Chart table, shelves, and clothes-hooks were built into its rear wall with the open space forward containing a brass helm, compass binnacle, engine order telegraph or EOT, peloruses, and polished brass voice tubes. The spoked helm connected to a steering engine in the auxiliary machinery room and linked through a shaft and cable arrangement, including two unassisted helm stations, to the single rudder.

Starke looked through its front windows, beyond the foremast's straw-yellow metal tube, bowsprit, and jibboom over gray water to the far shore then upriver. Off their starboard side were impatient line-handlers and shipyard trades on the pier then their escort moored on its far side. The small yard tug had a thin stack, nearly equaling two masts that rose from a deckhouse running most of the squat, scarred hull. In the wheelhouse next to her foremast, a tug master leaned against its doorframe; below the stack emitting a translucent column of gray smoke drifting above the river. Observing this, Starke saw the wind was veering north to northeast which meant an onsetting, negligible breeze for getting underway so river current would dominate.

Their pilot clambered over the tug's bulwarks, leapt to the pier, and crossed to *Calypso*'s brow where Martyn waited. As they came forward and up to the pilothouse, Watson passed Chief Weaver orders through a speaking trumpet and line-handlers began to retrieve the brow. Once that wooden bridge over dark camels floating between ship and pier cleared the bulwark, the gangway closed and Weaver waved to Watson, who turned to Starke, "Request permission to test engine, Captain."

Starke responded, "Very well," because subordinates used "Yes, sir" or "Aye, aye" in reply. The EOT arm swung to alert their engine room and instantly rewarded by its pointer signaling they were standing by to answer all bells. Slow ahead was rung up, held long enough for mooring lines take a slight strain then all stop ordered. The process was repeated with slow astern. Their steering engine was then tested by cycling her rudder as far right-to-left then left-to-right as possible without driving it into the stops. Watson then ensured aft steering was manned and ready. Emergency steering was also rigged since they were getting underway after major repairs.

Their dapper pilot was a lightweight Chief Weaver; well-respected and living near the chief's row-house. He was mourning a half-chewed tobacco wad cast into the river before boarding but grinned, "Looks a lot different from when she arrived," then, "What's your pleasure, Captain."

Starke nodded towards Watson, "XO's taking her out. Once away from the pier, we'll probably not require much from the tug. Wind's calm so the current should help breast us away. Stern could be a problem coming off."

The pilot considered the water, sniffed the air, and glanced at the familiar pier; a mass of fill and concrete surrounded by crush poles, "That'll work, Captain. Suggest a headline to pull us out. That and some rudder should keep her clear. Current here tends to push the bow downstream and stern into the pier."

"Agreed. Whenever you're ready Mr. Watson."

Starke normally rotated officers for each underway but this was the first after repairs so Watson would take her out. Thankfully, they would not go to general quarters since the chief engineer drove for that and only O'Leary remained. Starke regretted losing Osbourne to a new gunboat and guessed the next time they met would likely be at Watson's wedding to the elder Albert sister; since their previous chief engineer seemed taken with the younger.

Watson and their pilot stood on the port bridge wing as the tug came round her bow, made a sharp turn, and sent a headline over midship. While the pilot ensured it was properly made up, Watson crossed to starboard, had mooring lines singled, and ordered them cast off after seeing the pilot nod. As the last was lifted from its large pier cleat, *Calypso*'s ensign raced to her main mast truck and whistle sounded. Looking between pier and ship he watched the bark's wood hull breast slowly away, leaving camels and surface trash floating free; then left Blair to deal with the pier side and rejoined their pilot. With mooring lines clear, the tug emitted a cloud of black smoke as it backed down on the headline. This, with starboard rudder, moved *Calypso* out and into the stream. The solid pier diverted current and wind negligible so that line came off when *Calypso* was clear, her rudder centered, and full ahead rung up.

White water roiled beneath the fantail stern then turned muddy from her spinning screw forcing steerageway to clear the concrete pier and counter river current pressing her bow. *Calypso*'s 220-foot hull and 1,100 tons initially moved by inches then gathered momentum with Quartermaster Marius Moreau, a Newfoundlander veteran of fishing and merchant fleets, on the helm. Starke watched the brass wheel spin, forcing *Calypso*'s bow upriver against the current while holding her stern off. He and Watson checked again for traffic as they cleared and a series of whistle blasts signaled *Calypso* entering the channel under her own power. Seeing Moreau center his wheel once the pier was astern and current setting them downriver, Watson ordered starboard helm and a new course. Bowsprit and jibboom swung to port then steadied on the outbound track as Moreau met her and increasing speed gave the rudder bite. The tug fell in astern for their run to the bay.

Starke monitored Watson's commands, felt the ship throb through his feet, and kept lookout for traffic as early spring scenery passed and they steered towards the black Buoy S1 to clear coal pier traffic, minimize wake, and pass south of Newport News Middle Ground. Warwick Hotel emerged from the tree-lined river bank on high ground sloping to the river, beyond a cleared expanse after casino, academy, and pleasure pier. Next to pass were the rail station, tall coal trestles, cotton sheds, and grain elevator. The next course left Buoy S to starboard, marking safe water south of Newport News Middle Ground Lighthouse. Two white boats hung from davits on the six-year-old caisson-style structure with its round, black, concrete-filled iron base supporting a brown tower. The shoal's up and downstream limits were also marked by can buoys, except during winter months when exchanged for the spar variety.

Calypso had company this morning. The Virginia Navigation Company's walking-beam, side-wheel steamer *Pocahontas* was coming down the James River from Richmond, a Norfolk ferry left its landing, two tugs were making up to barges, and one schooner underway. Ship-rigged colliers were at anchor, waiting their turn alongside the coal piers. Few small craft moved along the shore except those fishing or on errands since unpleasant weather cleared river and bay of pleasure seekers.

Coming northeast, *Calypso* aimed left of Fortress Monroe to leave Buoy S3 to starboard while holding to the broad channel's south side. On Old Point Comfort the Hygeia and Chamberlain Hotels lay under that fortress near the tug station able to assist once their escort turned back at Fort Wool. Darker clouds were rolling in over the Atlantic to their northeast and an intermittent mist settled on the ship as it went forward into what must be light rain or snow.

Starke looked reflexively towards Craney Island Flats and buoyed channel into Norfolk during the turn. The Academy training ship *Essex*, crewed with naval apprentices, was one of several moored or anchored near where *Doireann Bannan* rammed *Calypso*. She just returned from Europe according to the pilot, and considered the Navy's best steam screw sloop. Donald McKay designed the bark first commissioned a decade after the war. Shorter than *Calypso* with shallower draft, she still displaced more. Her harbor furled sails were bent to three masts supported by a bowsprit protruding far up and out over a cutwater bow. There was an ochre stack between fore and main masts, midship pilothouse, and white boats swung out over a black hull fitted with six breech-loading guns clearly visible through binoculars.

Starke glanced at Watson then darkening clouds ahead. His executive officer took the hint and directed Blair to send those topside below for foul weather gear, dispatched the master-at-arms to reinspect preparations for sea, and had the ready lifeboat swung inboard and secured. Weaver sent petty officers to check standing and running rigging for chafing and within thirty minutes everyone outside the pilothouse wore pale-yellow canvas outfits sealed with marline which, unless inundated, kept rain mostly out and perspiration always in. Yamashita brought Starke his personal rubberized officer's coat that hung from a peg in his day cabin, with panels under the arms and a back flap for ventilation.

After passing south of a mid-channel wreck buoy they planned to exit Hampton Roads and enter Chesapeake Bay by steering closer to the low, gray Fort Wool than far larger Fortress Monroe. A shore battery had been added under the fortress. Watson heard it protected a minefield the Revenue Service Cutter *Alexander Hamilton* was about to plant. Starke identified her with binoculars. Anchored off Old Point Comfort, she had a black hull, white deckhouse, and a thin stack rising two-thirds the height of both masts. Their pilot observed the iron-hulled ship rigged as a topsail schooner had a single screw and less capable 4-inch gun than *Calypso's*.

Starke's attention shifted to the Hygeia's pier he walked with Katherine after dancing on the hotel's waxed parquet floor under the stars and open to the bay. It seemed ages ago and now, after one Havana night, she gave him a son but no reply to his proposal. He felt a chill and her face seemed less distinct as Watson requested permission to feed the crew by mess. Blair pointed out the Fortress Monroe weather station's flag and pennant hoist separated by streamers was warning of hazardous weather. Starke nodded and sailors began leaving to eat as *Calypso* shaved Fort Wool close enough to see the individual gray granite blocks of its low walls and foaming white necklace created by the bay pummeling riprap. Their escort put on a burst of speed then came alongside sounding several whistle blasts. The pilot waved to her tug master as she pulled even with the bark's pilothouse then reversed course by hauling off in a wide turn to port that carved a turbulent, white wake through gray water with a dusting of small whitecaps.

Starke could make out the Newport News grain elevator astern as their pilot guided them northeast past Willoughby's

Banks for the octagonal Thimble Shoal lighthouse on stilts and girders. Through binoculars, he picked out a red warning flag flying from the flagpole above that screw-pile light's cupola and a large fog bell over its entrance. Their well-maintained lifeboat swung from davits below its main door; kept ready to lower since the lighthouse was struck regularly. *Calypso* used it to turn southeast on a course between buoys marking the channel south of Middle Ground and Tail of the Horseshoe. As Lynn Haven Roads passed to starboard, a pilot schooner inside the entrance spun on her heels then made for *Calypso*; cutting close astern of the Merritt tug *Chapman* on her way in; after taking a savage beating.

Neither *Calypso* nor her crew had been underway for months and leaving a shipyard invariably meant things would fail, items fall, and something poorly secured. Their port anchor was ready to drop, so Starke could run for safe anchorage or continue into the Atlantic. Northeast winds made Lynn Haven Roads risky since it meant anchoring in three to five fathoms less than a mile off the lee shore, but coming about to head deeper in the bay could mean anchoring in bad weather. No anchorage guaranteed safety and could turn dangerous in storms; as demonstrated during the Samoan hurricane where German and American ships were driven ashore. A liner some distance ahead was not turning back so Starke was sensitive to crew confidence in their capabilities and ship. Against this, *Calypso* was riding light without stores and ammunition. Continuing would have been absurd except her coal bunkers were three-quarters full and freshwater tanks topped off. There was also adequate crew to work the ship. He weighed all, extracted an unlit pipe from his sparse beard, and turned to Watson, "Secure the anchor for sea, XO," then to the pilot, "Captain, I believe your ride's coming alongside. Perhaps we'll see you on our return."

The pilot grinned as they slowed, grasped Watson's hand, and left the pilothouse with Blair. Weaver directed sailors on the forecastle securing their anchor while Martyn saw fenders went over and preparations made to receive the pilot boat. These were mostly wood-hulled schooners, although a steamer operated out of Maryland. This one was sleek, black-hulled, and gaff-rigged with two masts and no bowsprit. Newport News was painted across her main sail in large black letters. She made the approach and soon caressed *Calypso's* flank with her bow; gently compressing rope fenders just aft of the main yard. Their pilot crossed with practiced agility, the schooner hauled off, fell into their wake, caught the wind, and was away.

Blair added another brief dilemma as *Calypso* gained speed despite plowing into worsening weather and growing seas. The pilot boat had passed a message during transfer, "Be advised, British steamer Gleadowe - two masts, 1,400 tons, 285 feet - went aground at 1100, two miles south of Cape Henry lifesaving station. Merritt tug Chapman ordered back. Lifesaving Service at scene."

Starke read the note then passed it to Watson for logging. *Chapman's* battered state was explained and *Calypso* could do nothing but stand by if she diverted. Any ship attempting to tow the steamer off a lee shore was more likely to join her. The liner must have been running before the storm, misjudged the entrance, could not reverse course, and went aground near the lifesaving station. Rescuers from shore might get a line to her since most stations were equipped with a special surfboat, Lyle gun, other gear, and shelter. However, not all stations were continuously manned despite the Lifesaving Service expanding since the war and adding facilities in areas ships could or had gone aground. Starke's choice was hard but clear. *Calypso* could do nothing except distract from the rescue, especially if she went aground.

Before clearing Cape Henry, Ensign Dunbar recommended steaming due east to leave two buoys and the Cape Charles lightship to port, come northeast into wind, and then steer to avoid a beam sea. Starke agreed. Once in the Atlantic he looked back towards the bay's mouth in time to watch a prolonged wind gust heel the pilot schooners as they reefed or lowered sails. *Calypso* plunged deep into heavy seas; drenching those sailors still on her forecastle. Further down the coast, beyond the Cape Henry lighthouses framed by an eighty-foot sand hill covered with brush and trees, was a dark form where *Gleadowe*'s fate was being decided.

⁓ ❧❀☙ ⁓

Chapter Fourteen
Heavy Weather

Regular underway watches commenced with Ensign Blair's starboard section. Before the collision, Naval Cadet Timme would have assisted but he and Naval Cadet Caldwell were ordered to other ships. Commodore Farquhar arranged that with Starke's full support since languishing in a shipyard while their competitors spent a full two years at sea after graduation would reduce their ability to obtain a commission; limited by law to available fleet billets.

Blair checked the compass binnacle then noticed Chief Quartermaster Paul Owen open their cupped anemometer's wooden box. His quartermasters would get a reading then calculate true wind for the deck log. Starke was studying the Atlantic and concluded this was the storm *Gleadowe* ran from so they would likely see fifty to sixty miles per hour winds, with higher gusts. *Calypso* pushed east as the sky blackened and ocean turned dark gray with white crest lines, spray, and forty-foot seas. Increasing wind sheared off wave crests and hurled water downwind in sheets of spray, rain, and light snow that battered windows and left a salt crust, further reducing visibility.

Calypso was heading east and had turned into the wind before the tempest's intensity made maneuver perilous. Heavy weather netting and lifelines were not rigged so Starke held the crew below. Without steadying staysails, their bark assumed a steamship's abusive gyrations so this, and months ashore without time to adjust, was worsening cases of seasickness, especially among riders. Starke felt weakness and rising nausea. He was seldom afflicted beyond that but concerned for the crew. The unaffected sometimes induced it for entertainment, seeing it as lack of masculinity or courage, but Starke viewed it as an illness and Watson agreed. Lord Nelson's continual struggle helped advance public perception and attempts were made, unsuccessfully, to design ships that avoided it.

Surgeon Conrad was susceptible so he characteristically developed an interest studying it along with yellow fever. Unless overcome, he rode out most storms in his whitewashed sickbay, low and forward, where he stood by for the inevitable injuries and burn cases. Even now he was alone at its large desk anchored near two coffin-like berths suspended from the overhead. The new apothecary and their baymen were checking medical storerooms so there was nothing to divert attention from a stomach signaling the need for another sugar loaf laced with creosote. They seemed to prevent nausea from becoming vertigo then vomiting but little could be done for those suffering the advanced stages. Most regained sea legs within a day or so if not too long ashore, a few might take a week, and those cured only by calm water would go before a medical board to be condemned and discharged.

He read the well-known physician Rosenbach theorized it was a malady of the senses despite the common belief a stomach disorder caused it. Conrad was coming to the German's view after months at sea. He put patients to bed before nausea became acute and found it helped; while observing vomit's stench affected sufferers too fast for a germ. Similarly, roll proved a greater factor than pitch and one experienced surgeon claimed sailors without symptoms on one ship often suffered recurrence after transfer to another;

especially from sail to steam. Remedies included cocaine, chloroform, hydrocyanic acid in water, and tight belts. One favorite was alcohol, which caused several sailors to seek relief from the sickbay medicinal brandy stock. He conducted tests despite their impure motivations and found it shortened duration but worsened intensity. His preferred approach was hard candy sticks or crackers for mild cases, loaf sugar laced with creosote for more advanced, and cocaine lozenges for the worst. A few fatalities were documented, and one landsman during the ship's first transit would have been a candidate, but most adjusted eventually or were sent ashore before that.

Calypso's translucent gray-black smoke tail dispersed immediately as she settled into a mishmash of pitch, roll, yaw, surge, sway, and heave. Her clipper bow was taking the sea on its port side, cutting down and forward as a single bronze screw thrust the black hull ahead; submerging it to the bobstays then recovering with water spraying up and over the deck. More than a ton of roiling gray-white sea was intermittently scooped up to cascade aft before escaping through scuppers and spaces under bulwarks. During each cycle, the rising bow rolled starboard, shook, hesitated, then returned to port while descending into gray seas with white stripes. Her fantail stern crashed down each time; reminding Starke it not only contributed to the bark's clean lines but caused excessive pounding aft and was a liability. The triple-expansion engine added to this cacophony when her screw lifted; causing its steady throbbing to suddenly become an unnerving scream as the unloaded plant spun freely until its bronze blades once again submerged.

Starke inserted a worn briar pipe, passing unlit through his sparse beard, and studied the volatile gray seas with spindrift streaming from every wave's crest line. This pipe stayed in the pilothouse on a small shelf set aside for his binoculars and personal items. He often felt the urge to charge it but that was not allowed in the pilothouse, even with the smoking lamp lit. Instead, he clamped down on its mangled stem and looked aft. Surrounding watchstanders were wedged in any available corner or standing with legs apart while rotating knees to maintain balance and contact with a gyrating deck. Their helmsman was lashed in place and relieved every half-hour, exhausted. Those unsecured or caught off-guard half-hopped across the deck before slamming into the opposite wall or sent sprawling. Blair was staring beyond bow and jibboom where increasing rain lashed the violent sea. Starke intended to hold course overnight since it best balanced pounding, water shipped, and the excessive rolling that might damage spars and boilers; besides a significant alteration risked sliding into a trough where they could swamp or capsize.

Engineering spaces moved less violently, being nearer the keel, but deck plates became precarious, bilge gas soured stomachs, humid heat took a greater toll, and these spaces were filled with searing pipes, valves, and boiler faces. Without steam reaching engine, dynamos, and pumps *Calypso* might be driven onto the Virginia shore or founder. O'Leary also put their donkey boiler on line to ensure continuous steam for bilge pumps handling higher water levels from constantly working sheathing and greater intrusion from the main deck.

Evening's approach brought ever darkening skies as Starke went below to find his meal prepared and cabin secured for heavy weather. Yamashita had done well, as always, in spite of rolls, thrusts, plunges, and surges. The desktop was shut and fastened, chair lanyards doubled, bookshelf bars in place, and window lids latched. The table's spider was also rigged to restrain his coffee, bread, rice, and sliced ham; bland food that helped adjust to heavy seas.

Calypso's commander toured below deck before eight o'clock reports. A surreal light permeated these moving, confined, close spaces. The smell of saltwater, coal, sweat, and vomit competed with food, paint, and canvas. Sailors could be found in several states. Some working or trying to, others bragging, but the majority resigned to near stupor. A few with oilskins gathered near one weather-deck door, waiting for the call to go on deck. No one moved quickly and everyone, including Starke, committed one arm to grasp something solid while intermittently fending off bulkhead, wall, or object with the other. Berthing deck portholes submerged to grow dark with solid water rushing past then lighten as the opposing roll resurrected dark foam, waves, and sky.

Noxious bilge gas, humidity, noise, and extreme temperatures transfused every engineering space. The fire room soared well over 100 degrees with main boilers on line, even in cool weather, and the engine room fared no better. Leaving port into a storm was especially unsettling. Some denizens leaned or slumped against bulkheads to be left alone if only moderately seasick. Those with bad cases, heat exhaustion, or both would be helped to marginally cooler spots or sick bay. If unable on their own, they were extracted when opportunity presented since two engineers were needed to remove one, and work could not be disrupted. O'Leary also kept everyone on station to permit short respites in this humid, hot, rolling, dropping, twisting world. Trimmers, passers, and stokers steadily broke coal loose, prepared it, and fed the boilers. Water tenders' skills and stamina were pushed to the limit as they stood at each boiler face, fixated on dancing water levels in sight-glasses while working steam and water valves to compensate. Too much could send water rather than steam into cylinders and cause catastrophic failure but too little might empty boiler water tubes and precipitate an explosion.

Lieutenant O'Leary and Chief Machinist Baasch spotted Starke coming down the ladder and crossed to greet him. He supported the black gang but they hardly expected him in engineering during a storm. Starke took them aside while lead stoker Jones coached men at the aft boiler face to feed its glowing white-hot coals behind heavy iron shutters that rhythmically swung open and shut over stokehole doors. Without delaying a call for coal from trimmers and passers, he grabbed one stoker about to back against a hot face. Jones was thin for a stoker, with pointed nose, matching face, and a sparse scalp hidden by the dirty white cap pulled down over his ears. Rivulets of sweat leaked from it to run down the sallow cheeks' shining stubble.

Starke continued to the engine room where three massive connecting rods flashed in a metal framework filled by pistons and cylinders. This space offered a different miasma of bilge gas, steam, lubricating oil, and vomit. He took care to avoid disrupting work there or in the auxiliary space forward since the operators' concentration was critical, especially in storms. During calmer weather he often obtained some small bit of information on a particular sailor from the executive officer or a chief then remark on it during what seemed a chance meeting. Few officers and almost no commanders spoke with sailors, except favorites who were often shunned, so this was well-received until the man began wondering what else their captain knew. It promoted honesty and seemed to remain undiscovered. Even Jones was surprised when asked about his brother's recovery from a kick administered by one of the small ponies kept below ground in the mine to pull coal cars.

Their ship's cat, Thaddeus, weakly announced his presence from a refuge deep in the ship where he waited out storms.

The nondescript gray and black tom's white belly had expanded considerably since *Calypso* sailors rescued him from an irate Key West bartender. That proprietor had his fill of a street cat strutting down the bar to search out customers' whiskey and went for the feline with a truncated, two-foot boat oar. *Calypso* sailors rallied to prevent the slaughter and, sensing fellow travelers, the cat trailed them until lifted and carried aboard. Cleaned, deloused, and dried out; Thaddeus was dismayed to find alcohol off the menu but adapted to a perpetual food quest, frequent naps, and friendly stroking.

Starke was in the day cabin with a pipe when Watson brought the night order book for review and signature. With difficulty, they sat at the table while Starke read and Watson stood by to answer questions about position, course, operating details, and anything else for the overnight watch. It stated the captain intended to maintain course until first watch then come northeast and ride out the storm. They would adjust later to accommodate the trials then return to Norfolk early on March 7, 1898. After signing, Starke reviewed deck and steam logs until evening reports then retired for whatever sleep the storm allowed.

Calypso's commander stripped blouse and shoes to wash then used the commode, basin, and water closet wall to brace against. Bare feet gave his toes a grip on shifting wood planking and a small amount of soapy water slipping across the basin's bottom tracked the bark's gyrations. Freshwater was limited. Boilers and drinking water had priority since the only sources were onboard distillers or lighters. A daily freshwater allowance for drinking and washing was set by regulations at no less than one gallon. Some ships barely met that so veteran sailors kept canteen-like containers near hammock or bunk. Seawater was unlimited and used to launder, flush heads, wash decks, brush teeth, and other requirements. This proved beneficial preserving decks and teeth but lathering was out of the question, even with special soap. After completing his ablutions Starke left the day cabin and climbed to his sea cabin behind *Calypso*'s pilothouse for whatever snatches of sleep fate permitted.

When Martyn's port section relieved Blair's for the first watch, lasting until midnight, the ensign greeted Starke then retreated to a secure spot between magnetic compass binnacle and the pelorus used to mark an object's bearing off the bow. He peered regularly into the binnacle's single, faintly lit oval opening above its dancing black needle card divided in points and fractions for the helmsman. He later came northeast into the storm for a better ride, as night orders required, then informed Starke. Martyn's section appeared well-run and alert despite the storm; telling Starke their ensign was gaining more self-confidence and shedding some hesitancy to act. He suspected this was partly due to the watch when *Calypso* narrowly missed a derelict schooner that crippled *Gamma*.

Calypso's commander visited the pilothouse each watch. Moving cautiously to its forward windows, he intermittently lifted binoculars dangling from his neck to scan the darkness though rain-coated glass as *Calypso* crashed through thirty or forty-foot seas and spasmodic downpours. Sheets of seawater mixed with rain hit the panes hard; allowing brief snatches of visibility that revealed foremast, forecastle, and jibboom. Sometimes, areas of greater or lesser blackness further out marked the horizon. Convulsing waves, separated by deep troughs and crowned by spindrift, smashed against the port bow forcing a starboard roll as it lifted. White water exploded each time the bark's stem sliced down. Bowsprit and jibboom remained mostly above the confused surface but a few starboard heels partly flooded her forecastle; forcing seawater to escape through slotted openings above the sheer strake.

What wake there was remained visible only a few feet before the sea swept it away. Starke found the solitary existence at sea comforting but total isolation on such nights rattled the most stoic since more modern ships often vanished or reemerged as derelicts.

Starke endured half-sleep in his sea cabin when not in the pilothouse; adjusting to irregular motions and waking when an unusual wave struck, the engine spun freely too long, or abnormal hesitation came at the end of a roll. Dunbar called him back several times for permission to adjust speed, except for one occasion. Starke's eyes went first to the telltale compass over his bunk then a nearby wall clock when Martyn's messenger woke him to report Seaman Dorian Kearney had sighted lights off their starboard beam. The Irishman was perhaps their best sailor when sober, so Starke left immediately for the pilothouse. Using its door to deflect windblown spray, he spotted a large ship. Her lights were too distant to identify as they drifted aft then passed astern. Small rivulets of water penetrating his waterproof's collar competed for attention while ensuring the event was logged. Shipping routes intersected east of Norfolk but *Calypso*'s northeast track left the densest traffic south. Still, steamships from the Caribbean, especially Havana, and the States' southern coast, might transit the area then continue up the seaboard or swing northeast to Great Britain. Sailing ships turned northwest at lower latitudes so one of that variety was possible, but such violent weather would slow progress or force them to lie-to.

Calypso's rhythm grew gradually more regular once the storm passed astern late in the middle watch, and it seemed their morning watch would see fair weather. Starke was awake when the sections relieved, spoke with Martyn, scanned a horizon struggling to light, and left for his day cabin. Yamashita had a freshly laundered uniform laid out and his toilet took place with movable items showing less violence and motion. Starke opened the drop-front desk and restored order to its contents before rejoining Dunbar and Owen for morning twilight. The cabin steward laid on a breakfast of bacon, eggs, rice, toast, and black coffee. Rice instead of potatoes had long since become normal and Starke had come to agree with Yamashita it traveled better at sea; just as his steward now accepted sauerkraut's similar qualities; including sweetness when soaked long enough.

Calypso's navigator worried stars, planets, and horizon might not be visible for morning twilight but called observers together when clouds thinned. The navigator, quartermaster, and two sailors stood on the flying bridge waiting for sunrise; armed with sextants and a pocket chronometer. As Starke joined the party, he surveyed the area created from the pilothouse overhead with its compass binnacle, pelorus, and voice tube encircled by white canvas screens. One arm tightly held his father's Parkinson & Frodsham sextant, a reliable instrument meticulously maintained and readied for their morning shoot. As the moment neared, those holding sextants swung them back and forth while peering through eyepieces at the emerging horizon and fading celestial bodies. Yeoman Samuel Pond stood ready to pencil each reading on small sheets after Seaman Moreau called time from the pocket chronometer synchronized with the ship's instrument a half hour earlier. During the brief interval horizon and celestial targets were visible, each observer aimed at the one called out, moved his sextant, swinging its arm until horizon and body met in the split view, then gently twisted its tangent screw for accuracy. The shoot went well despite weather conditions and months without practice.

Running lights were doused minutes later, confirming a new day, as the first lookout climbed weather ratlines to the foretop above *Calypso's* flying bridge. It promised to be brisk but clear with moderating seas; and smelled of rain or snow. Agitated gray seas remained but subsided somewhat and lacked whitecaps, crests, or spindrift. The ship's wake lengthened and stack's translucent gray smoke trailing astern widened, became thinner, then settled on the dark sea; leaving an acrid tinge of burning coal and steam to flavor cool, crisp salt air. Dumping garbage might attract a shark or two but other sea life and birds were absent; a temporary state with floating refuse and easing weather.

Starke left for the day cabin to reduce observations while Dunbar and Owen calculated their fix. Through cracked windows Starke listened to *Calypso* come awake from rough handling. The early morning routine included sweepers, clothes washing, and stowing hammocks in the nettings, after passing each through a sizing ring. Once the main deck was swept, sailors scrubbed then hosed it with seawater to clean, preserve, and swell planking. Holystoning was no longer allowed since it wore away wood but daily saltwater brushing ensured decks stayed watertight and left them a nearly white tan. The crew then breakfasted at tables lowered from the overhead. Messes were assigned lockers for their supplies and utensils. Retrieving what was needed from them, berth-deck cooks prepared food to be taken to the galley for heating. It returned hot, along with boiling water to pour over ground coffee. Ship's routine normally resumed after breakfast, but not today with crew and shipyard trades emerging from a jarring night to repair damage, complete repairs, and conduct tests.

Starke consulted with Watson, Dunbar, Owen, O'Leary, and their INSURV lieutenant in his day cabin while smaller items were corrected, adjustments made, and deficiencies recorded. The storm disrupted their planned track so Chief Owen spread a marked-up chart over the table and placed weights on it as Dunbar spoke, "Captain. We steamed east for five hours at eight knots after leaving Chesapeake Bay then northwest into the sea during first watch. Around six knots were made good on that heading and this morning's fix puts us sixty-six miles due west of the coast and eighty-five miles east-northeast of Cape Henry; and since morning sights we've advanced roughly eighteen miles."

Starke selected a cinnamon brown meerschaum pipe from the rack, dredged it through his worn leather pouch, and then used his thumb to press the pleasantly moist tobacco, "Your recommendation, Mr. Dunbar?"

"Hold course until noon sights are complete then turn due south, Captain."

Watson considered this, "We can test equipment on the run south, conduct monthly muster, have church service, hold rope-yarn, and enter the bay after sunrise Monday."

O'Leary added, "We need six to twelve hours of calm seas for a full power run and I doubt we'll have it this afternoon, Captain."

The INSURV lieutenant agreed so Watson interjected, "With your permission, sir, we could test the main battery."

Starke released a small blueish cloud of smoke, "Very well, XO. Gentlemen, I believe that settles it. Mr. Dunbar, please lay out our new track before turning south."

Watson and Dunbar's proposed track formed a right triangle with the current course as hypotenuse. Once noon sights established *Calypso*'s position the ship would turn south for their next leg, conduct tests, muster, hold church service, and permit rope-yarn until, at Cape Henry's latitude, they would turn west, increase speed to 10 knots and raise the Chesapeake's entrance about five-thirty Monday morning.

The seas calmed enough by half-past one to test 4-inch mounts with service rounds so a skeletal general quarters was set that eliminated any billets unrelated to crewing the guns, fire, flooding, engineering, and navigation. Newport News riders found spots to observe with the least interference while a Government Department rider and INSURV officer climbed to the flying bridge, then stood near its aft lifelines. Today's firing was to confirm the guns worked so there was no target and they carried only six common rounds; four for the replacement mount forward and two aft. Starke hoped to retain their old gun captains, Grier and Kirby, but they transferred to a small cruiser after the collision. The receiving ship lent one that seemed capable but Chief Stefan Poniatowski still closely monitored gun crew practice sessions and their gunnery officer's attention appeared equally keen.

Martyn brought *Calypso* to a stable heading as the forward mount's barrel swung over the port side towards an empty Atlantic. Quartermasters raised the red burgee above pennant and flag to warn approaching ships downrange; although their thirty-three pound shells traveled five or six miles, well beyond effective flag signaling. Starke made a final horizon sweep with binoculars then gave permission to fire. Watson had emphasized safety over speed to Blair and his gun crew; which seemed to produce the desired effect. The first round lifted from its ready-use magazine was handled gingerly. Any one of several mistakes or malfunctions were possible whenever guns fired but initial testing always increased risk of a split shell case, hang or misfire, burst ear drums, or some other common casualty so Conrad prepared the wardroom for handling wounded.

Starke watched closely as three of the crew grouped around their forward black rifle with five others formed in a line behind; the mount's protecting tarp tightly bound and secured to cleats nearby with the muzzle bag used instead of tompion at sea. This gun crew was certainly more uniformly attired than its predecessors and lacked assigned boarders with sidearms. Blair stood aside, struggling to follow Watson's admonition to focus on safety and leave preparation and shooting to his gun crew.

The first 4-inch round, projectile and brass shell, went to the gun cradled in a loader's arms. A second man opened the breech to accept this offering then closed and locked it with a long lever. Two men beside the slide rotated bronze wheels that trained their mount side-to-side while the gun captain twisted a small elevating wheel beneath the breech to raise and lower its barrel. The ersatz gun captain waited until the ship began its up-roll, warned everyone to cover ears, and jerked the lanyard. The resultant click was inaudible beyond several feet but not the earsplitting flat crack accompanying a muzzle flash that pierced a gray-black mushroom cloud. The gunsmoke was soon shapeless, floating about its crew, settling on deck, or dispersing in the breeze. Despite recoil cylinders, the detonation shook *Calypso* and Starke felt muzzle blast pressure on the flying bridge. He blinked then saw a dark object arc from the ship, vanish, splash into the sea, and detonate with a white eruption that hung stationary several seconds before collapsing back into the water. The crew repeated this three times, went aft, and fired two rounds from there. General quarters ended and regular watches were set after inspecting both mounts. With that complete, the crew started operating, inspecting, and securing various systems from bilge pumps to the Ardois signaling system's four paired-lights hanging from the mainmast.

Captains usually left repair inspections to the officer Navy regulations designated but Starke observed these activities more than most so Watson anticipated company evaluating hull and compartment work for leakage. *Calypso*'s wood sheathing was not single planks but multiple layers beneath copper plating, which complicated efforts to locate leaks. The captain and executive officer's greater concern was that *Calypso*'s keel, hull shape, or both were deformed by *Doireann Bannan* since only fortune and nearby schooner's deck load of planks kept *Calypso* afloat with the V-shaped opening punched through forward. That mount was mangled, interior spaces wrecked, foremast backstays abused, and mainmast forestay stretched. The repairs appeared satisfactory but time and a full power run were needed to test hull alignment; and hopefully time under sail before the quarter's *Steaming & Sailing Qualities Report* was due.

Fire and flooding drills finished before eight o'clock reports then Starke signed the night order book and slept well in the at-sea cabin; wakened only once, just before midnight. A four-masted schooner ghosted down their starboard side a few miles off; little more than spectral shape with flickering green running light. Sunday morning was spent at his desk while *Calypso* thrashed through cold, gray unsettled seas under an ambivalent sky and O'Leary conducting the lesser version of a full power run; until a ship was sighted astern. She was rapidly overhauling them and would pass close aboard so he was summoned, set the conduct book recording sailor performance aside, and went to the pilothouse. The low, dark hull off their starboard quarter grew as he climbed. Martyn was waiting at the ladder's top. Starke returned a salute and reached for binoculars as the ensign began, "She's gaining steadily, Captain. Bearing drift is good but the speed and smoke mean that fellow's in a hurry."

Chapter Fifteen
Nemesis Passing

Starke retrieved binoculars from his shelf then walked to the starboard bridge wing and looked to the newcomer's port bow. Riding low and slicing through rolling seas like a shark, the lines and counter stern suggested warship or large yacht. Three masts would fit her superstructure but what remained was a vestigial bowsprit and topless main, just aft of a small pilothouse and flying bridge. Amidship forward of the mast was a much larger deckhouse, pierced liberally with large windows. There was also a short stack then four whaleboats in frames arching over the deck. She was clearly not designed for cargo and too small for passengers. Starke was suspicious but Junta filibuster expeditions preferred schooners, tugs, or small cargo ships. A press boat was more likely and odds favored her being on legitimate business. *Calypso* was also completing sea trials with tests ongoing, carried skeletal crew, and expended her ammunition. That meant a long stern chase if the other ship refused boarding but should she acquiesce, any possibility of finding something incriminating fell to zero. Starke could not justify acting but lingered in the pilothouse; suspicious, observant, and ready.

Carte Blanche's master studied *Calypso* from behind unscreened lifelines enclosing her small flying bridge. Fachtna Harler, better known as Captain Buff, felt his muscular neck compressing to fleshy rolls while throttling the Goerz binoculars bought in New York to replace his lost paired-telescopes. Beneath the heavy winter coat, sweat-stained white scarf, and dark visored-cap, his overnight exhilaration was turning to fury, despair, and determination. His long-used sobriquet was short for Captain Buffalo and solidified during his first voyage as master; before that he was just Buffalo. That was when his deeply tanned face had been framed by black, bushy hair and full beard. His manner included enough bison traits to encourage the comparison but, unlike that species, he was no herd animal. Older, balding, and clean-shaven, the veteran of unequal struggle during and after the war glared at a ship he thought never to see again, let the binoculars' neck strap take their weight, and remembered three previous expeditions that left *John Gwinn Williams*, *Rafael Riego*, and *Astraea* rotting on the seabed with friends, acquaintances, and sailors.

The Junta ostracized him after losing *Astraea* so he accepted the first mate berth on a small steamer carrying sponges and sundries between Florida and New York. While away from the trade, Pinkerton detectives ferreted out several small filibuster expeditions preparing to leave New York. Their ships were libeled, leaving cargoes concealed and stranded while Cuban events ground towards a climax. This forced Junta backers to buy *Carte Blanche* in an attempt to move the most needed supplies south. The bark-rigged steam yacht crossed the Atlantic for the 1896 America's Cup six years after commissioning then her owner went bankrupt. Scottish-built, well-found, with exceptionally fine lines, the 500-ton hull was 180 feet with a twenty-eight-foot beam and seventeen-foot draft. She once logged sixteen knots under sail and steamed at least that with masts and rigging removed.

Her filibuster conversion was quickly done under the guise of a press boat so she was soon fitted out and coaling. Explosives, rifles, pistols, machetes, ammunition, and medicine were loaded; a false manifest created; and then typhoid fever took her master. A desperate Junta approached Dynamite Johnny O'Brien's wife who suggested Captain Buff since her husband was away. They located Captain Buff in a waterfront bar and offered *Carte Blanche* less than a week before sighting *Calypso*. Although sympathetic towards Cuban independence due to his Confederate experience, he was not passionate about causes and resented past treatment. However, running contraband paid well, was a trade he knew, and meant a master's berth so he agreed to smuggle their delayed cargo to Major General Calixto García's insurrectos near Santiago de Cuba.

All satisfaction died when the black-hulled bark with straw-yellow masts ahead appeared to be *Calypso*; a ship supposedly run down off Norfolk. If her commander had not been relieved, he swore this expedition would not be taken by that bastard lieutenant with dour countenance and few words. A detonator in the forward hold was rigged to a five-pound nitro-gelatin charge for dynamite guns. The Junta planted it to ensure the Spanish would not obtain cargo or evidence. A score of those sailing with him died after first sighting *Calypso* off the Florida Keys and Captain Buff vowed *Carte Blanche* might end her days as a mobile torpedo but never be taken. Weathered muscular hands clinched, unclenched then raised binoculars. A British red ensign was hoisted once lettering across the transom confirmed it was *Calypso*. That flag matched his documents but not survive close legal scrutiny; and Starke would reject them anyway. It was possible the bastard was gone but he sensed the collision had not divorced him from *Calypso*. *Carte Blanche* was making nearly twelve knots with wind and seas astern and both boilers on line so he held course, detailed a man to dip the ensign, and prepared to trigger the charge.

Captain Buff felt the deck drop as *Carte Blanche* entered a trough then lift as she rose to punch through the next crest. Wiping condensation from binocular lenses, he sensed the gray surroundings with rain or snow in the offing fit his present mood. *Carte Blanche*'s bow drew even with *Calypso*'s stern; 500 to 1,000 yards off her starboard side. His man freed the halyard from its cleat and brought their ensign part way down. *Calypso* sailors under their steam pinnace waved, tarps covering 4-inch mounts shivered, wind blew translucent gray-black stack gas forward, and her ensign returned his salute. It seemed hours for *Carte Blanche* to crawl past, but Captain Buff added to the deception by a long wave that did not expose his face.

Starke studied the passing ship while *Calypso* acknowledged. He recalled hearing creditors libeled the large British yacht *Carte Blanche* during the America's Cup races two years before. Once she pulled ahead he made out that name in raised script on the stern and concluded she had most likely become a British press boat on her way to Cuba and a war that seemed weeks away. Once she was safely distant, the sighting was entered in their deck log and he left the pilothouse.

The brisk Sunday morning hurried work that began with sweepers, a saltwater wash-down, and hoisting ashes. While the rain held off, their navigator assumed the watch for a monthly ritual. The general muster in full dress uniform came first then a uniform, kit, and person inspection before Starke read from the *Articles of War*. Church service was then held. Regulations avoided religious endorsement and only boy apprentices were required to attend but, like most crews, everyone did because it varied ship routine. Their paymaster deacon's messages also fit his ad hoc flock's religions, shades of unbelievers, and agnostics since its words and message were universal and logical. Obligatory temperance polemics were expected and overlooked but most everything else was well-received. It was Exodus 22:16 today, no doubt prompted by returning to Norfolk, had Conrad's blessing, and encouraged Starke to consider writing Sir Curtis directly.

The afternoon rope-yarn group congregating aft for music found the lively deck and inclement weather too disrupting. Some sought favorite sheltered areas to talk or sleep while others, like Yeoman Third Class Matthias Eberhardt, turned to entrepreneurial pursuits. Their Hebrew paymaster clerk was saving for his own tailor shop and took over a supply space to work his hurdy gurdy sewing custom liberty uniforms. *Calypso*'s wardroom lost enough cadets and officers for the off-watch to prefer reading, writing, and working administrative tasks in their staterooms. Starke finished reviewing the conduct book and began writing to his aunt and uncle; partly to delay starting another to Katherine asking about their son and marriage. Yamashita served afternoon coffee with Thaddeus in tow scrounging scraps. Their tomcat leapt silently to the couch when the steward left for his pantry, then braced himself and curled into a languid, purring ball that moved with the ship except for intermittent jerks as if bitten or dreaming.

The last dog watch brought calls for sweepers then relief for night watches. Starke, Watson, Dunbar, and Owen compared calculations fixing their position and agreed from 1900 until sighting Cape Henry light they would steam west towards the shore at ten knots; cutting across coastal shipping routes. The Gulf Stream would set them north so their night order book stated that and the inherent danger of steaming towards a coast at night. Watson called officers to the pilothouse after eight o'clock reports to further emphasize this. Blair's starboard section relieved Martyn's port for the first watch;

which meant he would return for the midwatch and Martyn the morning watch when Cape Henry's light should be raised about an hour before sunrise. Starke reviewed deck and steam logs in his cabin, expecting sleep would come in one or two hour stretches.

After turning to latitude thirty-seven degrees north, Dunbar altered course slightly south of due west to offset the Gulf Stream. He anticipated raising Cape Henry and Charles lighthouses while dark and Chesapeake Bay's mouth during early morning. The northeast seas' twenty-five knot winds struck their starboard quarter. This tended to lift the hull and thrust it forward with rolling damped by jib and staysails set during the day by a grinning, vindicated Weaver. Even so, standing unsupported became difficult, undiscovered loose items appeared, and the stern subjected to an occasional slap or pooping. The brass helm spun constantly as each thrusting increased, steadied, and decreased rudder pressure while the main engine screamed madly whenever its screw lifted.

Dunbar had sailors in oilskins streaming the patent log each watch. These readings were compared with recorded shaft turns to dead reckon position. After evaluating results, *Calypso* slowed twenty-five miles from land with the morning watch straining to differentiate Cape Henry's steady white light from ships and shore. Dunbar and Blair calculated landfall might occur north of Chesapeake Bay's mouth, consulted the coast pilot, and set about spotting Cape Charles lighthouse's single flash or two fixed beams from its companion lightship. Light looms glowed on the horizon throughout the night, with occasional running lights from closer ships. Steam traffic was usually north or southbound and included coastal freighters, one passenger liner with a blazing light array, tug and tow that cycled the morning watch, and steadily increasing numbers of fishing boats. One large ship about to overhaul them during the midwatch slowed to take station astern as her master gambled their draft equaled or exceeded his own.

Turn-to, sweepers, and clothes washing were passed before Blair observed one light exceeded others in steady brightness, searched northwest for several minutes, found another flash of equal brightness, and then located a pair to seaward. He sent a man to Dunbar's stateroom, then captain's cabin where Starke breakfasted, before requesting Weaver to assemble sailors for heaving the lead. If night orders and coast pilot were correct, Blair anticipated they would soon enter thirty fathoms that would shoal to around twenty. There was safe water unless it fell below ten, but he began walking their speed down before Starke and Dunbar entered the pilothouse; then continued at a pace allowing the best ride possible with heavy seas working their starboard quarter. Dunbar soon verified Cape Henry lighthouse, Cape Charles lighthouse, and lightship. The compass and pelorus bearings held them slightly south of the entrance so their course was adjusted. The Cape Henry lighthouse was soon visible against the bald face of a wooded hill and a less easily seen Cape Charles lighthouse rose from the lowlands. The lightship moored southeast of Smith Island Shoal was confirmed last.

Starke pointed *Calypso* towards the lower bay without signaling for a pilot since he was familiar with the area. Even so, a schooner with block letters "NORFOLK" painted on her fore and main sails broke away from others loitering off the mouth in a smooth turn; then, heeling from the wind, gained speed through seas slapping her bow. A code pennant over two flags broke at her masthead. Chief Owen went to the bridge wing and raised his telescope, "The hoist is a code pennant over two flags; one yellow and the other vertically striped white and red. QH, Mr. Blair." Petty Officer Jason Smithers entered their *International Code of Signals* then called out, "Chief; it reads stop or heave to, I have something to communicate."

Starke lowered binoculars, "Slow and prepare to receive her alongside to starboard."

Watson was off to the bulwark's gangway where Weaver's line-handlers already put over woven rope fenders and hung a small pilot ladder. The schooner held off until fenders were in place and tickled by waves before her master came alongside, lightly crushing them and remaining just long enough for his passenger to get past the gangway with agility defying age and girth. The schooner fell off and away once he was safely aboard.

Starke watched the slickered figure cross from *Calypso's* starboard bridge wing and suspected they just acquired an unrequested pilot. Irritation vanished when he saw who it was. The man was often employed by his uncle's firm, clawed his way to a master's billet on bay freighters, and captained several boats during the oyster war between Maryland and Virginia. He was unusually amiable for a staunch temperance man and possessed detailed knowledge of the lower bay and Potomac River. Starke extended a hand, "Welcome aboard *Calypso*, Captain.

"And you to Norfolk, Captain. You didn't request a pilot but entered too far from the Cape Henry signal station so I asked to be put aboard. Seems your lord and master wants you anchored in Hampton Roads. No reason given, but here's a letter."

Starke considered the crumpled, but still sealed and waxed, packet; turning it over in his hands as the dripping figure continued, "Don't read other folks' mail but word's out *Montgomery's* taking relief supplies to Matanzas and *Nashville* to Sagua la Grande. Poor bastards are starving but the Dons don't relish our Navy delivering relief. Blood's up over *Maine,* especially in Norfolk so rumor has it their sensitivities have been ignored and you've been shanghaied."

Starke read the note while their guest glanced at a restless schooner standing off the starboard beam. Seeing this, he shoved the paper in his pocket then looked into the weathered face under an oilskin hat, "Captain, I take it the harbor master has an anchorage designated and would appreciate your getting us there."

The pilot grinned, waved off the schooner, and walked to the chart table where he took a pencil and lightly twisted its point on the chart. After a huddle with Watson, Blair, and Owen, the navigator made their recommendation and Starke agreed with some discomfort. They would not enter the Elizabeth River but anchor near where *Calypso* was rammed. Starke, Blair, and Watson shifted to the flying bridge as they passed into Chesapeake Bay between The Middle Ground and Lynnhaven Roads. *Calypso* turned docile as they lined up on Thimble Shoal lighthouse then held course until entering the passage between Thimble Shoal and Willoughby's Banks. Easing slowly southwest to pass between Old Point Comfort and heavily rip-rapped Fort Wool, *Calypso* entered Hampton Roads.

Their anchor party stood back as the leadsman reported depth and bottom. While the helmsman made minute corrections, quartermasters shot bearings using compass and pelorus. Dunbar adjusted for variation then marked the chart. Finally, with screw stopped, the ship bled off speed as she inexorably glided towards it. After Watson hailed the forecastle through his speaking trumpet the leadsman and lazy leadsman gathered their equipment while Weaver deployed his anchor party to release a blackened starboard anchor; swung out and suspended from its davit.

The anchor release was tripped over the mark, after easing past a four-masted schooner and cargo steamer. *Calypso's* massive iron hook pierced the surface then plummeted through opaque water to a mud bottom as its chain threw off clouds of red dust with deafening noise. The stocked anchor, trailing its small marker buoy, struck bottom, rolled, and buried one fluke. Weaver briefly snubbed then released the brake as *Calypso* backed then stopped her screw. Momentum carried them away from the anchor, laying chain along the bottom until the desired scope was out. Weaver set the brake and their anchor held; causing its chain to straighten, partly leap from the water, and then drop below the surface. *Calypso* had anchored in about four fathoms off Sewall's Point, slightly further west of Norfolk's channel than the collision site. *Calypso's* crew began cleaning once the accommodation ladder was rigged and gear stowed; except for a brief pause to swing out and lower steam pinnaces so fires could be lit in their diminutive boilers.

The pilot remarked *Winslow's* departure was storm-delayed but the torpedo boat left around noon the day before. The entire crew of the ship aground off Cape Henry was rescued after some anxiety while the Merritt Tug *Underwriter*, towing the derrick *Chief* to the *Maine* site, was thought lost until she entered Charleston with damaged tow, lost deck load of coal, and needing repair before continuing. The *Maine* inquiry remained in session and unanticipated Navy work was flowing into East Coast yards. Norfolk was already putting additional men on *Essex* and the monitor *Puritan*.

Calypso anchored north of Craney Island where she would swing little from tides or river current. The bark was encircled by sail and steam ships waiting to load, unload, be repaired, or go to sea. Several barges were on their way to attend deep-draft ships. The receiving ship *Franklin* was not visible but easily reached by steam pinnace. Once a small schooner retrieved the pilot and the Newport News Shipyard tug picked up their riders, Starke found Yamashita waiting with a warm meal. He ate then prepared to call on the naval district's commandant, Commodore Farquhar. Things could have changed while they were away on sea trials but *Calypso* still had a skeleton crew, lacked ammunition, and required a supply load out.

Chapter Sixteen
Unwelcome Cargo

Coxswain Melvin eased his pinnace slightly port towards *Calypso*. Hampton Roads seemed unpleasant and cold under gray skies with rain coming; matching his captain's mood since leaving *Franklin*. Starke never vented frustration or anger on the crew; but was demanding, aloof without arrogance, spoke sparingly, and appeared serious about all things. Smiles seldom altered his sparse, well-trimmed beard and few claimed seeing more than a chuckle. The captain was definitely taciturn, but what Starke said could be relied on.

The crew appreciated this predictability, consistency, and fairness but those near him learned to gauge any situation's severity by a tightening jaw and the abuse his pipe stem endured. He also was an officer who would stand and poor one to test. Their fight with the Spanish gunboat proved that; and validated Kearney's claim he displayed little emotion or compassion during such encounters. His typically discrete cabin steward, Yamashita, also let slip he overheard Starke brace the formidable Captain Buff in front of their executive officer, Mr. Watson. The captain's silent fury apparently encouraged Watson to consider finding cover; and he was cut from a similar bolt as Starke. Talbot Griffin, a seaman fond of drinking and fighting, was listening outside the cabin. He backed Yamashita, adding their captain was a right boyo;

something he had thought berth-deck rumor despite scarred hands not common with officers.

The coxswain suspected this mood confirmed rumors circulating on *Franklin*'s boat piers that *Calypso* would deliver relief supplies instead of cruising for filibusters. Their new mission would be strange to Melvin's way of thinking since war seemed inevitable, the *Maine* inquiry hung over everything, and newspapers trumpeted State's unvarnished refusal to recall the consul-general or confine relief supply shipments to merchant ships. It also seemed the navy yard was hiring to ready a large monitor, *Franklin*'s recruiting was brisk, and aftereffects of the States' own divisive war were noticeably fading.

That passenger studied his black-hulled bark with straw-yellow masts, and mahogany pilothouse. Starke knew he was fortunate to retain command after her collision but the one-sided exchange just finished left a bitter taste. Commodore Farquhar held to the party line but was obviously uncomfortable. State's position that warships were not warships if engaged in humanitarian tasks seemed a cockamamie response to the Spanish legation's threat to protest the Navy bringing relief supplies. In practice, however, *Montgomery* and *Nashville* were no longer delivering to Matanzas and Sagua la Grande. *Montgomery* would enter Havana; freeing the ex-lighthouse tender *Fern* to cover those ports while Ward Line ships served Cuba's south and west coasts.

Cienfuegos would be *Calypso*'s contribution since she was available, once a merchant ship, lacked her full complement, and in commission. This gave Spanish authorities less to complain about while allowing State to claim they were not bowing to pressure; and an opportunity for the Navy to scout a strategic port. *Calypso*'s complement was minimal before her collision and poached repeatedly afterwards. She counted sufficient engineers, seamen, and line officers to transport supplies but not fight since they lacked line officers, engineers, and seamen; both gun captains in particular. Sending a sparsely crewed warship into a potential adversary's territory made captain and commodore question the decision's soundness, but neither would voice it.

Starke believed commanders did not choose missions but were obligated to resign should the situation warrant. *Calypso* could complete this task in the existing environment even if he was uncomfortable and there was supporting logic; despite State Department silliness and naval history littered with dead bodies and trashed reputations of those sent with inadequate resources. There was another reason Starke preferred an anti-filibuster patrol. *Dauntless* might be under libel in Jacksonville but *Carte Blanche* was on an expedition. This was only rumor before Starke confirmed they sighted her but failed to board.

The next day brought fair, slightly warmer weather with light winds rippling the bay and a well-fendered barge laden with stores. Weaver rigged a gun tackle to the main yard before it eased alongside so once lines were secured they began hoisting single loads off the barge, swinging them inboard, and then lowering lifts into the cargo hatch or spotting them on the main deck for stowing. That barge left just before noon and was quickly replaced by the ammunition lighter. Red warning flags were hoisted, fire party stationed, hoses laid out, and uninvolved sent below. Watson, Blair, and Poniatowski scrutinized the marked wooden crates of 3-pounder, .45-70 and .38 calibers, and other munitions as they landed. Once these were stowed, the 4-inch ammunition came aboard, with each thirty-three-pound common and armor-piercing shell hand-carried to magazines.

Cienfuegos' relief supplies came early next morning. The manifest included clothing bales, bags of beans and potatoes, barreled codfish and cornmeal, bacon, lard, bagged salt, and condensed milk. Medicines taken aboard included carbolic, laudanum, quinine, and morphine. Everything was inventoried when landed then stored according to a plan Starke and Watson calculated to optimize weight distribution and security. Medical supplies were especially worrisome. Laudanum was a popular all-purpose remedy and morphine commonly added to alcohol for kick. Quinine was unlikely to be pilfered for pleasure, but malaria affected everyone in Cuba so it sold for a high price on the black market. For this trip, Starke would hold storeroom keys; like those for magazines.

Starke woke to an overcast day threatening rain, chilled by an east wind coming off the Atlantic, and expected to reach near sixty degrees. After washing, shaving, and tooth brushing; he went to his desk, set the calendar to "THU MAR 10 98" and reviewed correspondence going ashore. Everyone worked late preparing to depart Hampton Roads; and the black gang overnight. His mood improved considerably after a short but sound sleep then turned to relief knowing they would soon be underway. He took time to enjoy Yamashita's eggs, rice, and oatmeal then, after two cups of coffee, lifted the dark service overcoat and cap from wall pegs and climbed to the pilothouse. Watson already put sailors in rain gear to save sending them below later. Starke decided not to use a pilot after reviewing charts with Dunbar. He doubted Navy accountants would be upset at saving money.

Martyn and Weaver were stowing accommodation ladders and tightening boat gripes aft when the tug *Wahneta*, trailing gray-black smoke, cleared Elizabeth River off their port bow, heading for the anchored bark. The five-year-old workhorse could be identified by her tall stack, light superstructure and black hull just shy of 100 feet. *Wahneta* might achieve eleven knots at times but was designed to move ships, barges, and lighters. Starke watched her close then nudge alongside near *Calypso*'s starboard quarter. A sailor descended the ladder from her pilothouse to forecastle, received the brown leather satchel Yeoman Pound passed; then returned. With *Calypso*'s mail on board, she would stand by them to Old Point Comfort.

Boatswain pipes sounded quarters for getting underway once the tug backed clear and moved off a short distance. Watson took the deck, Blair the conn, and Martyn had main deck and forecastle. Once all stations reported, Watson tested engine and rudder then requested permission to get underway. The easterly wind and flood tide held *Calypso*'s bow just south of Fort Wool; more north than east. On Blair's command, Weaver began heaving round on the anchor while a fire hose scoured its muddy chain. Blair eased the ship forward then, just after the chain tended vertical, "anchor aweigh" came from the forecastle. Once clear of the water their stocked anchor was left hanging from its davit and ready for letting go. Starke wished stockless anchors had been included in the conversion but other work took priority and funding limited. The ensign broke at *Calypso*'s main mast truck and water frothed below her counter as the screw clawed steerageway. Her head came smoothly left towards the channel to Old Point Comfort. She continued to build speed, keeping the large fortress and hotels slightly off her bow. Wind crossing the deck began picking up accordingly and light mist gave bare skin a wet rasping.

Passing between buoys lining Hampton Roads' main channel, they steamed past Old Point Comfort Lighthouse, came slightly right for Thimble Shoal with its lighthouse, continued round to the southeast, and then set a course to clear Cape Henry well to starboard. Large liners were absent since they usually scheduled Wednesday or Friday departures but some schooners were under tow, a small steamer made its way north, and one tug towing a barge fell in astern. After passing through pilot boats schooling off the bay entrance and before staysails were set, an Atlantic roller lifted *Calypso*'s bow, momentarily held her, and then let the bark descend in a slow roll, first to port then starboard. Through binoculars, Starke picked out the lifesaving and signal stations south of Cape Henry's lighthouses and *Gleadowe* was swarmed by sightseers further down the coast. His attention turned to their Cienfuegos trip once both capes merged into the coastline.

Calypso's departure was good news during a black week that sapped Captain Albert's energy, enthusiasm, and spirit. Evenings at his red-brick row house in Washington's western section found him struggling to keep the Building at bay beyond its low concrete steps. Even the dismal weather seemed more so after sunset. The weekend forecast was for rain and mild temperatures but that might change over the coming days if the wind veered from south to east and brought cold Atlantic air. Tonight he relaxed in his comfortable stuffed chair, slowly twirling two amber shots about a squat crystal glass. His pipe rested on its side in an ashtray and through their bay window he studied young, spectral trees ready to leaf that cast flickering shadows over their asphalt street from haloed gaslights along it.

National insanity grew as the Havana inquiry dragged on. The press blamed Weyler, despite his removal, and Spain for *Maine*. Roosevelt was even more galling because he demanded judgement be reserved while insinuating those who suggested it was not a mine were colluding with Spain. Even Long was not immune and attacked by the press for suggesting it could be accidental; which hurt him with McKinley who was trying to avoid premature judgement. Speaker Reed was under constant pressure by jingoes who were shifting debate to reconcentrados; in case the *Maine* inquiry found her destruction accidental. To Albert, it echoed the 1860 assurances a short, glorious war would preserve the union but was instead long, bloody, and left a nation divided with one region dominant, another occupied, and thirty years of acrimony.

Albert knew those capable of seeing beyond slogans were hesitant to predict which course war with Spain would take. If Europe stayed neutral, it would be decided at sea. If not, general war across the globe was possible. His counsel during Building meetings, if limited to Spain, was to blockade the island, let insurrectos throw off Spanish rule, and then end the war. If other nations were drawn in everything changed. Falk believed European politics and alliances frustrated Spanish efforts to get support, despite general resentment of the United States' cavalier attitude about a continental war, growing industrial power, anti-colonial inclinations, and actions taken to enforce the Monroe Doctrine. Britain and Japan might support the States but France, Austria, and Italy sympathized with Spain. Germany saw opportunity but also risk to its immigrants and trade; while China and Korea were Russia's primary focus. Cuban independence, *Maine*, and reconcentrados carried little weight in a Europe where any change could threaten national interests, trigger powerful antagonists, and intensify instabilities. The Greco-Turkish War came within a hairsbreadth of this so every capital believed any Spanish alliance could trigger war with another power.

Impoverished Spain, struggling to hold Cuba and facing a renewed Philippine rebellion, possessed a press no less vocal than America's. That public watched blood and treasure lost stabilizing Cuba and resented the States' inability or unwillingness to end Junta filibustering and support. Their army in Cuba alone was many times that of the entire American military and the navy was seen as still transitioning to modern steel ships. American shipping was also tempting enough that calls for Spain to ignore an agreement to end privateering were gaining traction.

The American press was eroding administration efforts to avoid war since many papers influenced by jingoes were demanding it. Even Speaker Reed was circumvented to pass a House bill authorizing $50 million in war preparations that Tuesday. Falk was in the gallery and reported what passed as debate consisted primarily of legislators wanting their support on record. The Senate approved it one day later and he predicted passage would not only simultaneously inflame and demoralize Spain but ripple throughout Europe when they learned this came from a treasury surplus at the same moment Spain struggled to obtain $40 million from French Banks, British Banks, or the Rothschilds; depending on source.

Albert spent Tuesday morning with Long and his bureau chiefs developing a spend plan for their afternoon cabinet meeting since McKinley wanted detailed accounting. He then waited in his office across from the Executive Mansion while Long and Alger spoke with the president; which paused briefly for the Secretary of State to present Spain's arriving minister, Luis Polo de Bernabé Pilón, in the Blue Room.

Funding was assured by day's end with naval spending poised to exceed anything since the war. This included ships, tugs, and yachts; with foreign warship buys heading their list. The most significant were two Brazilian cruisers; causing Albert to ponder if Starke's father had a role. Enlistments were exploding with Navy and Marine Corps recruiters taking all physically qualified. Officers on leave in Europe had been ordered back to duty two weeks earlier and Lieutenant Gibbons was tapping some of the naval militias' 4,500 members. Rear Admiral Sicard's indifferent health meant the North Atlantic Squadron would likely return to Commodore Bunce or go to Commodore Schley.

Albert ended his contemplation, slowly twirled what whiskey remained, took a slow sip, lit his pipe, and scanned *The Evening Times* and *The Evening Star*. The second's front page carried the photographic reproduction of *Maine*'s current state; a new innovation that provided a facsimile of the ship Ramsay and Crowninshield promised him. Another article reported her executive officer's Washington home robbed. One of Starke's torpedo boat papers mentioned Holland's version; which just started submerged testing. Pennsylvania Avenue's electric street cars would hopefully return to service within a week then the Navy Yard line; ending temporary horse-drawn cars. He just noticed Sunday evening's *Maine* Memorial Fund Concert at the Grand Opera House as Abigail entered. The family was attending that event and probably National Theater's presentation of *The Ballet Girl* with its New York cast. Woodward and Lathrop's ostentatious pre-Easter advertisement meant sorties by Abigail, Olivia, and Isabella; and his wife would want to know next month's Columbia University lecture list was out. For now, he set the papers aside and listened to wedding preparations before climbing the steep stairs with Abigail to their bedroom.

The next week proved no better. Stewart Woodford, the American minister in Spain, reported six torpedo boats left for the Canary Islands en-route to Cuba. Roosevelt wanted to sink or capture any Caribbean-bound Spanish torpedo boats; then pressed harder when the naval attaché in Spain, Lieutenant George Dyer, reported their commander was Captain Fernando Villaamil, a respected officer known for his work with that type. Besides citing Starke's paper on the subject, Theodore emphasized, with his habitual gesturing, a Chinese battleship and *Maine*'s Brazilian equivalent were disabled by the same type so their arrival justified war no matter what conclusion the *Maine* inquiry reached. On Tuesday, Albert joined Falk, three bureau chiefs, the Navy surgeon general, and Department's paymaster to support Long's testimony before the House Committee on Naval Affairs. Wednesday found him in a study group the secretary established to recommend action. Roosevelt was chair and other members included Crowninshield, Sicard, Barker, and Mahan. Albert disliked the retired captain's involvement but he was too popular to ignore or exclude.

An unusually morose Falk visited after listening to Senator Proctor's report on his recent Cuba trip that began with a late February arrival in Havana on *Olivette*. While there, he went wherever possible to learn reconcentrados' true state. Proctor was a businessman who served as secretary of war and governor, was close to McKinley, and arguably viewed as uncommitted. Falk claimed he delivered the powerful speech like a dry, neutral report that transported the starving, diseased, and dying into the chamber. Havana, he claimed, was divorced from an island where Cuban insurrectos dominated two provinces, safe areas were limited to rifle range, all rail lines fortified, and rural areas denuded of homes, farms, and animals. He confirmed press stories of indescribable suffering with half of some areas' population lost to starvation or disease and another quarter to follow no matter what. After his estimate of 200,000 dead stunned the Senate he claimed Clara Barton's work and the American people's willingness to give constituted the only real hope for those remaining. Congress was left seething with sympathy and anger. Falk observed Proctor's speech aligned with

Starke's reporting to the Navy intelligence office except for conveniently excluding General Gomez's contribution to this disaster. In his opinion, it was a speech that would turn reconcentrados into a crusade and provide justification for war with or without *Maine*. Albert fingered his pipe as the younger man relaxed into the settee; thinking two years struggling to end filibustering and prevent war was in extremis, "You believe it's over then."

"Both governments are trying to avoid war but autonomy cannot work without insurrecto support and Spain cannot give up Cuba. Speaker Reed barely kept Cuban recognition off this week's funding bill and he's hemorrhaging leverage."

"Predictions?"

"Difficult, Captain. The Junta doesn't want us to replace Spain and its factions will fight each other after independence. Madrid is soliciting support in Europe but those governments fear a continental war unless all agree. Without an ally, neither Spain nor United States can invade the other. Their army in Cuba exceeds our entire military and is experienced fighting there but requires resupply. Ours must be built by assembling its scattered parts, expanded, transported, and supplied. Consequently, any war against Spain alone will be won or lost at sea. Even with insurrecto neutrality they could only prolong defeat, drive up costs, and attack our commerce."

"So everyone's standing into danger?"

"Absolutely."

Falk left when they finished reviewing filibuster prosecutions; leaving Albert pacing the office and desiring a ship. It was nonsensical but he felt the same siren that lured Starke. Roosevelt suddenly shattered this introspection. The younger man seemed constantly in motion and today was no exception, but he never came to Albert's office and neither man considered the other confidant or friend.

Albert swung his hand towards the settee, "A seat, sir?"

Roosevelt glanced at it then declined, "Captain, we're going to war with Spain."

Albert considered the man who worked tirelessly to bring it about and whose conduct bordered on disrespect, especially in one cabinet meeting where he demanded war, "Perhaps, but the president's working to avoid it."

"He'll not succeed after Proctor's speech. You know Edith and my son are unwell?"

"I was sorry to hear."

Roosevelt drove one fist into an open palm, "I'm determined to go."

"Despite your family?"

"My father hired a substitute."

Albert understood this was a sore point with Roosevelt despite being common practice in wealthy Northern families; whether they advocated war or, like Immanuel Starke, resisted it. This, with payments to avoid the draft that funded enlistment bounties in a bad economy, allowed Lincoln to expand his army. Roosevelt deplored a beloved father's choice.

Theodore continued without pause, "I've spoken with Black. He's not sure New York's militia will leave the state and a volunteer commission may not get me to the fight."

Albert contemplated his pacing visitor, thinking it might if jingoes brought about a broader war.

"My friends want to go as well."

Albert thought this unlikely to include those living across Lafayette Square.

"What are your thoughts?"

"Why ask me, Mr. Roosevelt?"

"You speak your mind."

It was strange timing with Albert wrestling a similar dilemma. The captain pulled a pipe from the rack, looked through the window, and turned back to his visitor, "We all must live with our decisions. You've no real sea experience and military operations are no frontier posse. A battle or campaign requires complex orchestration."

Roosevelt considered this then his eyes lit, "There may be a way. I'll take it up with Alger."

The assistant secretary left as he entered; leaving Albert to sit, roll his chair forward, gingerly tamp the pipe bowl, and light its center. Roosevelt obviously devised some sort of plan. Looking over the desk through his window, Albert thought *Calypso* must be entering Cienfuegos and a cablegram should arrive shortly. He leaned back and slowly released blue smoke. The folded newspaper leaning against his wood letter box brought thoughts of Starke's correspondent friend in Havana and the young female reporter who looked after his daughters at the inauguration ball.

Chapter Seventeen
Storm Warnings

Darwin Tyson left his Inglaterra room, passed below the lobby's carved ceilings and high arches, crossed tiled floors, and took an evening table on the patio. The small, cast iron affair encircled by four wire chairs offered a clear view of Parque Central across Paseo del Prado. Less visible was Teatro Tacón, where a concert to raise funds for a new Spanish cruiser was attracting crowds. Americans, even reporters, avoided these affairs since passions and tensions often overflowed around them; even a Spanish gunboat commander was stabbed at one concert. The Havana papers' rhetoric was intensifying and no tolerance remained for the States generally and its correspondents in particular. Rumors were circulating that reporters would soon be arrested as spies and Consul-General Lee had suggested they consider leaving in February, the month before.

He leaned back in his chair, absorbing one of the perfect Havana evenings that would soon end with the rainy season. Today was noticeably warmer than the previous week with midsummer humidity coming but not yet oppressive. He pulled the light cotton suit off skin that darkened only slightly since taking over the Laffin News Bureau office. His broad-brimmed, white sennit boater took its share of the tabletop but allowed room for the waiter to land a whiskey. The silver hip flask was back at the room and no longer his constant companion since Cassandra Evans began working with him.

This restraint did not extend to tobacco, with its widely acknowledged health benefits, so the result was a diminishing store of Turkish cigarettes. He extracted one from his gold-trimmed jade case, tapped it against the rim, and lit up. They were more popular with women but packed easier on trips like his latest circumventing the island; one he was fortunate to complete before all coastal ships connecting Cuban ports were requisitioned for transporting troops and supplies. This would further hurt island economy because main roads were lamentable across the island; with rail transport limited in the west and worse in the east.

His small coastal steamer left Havana then steamed west along Pinar del Río's low coastal plains. They put in at Puerto de Mariel then Bahia Honda as distant, indistinct, blue-gray mountains began appearing to port and the deep blue gulf to starboard before entering a navigable channel shielded by black coral reefs and small, mangrove-covered islands. Inshore of the blue and sometimes black gulf; water changed color with depth. Where less than three feet it looked brown or appeared as dark patches. Deeper areas were light green. Blue water meant fathoms, not feet, below the surface; and deep blue water, mostly beyond the reefs, assured safe passage for deep draft ships. A short distance shoreward was the coastal frontier; gentle surf, whitish sand, and green blend of brush and tall palms. Gray limestone lumps loomed further inland then the province's mountain backbone miles beyond. Between coast and mountains lay tobacco and sugar plantations; most deserted or destroyed and some still burning.

They turned south after Cabo de San Antonio lighthouse and passing Cuba's western tip, steamed through the Yucatán Channel, east to the Isla de Pinos, and then along a string of small islands before heading northeast for Cienfuegos and its huge sheltered bay. They left there for Manzanillo, one of few southern ports not entered through a break in the coast. His small liner resumed its journey east after clearing local shallows to slide past tall red, brown, and blue Sierra Maestra mountain range; just beyond the breakers along narrow, rocky beaches. Easing to port, they entered a narrow cut in the high coast; guarded by the light-gray Castillo de San Pedro de la Roca that appeared close enough to throw rocks from its ramparts to their deck. Once through, the steamer eased up a broad bay encircled by green hills to the island's second city, Santiago de Cuba. Tyson lost his British mining engineer traveling companion there; who explained local pilots were essential to cross a bar at the bay's mouth but the sea just outside was too deep to anchor. Most inland traffic, according to this informant, used rivers emptying into the bay since the solitary railroad was hardly worth mention and roads maintained poorly before the conflict were now completely neglected. An undersea cable to Jamaica and Haiti, well-known due to the *Virginius* affair two decades earlier, ensured the city was not isolated. When Tyson's steamer departed, it continued east along a high coast that rose from the sea, except for a few indentations. Guantanamo Bay offered a broader mouth. They passed through its large lower section to enter the small port of Caimanera just beyond a channel to the upper bay. Unlike the Cuba he knew, this region enjoyed unvarying weather, arid landscape, multicolored land crabs, and leather-skinned iguanas. The next leg took him around the eastern tip to Baracoa then up a coast that grew less rugged then flattened and added numerous bays. After Nipe Bay, they stopped at Puerto de Gibara, with a rail line to Holguín, then Nuevitas, with tracks to Puerto Principe, before standing further out to clear a thousand islands, reefs, and shallows before Cardenas. The final port call before passing under the Morro and into Havana was Matanzas.

Tyson spoke with authorities and people at every stop, explored what he could, and filled several black notebooks that grew stained and flaccid from humid heat. *Alfonso XII's* sister ship *Reina Mercedes* in Santiago had equally unserviceable boilers, and small coastal or river gunboats were present in larger ports. Autonomy was stillborn beyond Havana, since those discussing it risked insurrectos' machetes. The cities were fortified and their environs usually included at least one pathetic reconcentrado compound. Only three of six provinces claimed anything like a rail network and what trains still ran were heavily guarded. Main roads were often little more than paths and nature was reclaiming the rest. Insurrectos effectively dominated Puerto Príncipe and Santiago de Cuba provinces south of Trocha de Júcaro a Morón so travel required a large military escort. The four remaining provinces were nominally government-held, but survival decreased rapidly beyond fortified villages, cities, or plantations. Western provinces appeared hardest hit by reconcentration with their safe areas overflowing in sick, starving, and dying; while many once-prosperous residents unwilling to beg were quietly expiring at home. City councils were supposed to distribute food through cocinas económicas but supplies were scarce, organization poor, corruption rampant, and stocks guarded by unpaid, poorly fed soldiers. This excursion convinced Tyson that recovery, even if fighting stopped immediately, would be slow with thousands dead along the way.

Havana's defenses isolated it somewhat from the full effect and this sense of security bolstered in early March when the *Infanta María Teresa* class armored cruiser *Vizcaya* arrived from New York to bands, fireworks, and cheering crowds.

Almirante Oquendo followed four days later. These two ships possessed impressive range, armor, speed, and carried two 11-inch and ten 6-inch rifles. Their high freeboard, twin stacks, black hulls, and fine lines renewed Havana's pride and confidence; especially while anchored in sight of the Austrian steam corvette *Donau*, American lighthouse tender *Mangrove*, and small gunboat *Fern* beside *Maine*'s blackened wreckage. *Cristóbal Colón*, a newer armored cruiser was also rumored to be coming.

The American cruiser *Montgomery* arrived just before mid-month and *Fern* was briefly away delivering relief supplies to Matanzas. Animosity towards Americans escalated after the States refused to conduct a joint *Maine* inquiry but worsened when *Montgomery* was not represented at Colonel Ruiz's funeral and declined invitations to a naval ball held for *Vizcaya* and *Almirante Oquendo*. Some reporters were arrested, including Honoré Lainé who was taken from the Inglaterra, confined, and expelled after claiming he knew of a Weyler letter stating the harbor was mined. Tyson suspected this was a convenient excuse and Lainé let off lightly since his insurrecto sympathies and activities probably exceeded mere words. George Musgrave came next after his newspaper published stories written while he traveled with insurgents. The *New York Journal* press boat *Anita* brought a congressional party to examine the reconcentrado situation; which added more fuel. Americans, and foreigners thought to be, often received hisses, insults, and small rocks. The local press fanned resentment, war braggadocio grew, and rumors of dynamiting the Inglaterra and assassinating Lee became common. Foreign nationals and Spaniards begin taking any available ship out. The Spanish liner *Alfonso XIII* left with 1,000 passengers joining her sick and wounded soldiers. Those Americans choosing to remain were warned to avoid situations where they might have to defend themselves and to accept abuse.

Tyson crushed a cigarette against his heel then looked for Evans. After she updated him on what occurred while he traveled, they planned to dine at El Palacio de Cristal restaurant behind Teatro Tacón; but the theater's aggressive crowd argued for going elsewhere. She pursued several reconcentrado stories, covered Clara Barton's arrival, and was the solitary female correspondent remaining in Cuba for any time. Although she continued resisting entreaties to relocate to Key West, her departure could not be put off much longer since the Laffin News Bureau would soon leave Havana, expand the staff, and charter the steam yacht *Kanapaha*.

Francisco Hilgert waved as he left the Inglaterra. Associated Press' solitary reporter was odds-on candidate to follow Lainé and Musgrave, or worse, but remained as the foreign population dwindled. Curtis left mid-month on Ward Line's *Seneca* for New York then home on the White Star liner *Britannic*. This was the Englishman's second Havana visit representing British investors who bought the vacant Starke properties near Artemisa. Tyson visited that city twice, mill and plantation once; both times with Starke and Curtis. He found the younger man intelligent and articulate; like Starke but less enigmatic and lacking a dark nature. Curtis' sister, Katherine Ledford, appeared to more closely resemble his friend. She also seemed endowed with a suppressed ardent sensuality he suspected explained Starke's obvious attraction. Something transpired between them when she visited Havana with her brother but Starke never mentioned it.

A curious relationship also involved Starke and Evans. She made subtle inquiries about the bachelor naval officer and, despite her professional dedication, Tyson expected this would change after marriage, like Nellie Bly and Elizabeth

Bisland. His friend was an obvious candidate since he would become wealthy and seemed to possess a forbidden fruit quality attractive to some women. She also spent a New York City evening with him while *Calypso* was at the navy yard and her visits to the Starke mansion were no secret. Tyson lacked any overwhelming urge to seriously pursue women and those overtly displaying interest or matrimonial intent made him uneasy, despite it being natural and proper. He found this colleague more attractive than most of her sex but his financial expectations were less, he lacked Starke's rough allure or Curtis' culture, and his past involvements seldom lasted.

Evans appeared as if summoned, leaving Parque Central to cross Paseo del Prado for the Inglaterra. She altered course after spotting Tyson and he studied her during the approach. The unfashionable tan was limited to face, hands, and wrists but fit her half-dozen ensembles from Obispo Street stores appropriate for climate and fashion. Today it was a faded blue cotton skirt, long-sleeved white blouse with high collar, and gold-buckled black waist belt. A light corset accentuated her breasts to create an appealing profile topped by the broad-brimmed, straw hat pinned to a pompadour twisted from long sun-lightened auburn hair. Held close under one arm and adding a professional air was the trademark brown Brussels carpet bag displaying its hard use.

He rose, extracted a chair from under the table, and slid it beneath her as she settled; then returned to his seat. Her father published a small newspaper so she grew up with the profession, knew how to observe, and demonstrated exceptional interview skills. Evans was neither shy nor overbearing, posed solid questions, and easily spotted chaff; but could also sit, say nothing, and rake in what filled the void.

Evans closely followed Red Cross operations after Clara Barton arrived in Havana and fell under its seventy-seven-year-old matriarch's spell. She even went with her to the San Ambrosio Military Hospital where Barton's presence seemed a salvation to *Maine*'s wounded as she started a list to inform their families; as during the last war and after. The experience affected Evans more than she let on but Tyson learned later the wounds were so hideous even Clara Barton required temporary respite.

Evans also stayed near Barton during her short stay at the Inglaterra before transferring headquarters to a large house overlooking the bay that was lent to the Red Cross. She trailed the Red Cross founder around Havana and throughout an assessment tour visiting five cities in a week and found the older woman indefatigable, in constant motion, and injecting energy everywhere; whether cleaning hospitals, supplying doctors, or starting orphanages. Governor-general Blanco's favorable opinion of Barton brushed off on Evans so she enjoyed greater access to Spanish officers and autonomist officials than most reporters. This did not come without cost. Tyson watched pace and climate wear on her, knew fever season was approaching, and expected every correspondent's personal risk to increase. She was ill once in Havana and nearly perished so he hoped to coax and cajole her into leaving for Key West over dinner.

The opportunity came immediately. She looked across the table, summoned a weary smile, then slumped back against the chair; something she seldom did, "Barton's leaving in two days."

"Klopsch?"

"Yes. She feels he's undermining her and must return to deal with the politics. I'll have copy by morning."

"Why not travel with her to Washington?"

The smile returned, "Still want me out of Havana, Darwin?"

"Yes. War's certain and you'll be needed in Key West."

"Let's put off that discussion this evening. Anything new on *Maine*?"

The wreck continued settling in putrid harbor mud and now fully submerged except her main deck section twisted into the air and one mast that remained upright, with a half-staffed ensign. Expectant buzzards circled overhead or perched on twisted steel while American divers probed her interior and their Spanish counterparts the harbor bottom. What lay beneath was obscured by *Mangrove*, tugs, workboats, and the curious. Among them were small boats hired by reporters who roasted and scribbled in the sun as they loitered and watched for anything emerging from the wreck; or *Mangrove* where the secretive Navy inquiry held all sessions except a brief trip to Key West's Fort Taylor. That would change when its report left for Key West and Admiral Sicard's endorsement before continuing to the Navy Department.

Tyson lit a cigarette, "We've a Key West man on lookout. Sigsbee and Lee believe our investigation will say a magazine was set off by some sort of mine while Spain's report will conclude an internal cause."

"What do you think?"

"I've no idea. Lainé claims Weyler mined the harbor. If so, it's possible some faction wanted her to limp home; and rumors exist that people testified to having knowledge of a plot, then disappeared or died. Spontaneous coal combustion, design, and accident are strong possibilities but it makes little difference after Proctor's speech. Public temper's similar to what I witnessed in Greece last year."

Evans began to rise as she reached for the carpet bag, "A half hour to change then El Palacio de Cristal?"

"No. El Louvre. Best avoid Teatro Tacón this evening."

"If you insist, but that means an hour and you'll want to change, too."

He forgot El Louvre was upscale, or thought it absurd to dress for a restaurant equaling those in Paris then drive past houses and sidewalks littered with the starving. She was correct, so another cigarette was snuffed out in the ashtray, "You're right. Say an hour then? I'll arrange a carriage."

Tyson was on Havana's waterfront the next morning. After confirming the *Maine* report was leaving for Key West, he walked past Alameda de Paula's stalls and piers to the Women's Hospital of Saint Francis of Paula where Evans was nursed during her first Havana visit. His attention settled on the large, black-hulled cruiser *Alfonso XII* being taken from her moorings by tugs. She was worked through harbor traffic, with *Vizcaya, Almirante Oquendo, Donau,* and *Maine*'s wreckage as backdrop, to the arsenal's floating dry-dock built in Great Britain. *Alfonso XII* would serve for its operational test before the navy risked any more valuable ship. He returned to Machina Wharf the next day with Evans when Clara Barton boarded the Plant steamer for Key West.

Havana would become untenable once Marix delivered the report, if sources were accurate, and remaining Americans must expect the worst. Even Britons risked being mistaken for one or subjected to retribution for their government's alleged neutrality. Curtis had seen this coming, postponed rebuilding, and went home. Tyson calculated he should reach Liverpool within days, spend one on the London train, overnight at the family's town house, and finish with a short rail trip to Brydian Grange, his family's Dorset estate near Bridport.

Chapter Eighteen
Brydian Grange

Brydian Grange was a monastery's outlier confiscated during the dissolution, sacked by Royalists during the English Civil Wars, then rebuilt and expanded through buying land and obtaining enclosures. Unlike many, it then grew smaller as the family sold parts to finance investment; leaving roughly 1,000 acres and West Dorset village at the estate's western boundary. Rents and investments allowed Brydian Grange to pass through the 1870s agriculture disruptions intact and preserve their family fortune.

The holding's square arrangement was unique. Fields, grounds, and groves within its perimeter were sectioned using fences or hedgerows with a creek cutting diagonally through to the southwest. The northern half consisted of sloping ground. Three farms made up the western third. Its eastern side was mostly fields and woods with a pond in the southeast corner. Brydian Grange House was not quite center and its two stories rose over the servants' quarters with a rear formal garden then woodland to the northern property line. The estate entrance and gatehouse were at the south boundary midpoint on the road from a highway fork that sent travelers to the estate or West Dorset. A hard-packed dirt lane after the gatehouse led past farm buildings, crossed the creek on a stone bridge, and ended in broad pea-gravel turnaround fronting the house.

Edward Curtis was traveling that lane by carriage. The son destined to inherit estate, family fortune, and baronetcy gazed at early spring scenery and shivered from the cool weather. Landscape and sky lacked the Caribbean's vibrancy and color but it was home and welcome after the gale *Britannic* crashed through from Fastnet Rock to Liverpool. This would be a short respite before London and reporting mixed results to syndicate investors. Mill and plantation titles were secure, initial planning was complete, and preliminary business arrangements established but reconstruction must wait for the rainy season to pass and fighting cease since autonomy was dead for any foreseeable future and American actions might reshuffle the deck.

Returning home also meant facing Katherine after four months. His illegitimate nephew's birth strengthened their already close relationship before leaving but he revealed the birth against her wishes. Starke had been in Washington and not the Caribbean with *Calypso* so keeping his promise to her required deceiving a man he liked, respected, and was the father. He doubted Starke would take the child from his sister but how she would view this betrayal was unpredictable. Becoming a mother altered Katherine and her correspondence to Starke never revealed the pregnancy.

Noise from horse hooves and carriage wheels changed with the transfer from dirt to pea-gravel just before his right-side windows revealed the greeting party. Katherine stood clutching his six-month-old, well-bundled nephew. Behind her stood their butler, housekeeper, three maids, and two footmen; one of whom would serve as valet. His father stepped forward and Curtis climbed down to grip the extended hand, "Father."

Sir Miles Oliver Curtis would have been just another limb on the family tree except an heir, Oliver Barrington Curtis, went to Cuba 130 years earlier with the 34th Regiment of Foot under Pocock and Keppel. Yellow fever carried off the young, unmarried officer after Havana fell and he was buried near that city; leaving a sword, plaque on the church wall, and portrait overlooking their main staircase. The next legitimate heir was an uncle so baronetcy and fortune went to him despite several local families' claims that never escaped the pub. Lady Christiana Mari Curtis was at his side. Formidable, kind, and less passionate than Sir Curtis, she oversaw house and estate. Lady Curtis came from two industrial families, one Welsh, the other English. Her marriage added to the Curtis family fortune and produced the required heir and a daughter but no other sons.

Curtis acknowledged his mother before turning to the widowed Katherine. Smiling, she gently pulled back the light blue blanket; allowing Edward to touch Oliver just below the chin. There was a gurgling response as miniature hands grasped one finger and squeezed. Katherine moved back to the main house just before the birth and appeared satisfied with motherhood but amazed she survived.

Edward was resigned to the coming days' regimentation; unless in London on business or visiting a sporting establishment where his favorite was Katherine's onetime girlfriend and classmate. This routine began that evening by dressing for supper then discussion with Sir Curtis; which hovered around the United States risking a European war and the colonial system. Mornings meant time with Lady Curtis and afternoons riding with Katherine.

He soon felt soft ground sponge under his tall boots while a groom brought brother and sister two bay mounts. Recent rains erased all traces of snow but left the ground saturated. This would not change soon since the day's scent and chill supported gale forecasts for March, despite temperatures reaching mid-forties. He took his gelding's reins, felt a tug as the bay sidestepped, then turned when Katherine's hunter whinnied its greeting as she walked onto pea-gravel.

Curtis' costume was traditional but his sister wore her winter favorite; trousers and boots under full-length skirt, below a loose, long-sleeved jacket over white blouse and riding corset. Her light brown hair was center-parted and rolled in a tight bun beneath the solid bowler hat. The riding crop carried to open gates without dismounting was in one of her thick gauntlets. During warmer months, she wore the blue-black riding habit from Washington. Its straight-legged, trouser-concealing skirt, and mandarin collared-tunic with buttons running diagonally from right shoulder to left waist, set her apart from locals and added a hint of defiance. Curtis mounted while a groom assisted Katherine. He looked away to conceal a grin while she adjusted her flowing skirt to drape over the sidesaddle and some of her mount. His sister disliked help mounting and preferred riding astride. She and Starke were well-suited in that since he would care little how his wife sat a horse.

Katherine was obviously pondering something so they left at a walk without speaking. She was never considered stunning, but attractive and growing more so. Her oval head was split by a longish nose between large, faded-blue eyes below curved eyebrows. While concentrating, like now, the forehead acquired slight horizontal furrows. Just below her nose was a slight, permanent depression to the thin upper lip that pressed against a fuller version below. Well-formed facial muscles emphasized her cheekbones and the strong jawline curved up from a slight chin dimple. Katherine's mouth seldom moved more than required to speak or form a slight smile but he recalled the bubbling laugh before she began filling out and stopped swimming with his friends. That was just as well since he also noticed how they started viewing his little sister and he theirs.

He willingly served as protector until her marriage then reprised the role once she widowed. After a friend observed she exuded sensuality that overpowered all efforts to disguise it, and thinking change might shake her despondency, he invited Katherine on the extended business trip to America; never thinking she would return pregnant. He liked and respected Starke, and would welcome him to the family, but never suspected a relationship. Neither showed any interest when in company and Starke had little in common with her husband, Philip Ledford. They were both naval officers but she was never especially attracted to that society over any other despite excelling at its social obligations. The Starkes, like his own family, wanted their eldest son married and apparently viewed his sister as a desirable candidate; which her upbringing and other qualities supported. Starke seemed less enthusiastic and overly proper to his sister so Curtis was surprised to discover a strong attachment when Katherine's secret was revealed. He also appeared less willing than most to engage in amorous or sporting pursuits so Curtis believed Katherine when she claimed he did not initiate their night together.

Strangely, he only recently began to see his younger sister as a woman; mostly due to the birth and intimate discussion between sessions with her old school friend. Leonora Rhodes Triggs came from a titled family impoverished by the agriculture depression. She was as accomplished as Katherine, well-versed in necessary social graces, and fluent in several languages; but discovered a fortune was needed to entice young men of their class since many were in similar straits. Most in this state remained within the family or visited a series of relatives. Some persisted in their quest for wealthy sons and eventually succeeded but most did not; and even less discovered a welcoming profession. Leonora once observed she never suspected how quickly her window closed with younger girls constantly entering the competition. She refused to accept ancillary family status or impose on friends but substantial opportunities for unmarried women of their class seemed nonexistent. This desperation continued until friends in similar straits pointed out their skills were highly sought in certain sporting houses. Leonora also observed she would not hesitate if ever in Katherine's position; but Curtis sensed, like his sister, she was not yet willing to marry for status and security only; despite the risk.

Edward and Katherine's shod mounts took the muddy entrance road to the gatehouse at a steady walk with the occasional brief canter. Conversation was challenging except when their bays edged closer together. They passed Katherine's remodeled cottage, turned east beyond a stable and outbuildings, and crossed fallow fields to woodlands surrounding a pond. The spring landscape seemed barren at first but a closer look revealed tree limbs' hesitant buds, short shoots of grain that gave planted fields a bright green tinge, and the creek had recently overflowed then retreated to deposit topsoil and dead fish. Ground near the pond was too soft for horses so they halted by a leafless tree arcing out over flat water with their old rope swing's remnants. A red-orange flash gave one hunting fox away and disturbed surface along the creek meant otter. To this was added the throaty screech of a concealed water rail, while blackbirds, sparrows, and warblers fluttered between trees and bushes. The gentle harbingers of a Dorset summer helped Curtis understand his sister's attachment to Brydian Grange's pastures, woodlands, birds, animals, trees, and plants. He hoped to return often from London.

A stableman spotted their return from the east and was waiting in front of the manor house. His sister dismounted easily and the boy was soon leading their bays to cool down and receive a small handful of grain. As the riders turned towards the house, legs adjusting to a leather saddle's absence, Katherine paused, "Walk with me, Edward."

"Of course."

Riding boots crunched from pea gravel shifting beneath leather soles then grew silent as they entered the formal garden with forested, chalk hills to the north. Sliding her arm through his, she looked up, "Did you miss your nephew?" She quickly paused in mild disbelief, "I never thought I'd say that."

"Yes, both of you."

"We were concerned after reading about rioting near the Inglaterra."

"Jacob, too?"

Her eyes looked down and away, "Edward, it was like Philip and *Victoria* when *Maine* exploded; I just knew he was on board."

Curtis was now convinced his sister also possessed a strong attachment, "He's written?"

"And cabled."

"Have you replied?"

"Not since you told him of Oliver."

"For heaven's sake why not?"

"He wants to marry; as you well know."

"Yes, and you mentioned this to father."

"Not yet. You know his views on Americans and recent events have not improved them. Perhaps mother has. She sees all men pretty much the same."

"She's never met Jacob."

"Her circle measures them by potential contribution and view relations as means to an end. I suspect mother thinks Oliver resulted from some ploy to orchestrate a union so she does not condemn me for Havana but cannot understand the delay."

Curtis gently squeezed her arm. Lady Curtis found virtue more easily maintained than husband, son, and, apparently, daughter; but willingly overlooked these shortcomings in others. Until his sister was with child, he thought Katherine much like her; and Philip too much the gentleman to raise such issues with a brother. That she was not proved unsettling until confiding in Leonora, whose acquaintance he was considering renewing when Katherine sighed, "Mother says Jacob is Oliver's father, will inherit an income, and proposed; while I risk being seen as a widow whose exposed proclivities will attract men more interested in sport than marriage."

"What about you?"

"Philip was the best of men and deserved more than I offered. I sometimes sense he's still near but know that's impossible. Jacob gave me a baby and there will be more if we're together. I often ache to be with him but sometimes wish we never met; except for Oliver."

"Oliver will have questions about his father sooner than you expect."

"Philip was kind and I fear Jacob's not. It's difficult to imagine living with him far from here. Besides, you let me to control my fortune and that changes if I marry."

They rounded the brick house, his sister's arm still in his; then entered the main path between shaped boxwood hedges extending from its rear patio. Katherine appeared more receptive than usual so he pressed, "Jacob didn't hesitate. He wants to marry and neither of you appear indifferent."

His arm felt a playful or involuntary tug, "Edward; how many times do you want to be an uncle; besides you're due."

He grinned, "Perhaps neither of us will have who we want?"

"Leonora?"

"I cannot say."

"She's not American, so father would approve of that quality anyway; and I suspect you know her well enough."

Curtis looked at his sister; trying to decipher her meaning, "I suppose so."

He thought Jacob a good match, even if Sir Curtis disliked colonists. Since the birth his sister seemed earthier but also partially regained the old confidence and spirit that vanished with her coming out. It also appeared her ability to attract men's interest strengthened rather than diminished. Lady Curtis observed her figure recovered unusually soon after the birth but Curtis thought her breasts slightly more pendulous and after remarking on a spotted blouse was told their mother objected to a wet nurse. Katherine's movements also seemed more natural although they still retained the poise instilled in ladies of her class before their hair was worn up.

Katherine noticed him looking, half-smiled, and then blushed. She acquired a past from one Havana night, but not one sufficiently notorious to be socially irredeemable. On that solitary occasion, thinking herself barren, she gave way to passion and nature's base aspects; or was that all? She understood more after reading *The Science of a New Life* by Cowan while in the States and Constance Starke's views were nothing like Lady Curtis; who believed intimate relations a disagreeable necessity to provide issue and best completed quickly when required. Constance was more candid, seemed to take some pleasure in such activity, clearly welcomed an understanding with her nephew, and desired a Starke heir.

She was also devout with a strong sense of morality so Katherine expected an illegitimate son would end her good opinion, and let their correspondence tail off. Seeing Edward was studying her, she looked down, "Do I embarrass you, brother?"

He was startled but recovered, squeezed the right arm to his side, trapping her much smaller one, "Quite the opposite, Katherine. I see why Jacob loves you and thinking he deserves a reply. If nothing else, you must give Oliver his father's name and birthright; but don't delay because others will be less hesitant."

That struck home. Jacob whispered he loved her in the Inglaterra lobby that morning but she wavered and their moment passed. One letter also mentioned a New York City outing with Cassandra Evans to Delmonico's and Herald Square Theater. He was unaware of her pregnancy, there was no understanding, and she cared little for the city; but Evans was attractive, intelligent, and ambitious so those lines caused several depressed days. There were probably other women, too. Cynthia Jefferson, the Starke's senior maid, was attracted and both women sensed it; which is why they were never more than proper. There was also Constance, who would continue guiding eligible women into her nephew's path if unaware of Oliver; or perhaps double down because of the baby.

She raised her free hand, squeezed Curtis' arm, and shifted her body closer, "You're right, brother, but I must be certain."

Katherine handed a satiated baby to nanny that evening, pulled her dress above the corset top, and rose from the nursing chair. The child paid little attention as the familiar transfer to a cast iron crib was accomplished. Then, discreetly passing through the first floor, she ensured the library was unoccupied, lifted her dress hem, and climbed the main staircase. Looking up, Katherine sensed Oliver Barrington Curtis' portrait studying her ascent of the oak staircase. The young soldier buried somewhere in Havana not only surveyed family and visitors for over a century but inhabited her youthful daydreams. Glancing back, Katherine noticed her son's namesake grew younger each year. For the first time she realized the blue eyes, high forehead, disciplined hair, and fine features resembled her dead husband; except Philip Ledford was never a rake and lacked the canvas' stern countenance.

Wearing a loose-fitting gown with short, broad sleeves covering just enough shoulder to hang, she glided quietly to the writing table looking east past heavy drapes across darkening fields. Her exposed neck and upper chest served as a pale background for Philip's cameo and silver chain; but the jet mourning ring taken off in Havana was never returned to her finger. She dipped a pen in the inkwell, stalled with its salutation, and considered a cable before realizing everyone could read it including his aunt and uncle.

Emotions failed transition to paper. She traveled to the States with her brother hoping to avoid men thinking a widow would be receptive, increase their fortune, or both. Her initial impression of Jacob Starke was someone more masculine than handsome; stiff, unpolished, and uninterested. A natural trueness and bruised but optimistic approach to life emerged and his absence of attention beyond bare civilities became unendurable as her taste for his attributes slowly intensified. In one unguarded moment after a dinner party she asked him to write. It was, perhaps, a spurious attempt to safely replace what existed with Philip but Jacob unexpectedly agreed and filled that void for a time.

Each letter saw her thoughts increasingly occupied by him, resolve eroding, and the desire for a man's attentions that surfaced late with Philip reignited. Her shift from a widow's wardrobe grew more daring, perhaps because she was overseas or sought the affection Immanuel and Constance Starke enjoyed. She grew increasingly agitated then nearly overcome by emotions while dancing with Starke at an Old Point Comfort hotel. In Havana, these urges were denied and attributed to an abundance of gothic romances when young and her ancestor's spirit; until the night before Starke left. She heard thrashing in the next room, went to his aid, and unexpectedly lost control in the hot, exotic night. When her wanton overtures were not rejected in disgust and his lust matched hers all propriety vanished and self-control with it. She wallowed in debauchery and wanted more but left humiliated by her moral collapse; with the only mitigation knowing Jacob would not betray her.

The voyage home from Havana with Edward affected her more than their rougher passage to New York and pregnancy became certain some weeks later. She continued writing to Starke but did not expect to survive and dreaded his proposal or rejection; so it was never mentioned. Edward pressed her to reveal Oliver after the birth but agreed, along with the family, to keep her confidence. This arrangement sufficed with an ocean buffer and would have continued, even when Edward returned to Washington and Cuba, except *Calypso* was not in the Caribbean, her brother revealed all, and Jacob proposed. A response was now owed but words would not come as night descended. Impatient blue ink dripped from her pen, wasting a sheet of paper without marring the ornate writing desk. Her decision to marry Philip was calculated but this one lacked time and complete rationality. She still believed herself devout but had sinned and the result was a son she adored who was owed his father's name; but marriage to Jacob would be neither easy nor safe. Besides turbulent emotions, there were religious differences, adjusting to an alien culture, Americans being unwelcome in her society, and customary end of financial independence.

Katherine relied on duty, discipline and propriety since puberty to bridge recurring spells of dark emotion that emerged as she matured; and to avoid the bluestocking label when her intelligence became undeniable. She mastered all expected of upper class English women then ventured discreetly beyond. Longing, fear, desire, and uncertainty bound her to the desk but their household schedule seldom varied and privacy fleeting so she wiped her dip pen's metal nib, gently submerged it in the inkwell, and began. The letter must at least explain what was required to give their son his father's name and respond to the proposal.

Accepting meant her previous conduct would be repeated, which was discomfiting, and more pregnancies. Despite behaving no better than one of their mares, Jacob's last letter indicated his aunt and uncle were more than accepting and hoped to see their grandnephew. She felt Starke desired her and would remain faithful, unlike her father who was susceptible to impromptu liaisons when visiting country homes. Lady Curtis accepted these as relief from an onerous task, but she could not. Philip remained faithful despite her ambivalence in bed but once he and HMS *Victoria* settled on the Mediterranean floor she realized they loved each other and the missed possibilities of a child. Now there was a son and proposal from his father; a man she wanted to run from and to. After finishing, she left an envelope for posting on the desk; sealed and addressed to the Starkes for passing to *Calypso*.

Chapter Nineteen
Cienfuegos

On the south Cuban coast, Cienfuegos lay quiet beneath a gold-tinged morning sky on its immense bay with narrow entrance channel. A constant, gentle east wind flowing across abandoned farmland from distant mountains rippled the mirror-blue water's shining surface. Louisiana and Bordeaux French built the city on a grid surrounding its rectangular Plaza de Armas and their influence could be seen in government buildings, a theater, cathedral, and more. It was Santa Clara's port city; and that entire province contested ground between western Cuba, where insurrectos were just holding, and the east, where they controlled rural areas and anywhere not heavily fortified.

Beyond the placid bay and Castillo de Nuestra Señora de los Ángeles de Jagua, better known as El Jagua Castle, *Calypso*'s captain studied the channel through binoculars. He refused to enter until confident war had not come since leaving Norfolk. Their March 17, 1898, arrival would allow a committee monitored by the resident American consul to begin helping reconcentrados. *Calypso*'s modest cargo would prime distribution in the province; then a Ward Line steamer leaving from New York with 560 tons of Central Relief Committee supplies would deliver bulk staples like corn meal, codfish, lard, bacon, and potatoes to that port, Matanzas, Santiago, and Sagua la Grande.

Calypso steamed southeast from Chesapeake Bay around midmorning March 10, 1898, with one main boiler on line. She continued at 10 knots until halfway through the first watch then turned southwest to clear Cape Hatteras, follow the coast just inshore of the Gulf Stream's center, and avoid local traffic. A restless Hatteras offered little more than rough seas. Fog appeared north of St. Augustine but that was common in March. The powerful current flowing to Europe retarded their advance by a knot but the bark turned due south two days later, as mess gear sounded, to pass between Florida and the Little Bahama Bank; losing another half knot to the current. Sharks provided escort on and off until relieved by dolphins. Sailing ships passed silently as *Calypso* crossed their preferred track from The Great Southern Route to Charleston and Savannah. Steamers proved slightly more plentiful and a Havana-bound liner overtook them during the night. Tugs also made appearances. Lookouts went aloft as Gun and Cat Cay lighthouses were employed to turn south by west and a quarter west. The morning watch then scanned a brightening horizon for the first lighthouse in a line running down the Florida Keys. These reference points were essential to squeeze between the reefs and an outbound Florida Current that often attained four knots. *Calypso* increased speed to compensate, made Alligator Reef Light, and then headed for the Yucatán Channel. As they plowed deep into Caribbean blues and greens, only flying fish or dolphins darting under the bow disturbed a smoothly rolling surface. This daily splendor was more than matched by nights with a quilt of stars to the horizon, and wake glowing green with phosphorescence. On March 15, 1898, with dead reckoning holding them clear of Cabo San Antonio, *Calypso* turned south into the Yucatán Channel, fixed position using its lighthouse, and headed eastward; remaining well off the Gulf of Batabanó's shoals, reefs, and cays. Clear water let sailors watch the white coral bottom, dark reefs, and marine life pass below. As evening came, *Calypso* turned north, the bottom dropped from sight, and they arrived off Cienfuegos; where Starke loitered until morning.

Calypso had both main boilers on line before first light and leadline party on her forecastle after breakfast. The leadsman protected by a heavy tarpaulin apron anchored his breast band to the starboard fore chains as an assistant laid out thirty fathoms of line in loops to allow free running. Heavier coasting or deep sea leads were worthless since the coast shallows dropped to an abyss within yards. The light hand-lead consisted of a ten-pound pendant armed with tallow to collect bottom samples and line marked with leather and rag bits.

A small schooner luffing near the coast saw *Calypso*'s hoist requesting a pilot, heeled slightly as it tacked, and steadily closed. She deposited a mixed-race guide with skin darkened by years of exposure; comfortably attired under a soft straw hat. Jose Marin was a small man with dark eyes flashing from a face like creased leather who assured Starke peace held, *Calypso* was expected, and arrangements made to offload cargo. He went to Watson's side after learning the executive officer was driving but Starke stood close by and Dunbar navigated from the pilothouse below.

Their leadsman leaned into the breast band, extending his torso out and away; paying out sufficient line to swing its pendant just above the passing water. Each pendulum-like cycle rose higher than the last until near collapse, then released to curve up, out, and into the sea. The trailing line whipped across deck planks until checked when up and down with no bottom.

The black bark came smoothly port using Punta de los Colorados lighthouse to enter a funnel-like channel. They steered nearer the green-banked passage's right side after passing between Punta de la Vigía and Punta del Diablo; using El Jagua Castle and Punta de Pasacaballos to avoid Punta de la Cocos. It seemed more broad river than channel with mangroves and brush along its banks. The lowlands to port climbed to higher ground near the fortress while terrain off their starboard side rose to a ridge carpeted by chaparral that followed the coast beyond a lighthouse and undersea cable station.

El Jagua Castle was situated where the left bank began its rise to higher ground and marked the last narrow leg beyond a turn with dangerous currents pushing ships from several directions. The ancient fortress built into this slope had ramparts looking down channel and guns placed to fire into ships entering that perilous turn from the sea. The main battery encircled a higher central structure capped by a tower while white houses with wraparound porches and mature trees were scattered along slopes below.

Their pilot coached Watson with serviceable English as *Calypso* neared the turn; explaining that maintaining speed while avoiding hesitation was crucial to avoid careening into the shore. Starke was confident in his executive officer but uncomfortable since a misstep could prove disastrous and the captain always accountable. They passed through with his unlit pipe's battered stem intact then entered the curving stretch leading to a bay that seemed more an inland sea. The large, green Cayo Carenas forced a port turn that took them between that island and Los Paredones high ground off their left side, then up a narrow channel cut by one of three rivers feeding the expansive basin; while keeping slightly north to avoid shallows. A white sand bottom was visible before they jogged northwest of an invisible pinnacle-like obstruction. The harbor was south of city proper with dark wharfs and piers jutting into the bay. Their pilot explained ships with drafts to sixteen feet could go pierside at high tide, before guiding them to an anchorage designated by the port captain between two points of land. It was further out than Starke thought convenient, perhaps due to Spain's angst about warships delivering supplies, but allowed him greater control.

Calypso bled off speed while a small launch flying Spain's naval ensign emerged from the piers. Watson stood at the flying bridge lifelines with a speaking trumpet; his service dress blue uniform contrasting with white canvas panels. Through it, Weaver was told to secure sailors on the leadline and form an anchor party. Dunbar remained below in the pilothouse, plotting landmarks to fix position. Their bronze screw ceased spinning as two small peninsulas began passing down both sides and the bark coasted to a halt with Weaver monitoring small bits of floating debris. The chief reported dead in the water through cupped hands and heard "Let go the anchor," in reply. Once released, the ponderous black object suspended from its davit plummeted through clear water trailing chain links, battering the chain pipe, creating deafening noise, and raising clouds of red dust. The brake was set after it struck bottom then released as Watson backed down to set the stocked anchor and lay chain. It was reset when enough scope clattered out, causing the chain to straighten, break surface, and re-submerge. An anchor watch was set once *Calypso* settled and bearings taken; then gear was stowed and cleanup began.

Starke watched the small Spanish boat come alongside and officer climb though their starboard bulwark's open gangway. Teniente de Navio Roberto Flores from the Spanish torpedo gunboat *Galicia* scrambled aboard, adjusted his uniform, went to the flying bridge, and saluted Starke. The gunboat's executive officer offered a courteous welcome to Cienfuegos. He represented *Galicia*'s commander, Teniente de Navio Jose Maria Arino y Michelena; senior naval officer and *Calypso*'s host. Flores clearly found this duty distasteful until recognizing *Calypso* as a ship that sank filibusters. Assured gun salutes would be returned, *Calypso*'s forward 4-inch mount began the timed firing of blank charges to a traditional rhyme. As *Galicia* returned gun for gun, Starke felt an involuntary chill observing the torpedo gunboat fire. She was *Pedro Menéndez de Avilés'* sister ship so rounds clawing that gunboat during their brief exchange returned.

Besides his ship, Flores proudly pointed out three torpedo gunboats, a small gunboat, and four others that were more realistically armed launches. Starke left the flying bridge for his cabin once the ensign was away and found Yamashita had already laid out a dress uniform for formal calls ashore. He still delayed leaving the cabin to give Weaver enough time to swing out and lower one of two white steam pinnaces in boat skids under round bar davits aft. Coxswain Melvin's diminutive command was again serving as his gig since warships' reputations in port were set by their boats' appearance and handling.

Coxswain Melvin, in dress blues, had removed the steam pinnace's boat cover then stocked his small command with items regulations required and those conveniently overlooked by his chief. The pinnace could not be swung out and lowered until anchored, since they were shorthanded, but once floating alongside his engineer and fireman stoked the blackened boiler with miniature hand-picked lumps until a shimmer of translucent smoke rose from its polished brass stack into a light harbor breeze. Satisfied, he took a deep breath and prepared to face the boat officer. Ensign Blair seldom ladled out the same grief to him as other coxswains, generally those the least bit slack, but had definite sundowner tendencies. That officer oversaw Chief Poniatowski's gun division so their paths only crossed when the ensign was his boat officer. Melvin did not reflect long before called to help his bow and stern hooks spread and lace the white canvas canopy. Once the ship's accommodation ladder was rigged, he maneuvered his steam pinnace alongside its lower platform and steadied the gig with lines.

Calypso's commander left his cabin accompanied by the executive officer. One glance at the boat's appearance, a pause to salute the flag, and he was through the gangway. Watson often selected Melvin's steam-pinnace as their gig; and Blair would complement their minstrel coxswain on this first trip. Starke nodded to the coxswain after sitting in the sternsheets, Melvin cast off aft, twisted his stern away, and then backed as the forward line came aboard. After pointing his bow at a large, covered quay the pinnace gained speed. Their pilot told Starke it was in front of the customs house on a waterfront consisting of something like eight wood piers on the smaller bay's north side. These were apparently of various widths, with lengths between 100 to 150 feet; except a railroad pier at the western end was nearer 200. Depth alongside that one was fourteen feet but the others were nearer twelve so ships with thirteen-foot drafts could moor at the head of some but anything deeper used lighters. Several derricks stood apart from masts of the small schooners moored along this crowded waterfront. Several one-story, white warehouses with peaked roofs and large doors flanked the customs house. West of this busy waterfront and just before the city cemetery was an open area that received all types of refuse and excreta. Flights of gray-white gulls could be seen in that direction, soaring overhead, waddling along dirt or planks, and gliding just above the bay to snatch small, surface-feeding fish then lift up and away with some unlucky morsel.

As Melvin turned slightly for the boat landing on the customs quay's west side, Starke caught a whiff of coal smoke slipping under the canopy to momentarily overcome an increasing stench of foul water and humanity. Another turn was needed to pass astern of a two-masted schooner under patched mainsail and jib; riding low with more bagged cargo amidship. Men forward were bending over its diminutive stocked anchor and one aft worked the helm. A longboat was towing astern and Starke concluded she was a sailing scow from the broad beam, overhanging counter, and, most likely, flat bottom. Different shades of rectangular patches where mainsail attached to boom and gaff showed she was also used hard on a tight budget.

Blair spotted the customs pier boat landing beside the quay's cement seawall. Like that roofed pier's other structures it was rough wood painted white and more utilitarian than impressive. Its wood frame girding several pilings with two broad planks serving as the platform had two steps leading to the pier deck. Melvin sent the bowhook forward, closed this framework, stopped his screw, put the rudder over, and backed. As they were about to drive into it, the bow twisted smoothly away, engine disengaged, and boat left parallel to and less than a foot distant. Boathooks thrust out fore and aft, caught this platform, and the steam pinnace was snugged in. Consul Owen McGarr waited on the pier beside a Spanish customs officer while his victoria on the packed-dirt wharf rocked slightly as its black gelding shifted in warming leather traces.

McGarr greeted Starke once *Calypso*'s captain stepped onto the pier's unpainted boards, "Welcome to Cienfuegos, Captain. May I present Senor Miguel Cisneros y Almodovar, head of customs and emissary of Santa Clara's provincial governor?" Starke walked with them to the carriage after firmly shaking one outstretched hand then another. Meanwhile, the pinnace left for *Calypso* where Ensign Dunbar waited to return the Spanish officer's call on board *Galicia*.

Their carriage clattered north from the waterfront on Calle de Santa Isabel then east to Calle de Clout, dropping the customs official on its way to the American consulate near Plaza de Armas. Cienfuegos' large customs house had five tall arches over its entrance and three windows, nearly as tall, on either side. A second story was set back between two small towers with a balustrade encircling its roof. Stretched along the waterfront on either side were small offices and warehouses. Most had peaked roofs but a few were flat or tiled. Some seemed to serve as barracks.

Cienfuegos' dry season continued beyond March with temperatures ranging between 70 and 80 degrees, muggy days with little change, and easterly winds; except at night when they often veered northwest. McGarr noticed Starke studying the passing city, "French from Bordeaux gridded it like Washington. There're wide streets and a Parisian-style boulevard called Paseo del Prado running north and south; but only three sewers. You caught the scent where they discharge on the waterfront. Streets collect standing water during our rainy season. Drinking water is boiled for safety but still tastes vile. An aqueduct like Havana's was planned then abandoned once fighting began. There've been no yellow fever deaths this month but we're on lowlands so the warmer seasons are quite unhealthy. Our more prosperous citizens leave during the worst months, like Washington, but only across the bay to cottages below the fortress. It's a pleasant city, except for summers. The queen palm trees add charm, if not shade, and hordes of fireflies put on a spectacular show."

Starke nodded politely. The macadamized street passing under their carriage seemed in poor repair but its roughly seventy-foot width with broad sidewalks carried a throng of people, riders, and vehicles. Among them was a Cuban oxcart threading through with a bulky cargo corralled by tall side poles rising considerably above its bed. This heavy load balanced on one axle with large wheels of planked wood was pulled by four light-red oxen under two yokes. Above some lower buildings, or though spaces between others, he could just make out the gray outline of distant mountains to the east, "What do you think of this posting?"

"Not nearly as cosmopolitan the Chile legation, but I prefer the climate over Ecuador and have been here since '95. Was with the Louisiana Artillery during the war, so anything beats that; but my trade is law. We'll circle Plaza de Armas since the government buildings and barracks are located there."

They turned west moments later and Starke saw a large building similar to Havana's Hotel Inglaterra. It had three stories with ground floor restaurant and rooms above opening to small porches enclosed by ornate iron railings. McGarr intruded, "Hotel La Union; best in the city; built around 1869."

Plaza de Armas was a block further. This central park was quartered by broad walks with street lamps and statues segregating plantings and royal palms. McGarr pointed out the buildings lining its surrounding streets. Many employed arched entrances or porticos. A cathedral with two tall bell towers was at the northeast corner. Nearby was Teatro Tomas Terry; a theatre seating well over 1,000 with phenomenal acoustics. The building McGarr referred to as the founder's house had a unique overhanging tower and living quarters above a ground floor warehouse. Besides Casa de los Leones, there was a new casino, the Palatino Tavern, army barracks, and more.

Once in the consulate office, McGarr closed his office door then offered Starke a cigar, "We can send your arrival cable, but you'll want to know our proposal for landing cargo."

Starke nodded, "I also need to develop an intelligence letter to the Navy Department so your thoughts would be helpful."

"Well, let's see. Santa Clara province is just west of the Jucaro-Moron Trocha so we're seeing heavy fighting. Sugar plantations are being devastated and a number owned or financed by Americans. Grinding's started and things will get worse if this harvest is not protected. General Aguirre has a full corps in the province with some of General Aldive's first division in Cienfuegos. My sources say the 36th and 54th infantry battalions, 23rd rifle battalion, 9th train company, and a 'Pando' infantry battalion of ex-insurgents."

Starke took advantage of a pause to ask about reconcentrados. McGarr leaned back in his chair, looked to the ceiling, and responded, "The fighting began driving our rural population into fortified towns before reconcentration. I'm reporting 15,000 destitute this month but that figure will increase. As consul, I work with local relief committees. Some of the $50,000 appropriated did arrive and was distributed to something like 132 of our citizens living here; but it's too much money and proving citizenship difficult. Your cargo, especially the medical supplies, will prime the relief effort and provide experience for handling the larger Ward Line cargo."

McGarr looked through the sunlit window then to Starke, "My tenure's nearing an end. William Fee's been appointed but I've no idea when he arrives. Perhaps the change is because I've been too candid with Washington. In my opinion, all but four provinces are nearly pacified. Insurrectos are losing ground generally, although that's less true in the eastern provinces. Spain prevailed using that strategy during the last war. It's a personal evaluation I believe realistic but didn't go down well back at State. I'm hearing the same clamor that preceded our last war and fear the nation's losing its head. This office will close when war comes so I've approached some of the twelve consulates. They're willing to act for us once their governments' agree, but Britain's the best bet due to our common language."

Starke listened then responded, "My uncle says much the same about public mood."

"He fought?"

"No; my father did, then went to Brazil."

"I see. You'll want to know the Cuban-Submarine Company cables to Santiago and Havana come ashore at the white building beside the lighthouse. Also, Ferro Carril de Cienfuegos y Santa Clara not only brings in the sugar harvest but connects to Havana through Santa Clara. There're no railroads east of here that amount to anything so traffic moves between small ports. Agricultural goods from the interior, mostly sugar, coffee, and livestock, pass through Cienfuegos, and smaller ports towards Santiago ship ore."

"What about fortifications?"

"They're formidable, especially for ships attempting to force the channel, but not yet sited. The fortress has a good location but is little more than ornamentation because its batteries are obsolete and vulnerable to shellfire. There are plans to build timber, sand, and earth fortifications. My informant claims at least a dozen Krupp rifles are available; probably 4 and 6-inch. Artillery units in Santa Clara could be here on short notice but they're mountain artillery, not coastal. I've no insight on torpedoes. You're a better judge of the naval side. *Galicia* is their largest ship and a torpedo gunboat; but I cannot confirm automotive torpedoes are available. Their smaller gunboats are more armed launches; but useful on the rivers."

"That's valuable information, Mr. McGarr."

"For our current exercise I propose landing medical supplies first then deliver them directly to the charity hospital since it treats reconcentrados. Supplies for the civilian hospital will go through committee. The military hospitals are excluded, of course, but there're two. One is on Tacon Street and the other a waterfront warehouse. Non-medical cargo can go to waterfront storage and since it belongs to our government normal customs procedures are suspended. If this is acceptable, lighters will arrive in the morning."

"What about security? An armed landing party is out of the question."

"I was about to mention that. The 9th train company commander agreed to provide pier sentries during tomorrow's offload then guard the warehouse. His quartermaster's quite honest for the trade, especially given Cuba's temptations. Without his help your cargo would have to be distributed immediately or vanish. The local press's been active so the city's become a tinderbox since *Maine*. Mobs are out most days to support Spain or protest autonomy. Chants against Americans are gaining popularity; and a number live and do business here. Which reminds; I suggest those coming ashore do so in civilian clothes."

"There is one other thing I would like to do before returning to the ship."

"Yes?"

Starke recalled Sigsbee's unintentional affront, "I assume an autonomous council exists and must call on its president and the military commander."

"I was about to suggest that. We'll do it now."

"Only if convenient."

The victoria that brought Starke to the consulate returned him to the covered pier behind the customs building just before siesta. Blair and Melvin finished conveying Dunbar to *Galicia* then drifted off the landing; maneuvering to avoid the sewer outlets' stench. Starke was unhappy about this since the canopy offered only partial sun protection and the effect obvious, but he had no idea how long he would be away from the landing and wanted to avoid conflict on the waterfront. Melvin and his crew were less concerned since loitering off the pier kept them away from equally hot work onboard ship.

Passed Assistant Paymaster Matthew Wiggs, Chief Boatswain Mate Braddock Weaver, Paymaster Clerk Matthias Eberhardt, and Assistant Surgeon Conrad already had the crew busy. Cargo was retrieved, staged, checked against the manifest, and sentries posted. Yards were rigged and sailors detailed to transfer cargo to a lighter alongside. Friday would be spent unloading and Saturday cleaning, but *Calypso* would not leave for Norfolk until Monday. Starke cabled the Department he was remaining in port Sunday for the required monthly inspection, church service, and *Articles of War* reading. That meant rope-yarn in the afternoon and time to relax, even if not allowed ashore.

Morning sun brought the first lighter from Cienfuegos' custom house pier. It looked like a dark water beetle at first; crawling over the blue bay trailing black smoke under high clouds trimmed with golden filigrees. *Calypso*'s crew was already up, breakfasted, and lowering rope fenders alongside. Starke went to the flying bridge where he could see everything but not insert himself; which proved a struggle. Starke firm cruises left him with greater expertise than Watson but this was their executive officer's show.

As the water beetle took shape, it was clear the approaching lighter and small, squat tug made an odd pair. The tow was once a flat-bottomed schooner; more work-worn than the one passing their steam pinnace yesterday. Masts and bowsprit were removed and rough planking with multiple layers of dark paint covered what had once been white. Woven rope fenders were draped to port and angling aft as they dragged water. One man at a long tiller guided the tug while others sat at what remained of a main deck once most was cut away to open her hull. The small tug lashed alongside was little more than exaggerated wood launch with a large boiler and more powerful engine. What passed for a superstructure was box-like and sheltered only its steam plant. A thick, black stack belched smoke from poor coal and, as tug and tow maneuvered, her helmsman could be seen at the exposed wheel aft; taking orders from the tug's master standing on the lighter.

This amalgamation eased alongside with a series of rasping groans before securing aft, where the first lifts were staged. The hulk's ten stevedores went below to receive cargo, leaving a Spanish sergeant on the main deck with eight soldiers in Guerrera uniforms of rayadillo under jipijapa straw hats. Leather harnesses and Mauser rifles marked them as regular army. The detail acted experienced and alert to pilferage; their honesty and efficiency marked by the thin physiques of being poorly fed and irregularly paid.

Calypso was no longer equipped for cargo-handling but retained a steam winch that was pressed into service. Offloading required using it and a yard swung outboard by hand for transfer. Once centered over the lighter's hold each lift was lowered into it. The cargo was staged so heavier goods went first and medicinals last to limit damage and remain in full view. *Calypso*'s small crew and lack of cargo-handling equipment meant all hands were involved; except Melvin and his mandolin who went to the flying bridge and played whatever tune came to mind.

Load after load transferred. Several times, one or another of the guard detail unslung their rifle. Starke was unable to determine if this was for comfort or to warn someone about to take liberties in the hold; but all showed great restraint and discipline. The diminutive tug eased this first lighter away once medical supplies were loaded and cargo covered with canvas tarps then made for the waterfront trailing black smoke bursts. *Calypso*'s assistant surgeon accompanied the medicine to consult Spanish counterparts and survey their hospital.

The tug returned with the first lighter's twin and placed it alongside. This exchange repeated several times before siesta; with Americans gratefully adapting to that custom after laboring in muggy heat with a fitful breeze and unrelenting sun reflecting off still water. Starke remained in his cabin when they resumed, reviewed periodic reports, and restarted a letter to Katherine since nothing arrived from her or Curtis. While the breeze crossing between open windows and raised shutters refreshed the day cabin, his steward looked from the pantry to see if Starke required anything. The crew finished early that evening then began unrigging gear and cleaning while Melvin's pinnace took Watson and Wiggs to confirm everything on the manifest was under guard in the warehouse. They were soon at his door with Conrad in tow. Starke invited them to sit at his table before pulling a browned meerschaum from the rack, dredging its bowl through the tobacco pouch, and pressing moist shards until satisfied. The match passed over center, ignited it, and then went out on its own.

Watson began, "Cargo's locked in a warehouse near the customs pier, Captain. Sentries are posted and the consul receipted for it. Their lieutenant seemed to dislike the affair, which is probably why we only saw his sergeant here. McGarr's man said some local officials view our help as a disgrace to Spanish honor; even if their poorly fed and unpaid soldiers further inland leave food on their plates for children to lick."

"I understand your feelings XO, but we can only do so much. The medical supplies, Doctor?"

Conrad's brow furrowed, "Army surgeons went with me to the charity hospital where our supplies are under guard and receipted for. They were talkative and one spoke English so he translated. It seems the city had no hospitals before the fighting but now there're four. The charity hospital is difficult to describe. Starvation cases are obvious, but I observed injuries and several diseases. It's beyond capacity and will be worse when yellow fever and other rainy season afflictions arrive. Most patients are women, elderly, and children since their young men are with one side or the other. We also passed the civilian hospital, two military establishments, and army quarantine building. I must emphasize the necessity to avoid distilling or unnecessary contact with local water; including wash-downs. Our anchorage is downstream from sewer outlets coming direct from three buildings; and one is the civil hospital. The wells are shallow and contaminated. Cisterns are no better and the river passes through sludge. Every water source requires boiling and I'm not confident how effective even that can be."

Starke listened then nodded, "Let's not make water until back at sea but ensure Mister O'Leary knows we'll depend on our distillers. Mr. Wiggs; I trust tomorrow's sermon is inspiring?"

The dapper paymaster with a distinct nose grinned, "Something using Colossians 3:17 should be appropriate; and writing it after today should not take long. Never thought I'd be doing the Lord's work like this."

Starke returned to reports and writing, reviewed the night order book, and slept well with windows open. He woke once to find Thaddeus curled at his feet. The cat had been investing more time in the adjacent pantry and probably slipped through its door. This companion padded off early the next morning while Starke trimmed his beard and shaved before one of Yamashita's rice and egg breakfasts. Later, he swirled morning coffee dregs, a thick liquid and grounds, around the bottom of his golden eagle-embossed, white china cup. Starke's thoughts drifted to Katherine, then *Calypso*. Yamashita had laid out his full-dress uniform and lightly oiled the sword's blade; an honest weapon the cabin steward placed special emphasis on. Captains might not be inspected but needed a flawless uniform in front of a crew since sailors meticulously prepared theirs. Pride or peer pressure were common motivators but if not clean, correct, and exact they also risked disciplining.

The master-at-arms knocked at his cabin door when everyone except those on watch was formed by division. He began at the forecastle where deck division mustered. Watson was waiting and Chief Weaver stood behind Ensign Martyn. The officer saluted and reported his men present and/or accounted for; then standing by for inspection. This was repeated for every department with formations opening ranks so Starke could quickly pass through, scanning each sailor top-to-bottom while Yeoman Pond recorded discrepancies. The ensigns had been with Starke since commissioning so there might be a few minor issues or uniforms blemished by a last minute brush with bulkhead or door, but nothing more. Afterwards, the crew went aft for their *Articles of War* reading then divine service. Wiggs' Colossians 3:17 sermon described conditions ashore and enumerated their blessings. The finale was a non-denominational prayer tailored to various religious views on board.

The Catholic cathedral was worth visiting according to McGarr and a number of *Calypso* sailors were of that faith. Starke or Watson usually ensured arrangements made for those wanting to visit a priest, but sending a uniformed liberty party ashore was too dangerous and enlisted sailors were not permitted civilian clothes. They would have to wait for Norfolk but everyone was free for the afternoon. The ship was too far offshore to be troubled by flying insects and only the tide moved *Calypso*, so those sun tolerant found a bulwark or bulkhead to sit against. Yeoman Third Class Matthias Eberhardt hunched over his sewing machine finishing seams on Seaman Cullen Flynn's liberty uniform; although the starboard section's redhead battler was unlikely to need it for some time. Others read library books, smoked in designated areas, or exchanged gossip with their messmates. A small number caught up on delayed tasks or correspondence.

Calypso would postpone breakfast to get underway with the seven-thirty sunrise. That would disrupt the day's routine and vex her sailors but things could be sorted once the bark cleared land. This was several hours after the first high tide but their pilot claimed waiting for the second that afternoon would not add much under the keel and going earlier meant transiting the channel against an incoming current. The second boiler's coals were spread while Starke slept and deck watches looked out over a quiet harbor, used landmarks to ensure the anchor held, spoke of many things, and readied to leave.

Starke climbed to the flying bridge as their underway neared, felt the muggy air, and saw distant mountains to the east take shape as they were backlit. The steam pinnace was hoisted aboard aft while an acrid smell of coal smoke mixing with steam covered the scent of shore and bay. As the crew went to station, one of the lights along wharf and piers began moving, broke from the rest, and was soon identified as the lighters' small tug. Its approach this time proved more considerate than previous visits; which deck division appreciated after repainting that area of the hull.

Ensign Martyn left main deck duties to Chief Weaver and escorted the same weathered pilot who brought them in to the flying bridge where Starke greeted him, "Welcome aboard, Capitán."

The pilot smiled as they shook hands then extracted a flimsy envelope from his pocket, "Gracias, Capitán; and I have been entrusted to deliver this."

Dunbar decoded the yellow cablegram from the Navy Department then passed a note to Starke, "Calypso to Key West. Orders to follow. Long."

Starke shoved it in his pocket then turned to the pilot, "Gracias, Capitán."

"De nada, Capitán; are you ready?"

Watson would drive out although ensigns usually rotated through each underway for experience. It was a tricky channel but Starke also thought their next entrance might occur without a pilot. Engines and rudder were tested while Starke observed the sun climb above far mountains, throwing light across a flat bay; turning some areas into a gold-tinged, multicolored palette bounded by the increasingly distinct shoreline. Partly obscured by *Calypso*'s stack and masts, Cienfuegos' awakening revealed low, white buildings with reddish brown roofs behind waterfront piers, masts, and derricks.

This underway began when their anchor chain straightened, briefly surfaced, and then submerged as Weaver brought the ship to short stay with a steam windlass. He paused for permission to continue once their stocked anchor was up and down. When it broke ground, *Calypso*'s ensign rose to her masthead, their steam whistle sounded, and Starke swept the bay for traffic. Fire hoses sprayed chain and anchor. Fished and suspended from a davit, it was being made ready for letting go when vibrations announced steam was starting to spin their triple-expansion engine and screw under her fantail stern had begun to bite.

Gaining speed and momentum, *Calypso* ran south, just far enough west to clear a submerged pinnacle to port off Punta Gorda, and then set a course for the passage between Cayo Carenas and Los Paredones high ground. The large, green cay blocked line of sight to the channel except for a masthead lookout. Today it was Doran Kearney, who had no regrets about missing liberty. Besides Americans being unpopular, liquor was readily available. He constantly fought the urge to indulge and regularly failed; but especially feared any recurrence while under a captain he respected since their time ashore in Alexandria after the British shelling. That cadet was now standing by his executive officer and pilot as clear water passing below offered glimpses of bottom. He remained alert for a pinnacle to starboard but the ship turned port and entered the brief passage between a low, green island and coastal high ground without it showing.

Watson followed the shoreline in an easy starboard turn placing *Calypso* in the narrow channel with lowland to port and high ground to starboard. Under the old fortress they found the pilot's advice accurate. Coming off the flood with less treacherous currents, the turning was smoothly accomplished and channel beyond El Jagua Castle rapidly widened to the Caribbean. As the bark emerged, a schooner off Puenta de los Colorados lighthouse tacked, made for

Calypso, came easily alongside, and retrieved the pilot Wiggs just paid in Mexican dollars.

Chapter Twenty
Reckonings

Captain Albert stood at the tall window in his east-wing office of the State, War, and Navy Building; taking morning coffee from a worn, white china cup. Slowly panning from the Treasury Building over the Presidential Grounds past the Executive Mansion to Lafayette Square's bustle, he thought of the walk to work through a warm southern wind bearing a coming storm's precursors. His three-year effort to restrict the Junta's illegal flow of men, arms, and munitions to Cuba was fast becoming irrelevant.

The *Maine* court of inquiry report would be presented to Congress before day's end but the press had its particulars; likely from Roosevelt who trumpeted war at the Gridiron Club's Saturday dinner. The assistant secretary's conduct had been that of an unabashed jingo but he at least seemed as keen on joining the fight as he was instigating it. Younger navy officers seemed equally enthusiastic while most army contemporaries compared Spain's military in Cuba with their small force scattered across the nation. War fever stoked by press and finally politicians seemed to reach a crisis after Senator Proctor's speech; trampling any opposition. Another, more welcome, casualty was the schism between North and South that had smoldered since the war.

Over the weekend, a letter to the ailing Rear Admiral Sicard relieved him of the North Atlantic Squadron. Captain William Sampson, his flag captain, would replace him. The choice was convenient, perhaps logical, but senior officers like Winfield Scott Schley were passed over. Schley, who would have been Albert's choice, visited Long at the Building on his way to Norfolk and command of the Flying Squadron. Both captains would have become commodores but Sampson was leapfrogged over Schley to rear admiral. Roosevelt knew something of Sampson so Albert wondered if he played a role, as with Dewey.

Albert turned and walked to his desk in the rolling gait that carried his stocky frame with a deepwater sailor's powerful arms and legs. He placed the worn cup with faded gilt eagle embossing on the oak desk, pulled out the rolling chair, sat, and then scooted forward over a Persian rug. Morning sun passing through his window illuminated the desk beneath a white glass and brass lamp hanging from ceiling medallion. The right corner was taken up by a correspondence box, mahogany pipe stand, and, towards the center, a small device with four rollers set to "MON MAR 28 98".

Two years ago he offered Starke *Calypso* from this desk and somewhere on it was a cablegram reporting her arrival in Key West five days before. The bark's return to Norfolk from Cienfuegos was altered when all available ships were sent to the North Atlantic Squadron in Key West or Flying Squadron in Norfolk. Long diverted his ferret despite protests she was unsuited for most missions and crewed to a minimum even before losing people during the yard period. His objections faded away when Crowninshield pointed out most of the fleet, including its armored cruisers, did not have war complements and a successful blockade required numbers.

Albert eased himself into the desk chair, leaned forward, passed over the briar pipe, and selected a meerschaum. Sitting back, he dredged it through a supple leather tobacco pouch, gingerly packed the bowl, lit it by passing a match over center while creating a draught, and then tossed the still-smoking match into an ashtray.

Oregon was underway from the Pacific, Marix was in Washington with the inquiry report, there had been a Friday cabinet meeting, the project to impede filibustering was over, and his portfolio exploded. Albert was with the assistant secretary on Thursday when they negotiated with Revenue Marine chief, Captain Charles Shoemaker, and Captain Gibson Fischer about transferring cutters to the Navy, *Vanguard* included. Those chosen would go to Norfolk for arming, then help bridge the gunboat shortfall or confront torpedo boats crossing from Spain. *Fern* relieved *Montgomery* in Havana. The Coast Survey steamer *A.D. Bach* brought *Maine* bodies to Key West then returned for more dead and salvage. On Saturday, the torpedo gunboat *Temerario* was reported to have suddenly left Montevideo, Uruguay. Roosevelt pressed hard for Long to change *Oregon*'s route; one more sign he was already at war despite the administration still working to avoid one. State remained in constant turmoil throughout the weekend.

Albert's musing ended with his bowl and he began sorting through items scattered across the desk. There was a meeting with Crowninshield later to decide what color ships should be painted since a Sunday cable from Key West reported they halted painting white hulls black and requested direction. He would advise the assistant secretary who would decide. Crowninshield put forward a dull tea color, like the last war. Roosevelt favored dull lead but thought it should be left to squadron commanders.

Falk's subdued visit after a day at the Capitol reinforced these morning ruminations. The president's secretary typed ten copies of the handwritten *Maine* inquiry report over the weekend and it was read to a Congress already familiar from their morning papers. Despite the neutral delivery or because of it, what little opposition remained crumbled and jingoes rose to their feet baying. The Spanish report was available but ignored. Albert heard little or nothing from his State contacts but rumor had them working with Spanish counterparts directly and through General Woodford, their minister in Spain. State successfully persuaded Spain to end their reconcentration policies, which was already accomplished in four provinces, but the peace faction was being crushed and the most ominous rumor was an alleged demand for full resolution of all issues before the month's close.

Albert's next three weeks were submerged in what seemed Congress' irrepressible rush to war spurred on by public opinion and press. Spanish newspapers and public were making similar demands while European diplomats' worried any war would entangle the powers and cause colonial upheaval. This inconstancy generated an irresolute diplomatic delegation to McKinley urging peace without strong British support. Sigsbee's unsubstantiated accusation of Spain's role entered congressional testimony on March's last day; followed by a reception for him that included political notables. Albert avoided the function by pointing out he was too involved in his latest task; helping establish an Executive Mansion command center. The rush for war slowed briefly during April's first week when Lee cabled State that Americans in Cuba would pay a price if war started without clear warning; and many were abandoning Cienfuegos, Havana, and other parts of Cuba.

Spain finally agreed to everything but Cuban independence; and promised that. The States viewed this as stalling and seeing neither side could back down, Consul-General Lee and his staff left Havana. Puerto Rico's consul shifted his office to St. Thomas when the president addressed Congress on the eleventh. That session's acrimonious debate pitted jingoes against those favoring Cuban independence before agreeing to a joint resolution authorizing force. McKinley signed it and the steamship *Condor* sailed for Cienfuegos the next day to retrieve Americans. Sampson left for Havana on the twenty-second with his North Atlantic Squadron, under orders to blockade sections of the Cuban coast. Roosevelt remained in the thick of this and more, despite his frustration with not securing a commission and worry over Edith's illness. Albert reviewed and staffed the unending memorandums flowing from the assistant secretary to his boss; including the most recent that advocated assigning people to explore Samuel Langley's heavier-than-air flying machine.

In Havana on April 10, 1898, Darwin Tyson sat quietly in the steam launch taking him to *Fern*, anchored off the city. Translucent gray smoke lifted gently from a stack between her two fore-and-aft rigged masts. On the Navy list as a gunboat, the Treasury Department steamer had been transferred and fitted with five 3-pounder guns. She may not be impressive but offered an excellent vantage point to report evacuation of Americans, Europeans, and Cubans from Havana since Consul-General Lee, Vice-Consul Springer, the Sagua la Grande consul, attachés, clerks, and reporters would be aboard for the trip to Key West.

Anxious Spanish authorities were assisting since they wanted these foreigners gone without incident. Casa Nuevo's absent American flag on Holy Saturday shocked residents since it meant war was certain. Men were being drafted and crowds gathering in Havana for passage out. The Plant Line's 182-foot coastal steamer *Margaret* left with refugees and Tyson spotted the Spanish tug *Susie* towing the schooner *James H. Dudley* through Havana's narrow channel into a deep-blue Caribbean. Lee advised her to leave without waiting to unload. Moored or anchored near *Fern* were the steamship *Evelyn*, survey ship *A.D. Bache*, and *Olivette*. Each master wanted to claim they were last out but *Fern* prevailed because Lee wanted to ensure everyone left before he did; and place their well-armed ship at the rear. One other master ignored Lee's warning and remained in Regla to unload.

Tyson looked at *Olivette* while his launch cut across odious harbor water. She and half-sister *Mascotte* made the thirty-six hour run from Port Tampa to Havana and back three times a week from November to May. This dropped to twice weekly during summers when disease hurt travel and *Olivette* took over a Boston-to-Halifax route. They were William Camp & Sons Ship and Engine Building Company creations designed to fit these slightly different tasks. Their black hulls were trimmed white with a rounded pilothouse, single stack, two pole masts, and white lifeboats along the upper deck; but at 291 feet, *Olivette* was eighty feet longer with a raised forecastle to accommodate heavier traffic on her winter and summer routes. The smaller *Mascotte* was designed slightly different and easily accommodated months with fewer riders.

Olivette was loading passengers ferried from the customs pier. Tyson arranged Evans' berth aboard her since the liner carried Clara Barton, a Red Cross contingent of twenty, and refugees. Evans' had stayed to cover Barton, which proved exhausting. The seventy-seven-year-old's energy, compassion, and steel took them to Artemisa, Sagua La Grande, Cienfuegos, and Santo Domingo exploring distribution sites with Dr. Monae Lesser, dark-haired chief nurse Sister Bettina Hofker Lesser, and four subordinates. In La Focas they discovered 649 nude, starving people covered with sores; a Havana food distribution center was opened on Estrella Street; and the list continued. Evans' only break came during late March when Barton raced back to Glenn Echo, dealt with

Red Cross politics, and returned in something like a fortnight. During her time with Barton, Evans' acquired more than copy by observing how she dealt with people and politics; even receiving Blanco's support while insisting on the truth about rumors soldiers took relief supplies. Evans was also with her at the palace when Barton regretfully informed Blanco she could not remain and witnessed his disappointment.

Tyson had been equally occupied since Starke and Curtis left. *Vizcaya* and *Almirante Oquendo* sailed in early April, allegedly to escort a torpedo boat flotilla. Wrecking firms working *Maine* were directed to leave about the same time. The battleship's executive officer followed within days; having spent no time ashore. Lee spent an evening with his Mexican counterpart, Andres Vazquez, and rumor had it Mexico's consul was approached because Britain's Consul-General Alexander Gollan sympathized with Spain and refused to accept any of the American consulate's tasks unless London directed. Local papers surpassed foreign press in rumors, mistruths, and outright lies until residents believed little that was printed; and many remained convinced autonomy was taking root and the States would yield to European pressure. Consequently, officials and public were stunned when reporters began leaving then shocked when flags above the wrecked American battleship and consulate came down.

Fern looked much like *Calypso* to Tyson as his steam launch chugged for her starboard accommodation ladder. The black hull's fine lines were hardly disrupted by a single line of white-rimmed portholes. Her low, white superstructure included a pilothouse forward and thin stack amidship with three boats slung in davits on either side of bell-mouthed ventilators. The union jack hung limp forward and ensign from her mainmast gaff when Ensign Charles Bookwalter welcomed him and two others at the gangway. Nearby, her captain, Roosevelt's brother-in-law Lieutenant Commander William S. Cowles, spoke with executive officer Lieutenant Frank E. Sawyer about getting underway. Tyson discovered Cowles was nearing promotion and, considering *Fern*'s wardroom, understood Starke's extreme fortune to have *Calypso* as a junior lieutenant.

He wanted a few minutes with one of the ensigns, Wilfred V. Powelson, to discuss the *Maine* inquiry but needed a more opportune moment. Sylvester Scovel, another *World* reporter, two from Associated Press, Redding from *The New York Herald*, and Akers from *The London Times* were available so Tyson compared notes, stowed his gear, then spent a few minutes in the close wardroom. When Powelson failed to appear he grew bored and returned to the main deck's sun. Havana was in siesta so little moved on the bay except for an intermittent stream of *Olivette* passengers arriving in small groups; at Lee's suggestion to avoid acrimony.

Lee and Springer boarded late that afternoon. The consul-general's bulk stood apart amongst ravenous reporters converging to ask questions. Despite Blanco having taken to wearing his campaign uniform Lee apparently attempted a final courtesy visit but the governor-general's secretary indicated he was unwell and in siesta so Lee's party left. However, Blanco met with British Consul-General Gollan shortly afterwards. Lee's courtesy call on the autonomous government's secretary general Jose Congosto was predictably disagreeable given the doctor's reputation. Lee described the consulate party's transit from Casa Nuevo to *Fern* as uneventful and that he anticipated orders from State in Key West. Later arrivals claimed they were taunted while passing through hostile crowds gathering from the Inglaterra to Machina Wharf. A few mentioned rumors circulating that

Britain would back Spain to protect its citizens' Cuban financial interests and investments in Spanish government bonds.

Shortly after five o'clock the consul-general conferred with Cowles then colorful flags raced up halyards. *Dudley* had already cleared when *Olivette* got underway with over 300 refugees, *Evelyn* followed with around 100, and *Bache* took twenty-six. *Fern* slipped her buoy once the others were away and the pilot guided her slowly towards high ground crowned by Fortaleza de San Carlos de la Cabaña before coming to port and entering the narrow channel. Those on board fell silent passing *Maine*, then returned cheers from a British steamer that dipped its union jack. Some claimed one of *Alphonso XII*'s Hontoria guns tracked *Fern* as she passed. Tyson was more interested in surveying crowds along the channel filling open spaces to the San Salvador de la Punta Fortress on the left bank and Castillo de los Tres Reyes Magos del Morro the right. People were especially thick along the low seawall with empty cannon embrasures; and close enough to hear. Each ship ran this gauntlet to a chorus of whistles, jeers, and gestures, commingled with shouts of "Yankee swine" and "fuego". British subjects mistaken for Americans or harassed because their government chose neutrality spurred one London correspondent to yell back he hoped every Yankee shell killed plenty of Spaniards. It was Springer, the thirty-year veteran of Cuba, who had the last word when he waved his hat and yelled back to the crowd they would return.

A waiting pilot schooner with tanbark sails saw *Fern* emerge, made for the American ship, came alongside to starboard in building seas, and retrieved their pilot; after Lee asked him to carry a verbal message to Blanco. Tyson extracted a Turkish cigarette from his gold-trimmed, jade case and waited on *Fern*'s fantail for the Cuban coast to close below a light tan Morro growing gray and less distinct as seas worsened. The last months in Havana and Evans on board *Olivette* consumed his thoughts.

Heavy weather engulfed *Fern* before evening became night. Caribbean storms were common but this one proved brutal for so early in the year. The seas, crowned by whitecaps in broken rows, turned deep gray then black. Tyson survived worse in the North Atlantic, but on larger ships. *Fern* was riding like a steamship and his stomach quivered to the familiar but revolting scent wafting through closed spaces from those who already succumbed. The smoking lamp was not lit so cigarettes were out, but a long slug from his worn silver hip-flask helped. Returning it to an inside jacket pocket, he staggered through gyrating passages to the wardroom. The little sleep he required was a lifelong curse and blessing so he spoke with reporters still able and filled the last of his Havana notebooks while *Fern* shouldered through confused seas. Whenever her clipper bow dropped into a trough the screw surfaced and engine raced; rattling the hull while emitting a tortured shriek. Noticeable between crescendos was the constant rattle of small items and dull slap of sea against wood which continued past midnight into early morning.

Olivette entered Key West around two o'clock Easter Morning and *Bache* about seven-thirty. Tyson was topside when *Fern* raised a gathering of ships off Whitehead Spit that included the North Atlantic Squadron. He surveyed horizon, small keys, channel and shore while they closed a guano-stained nun buoy lifting and dropping in the long swells. *Fern* slowed as she ran nearly parallel to, but seaward, of some miniature keys. Before they were abreast that buoy, the ship came starboard, steadied on course, and went up Southeast Channel as a red buoy passed to starboard. Halfway through this leg a second red nun went by and Tyson just made out the numeral four, partly obscured with guano stains. This fresh morning made up for the tumultuous night. He could see coral reefs outside the channel; barely above or just below the surface. Standing on them were sea gulls, terns, and brown pelicans; with more floating nearby in the sun. Salt air and sea smells enriched by land's scent rode a slight breeze. He could see the sand bottom pass below as their bow pointed to a black and white, vertically striped can buoy with requisite guano coating; then left it to starboard as their new course took them to the city harbor and wharfs up-channel from Fort Taylor, Marine Hospital, customs house, naval station, and a coaling cruiser.

A large collection of warships lay off the port and beyond its reefs. Tyson identified one *Indiana* class battleship and the distinctive armored cruiser *New York*. The rest were cruisers and gunboats; some with white hulls partly painted black. Monitors and green-hulled torpedo boats were anchored closer in and the naval station's three small harbor tugs were out and about. *Mascotte*, which brought nearly 1,000 refugees the day before, was loading pierside. One ship stood out so he extracted the small spyglass he carried. The black bark *Calypso* floated placidly on turquoise water with white boats tethered to booms below sailors preparing for Sunday inspection. Her stack exhausted small wisps of light gray smoke into the cobalt blue sky; probably from an auxiliary boiler. His oldest friend and confidant Jacob Starke was off Key West.

Olivette's refugees cheered *Fern* as she ghosted into the city harbor; just past the small naval station with its administration building, steel pier, machine shop, and new coal bins. The commercial port included piers, wharfs, slips, and docks up-channel from a horse-powered marine railway; with small schooners moored where their shallow drafts permitted. Beyond the waterfront, streets were laid out in a grid of houses, businesses, offices, warehouses, and peak-roofed wood buildings.

Carriages queued along the waterfront, beyond a larger crowd than usual; a gathering Tyson expected would include local correspondents he called lobby lizards. *Fern* anchored off the waterfront near *Bache* then began shuttling diplomats, reporters, and refugees ashore. Cowles and Lee were met by Commander Forsyth then guided through press, locals, and cheering Cuban refugees; the later boisterously grateful for their deliverance and the government lifting entry regulations.

Lee emphasized he was only in the city long enough to receive direction from State and would not discuss politics then a waiting carriage took the trio to Hotel Key West for an abbreviated reception. Tyson followed on foot since it was only a few blocks distant. Just beyond waterfront coal piles near the First National Bank Tyson turned up Duval Street towards the wood-framed, white hotel with broad, covered porch. Once there, he threaded and pushed through its congested entrance into a large lobby. The hallway to his right led to a bar and small parlor. It was tempting but he went left into the packed crowd. Cubans were shouting in Spanish with American refugees adding to the tumult as he slipped and elbowed through to the dining room in front of a kitchen and large storeroom. He heard reporters call out while others jotted answers, or lack of them, in notebooks. Since most questions concerned leaving Havana, and his copy was drafted, it was time to go. He retreated to the entrance and just stepped from the porch when he spotted Evans walking up the hot, dusty street; wearing a traveling dress and lugging her battered, brown Brussels carpet bag.

She smiled, "I thought you'd be here and there's a little time before *Olivette* sails."

"You're staying with Barton?"

"As we agreed; she's not coming ashore."

"It looks like the consul-general will join you."

"Perhaps I'll get an interview."

"Let me know, but I must get to the telegraph office before our friends."

"Of course; you're staying on?"

"Yes, I've a room at the hotel."

Evans laughed, "You'll find it a letdown after the Inglaterra."

Tyson paused momentarily to watch her sway up the street before sprinting towards the International Ocean Telegraph Company's two-story brick building on Green Street; in a race to beat competitors hoping to control the wire.

Forsyth and Cowles had the consul-general onboard *Olivette* by noon, although his staff remained in Key West. Lee intended to take a side-wheel steamer to Miami but worried he might miss the railroad connection until the Plant Line offered passage to Port Tampa and private car. *Olivette* moored there at three the next afternoon and that car was on the pier as promised. Barton rode with Lee to Tampa where over 1,000 cheering Confederate veterans greeted him. Evans followed. After turning in luggage for fumigation the two women lodged at Hotel Arno on Tampa Street; but Lee continued north with crowds gathering at every stop. Richmond's surpassed several thousand and he entered the capital on April 12, 1898, where a waiting carriage, escorted by two bicycles, took him to the State Department. After briefing Day he spent time with McKinley then testified before the Senate's foreign relations committee.

In Tampa, Evans left her second floor room for Hotel Arno's ornate front porch on the same level as her room. Barton had shifted to a house with her Red Cross staff while the reporter extended her booking in the three-story brick building since the stay's length was unknown and there was a first floor dining room and parlor. Five days later, Barton left for Washington without warning. The Red Cross leader found little for her in Tampa besides visiting locals, giving interviews, and a picnic. Evans was ready to leave for Key West when Tyson confirmed the expedition to take Havana would assemble then embark from Port Tampa. The delay proved providential for her since it aligned with several uncomfortable days addressing a periodic affliction, including one in bed.

Evans spent this interval in thought. The nation must change dramatically from the coming war so she was determined to cover it despite unsettling premonitions. These could not be described and she was unable to settle on whether they affected Starke, Tyson, herself, or anyone in particular. The naval officer seemed unable to avoid conflict, the correspondent's luck already carried him though one war she knew of, and the first Cuban affliction still haunted her. Strangely, it was the second she was most concerned with.

Tyson reluctantly joined bored reporters cajoling stories from sailors, workmen, and refugees flooding Key West; while monitoring the graying squadron. Temperatures often hovered near 100 degrees with expenses climbing faster. Obtaining a Hotel Key West room proved a genuine triumph with scarce hallway cots running five dollars a night. Everything on the island was shipped in so beer hit twenty-five cents, lemonade twenty, and water from the hotel's steel cistern was not given away. Meanwhile, his life after Havana devolved into short bursts of suspense punctuating constant boredom. In desperation and to escape the hot top-floor room he occasionally joined correspondents in chairs lining the long front porch; often joining *The New York Herald*'s Richard

Harding Davis and Walter Meriwether. Meals were taken in the hotel or across the street at Madame Bolio's. When he found nothing else to do there was always gambling at the Eagle Bird where Stephen Crane was a reliable patron. The famous author was an acquaintance from the Greek war; where Tyson also met Crane's extraordinary common-law wife, Cora. He filed stories on *Mascotte*'s last Havana run bringing out 900 refugees and the Plant line shutting down their Mobile route until its ships would be safe. It also sounded as if Captain, now Rear Admiral, Sampson was promoted over several others and a Roosevelt friend; but Tyson wanted to confirm that, perhaps through Starke.

This interlude ended Thursday when a boy propped his bicycle against the hotel porch and handed Meriwether a telegram; interrupting their critique of customers patronizing a cigar shop across the street; wedged between a tailor's establishment and drugstore. The wording was nonsensical code but told Meriwether a Cuban blockade was announced and war was coming in days if not hours. Sweat-stained correspondents exploded from island lethargy to gather reactions. Tyson headed for the naval station, thinking Forsyth might allow a tug to drop him off at *Calypso*, if already making runs. After turning at the First National Bank he passed civilian coal piles and sheds sheltering the Navy cache.

During his walk to the Navy's building he considered competing stories. There was the disaster in Alaska's goldfields, a British army was approaching the Mahdi's capital, and rumor had it Lieutenant Ramon de Carranza, after delivering Spain's report on *Maine*, planned to challenge Lee and Sigsbee to duels. Both suggested Spanish officers were the culprits during a Senate hearing and the lieutenant, who commanded a Cuban gunboat for three years, saw their unchallenged accusations an insult to Spanish honor requiring satisfaction. He felt obligated, especially with Havana's dueling mania, and was reputed to be expert with sword or pistol. An earlier generation of American naval officers and others would have been quick to give satisfaction but dueling had been prohibited for years in the Navy and out of fashion since the war. Tyson often wondered how Starke avoided challenges during his time in Havana then concluded it was down to a reticent nature, expertise with sword or pistol, and reputation for not making gestures.

Constance Starke was upset but sanguine when war came on April 25, 1898. It was no surprise despite some predicting a blockade would force Spain from Cuba without war. Madrid had been consistent in how they would reply and acquiesced in every demand except independence; which they promised in late summer. Washington dismissed this assurance almost out of hand, with some justification, as a ploy to gain time. Immanuel had warned acquaintances Spanish honor would not accept a blockade but his voice and others made no difference with both publics demanding war, the Junta blocking any compromise, jingoes baying loudly, and press attacking anyone not sufficiently belligerent as weak or cowardly. Her husband met with Captain Albert several times. Both saw war as inevitable in spite of Speaker Reed and the administration's effort to restrain this tidal wave. Albert also asked her husband to speak with their shipping firm's Jewish ship-chandler about providing information to Commodore Dewey since Aron Sharett retained a representative who made regular trips between Hong Kong and Manila.

Washington's weather turned cooler with northerly winds as the blockade began and Cortes Generales acted. Constance thought it too soon to close the mansion's parlor shades since her favored afternoon spot was an alcove formed by its large turret. Even on cold days, sunlight passed effortlessly through tall windows into the room. She was pouring coffee into a semi-translucent bone china cup when sounds of carriage wheels, horses neighing, and shod hoofs shuffling came from the street. Minutes later a second cup was placed on the small table as Altman ushered Clarissa Barton through. Short, thin, and vigorous despite nearing eighty, the old friend walked fully erect. Constance sent an invitation to Barton after her return and pleasantly surprised she accepted. The American Red Cross founder exuded firmness of purpose with dyed-black hair center-parted then pulled tight above dark eyebrows to frame a broad countenance with prominent cheeks, ears, mouth, and nose. They met during the war when a younger Constance helped raise funds and gather medical supplies; and more recently for the reconcentrados.

Constance stood, "Clara; I'm glad you could visit."

"Nonsense, Constance, I was in town to speak with the president and Secretary Long about our relief ship. Besides, it's my only opportunity before returning to Key West."

"So soon?"

"Yes. I'm already a day late after missing my Jacksonville connection. *State of Texas* left Saturday and should arrive late this week. I did obtain letters allowing relief supplies to pass though the blockade since reconcentrados are still starving. War requires nurses as well so we're ending our hospital's courses to support that."

Barton raised her coffee as Constance lowered, "I realize its sensitive ground but are you up to this?"

The older woman smiled, "I'm not yet on the shelf, Constance, and have good people. Hubbell and Duncan are on the ship and I travel with Egan, Cobb, and Lucy." She quickly changed subjects, "Cassandra Evans was with us until Tampa. She and Mr. Tyson spoke well of our effort in the newspapers.

I believe Jacob was in Key West at one point but never left *Olivette*."

"On his way to *Calypso*; I just received a letter. It seems the crew's too small and we're now helping filibusters so the Navy's trying to decide what to do with her."

Barton smiled from behind her coffee, "And still not married?"

Constance thought it too soon to mention their grandnephew, "I'm confident there will soon be something coming from him and Katherine Ledford."

Barton smiled, "Miss Evans would not be amiss either?"

"Perhaps not."

The Red Cross executive pivoted instantly to demands for trained nurses, recruiting problems, the Daughters of the American Revolution contribution, and plans to enroll immunes. Cynthia Jefferson straightened the table after Barton left then retreated to their downstairs kitchen. She once again seemed to have listened in on their conversation then went to Martella Young's domain. Constance might have thought this amounted to understandable curiosity but Cynthia remained downstairs some time; which usually meant she was after advice. Constance finished her coffee trying to understand why nothing had yet come from the Curtis family regarding marriage arrangements.

Katherine Ledford sat with her mother, Christiana Curtis, after America declared war on Spain. Brydian Grange's estate business was complete and the day's correspondence ready for posting so she could talk; and Katherine sensed this was no time to discuss marriage with Sir Miles Oliver Curtis. Her father was keeping to his study, he disliked Americans, and Starke fathered her son. Edward mentioned their father applauded the British and Egyptian victory over the Mahdists at Atbara River as payment for massacring Hicks and Gordon, but concerned with how Kitchener was limiting France's expansion in Africa. Europe seemed constantly on the brink of war. It came too close when Greece attempted to slice off more Ottoman territory and they were now back at the precipice with America provoking war over Cuba; so soon after backing Venezuela's dispute with Britain. Sir Curtis, like most Europeans, favored Spain but well aware without Great Britain leading a broad coalition the continent would split and trigger alliances. He was upset with Prime Minister Salisbury riding the fence since Britain's position was suffering from the Boer fiasco at the same time American and German industrial capabilities increased exponentially along with their naval ambitions.

Katherine remained conflicted about agreeing to marry but as the child's mother increasingly inclined to accept Starke. The letter offered his name to their son either way. Her brother became actively supportive after visits with his favorite lady at a house he frequented. She suspected this was Leonora Rhodes Triggs, the school friend lacking a fortune who chose one of few options open to unmarried women of their class. That choice and marriage severed their friendship but apparently not relations with Edward. Now that Katherine viewed herself as another fallen woman she felt morally free to surreptitiously renew it. Triggs was kind but blunt over tea. Jacob Starke was successful in a new country, of a prosperous family, and all but asked for her hand before learning of the child so, given the obstacles, must love her. Then, after some hesitation, Triggs pointed out this was Katherine's second opportunity for marriage to someone who appeared to love her when many women were fortunate to see one.

Lady Christiana Mari Curtis was uncharacteristically less delicate. She explained to her daughter that she grew to love her husband, did her duty, and understood men's needs but never encouraged those attentions. She emphasized families continued through women and Katherine's son was a Starke. Lady Curtis went further than Katherine experienced previously by summing, "I suggest you ask yourself if another child is possible were he here. I've never felt the passion you seem to experience with Jacob so the only question becomes whether he is worthy. We are often betrayed by strong feelings for the wrong sort since they sometimes exert the greatest attraction before marriage."

It was a strange conversation, probably the first and last such with her mother. That evening Katherine stared at her sleeping son for a long time then spent a restless night. As the morning sun illuminated her room she worried some did not return from wars.

❦

Chapter Twenty-One
War Cruise

Lieutenant Jacob Starke set his desk calendar to April 22, 1898, then left for the flying bridge. Sweepers were piped earlier and daily call to issue freshwater rations would follow. At seven-thirty, less than an hour away, the crew would breakfast in various messes. At the flying bridge lifelines, stripped of their canvas screens, he swept Key West's harbor and approaches with Bausch & Lomb binoculars. The North Atlantic Squadron under newly promoted Rear Admiral Sampson on *New York* was preparing to exit through the Southwest Channel then blockade Cuba's north coast. Some ships were from the European Squadron, recently called home. Once white and straw-yellow, they were now mud-gray. Some others in port were still partly painted black, the color originally chosen for war, but would soon be gray, except colliers, to comply with Department direction. *Calypso's* makeover continued, to Starke's distaste. Gray paint might confuse ranging and gunlaying but made an elegant lady dowdy.

The squadron flagship would not be directing the morning colors that officially began each workday in port. When *New York* was present the surrounding crews paused at their tasks while her band played *The Star Spangled Banner*. Afterwards, Day Orders that precisely followed the flagship's routine were executed and the steam pinnace began rounds. Since *Calypso* came from Cienfuegos a month before she floated placidly in a laminate of labor, frenzy, boredom, and ritual with early morning proclaimed by a brilliant sun boring through Starke's cabin windows. Navy and merchant traffic streamed through the port's channels with little control. Starke thought this cavalier with *Vizcaya* and *Almirante Oquendo* absent from Havana and a torpedo boat flotilla at sea since mid-March. Others shared his concern so all warships manned at least one mount. Many now coaled at Fort Jefferson in Dry Tortugas but black-painted water barges from Port Tampa still passed regularly. Fort Taylor and the Marine Hospital appeared unchanged but were undergoing modernization. Sunset soon became most days' highlight when the western horizon exploded into a kaleidoscope of colors beyond several small keys and intervening ships; while sailors searched for the green flash then lied about spotting it.

Starke was making headway on administration since *Calypso* was no longer chasing filibusters or delivering relief cargo; and still technically assigned to the Special Service Squadron. This ambiguity also left him answerable to Albert, two squadrons, and almost any senior commander present. Sampson's small staff showed little interest because a depleted crew meant she was poorly manned for any task except those better accomplished by a less valuable ship. To escape this limbo-like state Starke gambled on a candid letter to the Bureau of Navigation; including a specific request for replacement of the gun captains lost to a new gunboat that had yet to commission.

A letter received from his aunt described the rush to enlist and schemes proposing battalions of athletes, cowboys, female sharpshooters, Indians, and more. Meanwhile, firms like Starke Shipping & Shipbuilding, or people with expensive seaside homes, were less enthusiastic. Others panicked that a Spanish cruiser might visit them after watching American

Mutoscope Company's moving pictures of *Vizcaya*'s high, black hull slice through water off New York before racing down the East Coast for Havana. Like Plant, his uncle directed company ships to remain in port. The Navy had approached him about chartering *Eveleth* but Starke was puzzled there had been no Army inquiries since she was far better suited to carry soldiers than conversion to an armed merchant cruiser. His uncle was also frustrated American and British investors holding Spanish-Cuban bonds were more concerned with avoiding their repudiation than war. Some shippers were also cashing in on high profits by racing for Caribbean ports then transshipping cargoes to Cuba. A postscript asked about his son and Katherine; signaling there was still nothing from Katherine's family.

Ships off to blockade Cuba began lifting anchors and joining the outgoing gaggle. Sampson was forming his cruising formation in deep water beyond the sea buoy so captains were told to avoid hitting anyone then find their station. Those underway first were threading through anchored ships to assume a rough line beyond the channels; leaving long overlapping wakes and trailing light gray smoke that tinted a cloudless blue sky. The large armored cruiser *New York* was easily distinguished by distinct ram bow, fine lines, and silhouette displaying firepower and speed; aesthetics partly obscured by paint. *Indiana* and *Iowa*, along with *Amphitrite*, gave him added muscle. The first was part of a three battleship class, with two short stacks, low freeboard, fighting mast, two massive 13-inch turrets and four 8-inch mounts. The second was a faster, improved version with towering stacks, raised forecastle, and 12-inch main battery. The monitor *Amphitrite* was an anachronism that took twenty years to commission but her 10-inch battery contributed significant striking power. She also offered little in way of a target but low freeboard meant she plowed though most seas with main deck regularly submerged. Picking out the other gunboats and cruisers required familiarity, especially under gray paint. Some no longer bottle-green torpedo boats detailed as the large ships' tenders could be seen near their charges. The dynamite cruiser *Vesuvius* that Starke visited off Mayport stood out. She was frail, unhandy, and another miserable sea boat. The monitor *Terror* was left behind, like *Mangrove* and *Fern*, but visible at anchor from the flying bridge.

Starke was about to lay below when he recognized a vaguely familiar ship gliding up Southeast Channel with fine lines and counter stern suggesting ex-warship or yacht. A vestigial bowsprit and truncated main mast aft of the small pilothouse and flying bridge suggested she once carried a full sail rig. Amidship forward of her mast was a deckhouse with large windows; then aft of that a short stack and four boats under radial davits resting in frames that passed over and across her deck. He initially suspected she was one of many press boats trailing the squadron that experienced a casualty or arrived late and forced to coal. She could also be sailing for the Junta since filibustering was no-longer an offense. As this latest arrival passed, he suspected it was the ship that overtook *Calypso* during sea trials then confirmed it through binoculars by reading *Carte Blanche* on her counter.

Captain Buff stood inside unscreened wire rope lifelines encircling *Carte Blanche*'s small flying bridge, examining *Calypso* through Goerz binoculars. When he first spotted her amongst other gray shapes his powerful, sun-reddened neck compacted to fleshy rolls, sweat increased beneath his arms, and some trickled down from the dark visored-cap's hatband. The morning warmed quickly, but seconds later his attention turned to the quarantine officer about to board. By the time he looked back they were beyond the customs house piers and entering a congested harbor requiring full attention.

Tyson stood on the tugboat *Nezinscot*'s upper deck as *Carte Blanche* ghosted past the naval station pier. The air smelled of harbor, burning coal, and steam as a rising sun burned off what little temperature relief came overnight. This informal sortie was to allow Acting Boatswain John Holden time to become familiar with the roadstead. Besides supporting the blockade, she might be detailed to patrol port entrances, assist quarantine officials, and conduct local towing. Her Navy crew of fourteen was five more than in civilian service, the eighty-five-foot hull painted gray, and a 6-pounder mounted on her fore deck. The tug's solitary ornamentation was a golden eagle above the pilothouse's curved face. A thick, woven-line pushing fender cushioned her stem and sausage-like side fenders girded the steel hull.

Tyson heard Holden order mooring lines cast off as *Carte Blanche* cleared, felt the engine throb, and watched her stern swing out from the steel pier. More rudder and engine orders followed once the master was satisfied with his angle; then she backed into the stream, placed her stern up harbor, and headed south. The squadron's departure allowed Tyson to board *Calypso* for the first time during this stay. He had exchanged notes with Starke but they were of little or no importance since spies or rumors of them were plentiful.

Nezinscot hailed *Calypso* then touched her cushioned bow against the port side where no accommodation ladder was rigged. Tyson accomplished gymnastics familiar to pilots as strong arms helped lift him through the bulwark gangway. He spoke with Martyn who escorted him to the main cabin where Starke's table was obviously cleared of work just moments before. The owner stood beside it, hand outstretched, "Welcome aboard Darwin; please take a seat. I'd offer lemonade but we've none on board. Yamashita's finding supplies hard to come by ashore. There is wine."

"Thank you, Jacob. It was a hot trip out; perhaps some tonic water?"

The Japanese cabin steward anticipated this and brought two tall glasses of clear liquid from the pantry. Once he left, Tyson glanced about, extracted a flask from his jacket, and grinned at Starke before adding little better than a shot, "Some gin to ward off dehydration."

Starke twisted his glass, leaving a moist circle on the table, while his friend downed a healthy swallow, "I thought you'd be birddogging Sampson?"

"Lord chartered *Kanapaha* this month and sent her down for that, but I've no say in those operations. Laffin runs the news bureau so I expect some accommodation was reached."

Starke knew several press boats were ex-filibuster tugs so Pierpont Morgan's first yacht would stand out. She was schooner rigged with a thin stack rising from the sleek, black hull; and fast. Tyson continued, "Packard's master and Chamberlain's in charge. I'm to remain in Key West for my sins and coordinate our office but have limited authority to charter."

"What about Cassandra?"

"She's trying to go with the Army. I doubt they'll let her get near any fighting even if she gets credentials; and the Navy doesn't allow women aboard ships. I'm trying to convince her she's more valuable in Washington with her old sources but without success. What's *Calypso* up to?"

"Hard to say. There's crew enough for transport or running dispatches. If fully manned, she could scout but never face steel warships."

"I hear one Spaniard might disagree. Your fight with that gunboat off Pinar de Rio is leaking out. I assume you won't be coming ashore for a while."

"No; while we're at war I must remain . . ."

Starke was interrupted by knocking and saw Tyson's antennae quiver. The messenger reported a flag signal from *Terror* summoning *Calypso*'s captain so he rose, "It seems Captain Ludlow desires my presence and I doubt he's in a charitable mood after being left behind with *Fern* and *Mangrove*. He's senior officer afloat so I must go and don't know how long this will take. I can offer a ride."

"I would appreciate it, but Forsyth arranged for the tug to swing by. If I could interview some of your officers and crew until then?"

Loosing reporters on board was unpredictable but Tyson was a friend and once done it might fend off future incursions by the wolf packs prowling Key West. Besides, he deserved something. Starke called for Watson and began changing once they left for the wardroom.

His gig was one of *Calypso*'s steam pinnaces, already waiting at the accommodation ladder when Starke stepped into a midday sun. Coxswain Melvin stood under its spotless white canvas canopy as the compact boiler's polished brass stack released vapor into the heat. Watson and Chief Weaver saw their captain through the open gangway and watched him settle in its sternsheets. Besides the coxswain, there was Ensign Martyn, two seamen, a fireman, and coal-passer. Melvin cast off aft when Starke nodded, twisted his stern, and took in the forward line as he backed. Moments later they were chugging towards the monitor. *Terror*'s nearly 4,000 tons looked taller and more massive from a small boat. Most of the large ship lay below placid green water so she appeared more like a floating battery; especially with two large turrets housing a pair of 10-inch breech-loading rifles and squarish superstructure bristling with small-caliber weapons.

Terror's executive officer, Lieutenant Commander Garat greeted Starke as he stepped on her broad steel deck to honors. They entered the gray superstructure near her large aft turret, passed through a short hallway separating work spaces for captain and executive officer then went down a massive battle hatch into the berthing deck. Transition through the armored deck that let her fight with superstructure destroyed imparted mixed feelings of security and claustrophobia. They walked aft, around the turret base, and through a wardroom flanked by stateroom doors. Beyond a long table, solidly fixed athwartship, they went through another space before entering her captain's cabin. Below deck prisms lighting that cabin was a center table with one stateroom on either side.

Captain Nicoll Ludlow was sitting at the table but stood as Starke entered with Garat. The thin officer with center-parted white hair and prominent mustache commanded the steam screw sloop *Quinnebaug* a year after the Alexandria bombardment. The monitor's second commanding officer earned a reputation for incorruptibility and courtesy; as did his brother, an army colonel. Garat left quietly and Ludlow motioned Starke to a chair, "Captain, I felt we should speak in private. *Terror* leaves for Cardenas once repairs are complete; within the hour if all goes well."

Starke had thought it odd the monitor's canvas awnings were not rigged fore and aft if she was staying in Key West but sensed this prefaced something else so his response was limited to, "Yes, sir."

"I believe you arrived from Cienfuegos a few days before me. I need a tender when at sea and considered *Calypso*, but you were under the Special Service Squadron and lack a towing capability. Anyway, something else has come up. Sampson received orders to blockade Cuba but pushed back since there aren't enough colliers to cover its southern coast. Washington agrees but still wants Cienfuegos blockaded, so a fourth division is forming under Commander McCalla on *Marblehead*. *Nashville* and *Eagle* will join him if they haven't already. That gives him a cruiser, gunboat, and converted yacht. However, there's not a useful sail rig between them so they'll be returning here to coal."

Starke shifted uneasily as Ludlow continued, "The admiral's requested *Calypso*'s transfer to the North Atlantic Squadron but will join the fourth division as dispatch boat for the time being."

Calypso's captain was careful responding. In theory, she would only carry messages back and forth; but any blockading ship required a larger than normal crew. His was barely enough to carry out their filibuster mission before sailors were stripped away."

Ludlow looked at him sympathetically, "Manning?"

"Exactly, sir. I've crew enough for an armed transport or dispatch boat if not forced to fight or provide a prize crew."

"I spoke briefly with Forsyth. Supplies, coal, and munitions are pouring in without planning and he has only one paymaster. Replacements should be coming as well. His plate's full with Sampson at sea but has agreed to endorse your request and do what he can without a receiving ship. I suggest you make *Calypso*'s needs known before Commodore Remey and his staff arrive."

"I appreciate that and will get it to him."

Ludlow rose, "Excellent, Captain. Expect sailing orders late today or early tomorrow. Is there anything more?"

Starke sensed the meeting was over, "No, sir."

"Then I'll walk you to the quarterdeck."

They shook hands under a searing Key West sun and Melvin was soon pulling away from the low, massive hull. Steering for *Calypso*, he noted their captain's dark mood. *Terror* was underway two hours later.

Melvin was again summoned to ferry his captain shortly after *Terror* vanished. This trip was to the naval station's steel pier. After passing coal barges waiting on dock space and Army mining preparations, they moored then waited while Starke delivered a letter to Forsyth and visited Hotel Key West. The station commander agreed to cable the Department but cautioned *Calypso* was a minor item. His current priority was negotiating with the Army for ammunition bunkers; and leasing warehouses, wharfs, and dockage for the avalanche of supplies and munitions arriving. Bunkers for coal, dredging, and other construction projects were also beginning. Forsyth hoped Commodore George Remey's arrival from Portsmouth Naval Shipyard would alleviate some turmoil by establishing an officer under Sampson senior to any ship commander or captain in port; but was treading water until then.

Starke planned to visit Tyson before returning, and would normally send their gig back to the ship, but could not be ashore without transport during war so it must remain; with a crew restricted to the naval station. This would ensure they were available and was necessary because the situation ashore had changed. Mainland construction workers inundated the island and many shared the same fondness for drink and brawling as the fighting redhead Flynn. Some residents resented the 25th Infantry, a blue-uniformed Colored unit with a number of soldiers feeling the same about their hosts. Since the infantry outnumbered police, always less than a half-dozen, it held the whip hand. Forsyth said they just removed a comrade from jail several days earlier and locals were receiving little press sympathy, especially in the North.

Consequently, many Key West residents were keeping to homes and businesses.

Hotel Key West's front porch hosted fewer lounging reporters when Starke crossed and entered its spacious central lobby. The obliging desk clerk sent a runner to Tyson's room, which avoided squeezing through upstairs hallways filled with cots. Meanwhile, he took a table in its east-side dining room and waited.

The Sun correspondent, now Laffin News Bureau local manager, extracted a Turkish cigarette from its silver case as he sat, "This is a welcome surprise, Jacob, and perfect timing since I was coming down for dinner. Spent the day casting about to charter a filibuster and hire a master with experience making runs to Cuba."

"Any success?"

"Strangely, yes; I'm considering your old friend Captain Buff. *Carte Blanche*'s been working Pinar del Río and the south coast."

Starke looked at an amused Tyson. So the late *John Gwinn Williams*, *Astraea*, and *Rafael Riego*'s master now skippered *Carte Blanch*. He slowly rotated his wine glass' base; thinking water was an even greater a luxury on the island and how local sources made many sick unless boiled for tea, "On your head be it, Darwin. He's no amateur and not shy but the Spanish will kill him on sight and perhaps those with him. I've no interest since filibustering turned legal."

Tyson laughed, "He's not quite as charitable. I believe arrogant bastard was his kindest description."

"Not surprising. *Calypso* was involved in sinking three of his ships. Fachtna Harler's a first class filibuster so you'll get stories; but cost is the question."

"I prefer calculated risk over sitting on the porch like a potted plant or wasting time on timid masters; but what occasions this visit?"

Starke raised his hand and their waiter entered from a kitchen at the rear, "*Calypso* will be leaving for Cuba and I hoped to make up for earlier today."

They spoke throughout the meal then enjoyed a brief smoke in the parlor on the hotel's far side. Soon after Starke's return to the pier, Melvin's pinnace started down channel as evening began its lackluster effort to cool the day. The crew's time pierside, free of their daily routine, had been used for undisturbed maintenance so Melvin's mood was far better than his captain's.

The next day found Starke at the flying bridge's lifelines; feeling naked without their white canvas. With the number of ships in port Conrad was even more insistent they anchor in water flowing through the Northwest Channel and southwest of the Middle Ground; and fill tanks from one of the freshwater barges towed from Port Tampa. Just north of their anchorage, two buoys with fading paint and white bird droppings displayed no life beyond water lapping alongside. A white and gray seagull landed on one while others glided over it and the steam pinnace returning from a final mail run. *Calypso* was to rendezvous with fourth division off Cienfuegos on or about the twenty-ninth and the only response to his request for sailors was a coded Albert telegram stating he would look into it.

Calypso's accommodation ladder had been raised and stowed so Melvin maneuvered the pinnace under waiting boat falls where it was lifted from translucent emerald water, lowered onto boat chocks, and secured for sea with gripes. A light, intermittent breeze was flavored with the blended smell of paint, coal, grease, and harbor. With Sampson away, the port and approaches edged towards normal, although the waterfront below Man 'o War harbor was active with ships offloading to piers, wharfs, and warehouses. *Mangrove*, *Fern*, and several barges were also there. An adventurous or desperate dirty-white sponger was outbound under sail, towing small dinghies. Activity at Fort Taylor showed modernization work was beginning. Offshore were reasonably distinct buoys, small keys, bright shallows, and the distant, sparkling boundary between a clear blue sky and translucent blue-green sea with scattered whitecaps.

Watson intruded to report they were ready to get underway without a pilot. Dunbar had plotted their exit through Southwest Channel, Weaver stood ready with his anchor party, and engineering signaled ready to answer all bells. A depleted crew diminished fighting capability but not routine evolutions, their executive officer was a skilled shiphandler, and Newfoundlander Marius Moreau was on the helm. There was little for Starke to do besides give permission, watch for anything untoward, and prepare for some crisis.

The stocked anchor rose slowly from a hard sand bottom with little hosing required and soon swung from its davit ready for letting go. The instant it broke ground, *Calypso's* steam whistle blasted and her ensign went up the mizzenmast halyard. Watson came full ahead immediately, turning starboard towards Fort Taylor and the main channel. As the bark gained speed, Starke anticipated their next visit would be more challenging with the minefields planted; even if remote-controlled. Once in the channel they used Whitehead Point and Fort Taylor to alter course three times; steaming a path marked by buoys and obstructions. The Middle Ground passed after set and drift correction. The new course ran a southwest and quarter west bearing from Key West lighthouse until Satan Shoal was left to port. More gray smoke smudges than usual marred the bright horizon when Watson requested permission to secure for sea. Starke gave it then looked up as a solitary seagull glided smoothly overhead, its head looking down on the ship and orange beak squawking shrill warning. *Calypso* was at sea during war with a skeleton crew.

The forenoon watch was set and sick call sounded as the bark cut through a docile Caribbean. Their new course, held four hours, put off bucking the Florida Current and set them up for turning south into the Yucatán Channel. Shortly after noon sights, she heeled slightly while coming starboard to south by west and a quarter west. They held it twenty-four hours. Starke could have continued further south then followed the Pinar del Río coast but one of Spain's larger gunboats might be at sea and *Calypso* outclassed even with a full complement. Prize-taking was also out of the question since there was no way to hold prisoners and releasing them ashore with insurrectos about would be murder. Looking out his cabin's port side open window, while unconsciously adjusting to the bark's slow, rhythmic, gentle thrusts, Starke decided Pinar del Río's outlying islands, coastal, channel and shoreline must stay beyond the horizon. Even so, he pictured sand and shell beaches sloping up from shimmering blue and green-hued water behind black coral reefs and mangrove-covered islets running from Bahia Honda to Cabo San Antonio; with the green border of tall palms and bushes less than a stone's throw inland.

Staysails were raised for stability; square sails for practice and airing when the weather was favorable. *Calypso* turned due south after noon sights and entered results in the deck log for April 28, 1898. They transited Yucatán Channel without issue; passing within nine miles of Cabo San Antonio. From their calculations, Starke, Watson, and Dunbar agreed *Calypso* was on track despite lack of manmade navigational aids. Patent log malfunctions had ended, to Dunbar's relief, and they were registering nearly nine knots, with speed over ground close to seven on some legs; so *Calypso* remained an excellent steamer even on one boiler. Turn-to, sweepers, and hoist ashes were piped during the last dog watch; when they turned port to east by south. That course would clear the large Isle of Pines and avoid shipping lanes. Starke saw little value boarding any ships; especially since joining fourth division off Cienfuegos on the twenty-ninth was only just achievable and he had no desire to be late; especially if attributed to hunting prizes.

Dunbar called Starke to the pilothouse as the morning watch began, preparing for the turn that would take them down islands and shallows between Isle of Pines and Cayo Largo, then another port turn to nearly due east. The crew was familiar with the journey's clear shoal water and routine from their first passage. Starke ordered the second boiler placed on line that afternoon and speed increased. *Calypso* turned north for Cienfuegos when the first watch relieved and Dunbar estimated an arrival just after midnight. Starke wanted to keep to orders and stay alert since fourth division was blockading the port and *Calypso* would rendezvous in the dark. Despite and because of the war he had running lights lit and kept searchlights ready; but the only sightings were imagined by a nervous crew half asleep near their battle stations.

Starke spent the remaining night moving between pilothouse and flying bridge; then climbed the foremast just after their lookout went up at first light. Leaving pipe and cap to a sailor, he stepped up on the bulwark, then the weather shrouds, and began climbing with hands grasping shrouds not ratlines. The tar was tacky from a rising sun with almost no breeze as their ship moved slowly through a still morning.

Instinctively, he took the topman route using futtock shrouds rather than lubber's hole and acquired a thick black streak on his trousers Yamashita would find difficult to remove. Seaman Kearney was perched on an upper yard with one hand holding paired-telescopes and the other a section of standing rigging serving that kept grease and blacking at bay. Their best lookout had somehow avoided being poached while *Calypso* was repaired; or his propensity for drink was too well known. Below his climbing captain, Kearney saw sailors reclining near guns, their navigator watching Starke ascend, and Negro lead stoker Delmar Kemp jawboning with other black-gangers up for air. Chief Weaver and Landsman Mallory Hawk were examining an anchor's strapping on the forecastle and the captain's steward headed aft with fishing equipment; trailed by Thaddeus on one of his few underway paroles to the main deck.

Starke nodded to the lookout, caught his breath, and then asked, "Nothing in sight, Kearney?"

"Not a thing, Captain; looks peaceful enough over there. Fishing boats were coming out but saw us and went back up the channel. No ships and no smoke, a right fine morning."

Chapter Twenty-Two
Close Blockade

Calypso's commander scanned horizon then shoreline. They were roughly two miles off the narrow channel lined with mangroves. That twisting passage might be concealed but its location was unmistakable. Lowland on the western side rose steeply near the mud-yellow El Jagua Castle and its eastern bank lifted slightly to a chaparral-cloaked ridge just inshore from Puenta de los Colorados lighthouse and cable station. Local traffic, primarily the pilot schooner and fishing boats, was absent and no telling what lay over the horizon but he must assume the gunboats would be in port; including Teniente de Navio Arino's torpedo gunboat *Galicia*.

A sister ship, *Pedro Menéndez de Avilés*, was fought to a standstill by *Calypso* less than a year earlier but expecting anything similar against a lightly armored steel ship, even with the full crew, was unlikely. *Galicia* dominated the channel entrance with guns, torpedoes, and shore battery support. Given the opportunity, she might strike *Calypso* when her guard was down, sandwich her with the assistance of an arriving warship, or sortie to support a blockade runner. Starke recalled one Jefferson Classical and Military Academy lecturer. The bitter skeptic with bushy gray beard and wooden leg claimed all wars had six sequences. Under his schema, Starke saw *Calypso's* crew moving from naivety to anxiety with resignation, barbarity, remorse, and denial still in the future. He also urged students to recognize the uncertain balance between timidity and caution; and danger of decisions based expected actions rather than capability. Starke saw this play out during the Montana expedition but was just one of a thousand then.

He descended through the lubber's hole then retrieved cap and pipe once back on the deck. Blue-green water could be heard flowing along bark's flank in a stream of ripples and bubbles under the bulwark. Command seemed especially lonely and executive officers could be useful sounding boards. The increasing reliance on Watson and confidence in his ability resulted from the officer's performance since they first met in Albert's office. The Colorado sailor soon entered his warm cabin with light, faltering cross-breeze coming through open windows. Starke motioned him to a chair, "Good morning XO. It seems we're left to our own devices and I'd like your thoughts."

"Yes, sir. Fourth division's definitely pulled stakes."

"We're obliged to maintain the blockade until relieved or forced to coal but I doubt we'll be alone long since railroads linking Cienfuegos with Havana make this port one that needs watching . In the meantime, it's on us to avoid getting caught between any arrivals and the port's gunboats. We've enough crew to remain on station and can save coal keeping one boiler online and the other ready. Weaver can raise topsails when the wind favors. Have Blair and Poniatowski pick out and drill a forward gun crew and see what can be done aft. Also, revise general quarters billets to put the best sailors we have on our forward mount, one 3-pounder, and a Gatling. Your thoughts?"

Watson remained slouched in the chair, a favored thinking position, before responding, "One boiler's risky but it's that or return to Key West sooner. I've one suggestion."

"Let's hear it, XO"

"The Dons are digging in near the lighthouse. We could strike before they've placed artillery and might get lucky with the lighthouse or cable station. The crew would have an opportunity to shoot and *Calypso* to appear more threatening."

"Sampson's been ordered not to risk ships against land batteries but I doubt there'll be more than a few light field pieces or we're thought irreplaceable. Probing their defenses could prove useful. I'll consider it."

Calypso rang in May with four passes by lighthouse, beach, and cable station. These east-west runs were made 500 to 1,000 yards off Puenta de los Colorados to avoid the shallows between it and Punta de Barreras. Lighthouse and stone cable building, both painted white, were near the dark rock outcropping that dropped several yards to a narrow pebble and coral beach. Chief Owen sighted his stadimeter on the lighthouse, a known height, and then called out accurate ranges that steadily decreased. His was the only voice on *Calypso*'s flying bridge. Starke smelled coal smoke drift forward with a breeze from astern; only slightly faster than their passage through blue-green water. Three sailors stood at the forward 4-inch 40 caliber mount with the other five in its crew lined up nearby in various states of undress; as were the rest of the ship. The risk of a split shell case, hang-fire, misfire, or hearing loss clearly vexed the gun crew more than their benign targets. Starke could not say whether they found it a relief or unnerving Conrad transformed the wardroom to deal with these cases or worse; and Chief Carpenter's Mate Cheney Lefebvre standing up a repair party aft.

The guns were released to fire once they had a target so the forward captain motioned and a 4-inch brass projectile was lifted from the small ready-service magazine, brought to his open breech, and thrust home. After ensuring it was seated, the breech-block was closed and locked with a long lever. His two assistants then turned bronze hand-wheels to train the mount while he twirled a small one under the breech to point its long, black barrel; all while squinting through iron sights. Time passed and Starke reminded of two crack gun captains lost during repairs; then the sailor stepped clear, warned those nearby to cover ears, and jerked the lanyard.

There was a deafening crack and brilliant muzzle flash followed by a gray-black cloud enveloping the forward mount. This detonation transmitted throughout the ship and its muzzle blast reached the flying bridge. Starke thought he caught sight of the round in flight, but near pointblank range meant he could not be certain. It clearly screamed between lighthouse and cable station to explode against the low ridge, scattering dirt, brush, and chaparral. The portside 3-pounder followed with rounds glancing from the lighthouse into the brush or exploding near the cable building. It was poor shooting for near-perfect weather at stationary white targets little more than 500 yards away; but each pass improved and perhaps they damaged cable equipment or weakened thick lighthouse walls. Figures bolting from cover, most not wearing uniforms, confirmed improvised defenses had been under construction along the ridge.

A man knocked on Starke's cabin door while he entered the previous day's shooting in his personal log. Sunrise was just observed. His desk calendar read "MON MAY 02 98" and a look at the round brass wall clock showed eight o'clock was near. Boatswains piped their first iteration for stowing hammocks and Dunbar was reducing his morning twilight observations. The landsman from Martyn's morning watch entered, saluted, and reported smoke had been spotted along the coast below Puenta de los Colorados to the southeast just as they prepared to come about and steam due west past the channel mouth. Martyn was holding course and asking instructions. Starke thanked his excited messenger and said he would come to the bridge.

Calypso's commander entered the pilothouse, spoke briefly with Dunbar and Martyn, then climbed the foremast; passing through the lubber's hole since he carried Bausch & Lomb binoculars. The port section landsman, Hawk, was wedged in Kearney's perch and clearly uncomfortable with his captain's presence. Starke acknowledged him then scanned horizon and shore. Some masts and tall structures could be seen across the bay near Cienfuegos but no steamer smoke. Off the coast to their southeast was a blurred spot on the horizon. The distance suggested someone burning poor coal, but whether warship or coastal steamer was undiscernible.

At the rear of *Calypso*'s mahogany pilothouse, Starke bent over a chart to consider possibilities. There was no blockade along Cuba's southern coast so they were likely coming from Santiago or Jamaica. If neutrals out of Jamaica they would be merchants *Calypso* was obliged to board but Spanish coastal steamers regularly moved troops since roads were little more than paths besieged by disease, pests, and insurgents. One of these would add a bewildering plethora of issues, illustrated by the *Kowshing* incident four years before. It was also just possible this smoke came from *Reina Mercedes'* twin stacks. Her Havana sister, *Alfonso XII*, could not get underway since local Spanish warships suffered from poor maintenance and worse coal but *Reina Mercedes* was at sea long enough the year before to drop a round off *Valencia*'s bow. The steel-hulled cruiser carried six 160mm guns; half again the size of *Calypso*'s 4-inch mounts and three times as many. This overmatch held with 6-pounder and 3-pounder batteries as well. In speed, the three *Alfonso XII* class ships might match his on paper but were proven slow and unreliable. Starke was confident *Calypso* would have three knots advantage, and the same with

Galicia or most other gunboats. However, maintaining a blockade that satisfied international law was impossible if ships on station fled at every sighting. Starke turned to the deck officer, "Please set general quarters Mr. Martyn, reduce speed to three knots, and come right to southeast and a half east."

Starke needed time. Slowing bought it and the turn would place *Calypso* seaward of what now appeared to be multiple ships. One might be assumed a neutral or merchant but several meant warships or a convoy. *Reina Mercedes* and an escort might be bound for Cienfuegos and rendezvous with a Spanish squadron. *Calypso* could outrun her but not an *Infanta María Teresa* class cruiser. *Almirante Oquendo* and *Vizcaya* left for Spain but either could have returned. If even one of the approaching ships was that class or a similar, *Calypso* was finished unless Starke retired immediately. Chances of surviving improved if this was a convoy escorted by *Galicia* or some other small gunboat; but not successfully maintaining a blockade since speed was Starke's only advantage.

Teniente de Navio Emiliano Mendoza y Aguilar looked above *Francisco de Montejo* to smoke billowing rich and black from his *Hernan Cortés* class gunboat. Three coastal steamers, more or less in his wake at varying intervals, were producing enough smoke for a shortsighted lookout to spot miles off. He should be patrolling off Puerto Rico but *Francisco de Montejo* was drafted over his objections to escort three ships steaming from Santiago to Cienfuegos; despite convoyed merchant ships losing some protection under international law

His gunboat was in Havana delivering dispatches when ordered to Santiago de Cuba with boiler parts for *Reina Mercedes* before the blockade; which was announced as they left the Morro astern in a morning sun. Mendoza entered Santiago's broad bay on April 22, 1898, to learn Spain declared war once American warships arrived off Havana. The States reciprocated then back-dated theirs to cover that blockade. His cargo was critical but could not cure the ills rendering seven of *Reina Mercedes'* ten boilers inoperable; and war temporarily confined him to Cuba's south coast. The nearly immobile cruiser's commander, Captain Pedro Aguirre y Sáenz de Juano, possessed only the small gunboat *Alvarado* to escort this convoy from Kingston, Jamaica, with uniforms, medical supplies, food, and munitions on its next leg to Cienfuegos. *Alvarado* was unsuited and configured to plant torpedoes but *Francisco de Montejo* was available and would not disrupt minelaying. It did not take Aguirre long to decide.

After pilots guided *Francisco de Montejo* and her charges through Santiago's treacherous channel they steamed west along the coast to Cabo Cruz. After turning northwest towards Cienfuegos the ships kept seaward of the coast's broad shallows, profuse shoals, and hundreds of small cays. After Trinidad, they closed Cuba's mountainous shore, little more than a mile off, steering northwest and a half west. This was feasible only because shoal water abruptly ended just yards from shore with an undersea cliff dropping many fathoms. When the terrain began sloping down, Mendoza started to believe their short cruise might prove uneventful; except for herding merchant masters with his too-slow ship. Most frustration centered on one, *Delmar Maldonado*. The owners were squeezing one last run before an overdue overhaul so her breakdowns ensured a struggle to keep station at the malleable column's rear. This dawdling left them approaching Cienfuegos' channel during early morning under a rising sun that illuminated their progress along the coast and ruined plans to arrive when the convoy would be less conspicuous and blockading ships more so.

Mendoza raised Zeiss binoculars to study coastline and horizon through the small pilothouse's open windows. The seasoned captain first saw action along the Moroccan coast during Spain's Melillan Campaign and commanded *Francisco de Montejo* since the small gunboat commissioned in a Scottish shipyard. While in Cuba she intercepted *Rafael Riego* and built a reputation for aggressively pursuing filibusters. As the flush-decked gunboat's ram bow parted calm, blue water, he longed for the fifteen-knot speed her triple-expansion engine was capable; but that required quality coal, and an overhaul to fully recover from *Rafael Riego*'s attack. The best she could make was ten and that generated smoke enough to broadcast her presence for miles; and the sixty-seven tons of coal bunkered no longer achieved her 3,000-mile design range. Even so, the 156-foot steel hull, twenty-two-foot beam, and seven-foot draft made her relatively effective patrolling coasts. Her main battery also suited that role, the two reliable 57mm Hotchkiss quick-firing guns anyway. Their 22mm twin-barreled Nordenfelt guns might be able to pierce thin-skinned ships to 1,500 yards but used a lever-firing mechanism that made them unreliable. Far ahead, the smoke just off the channel was hazy but unmistakable. If not a Cienfuegos gunboat coming to meet them it was probably a blockader, and almost any American warship outmatched him. He glanced towards the gun crew, already at their open mount, and sent the rest of the ship to stations.

Starke studied four emerging shapes through binoculars. The loose column was nearly bows-on so distinguishing anything was difficult. The lead ship appeared lower than those astern and none displayed a cruiser's bulk, so he altered course slightly to pass less than 2,000 yards seaward. *Calypso's* two 4-inch breech-loading rifles could reach 12,000 yards and fire eight rounds every minute with fixed ammunition and a well-drilled crew. Losing the two gun captains would hurt today's accuracy and rate; while bowsprit, deckhouse, and masts limited field of fire. Consequently, Starke wanted to keep these targets just under 2,000 yards off either beam; also a good range for their rapid-fire Hotchkiss 3-pounders with a 7,000 yard maximum. The .45-70 Gatling guns could travel the distance but not be effective.

The Navy regulations, customs, and legalities of prize-taking reviewed before leaving Key West were not helpful. The time spent mostly reaffirmed his opinion those references better served debate than practice and explain why prize courts were contentious. Convoyed ships could be seized but must be stopped, boarded, and crew left unharmed. That required disabling or drawing off the escort, which better fit bygone sailing ship operations. In addition, every merchant, Spanish or neutral, must be boarded or the blockade was legally broken. If fourth division had blockaded Cienfuegos, how long they were absent before *Calypso* arrived and reason Commander McCalla left station became factors. Blockading and convoy rules were only two aspects; and straightforward compared to those involving ship registry, cargo owners, and passengers since each must be separately addressed as prize, contraband, or neutral.

Range to the leading ship looked to be four or five miles and decreasing at a seemingly more rapid rate when Martyn hesitantly approached him, "Recognition signals, Sir?"

"No, Mr. Martyn, let's keep them guessing."

No other American ships were present so they were obliged to engage the gunboat but Starke did not want to give the game away too early. He already decided against a ruse like flying a Spanish flag then exchanging it before firing. *Calypso's* large battle ensign should have scattered unescorted belligerents; so he chose to hold course and scan the convoy for a merchant cruiser, gunboat, or armed transport through binoculars. Within minutes he saw men forming around an open mount on the leading ship's forecastle.

Mendoza held off while his crew stood to their guns. The approaching ship would pass down their rough column just under 2,000 yards to port but its masts blocked a clear view of the ensign. The ship or bark rig meant it was still possible he was looking at a merchantman leaving Cienfuegos and the port open; until a gun mount was spotted behind the bowsprit and forward of the mast. Simultaneously, the ship yawed enough, or wind shifted, to reveal her gray hull and American flag. He motioned with one hand and *Francisco de Montejo's* forward 57mm Hotchkiss emitted a brief flash, white smoke, and deafening flat crack. His gun crew had been in action before but had little live-fire practice due to Armada finances; and the target was over 2,000 yards off the port bow so accuracy was more hope than expectation. The ship was large enough a hit was possible; besides, this was the agreed signal to scatter the convoy. When there were no splashes after several seconds, Mendoza knew their round hit or passed over but was at least in line.

Starke saw the flash, smoke, and a small black dot that grew rapidly larger before screaming past overhead. It was a lucky or credible first round and more would follow. He turned to Yeoman Pound, "Please log the lead ship opened fire at eight forty-five."

Their small adversary was most likely steel-hulled with a weak main battery but might carry mobile torpedoes. Those astern seemed unarmed merchants but it was far from certain some guns had not been mounted. The first steamed roughly 500 yards off the gunboat's starboard quarter, the next directly astern at around 2,000 yards, and the third struggled to stay in line with the second; creating two loose columns. If any were armed, he guessed it would be the one astern of the gunboat to shield those inshore. There was no time for coming hard to port, crossing ahead of the gunboat, and unmasking his main battery; besides that exposed *Calypso* to a mobile torpedo. He held course and ordered full speed, knowing it would take effect after the gunboat went down their port side at just under 2,000 yards, but the delay gave his gunners an opportunity. A second scratch-crew was at the aft mount so both 4-inch rifles might get one or two rounds off. The 3-pounders should do better, and Gatlings received permission to fire; more for practice and morale. He could bypass the escort and rake the ships astern, but international law and Navy regulations forbid attacking unarmed merchant ships without boarding or being fired on by them.

The gunboat turned ninety degrees port to cut *Calypso*'s wake as the convoy raced for a shoreline bulge four miles east of the channel. Starke came starboard to counter then steadied just over ninety degrees off base course. This prevented his opponent from raking their undefended bow or stern and left both on roughly parallel southwest courses with *Calypso* ahead by 1,000 yards and increasing speed. Starke could identify their adversary as a *Hernan Cortés* class gunboat because *Calypso* assisted Teniente de Navio Mendoza's *Francisco de Montejo* after she was hit by *Rafael Riego*'s dynamite gun then accompanied her limp back to Havana. Mendoza would be off Puerto Rico, or in San Juan, but this commander seemed equally capable. He already forced *Calypso* to deal with him and bought the convoy time; a sound tactical move. Starke considered the man's options. The best seemed a starboard turn to fall in behind the convoy scurrying up the coast so *Calypso* increased speed past fourteen knots, causing her bow wave to grow steadily. The gunboat maintained around ten; probably all it could manage. Two more rounds flashed towards the bark but neither 4-inch mount was unmasked long enough to reply. Ensign Blair was holding fire until his guns were clear which severely tested the young officer's restraint. It was uncharacteristic and Starke made note to mention it later since shooting away *Calypso*'s bowsprit was the last thing desired.

The warships steamed a little better than east-northeast with *Calypso* just off the Spaniard's starboard quarter and about to pass. Only the port 3-pounder added burnt powder to steam and coal smells but the gunboat's aft 57mm Hotchkiss could reply and did. Starke felt a crash and explosion aft that Watson would have to deal with. Thinking the gunboat's shooting might improve, Starke let *Calypso*'s head fall off slightly starboard. That and her speed advantage cleared both 4-inch mounts to port for an unobstructed shot at their opponent, about 1,800 yards off. Their port 3-pounder fired, a Gatling opened up, and the forward 4-inch mount let fly.

Gun captains Grier and Kirby were missed, as were enough drills needed for Poniatowski to produce anything like their shooting. Watson cautioned Blair about ignoring safety for speed so the forward gun captain squinted over iron sights, sensing his ensign willing him to fire once a 4-inch brass shell slid into the breech and long locking lever sealed it. Two sailors beside him rotated bronze wheels while he twisted the elevating wheel. It was now or never with a calm sea and pointblank range. He sighted below the stack on her dark hull, warned the crew, held his breath, and jerked the lanyard. There was a flash, explosion, and air pressure slapping his face as recoil cylinders reached their end of travel. His feet felt the shock transmitted to *Calypso*'s deck as gray-black smoke hid their target and coated the crew with gritty dust. From the flying bridge, Starke saw a dark spot strike the water, skip, and detonate over and astern; framed by a handful of small splashes marking the 3-pounder's efforts. Their aft 4-inch mount's scratch crew with a more restricted field of fire followed. That round did not arc towards their target but struck calm water halfway across, lifted, landed again, and repeated just before striking the gunboat's starboard side at a slight angle. When there was no explosion, Starke knew their one hit was a dud. The 3-pounder continued hammering and 4-inch mounts loosed two salvos before the gunboat was past and *Calypso* steaming for the fleeing convoy. Some 3-pounders hit, or appeared to, but their only 4-inch round on target was the dud; and yet the gunboat began to slow and ceased firing.

The ship that saved *Francisco de Montejo* less than a year before just mortally wounded her. Teniente de Navio Mendoza stared quietly astern watching *Calypso* turn north towards the retreating convoy. Their lethal duel was a short series of thrust, parry, and return that played out in less than an hour after sighting the bark. Starke fought *Calypso* well; better than her shooting. That quality seemed nothing like he remembered, but was enough. Several 3-pounder shells hit or passed close enough to unnerve his gun crews while Gatlings rippled the calm surface between their ships like an invisible claw. The 4-inch shells were more alarming but less accurate. Even so, they needed only one solid hit and he spotted that round skipping towards them. Mendoza hoped it would miss for what seemed an eternity before the ship convulsed as it was struck starboard hull midship under her stack, forward of the boat davits, and aft of the pilothouse. A second purgatory passed waiting for the explosion that never came, then a messenger reported the round penetrated halfway into their boiler room, was causing flooding, and now threatened to blow open her flank. Whether some expert gun-layer aimed low or a fluke; that armor-piercing shell designed to explode after punching through its victim's hide threatened to sink them slow or sudden at its choosing.

His segundo was soon reporting rising water forcing engineers from the boiler room and the remaining steam could not keep screws turning or pumps working. He also swore to remain at his post until ordered out; in case the shell dislodged. The petty officer messenger added it appeared the bruised projectile struck at an angle just below the waterline. Part of its length protruded from the hull, and steel plates surrounding it were sprung. The concussion also started several plates weakened by *Rafael Riego* and never replaced because *Francisco de Montejo* was needed in the West Indies and money too scarce for a New York docking. Mendoza put her on course for the channel, some four miles ahead, then had their starboard boat swung out before going below.

Boiler room deck plates were already awash in the close space, she was beginning to wallow and jerk from bilge water, and speed was bleeding away. Coal was being carried over wet decks to stokeholes but this could not continue much longer. The boilers would soon explode if their fires were not pulled; and yet *Francisco de Montejo* might still beach near the channel entrance if the round failed to explode and wound staunched. Discipline was holding, but black gang's fear of being trapped below was eroding it. He promised to look out for them then returned to the flying bridge. There was still a slight chance since *Calypso* apparently surmised they were hors de combat and went after the fleeing convoy. The straggler was *Delmar Maldonado*, a ship that barely made ten knots and was challenged to do anything swiftly. Yet, she might still prove useful if the time it took to board her allowed others to make the channel and his gunboat to recover. *Francisco de Montejo* was edging forward at less than three knots so Mendoza ordered her remaining whaleboats lowered. Four towing astern would be there for survivors and needed to reach Spanish lines safely should they beach too far from the lighthouse. The Caribbean dropped to fathoms only yards from shore so grounding was unlikely but possible if the boiler held out; and his chief engineer pledged to keep screws turning and pumps going to the last. Mendoza saw *Calypso*'s aft mount loose a round that went so wide he was convinced the one lodged in his gunboat's guts was there by chance, but it made little difference. He told their segundo to continue making for the channel then returned below to examine the dud and see what could be done.

An hour and a quarter after sighting the convoy Starke studied the gunboat 2,000 yards off their port quarter. Incredible luck crippled her but she bought time for the merchant ships moving along the coast towards Punta de Barreras. The leading two were more than 2,000 yards off *Calypso*'s port bow and the third lagging less than 1,200 yards off her starboard. That master faced an inhospitable coast to one side, *Calypso* the other, and no escape. Starke considered heading off the pair but gunboats might be coming to their rescue, his gun crews were shooting poorly, the crew would find it difficult to board even one, and *Calypso* accomplished enough to ensure the blockade held. He turned to Martyn. The chief engineer was supposed to conn during general quarters but O'Leary was needed below, Watson was with their ad hoc damage control party, and Blair had the guns. Martyn looked shaken but game so Starke gave what passed for a smile, "Signal that last merchant then lower the steam pinnace; we'll board."

Delmar Maldonado's master, Geraldo García, stared at the signal flags ending his time as captain. Sunk or captured, she was lost and the fools hoping to squeeze another trip before overhauling boilers and upgrading the engine were culpable;

but her fate rested on his shoulders, as with every master. Generations of the García family followed the sea. Some were represented in the Armada, one vanished with *San Telmo*, and there was a nephew on *Galicia* in Cienfuegos. He considered ramming. All illegality aside, *Delmar Maldonado*'s plant was about to fail and making the attempt, or forcing through, would be suicide since their cargo was munitions for Cienfuegos' new shore batteries and torpedoes for mining that harbor and Havana. García was a patriot so he slowed as if preparing to be boarded then put the rudder hard over. The lumbering, 240-foot iron hull turned from deep blue water and minutes later cut into the turquoise belt along a shore marked by short white bluffs at the edge of brush-filled flatland. Her riveted bottom was soon crashing through submerged coral heads to a slight surf; crushing and grinding until the bow lifted and hull canted slightly port. She finally came to rest hard aground off a portion of eroding coast that left small plateau-like points. The damage was fatal, he did not doubt that, but insurrectos were undoubtedly watching and soon descend to take what they wanted of the cargo; so his first mate was already setting charges. Spain's civil ensign was lowered long enough to add a striped code pennant over the "J" flag and "D" pennant; then the crew was sent to their boat, the fuse lit, and he went over last.

Starke watched her self-destruction and flaghoist through binoculars; considering the wreck for twenty minutes while Blair fidgeted. The gunnery officer's blood was up. He wanted to force the gunboat's surrender or board this wreck. Martyn, standing beside Starke, looked aft where their starboard whaleboat was at the rail; near where Melvin and his crew stripped items from their steam pinnace's remains. *Calypso* continued to cut circles 1,000 yards off the stranded wreck as the two other ships entered the channel; leaving *Francisco de*

Montejo crawling towards it and Punta de los Colorados at less than three knots.

Starke's caution rested on the absence of any sortie from Cienfuegos, the ship's sudden beaching and flaghoist, "You are standing into danger" flying below her civil ensign. The crew was also rowing for *Calypso* with an enthusiasm that did not fit; and gaining speed. After scrambling aboard, helped by *Calypso* sailors, García headed for the flying bridge at a pace that practically dragged Watson along. *Delmar Maldonado's* swarthy and ample master wasted no time approaching the taller and wirier Starke directly. Staring undeterred into the faded blue eyes below arching eyebrows in a face showing little emotion, he discarded formalities to warn the American his munitions cargo was set to detonate before sadly adding, "I could not let insurrectos have it, Capitán."

Starke now understood why the Spanish crew rowed for *Calypso* rather than a much closer shore, besides the always-ready machetes lurking there, and replied, "I thank you for your courtesy, Capitán. Mr. Watson, please see Capitán García and his crew are well cared for. Mr. Martyn, steer east and ring up full speed."

Turning due east opened the distance, placed the explosion off their starboard quarter, and crossed the limping gunboat's track far enough astern to lessen risk of being fired on. The freighter's abandoned boat floated tranquilly astern of *Calypso* for almost ten minutes before *Delmar Maldonado* erupted.

The 2,000 ton iron-hulled freighter rested placidly with calm seas caressing the battered hull until a bright flash appeared at the cargo hatch aft of her midship superstructure. It rapidly expanded to become a short, fat pillar of flames mixed with white smoke just above stack level. This remained for a second before billowing clouds forced from the gutted hull consumed everything then towered against a cloudless blue sky. Multiple explosions fused into the expanding brown, black, and white mass enveloping the old freighter as a deafening rumble and initial shock wave reached *Calypso*. Some sailors momentarily lost balance when their ship bucked as if struck. *Delmar Maldonado*'s superstructure and deck vanished. Her hull survived only long enough to vent most of the explosion upward, but there was enough left to blow out her bottom, disintegrate supporting coral, and create a debris-filled trench. Hundreds of fragments, mixed with larger pieces, dropped into the sea, peppered the shore, and landed inland. Starke glanced at García, whose warning saved lives. The master rose to his full height, "Capitán, I would be in your debt if you logged *Delmar Maldonado* blew up with her flag flying at nine-fifty, second of May, year of our Lord 1898."

Yeoman Pound entered the exact words in their deck log as Starke translated then added, ". . . and by doing so denied Cuban forces her munitions." The Spaniard's English was sufficient. He nodded, smiling sadly, "Gracias, Capitán."

Nothing more could be accomplished with the wreck; more easily seen by smoke and intermittent explosions than what remained. *Calypso* made an easy turn to starboard after crossing behind the gunboat then steered north by northwest, or about. She was off her adversary's port side at just over 1,000 yards by ten o'clock, with overwhelming speed superiority. Neither ship resumed firing but Spanish battle flags hung limply, when not sporadically fluttering in still air. She listed heavily to starboard and a few 3-pounder shell holes were visible. The ships were running parallel and slowly closing the channel, something like 3,000 yards ahead. *Calypso* would soon be within range of artillery emplaced near the lighthouse but to resume firing seemed murderous with the barely moving gunboat towing boats and guns silent. She could not be left to make port so Starke was about to resume firing when an explosion along her far side created a burst of white water thrown up and away from her hull. She staggered then coasted to a stop with smoke pouring from her stack as sailors surrounding open gun mounts began abandoning them.

Francisco de Montejo's commander, Teniente de Navio Mendoza, had held fire to entice her assailant closer since the gunboat could still shoot and might cripple the bark. *Calypso* refused to close so he hurried below to keep a promise. There was little time. He found fires already pulled and had turned to follow the last man up a ladder when the armor-piercing shell detonated. He was instantly lifted and hurled against a bulkhead, unable to see through the intense light and feeling only extreme heat; until striking steel. His legs crumpled and body failed as he sensed more than saw the sea rush in, quenching still-hot boilers in bursts of steam. Completely enervated, moving seemed hardly worthwhile, the rising water cool, and previous cares of no importance. Rationality gave way to unlinked snippets: something pulling on him, the gritty smell of coal dust, water flooding deck plates, items floating off, sprays jetting from hatch coamings, blue sky, and brilliant sunlight. Proportion went askew leaving the deckhouse lofty on one end, minuscule on the other. Masts tilted unnaturally and the world slanted. His body refused to respond when hot steel burned his back. Their segundo knelt beside him but speech was impossible. Strong arms roughly passed him to a boat. He tried to fight then all went dark. Mendoza was suddenly in Spain at his father's house with its interior courtyard channeling warm summer breezes through a single story.

Starke and others above deck saw the gunboat wallow and starboard side dip towards the surface while her whaleboats towing astern went alongside and loaded, despite the steel angling out over them. *Calypso* could do nothing but Starke ordered a whaleboat readied for lowering. Once the four Spanish boats loaded, they made for Punta de los Colorados, a little over a mile off, but he maneuvered *Calypso* to forestall escape. They rested oars once clear of their foundering gunboat and stared quietly. On *Calypso*, a panting stack and water lightly slapping alongside were the only sounds.

Francisco de Montejo's list eased and she began righting as turquoise water rushed over bulwarks and across the deck. Loose gear shuffled about or floated away as air vented in noisy plumes through open doors and hatches; flushing a figure from below who made for the bow then began waving frantically. Starke watched the sailor's shipmates gesturing at him. It never failed. Someone was always unwilling to hear, refusing to leave, or denying the inevitable. This fellow was savvy enough to understand none of the boats could risk returning, leapt into the sea, and paddled awkwardly from the 150-foot hull's 300 tons; now upright with bulwarks slipping below. The small superstructure and empty boat davits followed, leaving pilothouse, slightly raked stack, and masts above water. Small internal explosions vomited dirt, steam, and smoke through the stack. She died hard. Her bow reemerged briefly during the struggle then sank. A white boil sprinkled with debris briefly marred the blue sea before replaced by buoyant items on the roiled surface with more shooting up as she continued her journey down through many fathoms. The dying gunboat's last compassionate act was thrusting the swimmer away rather than take him down with her. A boat skirted around the grave to retrieve this last survivor; the courageous act of men who spent their lives fishing off the Spanish coast before conscripted.

Calypso was roughly 150 yards off the Spaniard's beam when she sank at ten-thirty. The boats reluctantly made for her, but until alongside most of two crews were unaware they once worked together to save *Francisco de Montejo*; now descending into eternal darkness. Conrad, his apothecary, and their baymen treated wounded on deck; mostly broken bones, cuts, and scalding. The worst case was Mendoza. Little remained of any uniform, his head lacerated and singed, back burned, and internal injuries unknown. The swimming straggler came through with only claw marks administered by the calico cat still struggling in his arms as he clambered over the bulwark. Starke's jaw tightened. The fool risked life and shipmates for a mascot.

Chapter Twenty-Three
The Cartel

*F*rancisco de Montejo's survivors were taken aboard but her boats kept alongside. Starke would not leave men in the open under a tropical sun, especially wounded, and *Calypso* sailors once worked alongside them; but their number and his depleted crew still made it a risk. He was considering how best to continue when a wispy smoke plume showed near the channel. Cienfuegos had gunboats and those kept in readiness would have taken about this long to raise steam and sortie. Starke quickly sent unwounded Spaniards to the hold, assigned a guard, and re-manned general quarters. Fighting was out of the question with *Calypso's* small crew, mediocre shooting, and prisoners. Their single advantage remained speed but he chose to cloak weakness with confidence and kept *Calypso* heading to the channel at bare steerageway with both boilers on line.

It was not *Galicia* but one of Cienfuegos' three *Alerta* class gunboats under a white flag. Her straight stem, single pole-mast forward, diminutive deckhouse at the slightly raked funnel's base, and overhanging stern, marked her as a third-class gunboat. Less than fifty tons, they were more accurately described as British-built armed-launches; but a shallow draft, narrow beam, and seventy-foot length made them useful for controlling rivers, patrolling the coast, and intercepting filibusters inshore. This large class was designed to make eleven knots but no Spanish ship spending time in the West

319

Indies avoided the ravages of poor coal and maintenance. Her open helm was aft and one whaleboat in portside davits was visible. The forward 42mm mount and aft rapid-fire 37mm cannon could be seen through binoculars but appeared unmanned. Spanish sailors standing topside stared at *Calypso*, as uncertain what came next as Starke.

The gunboat slid cautiously down *Calypso*'s side, reversed course, and then slowed to pace the bark 500 yards to starboard; roughly a third of the distance to shore. When sailors began lowering her boat, Blair detailed an honor guard, Watson took the flying bridge, and Starke went below to change. Leaving the deck was a gamble, but Starke knew the Spanish would never dishonor a white flag, Watson had proven capable, and he wanted to conceal *Calypso*'s true state.

Their reply to Weaver's hail revealed the whaleboat carried *Lince*'s captain, Teniente de Navio Salvador Gómez y Aguado. He approached Starke with hand outstretched after being piped on board. Starke grasped it then invited him below where Yamashita had refreshments. Too long out of port for lemonade, the cabin steward broached their wine store and quietly filled two glasses with a red. Both captains opened by saying they regretted the war, without mentioning politics or revealing useful information. Gómez was relieved Starke negotiated in Spanish, although his own French was passable, and began by asking for number and condition of survivors. Starke provided the latest count then offered to call his surgeon once Conrad could leave the gunboat commander; and only survivor in critical condition. The Spaniard obviously came to propose some sort of exchange but Starke could not guess what was on offer unless ships chartered by the States' consul in Jamaica had left Americans behind.

Gómez slowly twisted his glass before opening, "Holding so many prisoners must be inconvenient, Capitán. Perhaps you would consider repatriation on parole until some future exchange. It would relieve you of that burden."

The common enough proposal would resolve his dilemma, but Starke was unsure about the current view on parole or how to justify it later if questioned. Those paroled would not fight Americans until exchanged but insurrectos were a different matter; besides, only fools took the first offer when horse trading. Starke's sparse beard partly concealed the disciplined countenance as he parried, "I agree, but they'll soon be on a ship for the States and out of my hands, Capitán."

Gómez had little leverage. The austere officer across the table, perhaps inadvertently or as a ruse, suggested warships lay beyond the horizon or were expected. It was a possibility he could not ignore so Gómez approached the negotiation as if resolving a common problem, "Very true, Capitán; but perhaps some other arrangement is acceptable that would avoid passing this inconvenience on?"

Lince's captain clearly had instructions, but not something Spanish authorities would propose going in. That eliminated a confiscated ship, filibusters, or Americans. Starke took a sip of warm, red wine, "Everything is possible, God willing, Capitán."

"Very true, Capitán, but unfortunately insurrectos don't share that view. You heard perhaps of General Gomez ordering the murder of anyone willing to negotiate; even Lieutenant Colonel Ruiz?"

Starke waited a few seconds before responding, "What you say may be true but my country is willing to parley; not give up something for nothing, Capitán."

"We hold insurrectos that are equally inconvenient, Capitán."

Gómez just laid his hand on the table with one card face up. Starke countered, "True, Capitán, but why trade officers and sailors for peasants and desperadoes?"

"We've a senior officer and other insurrectos waiting for sentences to be confirmed."

Starke thought the move astute. Gómez offered at least one insurrecto leader of import and men while suggesting they would be executed should he refuse; something that would look bad in the morning papers. Starke probed, ". . . and the officer?"

"He is a comandante on General Rodriguez's staff."

Another card revealed. From his time with Lee, Starke understood Major General José Mayía Rodríguez was a cavalry officer commanding the insurrectos' Western, or Occidental, District. His staff officer must be an extremely inconvenient or valuable captive; which could mean one of those held by *Calypso* was equally so. That might be worth exploring further but relieving his ship of captives was more pressing. He paused to twist his wine glass and count silently to ten before responding, "Man for man, officer for officer, Capitán?"

"That would be acceptable, Capitán." The Spaniard's hand was fully played.

"There's one complication. Teniente de Navio Mendoza cannot be moved. I fear for his life if he is."

Mendoza was out of the war, they were friends of a sort, and Conrad's description of the port's military hospitals was not glowing. *Calypso*'s surgeon was first-rate and able to provide his full attention during a critical recovery period. If Mendoza was kept until out of danger he could be repatriated later; and stressing his wounds' severity might prove useful during any future inquiry over the gunboat's loss.

"Teniente de Navio Mendoza must be part of the exchange, Capitán."

"Agreed, but he can be returned under cartel when able, or travel to Spain through a third country. I believe your minister in Washington has left for Canada. "

Starke guessed the officers were friends or related so he strengthened the offer, "Our surgeon will provide any necessary medical assurances, Capitán." Gómez thought for several seconds, "Then, with your agreement, my boat will return Comandante Artemio Ochoa y Fermin with a list of names to select from, Capitán."

Gómez negotiated well. Spain would gain experienced sailors for Cienfuegos' gunboats and letting Ochoa select those exchanged would leave the worst in prison or with their date before some wall. Those released would return to the fight, which is one reason Lincoln halted the custom, but Starke viewed trading sailors for acclimated fighters defendable. The question became how. Exchanging seventy healthy Spaniards for an equal number of insurrectos coming from years as guerrillas then prison would leave *Calypso* worse off. These new passengers would lack shipboard experience, be hard to control, and carry any number of diseases. Starke held back, gambling Gómez was also instructed on the mechanics; which turned out to be freeing insurrectos west of the city in a disputed area just before *Calypso*'s were released at the channel mouth. Ochoa would lead the liberated insurrectos into Cuban lines then pass a signal to El Jagua Castle confirming this occurred. The fortress would repeat it to *Calypso* and Starke would release his captives just off the channel mouth. Success rested on Spanish honor, but Starke agreed since it would create good will early on and clear the ship either way.

The whaleboat that carried Gómez to *Calypso* returned for Ochoa; who stepped aboard, looked up at the flag, and cautiously relaxed. He had not anticipated this when ordered to wear his best uniform; a cotton blouse with large breast pockets and slightly darker khaki trousers. The triangular patch with white star had long since been peeled from his pinned-up broad-brimmed hat; and the tall puttees, cartridge belt, holster, long machete, and spurs were gone, along with a sash; but what remained was clean and presentable.

Ochoa believed he was being delivered to Havana for execution but instead brought to the cabin of an American warship where he listened to *Lince*'s commander explain the exchange then hand him a list of names in front of Starke. After Gómez and Ochoa returned to *Lince* the gunboat reentered Cienfuegos' channel at what must be full speed while Starke resumed patrolling at a prudent distance. In the morning he brought *Calypso* closer in and met two harbor tugs under white flags that matched a set flying above El Jagua Castle. The first tug hailed them then gently nudged *Calypso*'s gray hull to board passengers. Starke noted how carefully the masters handled their craft this time. Once transfer was complete, both tugs disappeared upriver under a glaring late-morning sun that engulfed the calm sea, beaches, and green shores. *Calypso* lowered her truce flag and took station beyond effective artillery range.

The remaining day was hot but uneventful. Blair and Poniatowski drilled gun crews, pushing hard enough for Watson to hover nearby; concerned their enthusiasm might risk sailors, guns, or confidence. Melvin finished removing all salvageable parts and equipage from his beloved steam pinnace then watched engineers cart off what they wanted, followed by Chief Lefebvre's sailors. What remained went over the side in pieces to sink immediately or later.

Starke reset his mechanical desk calendar to May 4, 1898, the next morning, enjoyed breakfast, and set *Calypso* steaming west along the coast. Nothing was visible for a dozen miles except deep blue sea, white breakers lapping broad beaches, eroding low bluffs, and brush-covered flatland. Their destination was a triangular inlet since water offshore was too deep for anchoring. Comandante Ochoa wanted to confer, confirm the exchange, and open communication. Starke went ashore over Watson's protests but had him loiter off the coast within easy range of 4-inch and 3-pounder guns. A whaleboat was chosen to pass through rolling surf while the remaining steam pinnace stood off under Ensign Blair with a landing party carrying .38 caliber revolvers and .45-70 Remington-Lee magazine rifles. Starke carried his personal .45 caliber revolver and immediately saw Weaver's hand in selecting this escort: Seaman Kearney, a man who would stand; the fighting redhead Seaman Flynn; and Seaman Talbot Griffin, a reliable soul when sober.

Melvin guided the whaleboat expertly through unfamiliar surf, deposited his captain on a hot shell beach, and helped the crew steady their charge since he had little faith in the boat anchor's grasp on an underwater cliff just off the beach. Starke's party chambered rounds as Comandante Ochoa and two menacing-looking men emerged from the brush to walk towards them. The searing beach, high humidity, and absence of a moderating breeze shortened preliminaries but the brief exchange was completed and Starke handed a set of signals. He also discovered their fourth division and Cienfuegos gunboats clashed the day *Calypso* arrived. *Galicia* took rounds through stack and boiler so she was being repaired, and would be for several weeks; which explained the convoy's lack of support. Nearly 2,000 Americans already left on the Norwegian liner *Condor*, but those remaining were not detained and allowed to send cables requesting removal. The worst news was Commodore Dewey's Asian Squadron entered Manila Bay and engaged the Spanish off that city four days before. Heavy fighting and losses were reported before the submarine cable went silent. Ochoa also asked for whatever military supplies could be spared. Starke agreed to arrange something; but hesitated since *Calypso* was commissioned to prevent this.

Starke considered steaming for Key West but chose to continue blockading until relieved or driven away. That came two days later when smoke plumes topped the horizon. He immediately took *Calypso* west to gain sea room and avoid getting trapped against the shallows west of Cienfuegos or the coast.

Fight or flight was resolved when the lead ship hoisted a recognition signal. It was their fourth division's unprotected cruiser *Marblehead* and gunboat *Nashville*. The pair appeared similar, with two tall masts and funnels, combination pilothouse-flying bridge, and less than fifty feet difference in length; but the unprotected cruiser was 1,000 tons greater than *Nashville* and included torpedo tubes in her heavier armament. A second flaghoist broke at the cruiser's port yardarm as they closed. Chief Owen entered the tactical signal book while Starke waited for him to confirm *Calypso*'s captain was summoned.

Starke shifted to a clean dress blue uniform as the ships converged and directed a whaleboat be lowered then outfitted as gig. Melvin was soon steering them towards the towering cruiser. He responded to *Marblehead*'s hail then took them alongside a Jacob's ladder lowered just forward of one 4-inch rifle's hull bulge. Starke climbed to the main deck then went through her port lifelines under the whaleboat and launch secured in their overhead frame. *Marblehead*'s commander waited a few steps forward.

Commander Bowman McCalla earned a reputation for action but the cost placed him below where he should be. The American with Scottish parents preferred West Point but ended up graduating fourth in his Naval Academy class at Newport then going to war in the side-wheel steam frigate *Susquehanna*. He fought along the Atlantic and Gulf coasts and later commanded a naval force under Admiral Jouett that landed in Colon, crossed the isthmus, ended rebel hostilities in Panama City, and held it until Columbian troops arrived. After a tour as *Powhatan*'s executive officer he was assistant Bureau of Navigation chief and commanded the steam frigate *Enterprise* during her independent cruise into the Baltic Sea, across the Mediterranean, and through the Suez Canal. She not only showed the flag but located the missing schooner *Starlight* off eastern Africa. Strict but consistent, he was popular with crews but no shrinking violet; which resulted in a court-martial for laying the flat of his sword on a drunk sailor. That cost him lineal numbers, a three-year suspension, and promotion denial for the same period. He was reinstated but remained a commander since 1884. Even so, he was not easily cowed; as a Mare Island Naval Shipyard contractor learned during McCalla's equipment officer tour.

Marblehead's commander was tall with little fat and bulging eyes separated by a large nose. Sideburns flowing from under his undress blue cap became mutton chops that merged into a large mustache. McCalla grinned while extending a hand, "Welcome, Captain. You've been holding the fort while we coaled?"

"Yes, sir"

"Let's go below."

Marblehead's cabin was steel, trimmed with wood, and newer than *Calypso*'s but had airports instead of windows and lacked warmth. McCalla invited him to its table then listened to Starke describe arriving, finding no ships, firing on Punta de los Colorados buildings, and engaging the convoy. His questions mostly concerned Starke's parley with insurrectos, their arms request, and *Calypso*'s current state.

McCalla's hand brushed his chin as Starke finished, "Well done, Captain. *Calypso* was fortunate but accomplished more than could be expected. *Eagle*'s due on the seventh. She's an armed yacht and Lieutenant Southerland's not bashful either; took on *Galicia*. We had planned to intercept a group of armed transports but they slipped through before our arrival. The Don came out to clear the way for *Argonauta*, but was shot up for his trouble and we took the transport."

"Yes, sir"

"You took a lot on yourself shelling Punta de los Colorados but it was appropriate. The Department's approved cutting those cables so I plan to do that and destroy the lighthouse once *Windom* and the collier *Saturn* arrive. That should end night blockade running and easy communication. You also prepared the ground for supplying insurrectos and we brought additional munitions for that."

"Yes, sir."

"I'm sorry to say, but *Calypso*'s ordered to Key West, Starke. I would like to keep her but you more than anyone know she lacks crew."

Starke expected as much and about say so when McCalla injected, "I hope you're fully manned and return to fourth division. I've something you may find interesting."

Chapter Twenty-Four
Fortunes of War

Captain Albert observed the morning sun light edges of a solid curtain covering the Executive Mansion's tall, multi-paned window. Sequestered behind these curtains, he missed quiet mornings sipping coffee at his Building window. It seemed increasing periods were now dedicated to this second floor, southeast corner, telegraph and cipher office.

The rectangular space with marble fireplace on the eastern exterior wall had been a suite's sitting room before Lincoln. Its adjacent bedroom was now the president's office and near one window a box-like affair was jammed with wires. Typewriters and line of telegraph paraphernalia on diminutive desks shared its long interior wall with an uncomfortable leather couch used by the president for short naps during busy or tense nights. Maps and charts with pins puncturing thick paper filled the wall above. A large roll-top desk and small table bit into fussy, worn carpet under an ornate five-globed gasolier hanging from the high ceiling's center. The desk's primary occupant was Captain Benjamin Montgomery of the Army Signal Corps. Before war came he was the president's telegrapher and cipher clerk but this sturdy man in civilian garb with dark, center-parted hair and mustache now ran the war room, regularly exercised a typewriter on the small table at one side and often on the telephone.

This was a new experience for Albert and others. One room contained the military telegraph, Associated Press and *The Sun*'s news bureau feeds, telephone lines to key department offices and selected officials, and shortly a link to Major General William Rufus Shafter's Tampa headquarters. The signal corps was also recruiting qualified volunteers to control the nation's telegraph network, install censors, and eventually establish lines from the Cuba front. Albert was impressed with signal corps' eight officers and fifty enlisted compared to the War Department's other branches. He credited Chief Signal Officer, Brigadier General Adolphus Greely; an explorer and disciplinarian known for leading the costly, controversial, and valuable expedition Commodore Schley rescued from the Arctic.

Change was also spreading in the Building across the street. Day was finally Secretary of State in name, which improved stability, while Secretary Alger and Commanding General of the Army, Nelson Miles, were at each other's throats over their department's readiness, role, tactics, and strategy; despite or because both had military experience. While their leaders clashed, a small regular army scattered across posts throughout the nation consolidated, expanded, and prepared to engage hundreds of thousands of acclimated troops on an island known for diseases that gutted invasions, occupations, and business ventures. Long's steady hand and Roosevelt's energy guided the Navy Department so, despite previous years of neglect, the fleet was modern and tasked with achievable goals: establish and maintain a blockade, dominate the Caribbean, and block Spain's navy. After an exuberant swearing in as lieutenant colonel in his office, attended by college friends and well-wishers, Theodore was off to join the volunteer cavalry regiment he helped establish. His replacement would be Charles H. Allen; someone Albert viewed as less disruptive but more concerned with political and entrepreneurial ends than the Navy.

Late April's strategy was to strengthen the blockade and land a substantial raiding force east of Cienfuegos near Cape Tunas. This was quickly abandoned once Cervera's squadron, designated the Cape Verde Fleet, left those islands. The revision McKinley, Alger, Long, Miles, and Sicard agreed on would land 40 to 50,000 troops at Mariel, besiege Havana, and force Spain from the island; but this collapsed during a cabinet meeting when Alger emphasized the Navy must neutralize Cervera's squadron before troops were sent and Long responded the Army was nowhere near ready anyway. When Miles sided with Long against his secretary, Alger ordered the general to immediately move on Havana with 70,000 men. The commanding general bypassed him and appealed to McKinley who postponed the invasion.

The Navy could act and did. Commodore George Remey was detailed to oversee Key West, a blockade established on Cuba's north coast, prizes taken, and expeditions began deliveries to insurrectos. McCalla already fought Spanish ships off Cienfuegos, coaled, and returned to cut undersea cables. Matanzas was shelled, a sharp action took place in Cardenas harbor, and San Juan bombarded.

For several days after the Manila cable was cut, anxiety permeated war room and nation. Little was known except there had been a battle with heavy losses; until a cable from Hong Kong reported Dewey's squadron destroyed Spain's fleet. Although the nation celebrated, this victory not only worsened relations between Long and Alger but widened a breach between the commanding general and his secretary of war which opened further with prodding by an intoxicated press and surging public patriotism ignorant of War Department realities.

Even State was getting more favorable press. They worked closely with Navy to ensure bewildering international agreements and customs were followed regarding neutrality and prizes. Their consul in Jamaica chartered neutral ships to extract Americans left in Cienfuegos and its diplomats appeared to be coaxing neutrality from an unsympathetic Europe perpetually at the brink and now anxious about their Caribbean interests, shipping, and colonies.

Their remaining neutral was critical. Besides merchant shipping, the British navy maintained a North American station that included the West Indies, one Austrian cruiser was already in the Caribbean, a French cruiser passed through the blockade for a Havana port visit, and Germany's *Grier* visited Cienfuegos and Havana before entering San Juan to join the French cruiser *Amiral Rigault de Genouilly*; so foreign ships were in that port when Spanish land fortifications and Sampson's ships dueled.

Albert's efforts to disrupt filibusters and his authority over *Calypso* ended. She was temporarily placed under the North Atlantic Squadron, despite a threadbare crew, to extract her from organizational limbo. Her future employment, however, remained uncertain. Some argued she should supply insurrectos while others wanted her used to placate one of the ports and wealthy communities demanding protection. A proposal to decommission and use crew to fill other ships' shortfalls also crossed the table. Albert argued her design as a commerce raider with unlimited legs under sail, easily repairable composite hull, and updated battery made her ideal to go after Spanish trade without pulling modern cruisers from the Flying Squadron. Roosevelt supported this, got his way, and directed her full manning before leaving; and later touted *Calypso*'s actions off Cienfuegos that preserved the blockade with a token crew while destroying a munitions ship and small gunboat.

Albert wanted *Calypso*'s resurrection to include restoring her original crew to the extent possible before adding sailors. Past collusion with her executive officer meant most key people were there to form the nucleus; and a possible donor existed. *Flint*, the final *Annapolis* class gunboat, was building at the same New Jersey yard *Princeton* would soon commission from. Using sailors ordered to her would provide Starke both gunner's mates he requested, some other sailors taken from *Calypso*, and men familiar with each other from *Flint*. Wardroom expansion was more challenging since most staff officers remained but the steam engineering and line officers assigned were a bare minimum before several were ordered off. Higher priority ships were also strapped so he decided search out previous cadets then enlist an act recently passed that allowed temporary appointments. For the remaining billets Albert would grudgingly look to naval militia or landsmen. It was a feasible approach he hoped to be well into before a Starke dinner party that week.

Constance Starke approached society as a campaign to support their business and this dinner party one more engagement. Handwritten notes were delivered and the invited either accepted or sent regrets. The staff had been cleaning, polishing, and shopping city establishments to complete preparations before Constance and Immanuel started to greet arriving guests at fifteen minutes to eight. Altman took each couple's outerwear as they entered then guided them to his master and mistress waiting at the large parlor's double doors. Exercising the hostess privilege, Constance chose a light blue and satin tea gown with silk gloves, drop earrings, silver bracelets, and wedding band. Her husband never varied, so he wore a black wool tailcoat, waist coat fastened with Mexican silver studs, starched white shirt, straight-legged trousers, white kid gloves, and patent leather shoes.

Clara Barton had returned to *State of Texas* in Key West and unable to attend but wrote a brief letter. It appeared the most in need of immediate attention were around twenty Spanish crews interned on prize ships. She also viewed medical preparations for war inadequate, wrote that Sampson refused to allow women on ships, and heard the Army intended to keep them far away from combat; particularly her. She also worried about familiarities developing on *State of Texas* and Red Cross political intriguing. Captain Fischer was unable to attend because the Revenue Cutter Service was struggling to cover increased duties while supplying cutters to the Navy. Evans was back in Washington applying for Navy or War Department credentials but unable to attend because she lacked time to arrange an escort. She did leave her card and promised to call the following afternoon.

John and Anita McGee accepted. She was a medical doctor with the Daughters of the America Revolution who managed their preparations to offer trained nurses. Captain Albert and Abigail brought their escorted daughters. Olivia came with an officer standing in for her fiancé and Isabella enjoyed the company of *Calypso*'s first chief engineer, Lieutenant Adrian Osborne; down from the Camden, New Jersey shipyard where *Flint* was under construction. Maximilian Falk and the Cuban woman he brought to the Christmas ball were last to arrive.

Constance led their guests across the main hall to the second floor dining room at nine o'clock; each lady's right arm resting lightly in their escort's crooked left. An extended mahogany table and chairs waited in that rectangular room with windowed alcove on its street end and morning room at the other. Suspended from a high ceiling framed by square beams were dark-crystal gasoliers; mellow gas lights being preferable to harsh electric. Varnished doors, trim, and moldings were waxed then polished until the wood shone like dark glass. Wall panels rose from the oak parquet floor to meet intricate gold and rust wallpaper serving as background for a half-dozen oil paintings. Besides the large buffet set against its interior wall there was a black marble fireplace with brass fittings.

Two pedestal cake-stands, off-white bone china, crystal stemware, silverware, folded napkins, handwritten placards, and menus populated the white linen tablecloth with a centered floral arrangement. Immanuel went to its head and stood facing the alcove. Constance remained on his right until guests were seated. She then sat followed by her husband. Gloves were removed and meal begun without prayer. Constance guided conversation, putting everyone at ease by diverting all discussion drifting towards food, politics, or other trying topics. Footmen ensured food came appropriately hot, warm, cool, or cold; with spring water then wine between courses. A consommé was served, then oysters on the half shell, side dishes, and sorbet. The main course was roasted spring chicken with cauliflower, broccoli, and carrots. Nuts, chocolate, candied fruit, and jellies sufficed for dessert. Finger bowls of lemon water were placed on the table just before Constance signaled the women it was time to rise. The original column then reformed and snaked down to the parlor for tea and coffee since she seldom separated sexes after dinner; but accepted some men would eventually drift to the library.

Parlor discussions were unrestricted so, except for brief exchanges on direct election of senators, most centered on the war; and European ships strictly adhering to international agreements when passing through the blockade. The French,

German, Austrian, and possibly Italian governments tended to favor Spain while Great Britain behaved with studied ambiguity to deter any rising coalition. *Charleston* was leaving for Manila with munitions, seamen, and marines to exploit Dewey's victory; and 1,200 more would follow within days on *City of Peking*. Also in the west, General Wesley Merritt, favored to be the Philippine military governor, was assembling more units for the islands. *Oregon* was still steaming from California to the Caribbean. The press falsely reported she was in difficulty but that was not surprising since the Navy Department was closed to reporters. Equally inaccurate accounts of a lurking Spanish torpedo boat and torpedo boat destroyer off Nantucket had disrupted the war room more than most sightings coming from Atlantic and Gulf coast informants. Constance was interested in reports sent from St. Thomas that Sampson fired on San Juan since *The Sun*'s press boat *Kanapaha* cabled this news and her nephew's friend might be aboard.

The nation reuniting after long years of bitter acrimony was another well-plowed topic since the president commissioned Lee and Wheeler, who served in the Confederacy as young generals. Besides obvious politics, this gave the Army two men who had maneuvered large commands; skills few on active service possessed. In addition, Lee was familiar with Cuban politics and "Fighting Joe Wheeler" earned the sobriquet on the battlefield then buttressed it in Congress. Doctor Anita McGee discussed her work as director of the Daughters of the American Revolution Hospital Corps. Both Army and Navy contacted her organization about recruiting contract nurses; and the Army approached several Colored society women for immune nurses. Namahyoke Sockum Curtis was the most notable since she helped open the first Colored-owned and operated hospital in Chicago then came to Washington with her husband; the Freedmen's Hospital superintendent. Constance noted Cynthia and the Albert daughters were intently following this conversation.

Immanuel Starke, Albert, and Falk slipped quietly off to the library. The room was too warm for a fire but bookshelves, oriental rugs, large floor globe, plush chairs, and wood desk with brass lamp made it a comfortable retreat. Bourbon flowing from a crystal decanter added to this congenial atmosphere. Albert sipped the clawing liquid before repaying a favor, "Secretary Long wished to pass his thanks to your chandler's Far East contact; who'll remain nameless of course. Admiral Dewey had very little to act on except his man's observations and our consul from Manila."

"I'll certainly do that. He'll appreciate it." Immanuel's Jewish associate and longtime friend, Aron Sharett, deserved more after that and assisting *Calypso*; but preferred anonymity as his business clients were international.

Falk leaned lightly against the mantel, holding a crystal glass with amber liquid slowly moving about its base, "The Philippines aren't monolithic and have constantly posed a problem for Spain so I'm not sure what we're stepping into. A coaling station might prove useful but our concerns must remain Cuba, Europe, and Cape Verde Fleet. Cervera's one of their best admirals. He's an astute commander, innovator, and excellent administrator when allowed; which he hasn't been in the past."

Albert's gaze drifted to the globe, "He could accomplish much given free rein. Three *Infanta María Teresa* class cruisers with torpedo boats would be formidable and there's a fourth armored cruiser with them. Cervera putting in at Martinique was unexpected and there've been sightings off Curaçao. Nobody's certain what's planned but some claim he's escorting a munitions convoy to replace the cargo *Calypso* destroyed off Cienfuegos."

Immanuel poured another amber shot, ". . . or attack commerce. Only *Brooklyn* and *New York* could catch them; and then there're the torpedo boats. My ships will stay in port, especially *Eveleth*, even if it keeps Captain Schumacher on pins and needles."

Falk moved slightly from the hearth, "Cervera's probably hamstrung by Madrid. Your nephew once mentioned planning against what your adversary could do, not what you expect; but we don't know the Cape Verde Fleet's actual capability. He's without reliable coal sources and Madrid will not allow any operation that does not directly support their army in Cuba. If so, he's limited to raising the blockade, attacking our invasion force, or supplementing Havana's defense."

Immanuel looked at him then across at Albert, ". . . and striking supply ships."

Albert set his glass down, "Which raises another topic; chartering. Has the War Department approached you?" Falk walked to the globe and gave it a slow spin, then stopping on the Philippines. Immanuel edged closer to Albert, "No; which I find odd, especially regarding *Eveleth*."

"The Navy might charter and fit her out as a merchant cruiser; like *St. Paul*."

"I heard Sigsbee will command *St. Paul*."

"That's true."

"I considered it but will not displace Captain Schumacher. He's a loyal master and cares little enough for our government as it is, so he could only see it as betrayal."

"I've never met the gentleman."

"What his family didn't lose during the war went soon after."

"And your brother? Will he sell or charter ships to Spain?"

"His loyalty is to Brazil and has no reason to support the States, except his son. Which reminds, can you say anything about *Calypso*'s role?"

"Her crew is being increased. It would be hard not to after the Cienfuegos action. After that it's probably blockading or scouting. I've suggested using her against commerce, since she was designed for it, but she'll remain anchored in Key West for the immediate future.

Chapter Twenty-Five
Key West

Calypso made Key West and anchored in water their surgeon preferred. Starke reported in and arranged for Mendoza's care at the Convent of Mary Immaculate; offered to the Navy as a hospital by its Mother Superior but rumored to be taken over by the Army in the near future. Conrad cared for him during the voyage from Cienfuegos and now the sisters. Since then, *Calypso* floated seemingly unnoticed in the outer anchorage.

Starke breakfasted on eggs, rice, ham, and coffee. Reveille was at five and sunrise later that hour. During morning twilight, one then another of the encircling ships emerged from the shadow after being darkened for night. Although shore-controlled minefields existed or were building, each warship manned one or more mounts should there be an attack. Pipes called for stowing hammocks, lighting the smoking lamp, signaling turn to, hoisting ashes, calling for sweepers, announcing their market boat's departure, and sending side cleaners over. *The Star Spangled Banner* would not be played for eight o'clock colors today since the band was on Sampson's North Atlantic Squadron flagship; somewhere off Cuba or searching for the Cape Verde Fleet.

The ex-lighthouse tender *Suwannee* was Commodore George Remey's latest flagship and her crew of less than thirty did not include a band or could offer much support. Rumors had the steam sloop *Lancaster* being ordered to Key West at the end of May to assume flagship duties and act as local receiving ship. She just recommissioned after a yard period so, like *Calypso*, her black hull was being painted gray using the repulsive concoction of white lead, linseed oil, japan dryer, turpentine, and lampblack oil. Starke tried recalling all the modifications since last seeing her off Alexandra, Egypt in 1882. Also expected was Commodore Schley's Flying Squadron, formed to protect the East Coast and destroy the Cape Verde Fleet.

The day cabin's open windows, glowing from mid-May's rising sun, allowed a slight morning breeze to clear away stuffiness and waft the sea's tart fragrance past table and desk. It promised to be another day's administration with an occasional main deck tour breaking it up. Watson ran the ship well so there was no justification to interfere and little enticement to go ashore. Key West had become the hub of Navy operations while *Calypso* swung at anchor. Washington intended it to be the Army's embarkation port as well until they finally accepted an acute water shortage existed. The island had cisterns but no wells so what drinking water rain did not provide was barged from Port Tampa. A distilling plant was being constructed and more planned but none would finish soon enough and a dry spell was in progress. Washington grudgingly accepted this reality after increasingly shrill warnings and designated Port Tampa as the assembly point for their Cuba expedition. Navy bureaucrats proved deaf or recalcitrant so the station commander was forced to beg water from the fort on more than one occasion to supply ships.

Commodore Remey had arrived in Key West a week earlier with flag lieutenant, John H. Shipley, as the only staff, rotating flagships based on availability and using a borrowed office in the customs house. The naval station was forced to provide his staff support when it could not meet its burgeoning responsibilities; leaving Forsyth so overwhelmed Starke had not visited since submitting his arrival report. The station commander lived alone in Quarters A, with cipher codes under his bed, and slept little. His paymaster, next door in Quarters B, was worse off and nearing exhaustion because the department continued sending everything imaginable except help. Paymaster Wiggs made regular trips ashore and reported the man trying to accomplish what called for a staff of six or seven. Consequently, requisitions were recorded by memorandum or not at all and *Calypso*'s paymaster claimed himself and others often rooted through available stores in what amounted to scavenging since some areas were neither locked nor attended.

The ad hoc First Marine Battalion, arriving just before May on a grossly overcrowded *Panther*, was waiting for orders and sending marines ashore to drill. There was talk of their establishing a Cuban coaling station but no one knew where. In the meantime, some were detailed to patrol city streets at the U.S. Marshal's request since sailors, soldiers, laborers, and others flooding Key West continued to make life difficult. The mayor supported this but unwilling to openly request it.

Correspondents from across the nation and Europe, Great Britain in particular, inundated the city. They combined with military officers to overflow rooms, porches, and lobbies of Hotel Key West, Duval House, smaller hotels, and rooming houses. The censor was an army lieutenant who regularly passed through Hotel Key West's porch. If not there, he was usually at the red-brick telegraph office on Greene Street; with concrete steps below its second-story cast-iron porch that served as finish line for correspondents racing to file. When not in competition, many joined novelist Stephen Crane at the Eagle Bird to play cards or joust the roulette wheel.

This transient population suddenly decreased when Sampson's flagship *New York* took the squadron out with a flock of press boats in tow; *The Sun*'s chartered *Kanapaha* among them. Tyson did not go but managed to get a correspondent on *New York*. He was fully employed managing the office and obtaining Lord's approval for a second press boat. This led him to the ex-filibuster *Carte Blanche*. During one of Starke's infrequent visits Tyson obtained his recommendation for a local surveyor used by the family firm. The steam yacht was deemed sound and Starke's reluctant but relatively fair evaluation of Captain Buff convinced Tyson his best choice for master was the recent filibuster.

He also decided to jeopardize career and reputation by including Evans in that press boat's complement. *Carte Blanche* was built as a yacht, he valued her abilities, and Evans had cabled Long would not issue her credentials because women were not allowed on Navy ships. The War Department was nearly as reticent but already pressed hard by the Canadian journalist, Kit Coleman; a vexatious woman Evans disliked intensely. Tyson toyed with keeping Evans in Washington to exploit her old sources but knew she was keen to return so he cabled his approval then informed an annoyed Captain Buff.

Edward Curtis would also be aboard. He arrived in Key West with a British paper's credentials; apparently convinced it was the best approach to monitor his investors' interests, prospect new opportunities, and join a great adventure. Tyson had seen the elephant and would not recommend it but knew Curtis would stand in a tight spot and any favors *The Sun* did for a foreign press could prove useful in future.

Today, Tyson hired a water taxi to visit *Calypso* and survey warships anchored in the outer harbor. Curtis wanted to see Starke on some personal matter and the excursion would give Tyson a chance to solicit his friend's thoughts. As a courtesy extended to all captains by visiting reporters, they would take the latest papers and some scarce luxury items.

Their small steam launch, clearly ridden hard, floated at Government Dock where press dispatch boats disgorged correspondents who raced for the cable office to lay claim on one of two lines to the mainland; the second being limited to military traffic. Their helmsman backed clear, twisted, then picked up speed chugging down the channel trailing gray-black smoke. The port changed considerably over the last few months. Everything was still imported but there was now a fleet, expanding Key West Barracks, and modernization work on Fort Taylor. March construction included plans for dredging a channel and building storage for the now daily arrival of stores, ammunition and coal that filled usable structures, open warehouses, and fort.

Tyson felt spring's heat penetrate their gently pulsating, canvas canopy as the customs house passed and dirty water flecked with trash slipped along the hull. Smells of harbor, steam, and burning coal were pervasive in a ship channel used by schooners, barges, press boats, liners, freighters, and smaller warships. Several torpedo boats were nested close-in; their once bottle-green hulls now matching other warships' gray with black bands around stacks. Colliers alone escaped repainting because black hulls might let them pass for neutrals; and foreign flags issued to aid this deception. Over two dozen prizes were moored above Key West's inner harbor with only security guards on board. Their crews had been running out of supplies and facing starvation when Clara Barton, on *State of Texas*, appealed to locals for help and residents responded. Local Cubans, however, began rowing out to threaten and harass interned crews so armed guards with permission to fire on suspicious boats coming too close were being considered.

The size of anchored merchantmen and warships increased further down the channel but Key West's roadstead was less congested without a squadron. The converted yacht *Wasp* could usually be found there or off Sand Key. Ponderous monitors, often with a coal barge alongside, and torpedo boats, were regularly present as guard ships since the first were designed for coast defense and the second type all but uninhabitable underway. Monitors, whenever present, were hard to identify in gray paint since an almost nonexistent freeboard made them all look like floating batteries. The single exception was *Puritan* because she was larger than *Miantonomoh, Amphitrite,* and *Terror* by 2,000 tons. Another fixture was *Suwannee*; a new Lighthouse Service tender less than a year before had transferred to the Navy as an auxiliary cruiser. For this latest role she received two quick-firing 6-pounder guns and single 1-pounder. The new addition was 164 feet long with a thirty-foot beam and displaced 630 tons. The aft superstructure consumed two-thirds of her length and separated from the raised forecastle by a short main deck section. A tall stack rose amidship, with pilothouse forward and pair of boat davits aft. She lacked sails but had two masts to work holds, raise signal flags, and display lights. Water-tube boilers and compound engines limited speed to about ten knots but her eight-foot draft and two shafts ensured she was useful in the shallows.

Lieutenant Commander Delehanty had been supervisor of the harbor at New York before becoming her captain. Within weeks of commissioning she arrived in Key West and became temporary flagship. Tyson understood Delehanty had been no more satisfied with this arrangement than Remey's staff and supported the flag lieutenant's continuing efforts to arrange more suitable office space. The naval station commander needed little encouragement since a commodore, even if one on temporary assignment from the navy yard at Portsmouth, Maine, ended his having to readjust for every senior officer arriving in port; and operations were already improving.

Their launch chugged past the white Marine Hospital building, eased starboard before Fort Taylor, and struck out for *Calypso*; anchored further out than in the past. Her fine lines were unchanged but gray paint made the bark appear less elegant than the original black and straw-yellow scheme. Even so, Delehanty and others must be envious of the junior lieutenant commanding; despite her poor manning and lack of tasking. The harbor water began to clear then turn crystal-green soon after leaving the channel. Several hundred yards later *Calypso*'s watch hailed them and within minutes, Tyson and Curtis were leaving her accommodation ladder to pass through the gangway.

A pleasantly surprised Starke greeted his unexpected callers before guiding them to the main cabin; a welcome relief from the sun since it was warm but not sweltering and enjoyed a gentle cross-breeze. Tyson laid his small trove on the table as Starke, in service blue undress uniform, motioned them to chairs. He particularly wanted to speak with Curtis about Katherine but instead ventured, "I did not expect you, Edward."

Tyson grinned, "Our friend's decided to try his hand at scribbling."

"A correspondent?"

Curtis mustered a smile, "Credentials I have, the rest we shall see in time."

Tyson observed Starke dredge a briar pipe through the supple leather pouch's moist tobacco and decided it was acceptable to broach his gold-trimmed, jade cigarette case, retrieve one, tap the selection on an edge, and light up. Curtis, as always, kept smoking to its proper time, place, and attire.

Outside, they could hear sailors sweeping main deck planks bleached to light tannish-white by morning saltwater wash-downs and a harsh sun.

Tyson released a puff of smoke, "Newspapers are interesting. Dewey's shaken things up. The Manila garrison's trapped between his squadron and Filipinos surrounding the city. Without a Spanish fleet, their other cities are cut off and under siege as well, but it'll remain a stalemate until *City of Peking* and *Charleston* get there with troops; unless Dewey joins with Filipinos and shells Spanish positions. Edward's more familiar with Europe but Chamberlain's apparently blocked continental efforts to intervene and may end Britain's arms-length policy there. Some predict the end of Spain's monarchy and most Europeans want our gains limited to the West Indies. Cervera's left Fort de France and been spotted off Curaçao. Some reports claim his Cape Verde Fleet is returning home but most have them headed for San Juan or Cienfuegos. *Geier* left Cienfuegos, entered Havana, and was in San Juan along with a French ship when Sampson shelled the port. There's more, but I'd like your take; only as a knowledgeable naval source, of course."

"All I can add is *Calypso*'s still on the shelf."

"I doubt she'll be there long after sinking a gunboat and supply ship but Dewey pushed you off the front page."

"I've no complaints there. Anyway, I would guess Cervera's best strategy is to weaken our blockade by drawing ships from Cuba. Three or four armored cruisers could accomplish that but would require a steady coal supply. Without one, he must return home, intern in a neutral port, or risk being trapped in a Spanish one."

Curtis' forehead showed the same lines as his sister's when Katherine considered something of interest, "When I left England, the Spanish public seemed certain Cervera will break the blockade and defeat the States. Most British naval officers I spoke with think it unlikely but they were wrong about Dewey."

"Dewey was a long way from support, extemporized what he could, and then fought a squadron just off its fortified base; but his ships were better and I suspect Spanish missteps. Cervera's one advantage is speed and he's too savvy to squander that taking on battleships. Every West Indies port is a potential trap for him so I doubt bringing those ships over was his strategy."

Starke noticed Tyson and Curtis scribbling as he released a translucent blue-gray cloud of pleasantly scented smoke, "So how are you and Captain Buff faring?"

Tyson looked up with his best death's head grin, "You're the better judge of his ability but *Carte Blanche*'s crew toes the mark and he seems to know filibustering. Whenever I mention *Calypso*, his neck becomes three red rolls; sort of like a snapping turtle."

"I won't say he's a good man but he's capable and will stand. Take his advice if you get in trouble."

"Will do; Jacob. With your permission, Edward has private business with you and I'd like to speak with your wardroom."

Watson was summoned to escort Tyson. Starke anticipated with no little anxiety he would pick up some embroidering of *Calypso*'s two Cienfuegos visits.

Yamashita placed three glasses of lemonade on the table. Starke nodded at the third, "Mr. Tyson's left for the wardroom. They'll offer him something so that's yours if you want." The Japanese cabin steward nodded then slipped quietly into his pantry.

Starke gave Curtis room. After long two sips of tart lemonade, the Englishman adopted a more formal tone, "Katherine's asked me to begin negotiations if your proposal's still open, but wants her son to have his father's name in either case."

Requesting this response from Katherine differed from receiving it and his reply would alter three lives. Starke's shock was reflexive and momentary since that decision was made during their night at the Inglaterra then cemented by a birth; and his uncle and aunt welcomed the union as natural and proper, even if out of sequence. Glancing at the door Tyson passed through, Starke allowed a smile. It might also mean a shift of his aunt's matrimonial ministrations to that quarter.

Curtis noticed the distraction through his friend's thin beard but pressed on with some discomfort, "I see our mother's hand in this since Katherine's cable made no mention of father. Perhaps that's why your proposal unsettled her, but I don't doubt she loves you."

"And I her; so what is the custom, Edward?"

"The marriage's financial aspects must be settled, which we can work. Sir Curtis will announce the engagement once your father agrees. As for the rest, I expect your aunt and our mother will have the largest say."

"My father's a formality. I will cable him so he's prepared."

"To be honest Jacob, my sister understands navy demands as a society but you'll both have much to reconcile. For instance, you're required to be in England when the papers acknowledging your son are signed; and where you'll live must be agreed."

Starke loved Katherine but understood her feelings for Brydian Grange more than equaled her distaste for the States. There were also the religious differences, though probably not as deleterious as they could be, and Curtis mentioned how she changed with the pregnancy. Starke took up a pencil and began writing as her brother waited anxiously.

He handed two drafts to Curtis, "Will this do?"

Curtis read the cable to her father then a second to his sister. The first said, "Spoke with Edward - request honor of daughter's hand. Regret war prevents calling." The other was even less verbose, "A thousand times yes." As Curtis finished reading, Starke added, "I will write letters to Sir Curtis and Katherine, get your thoughts, and would be grateful if you could see they get off. We can start working the rest tomorrow or at your convenience."

Curtis finished the lemonade dregs in one long drink, noticed Starke's was untouched, stood up, and offered his hand, "I will brother."

Starke and Curtis spoke a few minutes longer about Katherine and her son before Tyson returned and other subjects substituted while the water taxi was hailed. Starke walked his guests to the gangway when it arrived then watched an overworked steam launch chug off, leaving a dark smudge against clear blue sky.

Curtis returned the next day to discuss financial arrangements. He explained this was normally negotiated by lawyers but his future brother-in-law already willed the son everything, which was Oxen Grove Plantation and some investments for the moment; accompanied by a letter the flattered Yeoman Pond witnessed recognizing Oliver Barrington Curtis as Starke's son. That left her dowry as the remaining issue and one proving particularly odious for Starke. He disliked the idea and large amount until Curtis explained it was an inheritance and the custom protected her. With the war and lack of time, Starke suggested they reinstate the agreement used for her first marriage to ensure Katherine's security and independence. However, during these negotiations something strange appeared to come over Curtis. As their final session came to a close he reflected, "This will not be easy for you and Katherine, but made me to look at my own situation." He did not elaborate and Starke decided not to pry.

Calypso's surviving steam pinnace came alongside soon after Curtis left. Melvin was trading off with another coxswain until a replacement boat could be located. Watson appeared excessively confident that would come soon; perhaps relying on the number left behind by ships blockading Cuba that wanted to clear batteries and limit splinters. Until then, the one pinnace they possessed made regular trips to the naval station and two daily mail runs from their anchorage, since rowing was impractical and sailing unreliable. Starke was reviewing an engineering report when Yeoman Pond brought the last arrival's sorted cables and mail. Topping the small stack left on the table where he preferred to work official correspondence was the dull yellow envelope of a cablegram so he left his desk to decipher it.

Watson was on deck inspecting their whaleboats when summoned; so it took several seconds for his eyes to adjust to the main cabin's interior. Starke was at the table and invited him to sit. With one of his captain's familiar expressions, a marked up yellow paper was nudged across as Starke calmly said, "Looks like we're back in the wars, XO."

The decoded message read, "Restore Calypso for future operations soonest. Submit requirements. Crew assignments ongoing. Long."

Starke assembled officers and chiefs in the wardroom to explain they were to prepare for sea but there was no additional information. Blair clearly struggled to control his excitement. Since the blockade began, Watson believed the ensign's only self-reflective pause came when Ensign Bagley's remains were shipped home after the Cardenas fight.

A messenger woke Starke shortly after falling asleep. He instinctively glanced up at the telltale compass above the berth, his wall clock, and then calendar. Midnight was just over an hour off so it still read "TUE MAY 17 98". The landsman said Ensign Martyn was manning their forward four-inch mount, a 3-pounder, and one Gatling gun because a column of ships had been sighted.

Starke went quickly to the flying bridge and arrived to see a patrolling torpedo boat speed past; bow wave and wake clear against the calm, dark sea. Anchored monitors' dark bulks were also stirring as Ardois lights flashed recognition signals against a night sky. After the column's lead ship answered their challenge correctly Starke remained to study each passing arrival through binoculars. *Brooklyn* led from channel to anchorage, with a torpedo boat guiding them past tethered mines just below the surface. The armored cruiser was easily identified by her size, 100 feet longer than *Maine*, high sides with pronounced tumblehome, and three tall stacks. The battleship *Massachusetts* trailing her was not as long, had short stacks, low freeboard, a fighting mast, and massive 13-inch turrets. The second class battleship *Texas* followed with side-mounted turrets and speed enough to keep pace with the flagship. The protected cruiser astern was *Minneapolis* since there were only two stacks; so the four-funneled *Columbia* was missing. The pair looked different but of the same class and designed for commerce raiding. Sleek, long and fast, the two ships were engineering marvels but under-armed and coal-hungry; making *Calypso* a better choice for that role. He did not recognize the other silhouettes but what he saw was enough. Commodore Winfield Scott Schley's Flying Squadron was entering Key West on its quest to find and defeat Admiral Cervera's Cape Verde Fleet.

About the Author

ichael T. Ribble was born in Lapeer, Michigan, and raised on farms near Davison. He received a Bachelor's Degree in journalism after attending the University of Colorado in Boulder and Central Michigan University. During high school and college he worked road construction, farmed in Colorado, helped construct a feedlot, harvested sugar beets, and spent one summer as a YMCA camp counselor/rifle instructor. After enlisting as a seaman recruit, he attended basic training in San Diego, served on minesweepers, a guided missile cruiser, destroyer, and frigate before retiring from active and reserve service as captain. After obtaining a Master of Business Administration degree from Florida State University, he held integrated logistics support, program analyst, and cost estimating positions at Naval Sea Systems Command and Department of Homeland Security. Besides a year in Guantanamo Bay, Cuba, he participated in towing de-fueled nuclear submarines and early *Virginia* class submarine development, taught naval science at Northwestern University, facilitated the National Naval Reserve Policy Board, and completed the United States Naval War College's continuing education program. He served on steam and diesel ships as a Surface Warfare Officer and has crewed in annual sail races down Chesapeake Bay. Besides three previous Starke novels, his work appeared in university publications, newspapers, and U.S. Naval Institute *Proceedings*.